CW01521663

SUNSPOT

Garth Jones was born in Cheshire in 1948. He was educated at the King's School, Macclesfield and studied Physics at King's College, London. Never managing to escape from the South of England since, he now lives in Buckinghamshire. He is married with two children and four grandchildren.

His career, in the I.T. industry, has ranged from programming through to management in the private sector. Apart from his writing – *Sunspot* is the second in a series of science fiction works – his interests include music composition and sport.

He is currently working on his fifth novel.

SUNSPOT

Garth Jones

FrontList Books

Published by FrontList Books
An imprint of Soft Editions Ltd,
Gullane, East Lothian, Scotland.

ISBN 1-84350-088-4

For Peggy Holt

1

The stars were sparse in this part of the galaxy. Steady streams of fleeting light, passing through in search of more prosperous, populous places. They might have looked to an observer as if they were frightened of the huge, sucking blackness that engulfed them as they clustered together in small patches of dwindling brilliance. The distant sun, *Millar Vorspak*, looked all the more lonely amongst them as it claimed its place as the brightest object in the enclosing darkness.

The slender threads of stranded light bent and quivered as the small space ship returned, back into the real universe. Its black, cylindrical body had emerged at a speed that had matched that of the shifting starlight, but the last twist of its transfer from wormspace, that breaking through of the final membrane of its transit cocoon, had decelerated the gleaming, ebony canister to a more plausible speed. Still it shot through the frictionless vacuum like a bullet aimed at the heart of the cowering *Vorspak* sun. Or perhaps as a deluded moth might fly blindly towards the deceptive allure of the cold flame.

Inside, there was only room for one occupant, stretched out on the transit couch. He lay six feet and three inches long and dangerous. Forba Curzine was still asleep. Although the journey across two thousand light years of empty tract had only taken six weeks, still he had chosen the long sleep temporal option. There was hardly any room to move in the tiny vehicle, and he was not good at passing time with only himself for comfort and company.

Millar Vorspak had grown in confidence and size by the time Forba was revived from his state of near-death. It was drenching the front of his tiny, blunt *Capuletti* space ship with generous bands of lethal radiation. As consciousness trickled into Forba's rounded skull, like rain through a neglected roof, he felt that his meeting with death must have been a very close encounter. Everything ached, but worst of all was the need to slowly peel his caked tongue away from the dry skin at the roof of his mouth. There did not seem to be enough muscles in the right places for such a strenuous manoeuvre.

He rolled over from his back to his side, and took a mouthful of wash from the valet tube. As he collapsed back, exhausted by his efforts, he slammed his right wrist into the medi-comp's padded receptacle. Contrary to his expectations, the depth screen above his head told him that he was in perfect health. It confirmed that his hibernation steroidal program had successfully added ten percent to his muscle mass during his slumber. He sniffed with satisfaction and took deep breaths of the cool air that was now circulating more vigorously around the inside of the speeding survival pod, automatically reacting to his strengthening vital signs. He lifted his head and looked down the length of his naked body, taking pleasure from the smooth curves of his torso. He twitched his phallic sinews and glimpsed his magnificent weapon as it peeped briefly over the haze of pubic shrubbery. Like a humpback whale breasting the spume, he thought. All was well if that was well. He examined his long hands. Warrior's hands, strong but smooth and sensitive — unspoilt by the ugliness of labour.

Forba tried to enjoy the remainder of his trip into the *Vorspak* system. The *Capuletti* was so small that he could not stand up or move about, other than on his expansive couch. But he could lie on his stomach and look forward through the nose window. He liked that. He had the gossamer-thin ambience sheet draped around his broad shoulders. Looking back over them he could see his large buttocks swelling beneath its silken caress. It all reminded him of when he was a small boy, tucked up in his warm bed. In bed, yet imagining that he was surfing along the moonbeams and gliding down the storm trails of the vacuum. It still gave him a small thrill. He could not help but move his groin in small circles on the compliant fabric of the transit couch, which he had adjusted, now, to a more luxurious softness.

It took a few days for him to penetrate properly into the body of the *Vorspak* system. Forba had many ways to fend off the cold winds of boredom; he used all the small ship's alternative environments. They were not of the highest quality. The synthesised beach was what he liked the best. The couch took on the heavy dampness of wet sand, and if he kept his eyes closed under the wrap-around shades, he could believe himself elsewhere. He moved the sun across the sky in hourly cycles and reduced the salty breeze to the gentlest waft. He enjoyed the feeling of the perspiration as it ran over his dark, bronzing limbs. It was trickling into secret places where many women had sought their own dreams in the past, when he was back on *Sumesotta*. He could doze, and feel no desire to move away from the torpor of the surf-line. The illusion was only spoiled when he stretched his long arm too far, grazing his knuckles on the distant, rocky headland that was actually a hydraulic valve, standing proud from the ship's inner skin.

As his arrival hour approached, Forba disconnected himself carefully from the abdominal and intestinal ducting. He started to end his fast with small, regular morsels of paste and thereby distend his shrunken stomach. And so, with the inevitable precision of fail-safe computing, the *Capuletti* fell into orbit around *Pirismus*, second planet of the mother *Millar Vorspak* sun. But even her frightful, unblinking glare would not provide protection from the hungry gaze of the new arrival.

Forba looked down on the rich world and smiled. Here was his new territory, his hunting ground. It was awash with easy wealth and docile creatures. He would stride through it as a colossus.

In his black coffin, which now reflected the luminance of the planet's sweet atmosphere, Forba savoured the moment and his ethereal position of power. He hovered like a majestic bird of prey. Many timid, scurrying victims would feel his dagger-talons before he selected his ultimate quarry. They did not yet realise their peril. The great and implacable predator had arrived.

Forba broadened his smile and licked his black lips. From his thick, powerful neck he indulged himself with a low, throbbing growl.

Far away yet at the same moment in time, a dense jungle lay beneath a wild sky. The treetops were whipped by strong winds, under great columns of torn cloud. The continuous motion of millions of leaves created a perpetual but pulsating background of whispering sounds.

In the calmer, darker depths of the forest the undergrowth was parted by mighty shoulders. Bright eyes watched the brushwood, where lesser creatures cowered or fled. Long, white teeth shone in the gloom as if radiating, not reflecting, the watery, filtered sunlight. Great paws weighed gently on the soft decay of the jungle floor. Sharp bristles of black and orange hair stood erect on the wide, muscled back as the animal padded down towards the slow waters of a great river. She surveyed this newly revealed tract of her domain.

The predator had arrived, but was unaware of her own majesty.

2

Sarnia Galant looked out from her bedroom window. Dusk was gathering outside and she could see herself in the pseudo-glass. She smoothed her dress across her flat stomach, pleased with the tautness that she felt beneath her small fingers. She often came here at this time, just as the sun had sunk behind the distant line of trees. In this light, her reflection looked very much as it had done when she was a young woman, before she was married. And now she was a grandmother, but her legs were still slim and her waist narrow. She tilted up her chin before looking into her own, darkened eyes. Her face, too, was still the same. High cheekbones and full mouth. The cloudiness of the window obscured any unfair lines that the years had strewn across her fragile skin. She was satisfied with what she saw.

Downstairs, in the kitchen, she could hear Warren's dinner cooking. She liked the sound of bubbling water and escaping steam: it gave the house a homely feel. She had first started to use the sonic and aromatic features of her food system when the girls were at home. She wanted them to have strong, happy memories of their childhood days, reinforced by vivid sensations that would forever bind them to her motherly love. These days she did not program in the cooking odours. They were a little too difficult to dispel, afterwards. Sound was enough.

She turned round and looked over her shoulder to see her shapely backside, well defined by her thin dress, reflected in the darkening window. Young men would still watch her as she passed them in the avenues. When she was in her teens, her mother had said that she looked very much like Morfa Nevin, the actress. Morfa was also a pretty, slim girl at that time. She had a quick, bird-like quality that men found attractive — small-framed but swelling subtly in very womanly places. She had just risen to prominence in the film *Standing Room*. Sarnia had hoped that everyone assumed that her breasts were as lovely as Morfa's. In fact they hung a little lower and somewhat further apart, but Sarnia saw no reason to make an issue of it. Morfa had become notorious, after this first success, as an independent and aggressive woman. Her affairs were reported in detail in the media. There were many simulations of her bedroom encounters on the smuttier holo-channels. Of course, when these carnal matters were discussed amongst Sarnia's friends, she distanced herself from the star, saying that outward appearances meant nothing.

"You can't judge a book by its cover!" she would claim, using the ancient saying — which most of her friends did not understand. But secretly Sarnia knew that she, too, was a deeply passionate woman, even as her fiftieth birthday drew close. Like Morfa, she took great pleasure in her own body and also like Ms. Nevin she regarded the male physique as a delicious feast of meat and drink. Her urges were grindingly powerful but she was proud to reflect that, unlike her profligate star doppleganger, she kept these passions in check. She felt that the exercise of restraint gave her an inner strength.

She reminded herself that she loved her husband, Warren, and that she was looking forward to his return tonight. But she had to admit, only to herself, that their sex had always been less than she had dreamed about when she was a girl. He had never been down on his knees before her and worshipped her in the ways that she longed for. Not in the unbridled manner of a fully free, unrepressed male searching for new openings. And so she had not used her own mouth and tongue as she would have liked. They had never spoken about these things and she would not be the first. The matter would remain another source of her inner power. She took consolation by believing that her untapped potential shone through from her bright eyes and elegant body.

She could not help but sigh, though, as she turned back to look out on the rapidly falling night. Presently she saw two small lights appear over the distant line of trees. One green, one red. They wobbled in familiar greeting. Warren was flying in and would be landing within five minutes. She did feel a little warmth fill her stomach at the expectation of her husband's arrival.

She waited by the window for another minute so that he would see her wave, as always. She knew that she would be a lovely sight.

3

The city was a fine sight from the distance. Its jagged skyline stretched for fifty miles along the river, to the point where it broadened its waters in preparation for confluence with the ocean's wash. The urban buildings looked perfectly clean, when viewed from the boats that churned through the *Timorillo River's* muddy currents. They were mainly constructed of glass, and their cleaning systems kept them pristine. Not for the benefit of sightseers, just for the people who looked out from their offices and apartments.

Cheng Ham Tung thought that this was a waste of municipal resources. He knew that down at street level things got a lot dirtier. It felt neglected and dark where the towering pinnacles of metal and glass finally met the humble ground. He did not like the skyscrapers. He knew that they screamed at the heavens without respect, like dogs howling up at a tree-trapped jaguar. He heard them cursing as the wind swept between their teeth and whistled through the lips of their parapets and balconies. One day he would understand their language. He had a very good ear.

Tung had lived in *Dass Urmistam City* all his life. When he was a boy, he had lived with his family in the low-rise eastern suburbs. From their small garden his mother described the sight of the city to him as he sat on the grass lawn. To his young mind it had sounded wonderful. Even then he thought that he could hear its quiet whispers. In his bed at night he used to speak back with his mind.

But that was more than forty years ago. His mother and father were both dead now. He had been moved to one of the high towers on the south side. It was two hundred stories tall, a giant by any standards, but its neighbours were all half as tall again. The other residents of Cashen Column often complained about how the view was spoilt and the sunlight obscured. They would have been able to look across to the *Opel Ocean* if they had clear line of sight. But Tung did not care.

He did not like the high city after all. It had disappointed him. It was cramped and hard to get about. Although his rooms were near the very top of Cashen, he preferred to be out in the streets where the wind funnelled at high speed around the feet of the swaying giants. He could walk down there. But he also learned that she was not a clean place. For many years he had tried to keep the sparkling picture of *Urmistam* that his mother had put into his mind. But the damning evidence had gradually built up against her. She wore a pretty face and kept it clean, but her lower regions were less sanitary. In fact, she had many putrid parts to her anatomy. Tung knew this, because he also had a very keen sense of smell.

Of course, many of the office workers lived outside of the city. They flew in as the sun was rising, like anxious flocks of roosting birds. They came by the thousand in their fly-cars. Tung heard the buzz of their engines outside his apartment windows. They never touched the ground, these city flitters, especially the executive classes in their top floor suites. Tung was pretty sure that they all left plenty of detritus in *Urmistam* before they winged away to the dormitory towns which lay further along the sea coast or up in the wooded hills, inland. They were quite a sight as their navigation lights twinkled in the dusky sky, apparently. Tung was normally taking his evening walk at this time. Down on the sidewalks he pottered along and tilted his head as some reckless driver above banked his car around the tower gaps with a squeal of air brakes.

So Tung lived without any great happiness. He considered it a mere existence. Something had gone wrong in his life: his mother had told him that there were great things in store for him, but in reality there was nothing left to him except his pride. He still knew that he was special. Despite the dingy city that pressed all around him, he kept himself impeccably clean, and he behaved with dignity in public and in private. He could not always distinguish one from the other. He had even had his sexual functions disabled in order to remove any temptation towards unclean practices. So he kept his self-respect, which barely fell short of arrogance.

Some things made him very angry. As he got older, their number and intensity grew. For many years it had really rankled when people told him that he was living in the most spectacular city on *Pirismus*. Despite the dinginess of its alleyways and sewers it was regarded as a wonder. Its looming forest of buildings raked the stars from the sky and blazed as brightly as the *Vorspak* sun. Everyone said the city was a marvellous sight. But Tung would not agree.

Tung was blind.

4

The shuttle time from the *Vorstella* orbiting space station down to the surface of *Pirismus* would be five hours. Forba was not enjoying the experience. He had more claustrophobic reactions to the cramped seating arrangements now than at any time in the tiny black coffin of the *Capuletti* long-haul transit module. The shuttle carried six hundred passengers in its long, tubular fuselage, and this seemed to make it hard to breathe. And they were all crammed into seats, shoulder to shoulder. No luxurious stretching out on his couch this time. Forba had to sit quietly in his narrow chair and submit to the torture, bound by the indestructible bonds of good manners and social protocol. He could hear the shuttle skin groan and creak every so often as it accommodated the vast temperature differences that abused its stubby wings and long body. Forba felt like he was in a similar state of conflicting, suppressed tension.

At least he had been given a window seat, so he had only one immediate neighbour. He could look out of the thick plyspex porthole and admire the sight of the planet's swirling weather systems as they played around the dark blue oceans and brown landmasses. Despite his research at the *Vorstella* station bibliovault, he was still optimistic about his prospects for finding suitable quarry on the rich, populous world. He had spent a week at the station, after his *Capuletti* had been slowly sucked into the tractor paths of the planetary depot complex, and then shunted into the *Vorstella's* docking bay. He had rented a cheap room in one of the inner habitat rings. He had not brought very much money with him from *Sumesotta*, because he had never had very much, and the unfavourable exchange rates had made it dwindle even further. He could not afford any luxuries, not until he had started to feed on the wealth that was scattered like diamonds across his new planet's surface.

Sumesotta was his birthplace, and he gave it due credit for this service. But it was relentlessly poor amongst the planets of the populated galaxy. It was dry. Water only survived below the surface or in deep, shaded lakes in the foothills of the massive mountain ranges, and as ice at the poles, where thousand mile long glaciers ground their way towards the equator and trickled their precious moisture into the cracked skin of their mother earth. There was no rainfall, and the atmosphere was painfully thin. Fortunately, there was very little meteorite activity in the area. The protective girdle of gases would offer only a poor defence. But it was the lack of material wealth that had driven Forba away. *Sumesotta* did not have enough rich women for Forba's taste.

As his breath misted the inside of the cold plyspex window, he could tell that *Pirismus* would be different. He imagined that he could smell the currents of lucre as they flowed between the giant cities like canals of liquid gold. He sat back in his seat and breathed deeply, feeling reasonably relaxed for the first time since he had boarded the *Netrack* shuttle.

Unfortunately, the passenger next to him seemed to take this as a sign that he could begin to engage him in conversation. He was a small rat of a man. Forba observed his thinning hair, thin lips and thinner voice with disdain. He looked down his straight black nose with eyes filled with contempt, but his elbow-mate seemed to be immune to such discouragement. Perhaps he was too used to such treatment and regarded it as polite interest. In any case, he would not be interrupted now that he had locked on, like a pilot fish below the jaws of a great shark.

The thin man treated Forba to a sample from his collection of witticisms. His gold-rimmed spectacles gleamed in the shuttle lighting as he tilted back his webbed chin and laughed at his own stories. He had started badly enough.

"Of course my wife has been trying to improve her figure recently. She's been looking through the surgery catalogues. She's seen me watching some of the heavy smut channels, and so she wants to have bigger tits, like some of those babes. I told her that she didn't need any implants. She looked real pleased and came and sat by my side. 'Why is that, Honey?' she asked me, expecting some kind of compliment. I just undid her blouse and put my hand between her two flat sacks. 'No, all you need to do is wash between here with some soapy water and then dry it with nice, scented warm air.' She looked puzzled. 'Will that really make my breasts bigger, Hun?' she asked. 'Sure,' I said."

Thin man leered at Forba in order to savour the moment, and to wait for the advent of dramatic effect. But Forba knew what was coming. He had heard it before.

" 'Sure, sweet, much bigger,' I said. 'It sure worked fine on your ass!' "
Thin man wheezed with laughter and was unaware of his audience's
indifference.

Forba became uncomfortable again. He looked longingly at the aisle
seat, six places away. If he had been sitting there, he would have been
able to take a stroll or look across at the windows on the far side of the
fuselage. And he would have been able to feel the stewardess' body
pressing up against him as she served the refreshments. She had
exchanged a few long looks with him already, of course, and he knew
that she would have been very pleased to apply such surreptitious
pressure. But he was trapped as the shuttle slid like a razor into the
tender cuticle of the planet's atmosphere. Thin man's jokes kept stinging
his ears. Finally, it went too far.

"Here's one you'll like. These two drug dealers were up before the
judge. He told them that they had two choices. They could either go to
jail for ten years or else they could promise to cure a hundred users of
their addiction to Trick. They would have to come back in one week
and report their progress. If they had not succeeded they would be sent
back to prison. They took the promise.

"A week later they were back, and the judge asked the first dealer
how he had got on. 'I have converted two hundred addicts!' he claimed.
'Good!' said the judge. 'How did you do that?' 'I showed them two
circles on the computer screen. One big one and one small one. I said,
pointing at the larger, that this was the proper size of your brain. And
the small one was the size of your brain after taking Trick.' 'Very good,
you may go free,' said the judge and he turned to the second dealer.
'And how did you get on?'

" 'I have converted two thousand addicts,' said the man. The judge
was amazed. 'How did you do that?' he asked. 'I showed them two
circles on the computer screen,' said the dealer. 'One big one and one
much smaller one. I said, pointing at the smaller, that this was the size of
your ass hole before you go to prison.' " He cackled again. Forba's
stomach churned. He had to take control of the conversation before
things got any worse.

"We do not have such fine humour on *Sumesotta*," he said, deepening
his already deep voice. "We have to make do with words of wisdom."

"Oh yeah?" said the thin man, without enthusiasm.

"Yep," persisted Forba. "One of my favourites is about the dilemma of the artist or literary master. It contends that the greatest authors are never published. They critique their own work in their minds, and their standards are so high that they destroy what they have produced with ease, thinking it trivial. Only people who have to work hard consider that what they have written is good. But they are, by definition, poor judges. So the question is posed, are critics the only true artists?"

The thin man looked perplexed. This did not appear to be the way he wanted the conversation to proceed. Forba was merciless.

"I can see that you enjoy the challenge of philosophy. We also contend that high art is actually the lowest form of art. Consider, again, a literary masterpiece. The trouble with such a book is that it is obviously a one-man effort. No genius would share his creation. But all the best of human creations, like television programs, football matches, and so on, are team efforts. The solo creation is certain to be self-indulgent, introspective. Rarely will it sustain real quality. What do you think?"

By now, the thin man was looking longingly across the shuttle's aisle towards the distant window, where the curve of the planet showed a glorious blue. Forba thought it was time to try to get some sense out of his neighbour. He asked how he might get a job down on *Pirismus*.

The thin man at last showed that he did have some common sense. In fact, he was very knowledgeable about the commercial environment, being an engineering manager. He told Forba that he should start by going to the largest city, *Dass Urmistam*, and registering with an agency. He wrote several down on the shuttle's free data cubes. He also put Forba straight about women on *Pirismus*. Unlike on *Sumesotta*, they were not the main salary earners here, although he could still reassure Forba that there were some pretty rich bitches about, as he put it.

At last, his neighbour announced that he had some preparation work to complete: possibly he was tiring of sensible conversation. He plugged his mobile into the shuttle seat's communication port and blanked Forba out from his sphere of interest.

So Forba was able to doze off as the shuttle floated down and finally came to earth at the *Martel Ince* spaceport.

5

Jacques Bonne had nearly finished his shift. He had been out at the extremity of the construction site for five hours, and he was looking forward to a shower and something to eat. These space suits got quite uncomfortable when you were working hard. And he always worked hard, even when he was unsupervised, as he had been during the second half of today's stint. He liked honest labour and using his big, powerful hands. He enjoyed working out here, too, where he could keep glancing down at the luminous vastness of *Pirismus* as she turned slowly below his feet. And if he had to adjust his position as he assembled the complex cabling systems, he could see the rest of the universe looking back at him. All those millions of photons that had travelled across semi-infinity to end their journeys as tiny scintillations on his admiring retina. He liked it when his hands could keep on working as his eyes feasted on the black and white certainty of outer space.

Probably, he himself was not unsupervised today. His team leader had retreated out of sight, to another part of the platform, where they were having trouble fitting a newly constructed heat transfer engine. They had a lot of trouble with the big Crocodile fuel cells. But, in the time-honoured way of construction sites, there were quite likely to be a number of casual observers around the site. People had always come up here from the planet's surface to see the glorious sights. To put their own lives into a proper perspective, or else to cloak themselves in its reflected majesty. Jacques did not understand all the reasons why they came into space in their millions.

Once the land dwellers had been satisfied with coming into the depot network and staying in one of the great orbiting space stations. The habitat rings were many miles in circumference and offered relaxed viewing conditions. But, of course, this had not been enough for the voracious tourists, and soon the stations offered tours in small cruise ships, specially designed for pottering around the orbital netscape. And then the travel companies, who found that an ever-increasing proportion of their revenue was coming from the visitor entertainment sector of their businesses, began to offer personal carriages. Jacques did not approve of this. All these little vehicles buzzing around out here in open space. It was getting pretty crowded, where once it had been frontier territory. Jacques admitted to himself that he felt very proprietorial about the erosion of his own personal universe.

Now he had even heard that there were new personal transports that could bring people up from the surface in only half an hour. Flipped up on the recently augmented ionic magnetron beams. They were expensive right now, so they were only within the reach of the wealthiest of earth-leavers. But everything always got to be a lot cheaper over time. It could get very cluttered around here before long.

Jacques saw from his helmet display that it was just about time to pack up his toolset and begin his crawl back to the crew cabin. He could see its red, winking homing light in the distance. It would take at least twenty minutes for him to edge his way along the titanium alloy struts of the in-progress construction. Quite close to the cabin beacon was the huge, rotating company hoarding. Jacques scowled at it. Here was another sign of the increasing number of concessions and accommodations being made to the tourists. They were fifty miles above the planet's surface and still the company felt that it needed to advertise itself and the project. Five hundred meter high red letters spelt out to the universe,

"Boquat Incorporated. Proud subcontractors to the *Sunspot Project.*"

At least the luminance of the words served some useful purpose as it lit his workplace, augmenting the clamp lights that he had set up to point directly at his instrument frame. As he turned these off, one by one, his shadow was revealed more clearly in the sign's vulgar, red glare. He waved to himself and twiddled the stubby fingers of his space gloves.

As he extinguished the last lamp, he saw another shadowy figure lurking next to his own. It made him jump. Some damn tourist coming for a closer look, he thought. The idiot must have missed the 'men at work' transmission barriers. He was about to turn and give his unwelcome visitor some well placed directions, when the shadow placed a hand on his shoulder. He had not realised that they were so close.

Then the intruder punched him in the back, hard. He let out a quiet gasp. The blow seemed to go straight through him. His helmet heads-up display had flashed a brief warning icon at the moment of impact. Jacques did not know what to say, he was confused and hurting. Almost paralysed. He stared at the other shadow where it lay on the smooth, metal beam before him, as if looking into a mirror, searching for the face so that he could read the expression. And then there was another strike at his back. It seemed as if it carried a terrible cold with it, which invaded Jacques' body. He started to shiver.

The warning icon flashed on again, for longer this time. He knew what it was now. There had been a temporary breach of his suit. The active skin of the fabric had made immediate repairs, and the air loss had been minimal. But if something had pierced his suit, twice, then there was nothing to stop it entering his body. Near his kidneys, just below his systems back pack. And that was incredible. He smiled with his chattering teeth at the absurdity of it. But at the same time the cool part of his brain knew it to be true. There was something wrong inside him. The cold was spreading and the pain was making it hard to breathe.

His shadow attacker slowly turned him round and there was the dreadful, unarguable confirmation, flashing red before his eyes. A long, sharp blade was held up before his helmet. He groaned in despair. He watched as the knife started to saw through his umbilical cords. His arms would not move to protect him; his eyes could see nothing inside his aggressor's darkened helmet.

When the amputation was completed, Jacques' limp, helpless figure was thrown away from the rig and out into the uncaring void. He imagined that he must have looked like a rag doll. His dying brain told him that this was the proper phrase to use. He was a doll. Yes, he could see his arms and legs flopping about like a child's plaything.

As Jacques drifted away to his endless grave, the last thing that his eyes saw, before they closed down, were the lurid words, now in a shimmering, blood red.

"Sunspot Project."

6

Boquat Incorporated occupied five floors, high up in Tramalgar Colossus in central *Dass Urmistam*. At ground level, there were coffee shops and bistros, some of which Cheng Ham Tung visited when his spirits were up. His senses enjoyed the challenge of their aromatic, steamy, noisy interiors. But that was a world away from Warren Galant's office, on the one hundred and sixtieth floor.

Warren was Production Director at Boquat. It had taken him his whole career to get there. He had worked hard for it, starting at the bottom. And he was still working hard, because that was how he liked it.

He had been thinking about Sarnia as he drove in to work that morning. He had left the house before she was up, flying his *Chincha* quietly out over the line of trees just as dawn was breaking. He would miss the heavy traffic into *Urmistam* at this hour. He enjoyed driving the *Chincha*, because it was a quality vehicle. These days most of his fellow directors at Boquat were choosing the *Reisen Eight Series* fly-cars. They were supposed to be the choice of all real pilots. But Warren was quite satisfied with his *Chincha*. Even though it did have thirty thousand air miles on the clock, it still rode the air currents very smoothly, and there was plenty of power in the levitation pod. It was big enough for him to take Sarnia and their little granddaughter on the weekend, too.

He eased back in his padded seat as he skimmed over the *Urmistam* suburbs and thought about his wife. At the moment things were pretty quiet at work, so he could afford to indulge himself in this luxury. Although he had taken his datacase back home with him last night, as always, there had been no real need. He had been so relaxed that when Sarnia had come down to meet him at the garage door, he had kissed her in the special place. He gave her a peck on the cheek every night when he came home, but this time he put his lips a little further back, to the sensitive area just below her ear. He was sure that she understood the significance of this polite enquiry. This respectful suggestion that the evening might involve an early night. But Sarnia had just given him a quick little smile, in her startled bird kind of way. And, as he expected, shortly afterwards she had put her hand to her hip and given the faintest little sigh of pain. Just enough of an almost silent, unspoken complaint to let him know that her back was giving her pain again. It had never been the same since their second daughter had been born. Of course, Warren did not blame their lovely girl for this minor inconvenience in their lives, but he knew it meant that there would be no romance tonight.

Warren did not mind too much. He believed that a good husband did not make demands on his wife. He felt very lucky to have her. Sarnia was a beautiful woman and men were still attracted to her. Warren himself was no catch, physically. He was quite short and had been somewhat overweight ever since his mid twenties. Now, at fifty-five, he was distinctly portly and his face was redder than it should be. Despite Sarnia's frequent counselling, he enjoyed his food and drink. So his round face had got rounder and ruddier, in contrast to her pale, thin intelligence. Sometimes he wondered what she saw in him. He felt that he partly repaid her by not pressing himself upon her on nights like this. He had always thought that the whole sex thing was overrated anyway.

He had first met her on the planet of *Cosphoral* when he was doing his engineering postgraduate studies. She had been born and brought up there. Now that was a real pressure cooker of a society. They were beyond a meritocracy, particularly in the capital city of *Pontillac*, where he had gone to school. In their world, social standing was everything. But it was gauged not by one's own achievements, but rather by the people who acknowledged and entertained one. Warren thought of it as being a kind of anti-matter or negative version of what he was used to. He had been brought up to believe that you stood by your own achievements, your abilities and skills. That was the gauge of your worth. But, in *Pontillac*, it was the hole that you filled that counted. You would measure yourself by the position you occupied in the complex, hierarchical network of society. Who put you above, below, or alongside themselves. It was this carefully defined gap that you occupied that mattered.

Obviously your own proficiencies were a factor, but most important was the contacts you developed and held. Warren could not really cope with it, and spent most of his time on the school campus, amongst the other foreign students. He had met Sarnia when she had come with her parents to the University for another Faculty's graduation ceremony. No doubt they were seeking to make another small shift upwards for her through capillary action. He had gone because one of his block-mates was receiving his doctorate. Sarnia had been forced to sit next to him, because of a mix-up with the arrangements and, wonder upon wonder, she had liked him. There had been no turning back, and Sarnia soon told him how she would like to move away to a more relaxed regime.

She still retained some pretty acute acumen in society matters, though, and so Warren told her most of what went on at work. Her instincts and his intellect made them a good partnership.

Warren steered the *Chincha* into the parking floor and settled it down into his reserved bay. He liked the old-fashioned way it hummed and throbbed as it sank onto its haunches and powered off. He walked up to the office, swinging his datacase as he went. He might have whistled, had he known how.

Cass was already in the office, as usual, sitting behind her administration station and communing with the computer. She smiled as he came in and got up to get his coffee, without having to be asked.

"So, what have we got today, Cass?" he enquired, as she brought the steaming cup through into his office. Cass had already been sifting through the mail and reports for him. She lived closer, so could get in even earlier. Warren was not very good with the computers. She moved over to the window and looked out across the city. She could see the traffic building up already in the growing daylight. Thousands of small, hovering dots, buzzing around the city's honeyed towers. Their municipal traffic systems would safely stack them up as the airways began to clog. The sky was shaded from a pink horizon into a rich blue overhead, and for a moment her soul fluttered like a bird seeking flight. But her sense of duty tugged her back to the present.

Cass liked Warren and Sarnia. They had met socially on many occasions. Still, she liked to tease him a little and enjoyed trying to predict his reactions to events. This time, she thought that angry was most likely. She cleared her throat.

"OK. Well now. The month to date efficiencies came through at two percent above target. Jim Moffat would like to see you at ten o'clock in his office about budgets. I've prepared the figures for you from the North Coast facility, where we are running over plan. And you have a staff meeting this afternoon in the Board Room."

Warren slipped off his jacket and hung it up on the laundry hook.

"Doesn't sound too bad," he said, in a neutral tone. Cass felt a little guilty for toying with him, but then she knew that Warren actually liked emergencies. It was long range planning that he struggled with. Give him a good, old fashioned panic any day. Something to get hot under the collar about. She moved round in front of his large, shiny wooden desk.

"Oh, and Bryan called just before you arrived. There is some trouble up at the *Cassius Station*. On the *Sunspot Project*." She saw Warren stiffen. This was the big one. The one project that Warren needed to be seen by all as a great success, a last triumph before his retirement. Maybe this was the one place where he did not really want an emergency. She saw his face turn a little deeper red.

"Ugh! What's going on up there?" His second chin slid over his collar as his neck distended from the pressure of the breath that he held in suspense.

"One of the workers has gone missing." Cass wanted to get it over with now. Warren's eyes watered a little. Yes, angry was right. His breathing burst forth and started to come harder.

"Damn! Not another computer error! Get me Farr Litten on the 'phone straight away. Assuming that he is in by now. I suppose I'll have to sort them out again."

Cass went out to her own office and punched in an urgent summons. She was not quite sure how Farr had been fingered for this one, but it was always a pleasure to have him visit.

"Oh, and Melda Smith called." Cass directed the words through the door into Warren's office with a turn of her head. "She says that she is worried about the Crocodiles and would like the authority to take some local action."

"Tell her she can leave it to me," replied Warren.

7

Farr was at work, two floors below Warren, where the offices were smaller and busier. He had gone in earlier than usual to work on a special analysis for Jim Moffat. He had started it late the previous night. Although Farr had a head-count of fifty-three staff in the Information Networking department, he was handling this one himself. Jim had walked in to his office after all of Farr's people had gone home for the night. He had observed that they always had a knack of getting away just before trouble broke. He suspected that there was some system of jungle drums in operation around the building. Sometimes it worked faster than his own data hypernet.

His grey-haired guest had collapsed into the comfortable visitors' chair opposite his desk. Both the chair and his new arrival had exhaled noisily. It was obvious that Jim had a lot on his mind. Farr had pushed his terminal away with a reluctant shrug, so that he could pay proper, respectful attention to what the top man at Boquat had to say. He had known that he would not be able to complete his expense forecasts that night.

Jim had thrust his hands a little way down into his trouser waistband, in that absent-minded, disconcerting way of his, and rambled around the company's problem pages. Farr had heard a lot of it before. Inertia in the workforce. Lack of vision in the management. Lack of understanding from the shareholders. Not enough bright sparks of young executives to lighten his gloom. Farr recognised these themes, but he also knew that the company was doing all right. He assumed that nagging insecurity was a vital ingredient in the make-up of a top executive. He tried to communicate sympathy and support to the short but large, grey man opposite. He helped, with a few well-chosen prompts and reminders, to move the whole performance along.

Then Jim talked about the *Sunspot Project*. Farr sat forward in his hovering chair and pulled himself closer to his desk with his fingertips on the table edge. He could tell that Jim was getting to what was really worrying him. He was becoming a little moist around the temples. The subdued ceiling lighting was reflecting from his scalp. He stopped looking Farr in the eye quite so often.

The *Sunspot Project* was the biggest thing that Boquat had ever been involved in. They had won the contract over a year ago, and it still had another year to run, if it kept to schedule. It had been a real shot in the arm for the company, at first. It had captured the imagination of the whole workforce, as the marketing people had put it. Naturally, as with any engineering program, the initial euphoria had worn off and had been replaced by a crushing apprehension. Everyone realised that the company's whole future, and most of its resource, was invested in this single, make or break project. Unfortunately, there were plenty of distractions, and many other projects still reached out from the past with sticky fingers. Overruns and crises, designed to sap Boquat's energies, unless they were able to remain very precisely focused.

Jim was not sure what exactly it was that had him unnerved. He had a gut feel that things were not well. He was a detail man, always had been. And his memory was almost photographic. On traditional projects, this was enough to keep him ahead of the game. He could ensure that his subordinates were on their toes, through his often-superior knowledge of their own disciplines. But *Sunspot* was too big even for his high-powered brain, and he did not like the feeling. He conceded that it might only be healthy paranoia. It was just something he could not put his finger on. Something about the hundreds of thousands of resource requisitions, perhaps.

Farr offered to do some data mining and see what he could come up with. He saw a smile cross Jim's face at last, as if a great worry had been lifted from his brow. Obviously, a trouble shared was a trouble square rooted, as his father used to say. Farr considered asking Jim if he had taken the matter up with Warren Galant. It was his direct responsibility, after all. But Jim was already on his feet and looking at his watch.

"Hey! Mrs. Moffat will be wondering where I have got to. Dinner party tonight. Hate them! See you in the morning, and you can show me what you have chipped out from the information rock face." He blessed Farr with a casual wave as he left the office.

So once again the brave computer man was left in heroic stance, holding the future of the company in his slender fingers. He had worked through until midnight. He had only stopped when he had extracted and summarised all the data. He knew that the final analysis would be best tackled after a short night's sleep.

The next day Farr trailed up to Warren's office in response to a telephoned summons. He expected that the subject would be Jim's report. He was relaxed enough to notice that Cass was standing by the mask machine, tall and lovely. She smiled into him as he walked through and he gave her back that look of intrigue. It was a long glance intended to tell her that he would like to be hers, that he definitely would be hers given the opportunity. But he hoped it was also a subtly unthreatening approach that said "only on your terms". And he knew perfectly well that Cass was a happily married woman and so their few seconds of flirtation were safely theoretical.

Farr went into Warren's office with a light heart and came out bleeding. He had been so busy with Jim's job that he had not looked at the morning's exception screens. And none of his staff, he thought later with a touch of bitterness, had mentioned it either. So when Warren demanded to know why the *Sunspot* personnel figures had gone out of balance again, he had no answer. He fell into Warren's slavering jaws and felt himself being slowly chewed. On the stage of this minor corporate drama he could see that Farr Litten was the victim and that Warren was the expert assassin. The weapon of execution was the sharply bladed demand to know when things were going to be sorted out.

Farr considered pointing out that it was Warren himself who had decided against installing the personal accounting pads for all of their off-world project workers. But he had no evidence that this was where the problem lay, so he left with promises that he would sort it out and report back. Cass had her eyes downcast as he passed her desk again, which somehow increased his feeling of humiliation. Had she heard the tearing sound as shreds were torn from him?

Sure enough, when he got back to his own desk, there was a message that Jim Moffat had been asking where he was with his priority report. That was the kind of day it was going to be, clearly. Farr rushed up with what he had. Jim was not too friendly as he flipped through the paper output. Farr talked him through it, not sure whether Jim was listening.

"I can't see anything out of the ordinary, Jim. The spend lines are all pretty even, right through from project initiation. I've broken the revenue trends down by unnatural account and related them to other project profiles, but nothing unusual there, either. Seems like a pretty normal profile to me." He waited for some reaction from his grey, balding boss, who was still turning the pages. The minutes crept past with criminal silence. He thought of asking about last night's dinner party. It would be a test, so that he could hear the tone of Jim's voice. But then Jim looked up and snapped the sheath of charts back into neat order.

"Thanks, Farr. I agree with everything you've said. Only I think that is exactly what is wrong."

Farr knew better than to ask for an explanation; there were things that needed to be done down in his own department. He confirmed that he could break the figures down further, if required, and scurried away.

It was not until lunchtime that Farr was completely sure that there had been no problems with the computer systems. There really must be a personnel anomaly up at the *Sunspot*. He called Warren's office to attempt a little sweet, righteous revenge, but Cass answered. Over the screen she looked colder, older. She said that Warren had left for the North Coast site and would not be back until Friday.

There was no justice.

8

There was a light drizzle in the woods around *Mildeburg*. Down on the coast, the news reported that there was a band of clear weather. *Dass Urmistam* would be bathed in sunlight. The on-shore breeze was pushing the cloud back onto the *Chesfold Hills*, so that Sarnia was jogging through its haze as she took her afternoon exercise. There were many good routes around the house. Today, because of the weather, she was keeping to the shell paths, which crunched softly under her trainers. Even so, she would make sure that she clocked up at least three miles, as reported on the mileometer around her wrist.

She could hear the telephone warbling inside the house when she was still ten minutes away from her warm shower. It was probably Warren. It would be about work, not about last night.

He had come home in one of his happy moods. Strangely, she was pleased for him, because she cared for him, but at the same time also slightly aggravated. He did not seem to realise that she had had a bad day. Her cocktail morning with Tess, Christiane and the rest had not gone well. She had invited the new woman from *The Willows*, Castra, whose husband was in communications. Right at the very top in communications, mind you. He was really a top floor man, unlike Warren. And *The Willows* was a top-drawer house, twice the size of theirs. She wanted to be friends with Castra, and she wanted the new connections that it would bring.

But Tess had let her down. Why had she invited her? She should have known better. Tess was loud, grating, and kept talking about her husband. Not in a kindly manner, either. She even prattled about his poor bed-worthiness. Sarnia could see Castra making up her mind with every stupid word that fell out of Tess' big mouth. She had tried to repair the damage with flattering comments about Castra's house, but she had known that she was trying too hard. It was horrible. She doubted that she would be invited back to *The Willows*, and the absence of reciprocation was a real slight where she came from. She had moped around the house for the rest of the day.

And then, when Warren had come home, he had been light-hearted, not realising her inner turmoil. He had given her that kiss just below her ear, which he thought turned her thoughts towards the bedroom. Well it had done, once. But last night was the wrong time. She had turned away again, despite her passionate nature. And then she was angered by his easy acceptance of rejection. Again, she felt wasted, trapped in her high, romantic tower, waiting for something to happen.

Her resilience, of course, soon pulled her through and she was able to talk quite politely with her husband over dinner. This was their kind of intercourse. And as he told her all about the day's events, listening to her suggestions and interpretations, she forgave him for the transgressions that he did not even know he had committed.

After she had showered away the rain and perspiration from her jog, and was sitting by the fire poking the coals expertly with the burnt blade of their antique sabre, the phone went again. It was Cass. Warren had called earlier, but had not got through. He had to go to the North Coast, and would not be back until Friday night.

Sarnia liked Cass. She listened to her voice as it fluttered down from the sound system, crystal clear and intimate, just as if Cass was in the room with her. She heard the apology and sympathy, the small breaths and swallows from the woman fifty miles away. She listened for any tension, any strain or embarrassment in the disembodied articulations. No, Cass was telling the truth, as every other time. Nothing was being hidden. Warren really had gone away on business.

But it did leave her at a loose end. Restlessness suddenly descended on her. The opportunity for a quiet evening on her own did not appeal today. She mooched through to the kitchen and poured herself an orange juice. While she was there, she might as well take another look at her new pride and joy. She opened the door to the garage and stepped into the windowless darkness. She called out for the roof portals to open.

As the grey daylight sulked and dripped in through the new opening overhead, it revealed the dark, shining body of the *Tyratheon* space car. Its ceramic, black skin felt smooth and cool under Sarnia's fingertips. Its rounded, equilateral triangular form spoke of speed and power. And without deceit, for it could carry two passengers into low orbit within an hour of take-off. She had been up with Warren twice and already she had made three solo trips.

Warren had needed a lot of persuading before he had agreed to buy a *Tyratheon*. He had tried a lot of arguments against it. Not only were they very expensive, but he was unsure just how safe they were. This was the first ever, commercially available, private spacecraft. Some people thought that they would be banned once there had been a few catastrophic accidents.

But Sarnia had worn him down, as she always could when something meant a lot to her. And it was not just a status symbol, either. There was something that drew her to space. It was irresistible, the allure of spinning up amongst the stars, looking down on the child's face of the planet like a proud mother or goddess. She felt that a part of her belonged up there on the pedestal of high orbit.

She opened the hatch and admired the beautifully crafted interior, the sensual couches and the rich plastic controls. The wonderful, new, expensive smell rose up from the ship's sumptuous fittings. She felt a surge of almost sexual pleasure.

But this was no day for space hopping. She looked up at the dull grey clouds that skimmed over the garage roof and spat down at her. Not a day to be alone, either.

Back in the living room, she called her daughter and arranged to visit her for a couple of days. Within an hour, she was flying out over the treetops in her regular fly-car, leaving the dark, abandoned house behind her.

9

Two hundred miles away from *Mildeburg*, the weather had been ideal for a *Tyratheon* flight. Peet Vallew had been very excited about the prospect of his epic voyage of ascent. He had bought his triangular pride and joy eight weeks earlier, and he knew that this was to be his main pastime from now until the grave. Golf would just have to take second place henceforth. He would have gone up into world orbit every day, were it not for the safety warnings about excessive radiation exposure. The relative weakness of the *Tyratheon's* shielding, a concession to its overall weight, was one of the few parts of its configuration which warranted improvement.

For Peet, the time required to indulge himself in his new hobby was not a problem, not now that he was retired and widowed. Today he would be up there longer than ever before, because he was going to use his new float suit. It had just arrived and had checked out OK in the home quality assurance and self-validation procedure. Peet had made sure that he had followed exactly the in-built instructions. He expected to be striding across the planet for as long as he could in his first space walk.

He had set off straight after lunch; having made sure that Puff the cat's dispenser was fully loaded. He eased himself onto the cream navigation couch and selected his destination. He was going for a look at the *Sunspot* works. Although many of the construction components were already in transit to *Darius Proxima*, and so onward to the planet of *Morasmus*, the current configuration was supposed to be spectacular. Quite a few of his fellow members at the *Marshridge Hall Golf Club* worked for either the Towzer or Boquat companies, and they all said that there would probably never be anything like it built again. Seeing it for himself would be something to proudly talk about in the clubhouse, on the odd occasions that he now went there.

The *Tyratheon* shot straight upwards into the afternoon blue. He watched the world dwindle away beneath him as he pressed his face up against the shaded plyspex of the canopy. He felt as excited as a little boy, despite the weight and wear of his seventy-three years. To prove the point, he took a photo of Puff from his pocket and stuck it in the console grip. He had snapped her as she hung upside down from one of the dining room chair backs. Occasionally, she forgot her dignity and tried to kill one of the poor, dumb, innocent things. Her feline soul for a moment transported her to the blistering heat of the prairie and she became the mighty simba, pulling down great buffalo with her deadly jaws locked around their muscular throats. Some said that there were giant cats of this sort on the other planets, but it really seemed rather unlikely. Cats just seemed to be for fun. As Peet looked at his pet's image he could swear that, captured in her moment of savage rapture, she had an embarrassed expression on her startled face.

When he was out in orbit, released from the sweeping catapult action of the ionic beams, the *Tyratheon* nudged its way around the planet's halo and homed in on the *Sunspot* identification markers. Peet was impressed, all right, when he saw the construction site, hanging out like a brilliant necklace in space. It stretched for twelve miles, a thin linkage of thousands of pearl modules that had been thrown out, it seemed, by the centrifugal force of *Pirismus'* spin. Most of the work appeared to be on the inner sections, closest to the planet, which were bathed in light. The outer, completed units, which trailed away into the black void, were mostly in darkness, except where the standing beacons marked their presence.

Peet steered for a middle portion of the jewelled colossus. He took the ship right up to the point where it nudged up against the guard signals and anchored it to a convenient stanchion beam. He lay back on his couch and purred to himself. Puff would have recognised the feeling of inner contentment.

Peet unpacked the float suit and carefully manoeuvred his old body into its thick, supple folds. The best part was clipping on the big space helmet. He admired himself in the small on-board screen: he looked a real space hero in his bright yellow and black outfit, and it masked his true age rather pleasingly. The ship's safety systems gave him their own check over, and asked that he re-adjust his left glove to establish a better seal. Only then did the ship start to evacuate the cabin, sucking the air back into itself. Peet controlled his breathing carefully as he sensed the pressure lifting from all around his body.

Before long, in a glorious, dramatic gesture the *Tyratheon* released its canopy like a blooming flower, exposing Peet to the vacuum of space. He felt a moment's dizziness. It was like a spasm of vertigo as the swirls of the planet were revealed below, or above, him. He grasped desperately to the couch's arm holds, for fear of falling out into the world. A churn of nausea came and went.

Slowly his mind accepted that he was not actually falling in the traditional sense and he let himself go. He floated slowly out of the vehicle and into the body of the universe. He swam in the soundless currents of the ether and prodded himself forward with little dabs of his motion button. With each minute that passed he felt more content, more in the right place. He was an ancient cherub, smiling down on the face of humanity.

Along the thin miles of the *Sunspot* modules, he could see the various contractors' hoardings winking into the distance. Peet fumbled in the suit's side pouch and pulled out a small camera. He wanted to get his ship and the bright side of the planet in the same frame. His heart burst with pride at the thought of what a conversation piece it would be at the club. Better than any reported eagle or wonder putt.

As he slowly spun round towards his *Tyratheon*, he was surprised to see that there was another vehicle floating alongside. Now there was a peculiar thing. His ageing temperament wavered between anger that his privacy had been invaded, and pleasure at the opportunity of sharing the moment. He settled for a generous attitude and just hoped that his own darling ship was not about to be dented by its new neighbour. He pushed himself sluggishly back towards the two ships.

The newcomer's canopy slowly opened, and a little shiver went through Peet's heated body. The smooth movement looked somehow ominous, as if evil forces were being released from a long, embittering captivity in a coffin cage. Old memories of nightmare aliens slithered through his mind, and he knew that he was virtually helpless as he hung in the clawing, viscous grip of the vacuum. But it was not a monster. Instead, a silver-suited figure emerged from the cabin, moving even more gingerly than Peet had himself, he noticed. Peet gave a sudden grin of relief. It was presumably another adventurous pensioner. If this senior citizen hobby caught on, he thought, things might get as bad up here as at the golf course on a weekday. Full of old timers, retired from the real world and trying to fill the long hours of their shortening years. The hesitant figure swung a leg over the side of the cabin and teetered on the sill.

"Hang on and I'll give you a hand!" called Peet over the short-range radio. His companion looked up with a jerk of his head that freed him from his ship and set him adrift in space. He carried a long rod in his hand, like a walking stick. It seemed to confirm his appearance as an old, eccentric decrepit. The two suits floated towards each other like twin cherubim, gleaming in the planet-light.

Peet held out his hand as they came nearly within reach. He looked into the other's helmet and saw the eyes that lived inside it, behind the shaded plyspex. Fear returned to Peet like a mad dog, once shooed away but now returning with slavering mouth. Real fear flowed out from his trapped eyes but found no sea of pity waiting to receive it. There was no compassion there in that other suit, no humanity, no friendship. He drew his hand away, and in reply the other smashed his stick into Peet's visor. But it was not just a stick; it was a pointed metal rod, a sword possibly.

The first stroke did not pierce the thick, strengthened glass. Peet was shocked and immobilised by the fierce blow, right before his face. Adrenaline pulsed into him, demanding action, but another powerful stroke came at him. This one penetrated his weakened helmet, breaking into his headspace and right through into his left eye. It drove on and on so that he thought it might be emerging at the base of his skull.

There was no pain as the blade went cruelly, remorselessly on. His right eye turned inwards and saw the gleaming rod fitting snuggling into the hole in the visor. It made an airtight seal. He struggled to accept this reality into the clouded world of his shocked perceptions.

Then his worst fears were realised. His attacker started to twist and rotate the sword, so that its point ground around inside his head and the sharp edge of it widened the hole in the cracking plyspex. Here was real pain now. He could feel the roof of his mouth splitting and blood flooding into his throat. His ears burst like septic blisters. Peet screamed in agony and fury. And somehow he knew that his own scream was accompanied by the shrill whistle of his helmet's air as it rushed into the vacuum, carrying his terrified voice away through the breached glass.

His right eye reported to his convulsing brain that the whole visor had now shattered. Tiny round balls of plyspex were spraying out, leaving his face naked to the vacuum's kiss. In a desperate search for dying consolation, the remaining, coherent part of his mind sent out a prayer that Puff would be all right. Amongst the mad cacophony of other pains, fears, impulses, steel blades and terrors inside his head, this one tiny thought echoed with a vain hope that its pious sentiment might bring redemption. But there was no possible release, no escape as he was pinned back against the fabric of the universe like a moth.

It was not through pride this time, but very soon Peet's heart burst again.

10

It was raining in *Dass Urmistam*. The surrounding hills were sharing their gentle irrigation with the great, concrete forest that lined the *Timorillo River*. The taller buildings reached up into the low cloud, forcing the moisture-laden currents to part around their sharp edges and pointed towers. Sea birds had flown up from the coast and were circling in the grey sky or standing in leaden city lakes. Town grime was washing away down gutters and gratings.

Cheng Ham Tung liked this kind of weather. It made the city smell fresher and more strongly. His nose was a powerful navigational instrument at these times. He also thought that days like this, days of showering rain, gave the city's sighted citizens less of an advantage. They went about their business with down-turned faces, scarcely able to see better than he could himself.

He had been talking to his computer that morning as he sat in his room. They spoke about many things. And the computer's voice, which was Tung's own, told him that it was going to rain all day. He was pleased, even though he did have to go out soon.

He was going to the optician. His spectacles had been losing focus increasingly often, so that he had several bruises on his arms and shins from clumsy stumbles. He took one of his walking sticks from the hook by the door as he left his apartment.

Tung walked slowly through the city canyons, tapping the ground ahead of him in case of unexpected obstacles. He turned his face up into the gentle drizzle. Water splashed over his spectacles, but it did not matter to him.

The optician's was off the street at the base of Cashay Column, only a few blocks away. Tung took a seat in the waiting room, without being asked. He put his hands out in front of him, resting them on the top of his stick. There were some things that he needed to think through.

The first was his new neighbour in Cashen Column. The apartment next door had been empty for several months, ever since old Mandy Cortel had died. He had hardly known her, and she was certainly of no use to him, so he was quite pleased when she had been carried out by the city undertakers. He liked the quietness of the deserted rooms on the other side of his thin walls. He needed a lack of noise. His ears were keen and he wanted to hear the pulse of life in the city outside.

But then he had got in from his evening walk two weeks ago, and as soon as he was inside he knew that there was someone next door. Muffled bumps and scrapes pushed the silence away. Tung's jaw tensed and his teeth ground in annoyance, although he had to admit that things could have been worse. It was a single man, no children or squawking wife. And he was not noisy. In fact, in some ways Tung admired him, without ever having met him. He could tell that the man was powerful and intelligent. When he walked around the flat, Tung sensed the muscular body. He heard short, efficient movements; the man was organised. There was no angry scrabbling through drawers for misplaced belongings, no clattering of pans or scraping of furniture on the floor. Doors were not slammed and music was not played loud. Tung observed and recognised a man who had self-respect. He was so disciplined and organised that he might almost have been a blind man. Things had looked quite promising for a time. But then, there were the women.

Tung could have been very angry about the women. There were a great many of them; they came in the evening and they left in the morning. Tung himself led a chaste life. He had sacrificed himself to surgery to make it so. This debauchery might easily have driven him insane. He could not help but hear, and so picture in his mind, the carnal activities that filled the room with quiet gasps and touching flesh. But his initial outrage had been assuaged. And he knew why.

He could easily overhear those night-time conversations. Not the words, but the rise and fall of the speech. The duet of two separate performers, searching for harmony in the desperate, ancient dance of sex. He had initially expected to hear the wheedling, conniving, seducing sound of the man's deep voice. The sickening sound of his attempts to draw himself into the woman's favours, the croon of the seducer. It would have meant a failure by the man to keep cool, calm and dignified in the face of the terrible tyrant, the male sex drive.

That first night, he had already been grinding his teeth even before the verbal intercourse behind the thin wall had begun. But the music of those two voices had not been as he had feared. It was, in fact, the woman who spoke with a mixture of desperation and entreaty. And so it had been with all of her successors. They started calmly enough, thinking themselves secure in their position of sexual power and advantage. Then Tung could hear a huskiness enter their vocal chords as they began to fear that just perhaps they would not become the object of desire, the receptacle of hot male craving. And the man's voice remained composed and occasional. He seemed to deploy his influence without the need for speaking at length. He was not babbling and pleading for her favours, not in the least. It amused Tung to hear those women almost beg to be granted their satisfaction. And the lucky ones, those whose pride did not make them leave the apartment in a flurry of female indignation, were amply rewarded, he could deduce with ease.

Tung listened to the sex act, or more often plural acts, as he sat holding his breath with his knees drawn up to his chest. He could tell that the women did most of the physical work, despite the power and vigour of their partner. The hush said more about their ecstasy than any loud shrieks of delight. Even on his side of the divide he could feel the tension build and take form, drawn with great long brush strokes of passion. Although the creaking sounds were stilled now and then, he knew that the depth of the couple's desire would not be plumbed or sated until the lovers had plunged down onto the rock bottom of their lust.

Tung greatly enjoyed the way that the women had to surrender their accustomed position of sexual power. But most of all he was pleased that they never came back. He heard their submissive, imploring voices as they left in the morning, seeking reassurance that they be granted another visit. But they pleaded in vain. He came to gloat on the proposition. The certain fact that they would spend anxious days waiting for the summons that never came. Staring hopefully at their empty mail boxes, listening for the warbling netcall, never being without their handsets by their sides.

Tung was smiling to himself as he was called to the optician's chair. Doctor Mikuno sat next to him and examined his spectacles. He slipped them off Tung's head and placed them in the calibration frame. Tung felt exposed, naked without his black shades, and his hand edged up and covered his face. Mikuno was used to this.

"Well, Cheng Ham Tung, let us see how these are behaving. Forward scanning looks OK. The multi-frequency transmitter needs a touch of binocular adjustment. I'll just clean up the receiver patches with a touch of fluid. That should make things look somewhat clearer. Now, the sensory transmitters. This could require some retuning."

Mikuno gently pushed Tung's head back into the tuning cradle. The small inference stalks emerged and pressed up to his skull, just behind the ear.

"We've got to make sure the signals are getting through your thick bone and through to your receptor implants. Yes, this needs a few corrections. You sit here while I see to it."

Tung thought about the other thing that was worrying him. He thought that maybe he ought to get a job. Now that he had a new mission in life, his blind pension was running low. He really needed to augment it and acquire a salary. Before, he would have considered that taking a job was beneath his dignity. It would prejudice his purity. But now he had a higher purpose and such base employment might be excused. He needed to be able to afford more frequent visits to the club.

Mikuno returned and placed the opaque spectacles back on Tung's face. It took a few seconds for the instrument to make contact with his brain, and then the strange audio-vision was back. He could hear the shape of the objects in front of him, the standard optician's test set. He called off their co-ordinates to Mikuno's satisfaction. He once again had focused vision, to a range of around fifteen feet. Not good enough to see the features on a face, but enough to tell if it was wearing a hat.

Mikuno slapped Tung on the back as he showed him out of the shop, maybe as part of his customer service, maybe because he knew that it would annoy the small man.

It was still raining as Tung tapped his way back through the sodden streets. He could afford to walk a little faster now. He read the relief logos of the companies whose giant buildings stretched up above him. By the time he entered the portico of Cashen Column, he had made up his mind what kind of job to seek. Something in computers would be acceptable.

Farr Litten walked off the eighteenth green at the *Marshridge Hall Golf Club*, his round complete. He carefully peeled the glove from his left hand and folded it into his pocket, in no rush to be gone from this sun-blessed place. He had the feeling that he was leaving a theatre of dreams and was about to re-enter the mundane world; that cold realm of reality which swirled with the icy waters of demands and expectations. It was hard not to feel a tiny sense of dread at the prospect of relinquishing this brief time of leisure and returning to his life at work. It was only on these weekend mornings that he would spring out of his bed with exhilaration coursing through his veins. There was a very different feeling when he woke on workdays with a cold, tight compress gripping his heart. He would curse the alarm clock that had brought him out of sleep's sweet oblivion. It was not that Farr fundamentally disliked work. By the time he was a few hours into the day's routine labours he was content enough, sometimes even rewarded and motivated. But his intuition told him that his toil was draining the spirit from him, drip by drip. He gave his energy, his creativity and occasionally his passion to its demands, even though he knew there was no reciprocation beyond his monthly pay credit. The effect of time spent on the golf course was to allow him to plug back into some mysterious central power source and recharge his soul and his morale, or at least redress the balance a little.

Farr adjusted the bag to a more comfortable position across his back and, despite himself, turned his mind briefly towards affairs at Boquat. There were a few things that needed thinking through. The main issue was the *Sunspot* venture. There were more than fifty separate Information Systems development projects associated with *Sunspot* and the unthinkable was happening. Some of them were starting to run late. There were such reliable and well-established techniques for sizing and controlling computer programming these days that slippage was very rare. About the only thing that could cause it was if some areas of project control had been taken out of his specialists' hands. He had held a meeting with twelve of his managers on Friday, and his suspicions had been aroused. They themselves had not yet got all of the answers, but the tell-tales signs were there. There had been too much re-work, too many testing failures, an inordinately high staff turnover rate and numerous requests for re-assignment. It all smacked of user meddling. He would need to dig further.

Melvor caught up and walked with him towards the clubhouse.

"It'll have to be more lessons for me. You played well, though. Farr, I have a favour to ask. You know in my spare time I'm involved in the 'Workback' scheme? We provide sheltered careers for the challenged. I have a new quota to place. You mentioned how you are recruiting again. I wondered if you would have a look at a few of the better candidates? There are some with very good computing credentials."

"I'd be pleased to," said Farr. It sounded like a low-risk promise.

The other two players met up with them and all four golfers strolled into the clubhouse, blushed by the sun's tender burn and carrying in the tang of clean air. In the bar, there was talk about poor old Peet Vallew. He had been a member at the club for thirty years until he had been lost in space, five weeks ago. Most of the opinion was that he had been a little barmy to buy his own space ship, at his time of life. Farr was not so sure. There was an eternal lure from the heavens. He had never visited the *Sunspot* construction works, but he had seen the graphical representations and he knew that there was magic out there. The stars were able to tug at his imagination and pluck at his heart's strings even at his age. He guessed that the seductive caverns of space might easily rouse an old man's obsession.

Nobody knew how Peet had been lost. His corpse would never be found. This amiable clubhouse was probably the only place where he would be missed. He had no close family. In fact his disappearance had only been discovered because his home computer systems had complained to the local animal welfare agency that Puff's food had run out.

Most of the members thought that these individual spacecraft would be banned soon. It would not take many more deaths before they would be regarded as too dangerous. It was not that the vehicles themselves were unreliable; it was just that there were inevitable risks that would always accompany any journey into that ultimate, most hostile environment. Such sorties needed to be managed professionally.

As Farr was putting his clubs in the back of his fly-car, ready to leave, Melvor trotted over from his own vehicle. He had brought the data cubes of applicant details that he had mentioned out on the course. He handed them over with an embarrassed, sorry to be a nuisance, smile. Farr reassured him that he would take them seriously. He did need some new blood in the department, including a personal assistant for himself. Rachel had left to get married three months earlier, and his experiment of trying to do without her was not working out.

Farr looked down at one of the tiny, luminous identification badges. Picked out in small, orange dots was the name Cheng Ham Tung.

12

The *Sunspot* modules radiated out from the planet's orbit for fifteen miles. Their long chain was growing away from inner roots that barely tapped the outer atmosphere. Every day, a new module was born close to its mother planet and in its creation it pushed its brothers further out into the cold and dark of space, away from the glow of home.

Although most of the work was being carried out in this base region, where the module shells were fabricated and assembled, there was activity along most of its snaking length. Even at the farthest tip there were a few maintenance crews, preparing for the great construct's first and last journey. Most of the work out there was inside, within airlocks, completing fixtures and fittings. Applying many coats of luxury fit for the visitors to come.

Melda Smith was in charge of the Boquat Proletariat on *Sunspot*. Of the total Boquat work force of fifty thousand, two thousand were under her control. Jacques Bonne had been one of hers. Not many of the Boquat employees were required to go outside. Their responsibility was for the internal communications network and some of the computer sub-systems. Those, like Jacques, who had to venture beyond the safety of the huge inner space of *Sunspot*, received handsome danger allowances and their insurance provisions were substantial. So Melda had been surprised at how little excitement had been shown back at Tramalgar Colossus Headquarters. It was almost as though they had not believed her report, despite its various documents and attachments of corroboration. She felt that there was something wrong down there in the ivory tower these days. She had been with Boquat for twenty years, in their *Pirismic* terrestrial sites and now up here in space. This was the first time that she sensed confusion, indecision. But then it was the biggest thing that they had ever been involved in and perhaps this impression was inevitable.

For her part, she was a nuts, bolts and cable woman, not all that tuned into advanced computing. But that small inadequacy did not matter too much: the main thing in her job was man management, and she could handle that with her hands tied behind her back. She had always found it easy to command respect. Being six foot tall and two hundred pounds in weight helped. Her husband called her his blonde protector. Ted was still down on *Pirismus*, living alone now in *Mont Cebrane*, in the central highlands of *Kiceland*.

But she had not been able to protect Jacques, and that rankled. The disappearance of the old sightseer, Vallew, had worried her too. She had a sense that something was not right, out there where legend spoke of monsters and the unimaginable. The forward risk analyses had predicted a finite level of attrition amongst the workers, but the facts were now starting to surpass the grim forecasts. She had recently arranged that her out-workers operate in pairs, if they were not located in high-density sites. She had also decided to go out herself, even though it was not called for in her contract. Ted would have been very angry with her if he had known.

She did not know what she was looking for, or what she might do when she found it, as she patrolled her five miles of territory, spiralling all along the building line. She had acquired a mobility suit from one of the out-rig foremen, so she had a good turn of speed as she checked her industrious charges. There were at least six hours a day in which she was able to create a gap in her routine and go out into the airless emptiness. She did not mind having no leisure time left. There was nothing to do here anyway, even though it would eventually be the greatest entertainment facility ever built.

Melda had been performing her shepherding for five weeks, without anything untoward happening to either her people or to those darn sightseers who increasingly popped up from the planet to gaze in wonder at the monstrous fabrication. She was beginning to think that her fears of some malevolent intent had been unfounded. The company lawyers also seemed to have rebuffed the multiple attempts to have the project closed down, now that the losses had abated.

As she jumped out of the air lock and let herself bob amongst the stars, she thought this would probably be her last time. The scintillating galaxy had been pretty enough the first time out, but she was over all that now. She knew that some men found great and everlasting inspiration in the sight of those millions of distant suns. She was only a simple woman, but she had concluded that it was their sex's compensation for not being able to have children. The poor things needed something else to be wonderful in their lives.

She carried a soldering rod with her as she travelled along the *Sunspot's* skin, tapping it every now and then for her own amusement. It was the closest thing to a weapon that she could find. Because she was executing a spiral path down the structure, the horizon created by *Sunspot's* huge bulk was changing continually. She was always creeping around a sharp corner or scuttling over a rounded hull. She could have moved further away from the axis of her flight to have a better view, but that would have lengthened the distance she had to travel, and so the total transit time. She wanted this trip to be over quickly, partly because she had things to do when she got back, but also because she felt that inevitable and irrational fear that her last flight would be the one on which calamity would strike.

So she flew on in her bulbous suit, every second expecting something to appear from the other side of *Sunspot* and attack her. She did not dare think what it might be. And then again, it was possible that the threat would swoop in from outer space. She had to turn round and look behind her every few seconds, just to make sure that there was nothing but the unblinking stars. So it was that she was taken my surprise.

In Melda's suppressed imagination, she knew that it would happen like this. She was traversing a long, curved sweep of one of *Sunspot's* viewing galleries. The surface below her was of specially strengthened and tinted plyspex, which looked pitch black as there was no internal lighting behind it. It created a fairly good mirror, and she could see herself in its dark face. Even the brighter stars were visible, deep inside its secret interior, as if they had been caught and caged. She turned over onto her back again for a few seconds. She had not seen anything behind her in the accidental mirror, but there was no harm in checking. Maybe it had cunningly crept up so that she hid it from herself with her own bulk. As she flew on her slow arc, she generated her own planet rise. *Pirismus* appeared around the rim of her helmet and she had to watch it for a few seconds. She tried to recognise the continental shapes through their veil of swirling cloud. Perhaps she could give Ted a wave. She floated on her back and took a few moments to enjoy the sight. The planet's face smiled in response. It was the first time that she had relaxed her guard since she came out, an hour ago.

Then the gloved hand came over her shoulder, and the arm wrapped itself around her neck. Her body snapped into action, as if the attacker's limb was carrying an electric charge, but she was almost too energised. She had moved so quickly that she had let the solder-weapon slip from her grip. It had not floated away because of the restraining strap, but she could not get it properly back into her hand. Nor was she able to rotate herself to face her enemy. Melda knew that she was losing vital seconds as her attacker wrapped himself more tightly around her. She expected the sharp pain of administered death at any moment. But her adversary was missing his opportunity as well. She did, surprisingly, have time to locate her suit control buttons and was able to spin around to face him with her burning weapon at the ready. She pushed the heavy weight of him back, but his hand was clasped to her survival pack. She prepared to thrust the glowing point into his throat, her feelings fired into murderous resolve. She glanced into the space helmet that was almost touching her own and was now bathed by the gentle light from the planet below.

She was shocked again, this time the shock nearly making her spew. The face she saw there was horrible. Frightful. The expression was like that of a wild animal. It snarled. His lips were drawn back, revealing rotten teeth and gums. His black tongue was thrust out like a serpent's, sensing for her fear, mocking her feeble attempts at escape. Perhaps he had spared her for a few moments only to prolong his pleasure and her agony. Melda saw the eyes, too, wide and staring into her own. They were blood-shot, unmoving and unmoved. But, worst of all, was that she knew that face. Or she had known it, when it had been human. Then it had been Kennedy. Then he had been a pleasant man, about her own age, who had been in her maintenance crew.

The terrible, jarring recognition unnerved her again. She shut her eyes tight and pushed the evil transformation away with a tearful, weeping gasp, like a child rejecting a once favourite doll. And, like a broken toy, Kennedy floated away from her and she felt his hand disengage from her suit's supply tubes. When she re-opened her eyes, she saw the same horrible look on his face. But now it spoke of terror, not manic aggression. She realised, almost with relief, that Kennedy was dead.

Melda was a strong woman and she rapidly gathered her tattered nerves. She secured Kennedy to a nearby vent clamp and began to look for Mordichelli. They had been out together. They should have been working two modules further down the chain. She went four units along before she gave up, partly relieved not to have found another twisted corpse in the spectral light of planetary space. She towed Kennedy back alone.

Doctor Thebarius examined Melda first, despite her protests. Only after he had given her a mild sedative spray would he look at Kennedy's remains. He reported his findings to Melda and her supervisors after his initial, superficial inspection. He pointed out that he was not a qualified pathologist, and that a full post-mortem could only be carried out after Kennedy was transported back to *Pirismus*.

But he was pretty sure of the cause of death: there was not much room for doubt really. He had found at least forty stab wounds on Kennedy's body. He looked at his audience, as they sat before him in the conference room, and powered up the big display screen. He popped up a few of the less gruesome scans that he had taken.

"A long, broad blade was used. I think that we can agree that it was a frenzied attack. The cuts are all over his body. There's even one on his foot. The attack must have lasted for several minutes. He fought for a long time. Many of the gashes are on his arms. I believe that it was a solo assailant, and not very well co-ordinated, I would say. Virtually all of the wounds are in non-lethal areas. My guess is that Mordichelli was attacked first, so that Kennedy was alerted to the danger."

"So what actually killed him?" asked Costa Spratt. He was sitting next to Melda and he could see that she was beginning to tremble and go pale, which he was sure was from grief rather than any fear or squeamishness. He knew that she would not bring the explanation to a rapid conclusion herself, so he wanted it over with on her behalf. Doctor Thebarius heard the edge of irritation in Costa's voice. He looked to Melda and saw the situation immediately. He cursed his own enthusiasm and stupidity. He switched off the projector and straightened up from the table where he had been leaning.

"The fatal blow was to the heart, from the front. Judging by the dispersal pattern of the other wounds, it was almost unintentional. You might even call it blind luck." He had not meant it as a joke, and no one laughed. He watched as Costa helped Melda out of the room, with the others gathered round.

The doctor looked around the conference room and sat down to complete his report, before sending it down to Headquarters. It annoyed him that such an important document would be going through company channels, rather than straight into the judicial system. His faith in Boquat's procedures had been shaken over the last year. In his time up here, in the angel's sphere, looking down like a god on the turning throng of humanity, he had begun to feel like a transmitter whose receiver had been turned off.

But it did not stop him from doing his best as he filed and sent his document. As he left the large room and switched off the light, he looked at its future complex assignment tab indicating its ultimate purpose. In another year, this place would be a racquets court. He could do with a game right now.

13

Rattle Point curved out into the turbulent waters between ocean and estuary. To the west was the other world of the shifting, blue seas. Uncharted depths and mysterious species lurked there, more alien than anything that Forba Curzine had ever encountered. To the east were the brown currents of the *Timorillo River* as it spread out from its restraining banks to exhaust its floods in futile battles with the ocean swell. Birds wheeled around the landing pad, balanced at the extreme end of the Rattle, hoping for food.

Forba had parked his *Cabbilux* fly-car so that he could look out on either side of the point's rocky extremity. He had come here to eat his lunch, but the birds would cry in vain. He was not in a generous mood. Nothing had been going the way he had expected since he had made his predatory swoop on this fat, rich land. He had expected to be luxuriating at the top of society, splashing his muscular body in the opulent cream of their meritocracy. Instead, he was scraping around at the bottom of the pack, feeling the oppressive weight of near poverty on his broad shoulders. This was not what he had come for. The women were letting him down; he had no problem with the quantity, just the quality.

He broke open his meal pack and gave it a shake, allowing it time to heat up. He was alone in the car. He had dropped off his fare at *Gosbeck Bay*, fifteen minutes earlier. At least she had not made a pass at him. He had a good hour to go before he was due to be back on duty, but he took a little pleasure from the warmth of the sun as it shone in through his windscreen, and in the seascape that washed away to the horizon.

He had arrived on *Pirismus* with very little money. Although he had not found a rich protector within the first few days, as he had hoped to, this was not a major problem. He knew how to get by. He took his rooms as close to the centre of *Dass Urmistam* as possible. That way he could visit the clubs at night, but he seemed to have lost his knack with girls.

It was soon obvious to him that things were arranged differently here. He knew that there were a lot of career men, taking a lion's share of the planet's wealth and power. Women here were strangely satisfied with the situation, which surprised him. It cut down his chances, even though there were some female executives and widows to be found. There was still the incentive that these illusive few were immensely more wealthy than anyone on his home planet. In this respect his research had not let him down. He would just have to look more carefully.

The first night out, when he had gone to the *Starlit Canopy Club*, had been a bad start. He had to pay to get in, and then, after he had cruised across the dance floor, he had reached the bar without anyone offering to buy him a drink. Of course, as soon as he had a ten-dollar beer in his hand, blonde Corella had come across and asked him if he was a stranger. She was nice enough, but the bad sign was that she did not seem to think she needed to make it perfectly clear how well off she was. He would have liked to have known, but he did not wish to appear too mercenary. So he gave her some time.

Corella had dragged him onto the dance floor and made her intentions perfectly clear as she pressed herself against him. He had noticed her glancing across to her girl friends, who watched them from the shadows. His heart sank. He could imagine that she had been the one with enough front to close in on him, encouraged by the mixed envy and fear of her confidants. Her friends would have dared her to approach the big, strange man who was the best catch in the place. She was not his type, but she was not going to let him off the hook now that their proximity had allowed her to sense his impressive proportions. She clung tightly as the flog music thumped through their bodies and the holograms danced around their entwined forms.

Soon enough, she had slipped out of his arms and clasped his big hand in her small, cool fingers. She led him away, towards the door and her rising desires. Out in the cool night air, he had suggested a meal. He was hungry, and he thought it might calm her down. She reluctantly agreed, and they stepped into a nearby *Chompamat*. He tried to take his time over the thick pizza. He chewed slowly, hoping that Corella's mastication rate would also moderate in line with his own. But she was determined to get on with it. He guessed that she had a schedule in mind, one that would impress her friends in the morning telling. She disposed of her supper in no time at all. Then, for a horrible moment, it had seemed that he would have to pay. He had to fiddle around in his jacket for some time before she got the idea and popped her own card into the table slot.

They had gone back to his apartment. He could not find any way out of it despite his vast experience in these matters, and he knew that there was great risk in getting a reputation for spurning women. These things got around fast. He had offered her coffee and tried to talk about trivia. He spoke low and slow, but this merely seemed to inflame her further. He asked her about her life. Not that he had any great hopes of her, but there may have been clues for future use. She had their clothes off in no time. He had, he admitted, been pleased at the obvious delight she took in his body. He always was. She had purred and squealed as she lowered herself onto him. He could tell that she had never been so fulfilled.

But despite her multiple pleasures of the night, he knew that he would not see her again. When she left in the morning, she gave him a quick kiss on the cheek and a sad smile. She asked if they could meet up again and gave him her details, even though she knew that there was no hope. She seemed, thankfully, to be resigned to this and he realised that, partly, this was because she knew that she could not hope to keep such a man for herself. But, as ever, when he saw her pretty figure disappear behind the elevator doors he still felt used, a little pang of hurt stabbing him as he closed the door quietly on another fruitless escapade.

He put Corella down to experience, thinking that he would move on. But she had merely started a repeating pattern. Although he did not return to the *Starlit Canopy*, he only seemed to attract more Corellas. His reputation must have spread around club-land. Young women were queuing up, and he felt he had to oblige. He needed the meals that they bought him and they usually helped out about the apartment with a little ironing or cleaning, laundry and stitching. Very occasionally they left him a little money. Of course, during these brief liaisons he avoided sex if he could, which was hardly ever.

One morning, as he kissed a girl called Sonia goodbye, she said that he was just as good as Beryl had told her. And Beryl, he was pretty sure, had been about a week ago. What he had surmised about an orderly queue being organised by the impecunious club-land girls was suddenly revealed as fact. Sonia meant it kindly, as she oozed out of his life, but it hit him hard. He was being passed around like a toy. Like a freak, only good for one thing. He decided that he must break the cycle. He did not want that kind of reputation. He was looking for something secure, long term.

He needed a proper income and independence. So he had come by his job driving fly-cars around *Dass Urmistam* and its surrounding dormitories. It would do to fill in with, until he worked out how to break through to a better class of women. He sipped his meal pack as he looked out over the battling waters. He was not entirely sure that men were made to work all their lives, but this would do for a while.

When Forba returned to his apartment that evening, he approached his door with long, quiet strides as always. He well understood the need to avoid annoying the neighbours. The security scan on the wall had just verified his life signature, and the door was swinging open, when he felt a hand on his shoulder. He spun round, ready to strike. This was not how people greeted one another where he came from. But he saw that it was his next door neighbour. They had never met, but Forba knew that he lived between a retired lady and an old, blind oriental. He also knew that Cheng Ham Tung had the reputation for being extremely unsociable.

He looked down at the short man who stood before him, and was surprised that there was a smile on his round face. Not a very pretty smile; not one that had been practised in front of a mirror; nevertheless, it was an attempt at friendliness. Tung's head swayed from side to side slightly, helping his vision spectacles to get a broad impression of Forba's facial details, and he had his hand held out in greeting.

Forba spread his fingers and engulfed his neighbour's small palm in his own large, black fist. The feel of Tung's clammy grip was not pleasant, but he shook it warmly, nevertheless.

Tung let out a vague sigh of satisfaction, which sounded as though he considered them firm friends.

14

Chilly Perez floated round the kitchen on her puppy seat. She swayed her body to induce a rocking motion as it cruised four feet above the brown tiling of the floor. She swung her legs and cocked her big toes as another small biscuit popped out of the dispenser onto her tray. She sighed at the thought of having to suck her way through it, but she knew her duty. Outside it was another sunny day. The trees were swaying in a brisk breeze and she noticed the birds were having some difficulty as they fluttered over the garden, where their food had been scattered. Chilly wondered whether to express delight at their antics or begin to complain. She had been in her chair for at least an hour now, as it trailed around after the electronic lure in her mother's belt. She had been over most of the bungalow several times, scattering her playthings as she went. It seemed to be about time for another practice totter. Now that she was just over a year old, she felt she needed a lot more practice at getting about on her own. As she thought that she really must attract her mother's attention, the front door bell played over the wall speakers. She giggled as the puppy chair leapt away after the lady of the house and down the cool hall.

It was Grandma. Chilly was pleased to see her Gran's eyes go straight to her as the big wooden door swung open. She threw her sodden biscuit on the floor in greeting. Sarnia Gallant came in and kissed her Mum on the cheek, cleverly closing the door at the same time. Chilly's big eyes watched the act of supreme co-ordination with admiration. Would she ever be able to carry out these cunning manoeuvres, which the big people took for granted? She was still in a daze of contemplation when her Grandma swooped and gave her a kiss on the cheek, too. She started back in her seat. She should have known that was coming, it always did. She must remember to be ready for it next time. This memory thing must get better with age as well, she hoped. It was probably something else that needed a lot of practise.

Tania Perez made her mother a cup of coffee and another one for herself. Sarnia had been making frequent visits in the last few months. She did not mind. It was good to have her expert confirmation and advice about baby matters, even if she did generally choose to ignore it. It was easier to show the little marks on Chilly's skin when she was actually here, easier to let her mother listen to the occasional baby coughs and hear her mother say that it was not a problem. Her mother was coming more often because of Chilly, naturally, but she could tell that there was something else. Something that she would get around to talking about in the end.

The two women walked through with their mugs and out into the garden, with Chilly following behind on her floating plinth.

"Like a Mekon," her mother always said, not bothering to explain the reference. Tania took her baby out of the chair, taking care not to strain her back. She had often been given good advice about that. Some of her friends said it had spoilt their sex lives forever, that post-natal back twinge. Tania was still not interested in renewing that part of her life anyway, but she took the point. She set Chilly down on the grass, in amongst the inflated tubes of the lawn maze. The baby would spend a long time walking around the maze, or shuffling on her bottom, looking for birds to chase away. The women sat together on the sun chair.

"So, how are things at home, Mum?" asked Tania, sipping her coffee and thinking that she did not really need another drink.

"Oh, fine dear. Things go on as usual, you know. No major disasters like that time with Tess. I've built a few more bridges here and there. Climbed a few rungs up the stairway of life. I don't think your father appreciates it, of course."

"How is Dad?"

"He's fine. Busy at work. He spends a lot of time over at North Coast."

"I thought he was working on *Sunspot*."

"He is. But he says that it is important to keep Boquat's traditional business under control at the same time. I don't think he is all that keen about *Sunspot*, really. Its a bit too filled with modern technology for him."

"Really? I think it sounds great. When it's all put together it will be wonderful. Not that Rico and I will be able to go for a few years, not with Chilly." She looked accusingly across to where her daughter was toddling about in her safe prison. Tania smiled at the look of concentration that furrowed her little girl's brow. This was serious, growing up work.

"Yes, but Dad doesn't like Farr Litten very much. He thinks Farr has life too easy, playing with his computers all day. Pulling in a big salary when he has only got a staff of a few hundred to worry about. And it's not as if they are difficult people to manage. They are all intelligent, in a technical kind of a way, and self-motivated. It's easy meat compared to being in charge of several thousand production workers. He has had a few discipline problems to deal with, and these have always worried him."

Tania liked to pursue the truth.

"I understood that it's the computer systems that will make or break *Sunspot*. Not just the bits that keep it working, but the entertainment facilities it will have."

"Oh, I don't know. They call it a new generation of artificial intelligence, but Warren says that's just the marketing men's invention."

"That's a pity. It all sounds rather good in the magazine articles. They say that it will learn about every guest's personal preferences, and create a leisure environment to suit each individual's appetites. Exercise, music, films, food, drink and . . . other things." Tania thought better of describing some of the wilder suggestions that had been made in the last edition of *Perfect Woman*. She flushed a touch at the thought. Perhaps she would take extra care of her back. Maybe Rico was in for a pleasant surprise tonight, after all.

"Well, don't talk about it to your father when he comes over this evening," said Sarnia as she got up. She went over to Chilly, who was starting to rub her eyes and grizzle, and picked her up for a grand-maternal cuddle.

Later that day, in the early evening, the women were still out in the garden when the phone rang.

"That will be your father calling to say he'll be a little late. He will bring flowers to make up for it," predicted Sarnia, as Tania picked up the nearest handset.

"That was Dad. He's going to be a little late," she said as she hung up.

An hour later, Warren arrived with a bunch of roses. He wondered why the women giggled to each other as he gave his wife and daughter their kisses, but he knew better than to ask. He executed his usual arrival procedure, which he saw as completing the girl-kissing set, by tiptoeing into Chilly's bedroom, where she was sleeping in her protectacot. He gently brushed the sticky hair away from her forehead.

Over dinner, it was Warren who raised the *Sunspot* project, not the women. Sarnia knew that he was going to make a bit of an announcement. She could see him order his thoughts, although he had undoubtedly pre-prepared his little speech. She smiled as Tania put down her utensils and clasped her hands on the dining table, in the "paying attention to Dad" pose that she had adopted on such occasions ever since she had been a small child. Warren let it all pass over his head.

"I was in Jim Moffat's office today. I was explaining how the project was running late, all due to computer problems of course, and my plans for minimising the delay. I've taken some of the systems tasks off Farr Litten to get them moving and I've brought in some more Knowledge Engineers. But it still won't get us back on track in time."

"In time for what?" asked Sarnia. Warren fidgeted in his chair. Not a good sign, she thought.

"Not in time for the launch date."

"Well, that can be delayed, can't it?"

"Apparently not. Jim explained that bookings have been going very well. In fact so well that any postponement of the opening is out of the question. The compensation payments would be astronomic."

"So what are you going to do, Dad?" asked Tania, quite intrigued by the growing tension around the table.

"We are going to have to carry on working as *Sunspot X* is in transit."

"Well, that won't go down very well with your workers. And their wives will be up in arms. It's going to be an eighteen month round trip isn't it? Who would want to spend all that time in space?" asked Sarnia.

"No, it will not be a holiday. But Jim says that the work force will go along with it."

"Really? Why is that?" Sarnia thought that she knew the answer as she looked at her husband's florid face.

"Because he thinks that I should go with them," said Warren.

15

The desks of the Boquat Knowledge Engineers stretched in two straight lines under their indirect, pink, diffuse lighting. Acoustic hoods encased each station, stifling the noise of the computers' babble, like giant eggshells. A few of the Engineers talked into their terminals' electronic ears, but most finger-keyed and clicked their instructions into the patient machines. Some of the Engineers had decorated the insides of their transparent, plastic hoods. They chose pictures of brains and big ears. That sort of thing. The main thing was that the pictures were big enough or dense enough to give a degree of privacy by reducing visibility into their private worlds.

Izabel Torini kept hers clean. She liked to be able to look around when she was at work. She had just been watching Farr Litten as he walked down through the Department with Sandra, her supervisor. She liked Farr. He had a nice body. Good bum. And he treated his staff well. He was not over familiar with them; he kept pretty much to himself, in fact. But she could tell that he had respect for them. He told them the truth, and dealt with them as intelligent people. When she had started at Boquat, six years ago, she had toyed with the idea of trying it on with Farr, but she had thought better of it when she found out that he was married. Not only that, but married and nice. One or the other she could have handled, but not both. It was not certain that he would have gone for it anyway. She did not kid herself that she was a good looker. She saw her ordinary, round face and short, broad body in the bathroom mirror every morning. Bigger breasts might have improved her figure, but she was not going to spend her hard earned salary on such trifles. For her, it was sufficient that she had nice skin and big, brown eyes under her lustrous, straw fringe of hair. Men came along often enough for her. They did not stay around for long, though. They were usually a bit too dumb for her.

Although Izabel enjoyed observing the goings on around the computer deck, she was not a lazy worker. She went fast. Everyone knew her to be one of the speediest programmers, as she liked to think of herself, in the company. But you could not keep at it all day long without a break. This was creative work; you needed to recharge every now and then. So sometimes she would surf around the network, looking for interesting diversions. That was how she had found out about the new Coding Group in the Production Corps, three floors higher up in Tramalgar Colossus. There were ten of them now, and they had taken over the propulsion and environment systems development. This was work that other members of KE should have been doing. They had started to run late on the project, but that was because of continually changing requirements. It had been as though somebody in Design, or Management more likely, could not make up their mind; anyway somebody in the Production Corps. And now they had hired their own developers! Izabel's sceptical streak had noticed that, in business, it is very possible, even probable, that you get rewarded for your own mistakes.

In her moments of leisure, Izabel had been having a little fun with this group of newcomers, the Bugs as she called them. They were really not very good. She found some amusement in tampering with their work. Nothing too destructive or strictly against company guidelines. Just the odd voice interface made squeaky or the temporary introduction of an annoyingly sticky cursor. They were easy meat, or they had been.

But that had changed now, with their latest recruit. He was a more serious proposition. The first time that Izabel had left him with a friendly little virus, one that produced the sound of a sneeze each time that he hit the delete key, he had sent it back to her with the nasal explosion changed into a scream of pain. She had raised her security barriers straight away. It had not been funny. It was a real cry of tortured agony, too graphic to be a joke. The terrible noise had actually made her cry, sitting and sniffing inside her big, plastic cocoon.

She had kept her eye on this new Bug since then, peeking into the human resource folder every now and then. She followed some of his work as well. He was good, she had to admit. He was, oddly, a lot better than he was making himself appear to his supervisors. Like her, he achieved a lot in a very short time. Then he went off to do other things, which Izabel was unable to trace, they were so heavily encrypted. The net result was a level of output much like the rest of his group. She knew that he was fooling his team leader, but she did not know why. Something told her that it was not for any good reason.

Shortly after her screaming shock, she had the opportunity of asking Farr about the Bugs. She did not get many chances to talk to him, but that day he had asked her for a personal update on the progress of her Leisure Attitude work. He was really interested, a rare condition for a top manager in Boquat, she thought. It was good fun work, too, developing the interactive features of the robotic tennis player. She was using body language recognition techniques to ensure that the robot eased off if its guest was getting too downhearted. It was not just a question of looking for racquets being thrown on the court. It was able to detect much more subtle signals than that.

So before she went back to her desk, she had turned around at the door of Farr's office and asked about the Bugs. She was wearing one of her shorter skirts, and was pleased to see that Farr quickly cast his eyes up and down her legs. She rewarded him in turn with a willing smile, which said that she was not offended by his scrutiny. But she had been disappointed with his answer about the Bugs. He knew about them, but he was not annoyed or offended. He just said that he understood their position, and as long as it helped the project along, it was OK with him. This was one of the other things that had cooled her down about Farr as a potential bed mate. He just did not get mad enough. She had seen Warren Galant come down through the department, acting like he owned it, and walk straight into Farr's office without asking. They could all hear Warren pounding away about some imagined problem, as Farr sat and took it all patiently, without shouting back or putting Warren in his place. It always seemed to her to be another case of wrong winning through. And here again, Farr had no intention of going to Jim Moffat and insisting that the Bugs be closed down. She would have, in his place. You could take customer service too far. The users needed to be kept in their place.

Anyway, Izabel was going to watch the Bugs on her own initiative, even though Farr had not endorsed it. And if she found something really going bad, she would not sit back and let it happen. She felt quite personal about it. Even though the new Bug programmer, this Cheng Ham Tung, was a sheltered worker, she did not like him or trust him. She felt no compassion about his blindness. In their world, that was no great disadvantage. In their virtual, unreal realm of jagged logic and slithering inference he was not disabled at all. In fact he was dangerous.

16

Melda Smith looked out at the brilliant canopy of pure stars. Her gaze took her to the edge of infinity for an instant, but her mind recoiled from that unfriendly place. She was not drawn by the studded view of unreachable places and ancient times. It was here and now that worried her. From the observation bubble at the side of the *Sunspot* condominium she could look up the entire length of the module chain as it whipped out towards the cosmos. Kennedy used to call it the stairway to heaven. It did look like a giant's ladder, if you had that kind of imagination. He had had a poetic nature, Melda thought, recognising her own as more down-to-earth. Who said that women were the romantic gender?

Now that Kennedy was dead, chopped and slashed by some mad, tripper bastard as he floated in his helpless, straight-jacket of a space suit, Melda found she was remembering more about him than she thought she had ever known. Little things which he had said and done; sweet things, many of them. A few words here, and a facial expression there. A touch of friendship when things were getting her down, maybe. She had thought that her shock and grief were over after the first few days, but these memories kept the pain flooding back in waves. From this off-planet, infinite perspective of the universe, which somehow shrank the distance that lay between the living and the dead, she found that she was growing more fond of him every day. Like the scattered galaxy, he looked beautiful and clearly defined to the distant observer. At night she was crying tears for him, as if he was a lost lover. During the day, her mind was focused on preventing any further damage to her other charges. She hoped that she might to be lucky enough to encounter the murderer. She imagined plunging her glowing sword-welder into his black heart and seeing the flesh burn.

At last, through the great eye of the bubble porthole, she saw what she had been waiting for. The navigation lights of an approaching shuttle appeared against the blur of the *Pirismus* atmosphere. It hung next to the transportation module, in the base region of the construction works. A docking tube writhed outwards and connected onto the shuttle, like a slow snakebite. Melda knew that the ship had brought some Security Agents. It would also take Kennedy's body home.

Three hours later, Melda was in the main Conference Room with the other contract managers. The site Overseer, Standish Klinedorf, introduced Agent Feliskaya who had come with four other security specialists. Not really enough to cover what was, by now, twenty-two miles of complex building work, thought Melda. And Feliskaya, a big blonde woman with aggravatingly large breasts, started by explaining that they were here to give advice only. They had no instructions to conduct policing operations in space. Opinion back at Headquarters was that any further attacks could be forestalled by improved working practices. Melda started to lose interest. This seemed like another case of too little, too late. Her annoyance was only increased by the sight of the men's eyes as they followed Feliskaya's chest, pacing to and fro at the front of the room. She doubted their ability to hear the blonde woman's words with objectivity.

Klinedorf rounded the briefing off by trying to give them comfort and assurances. One of the things that he thought should set their minds at rest was the knowledge that the *Sunspot* surveillance and support systems were now being monitored down on *Pirismus*. Teams from the main contractors, Towzer, Boquat, Signal Hudson and Freestone were covering things round the clock.

Melda was not reassured. Her instinct was to close up with her team, here on the edge of space. To huddle together and take their own precautions against the unknown threat. Exposing themselves to indifferent strangers, safely sipping their coffees down on the planet, where there was not the constant threat of the air being ripped from their lungs, made her feel cold, not snug and safe.

When the meeting was all over, Klinedorf came over to her. He had not seen her since the loss of Kennedy and Mordichelli. He put his arm around her big shoulders and told her of his sympathy. She did not mind, as there was a genuine touch of sincerity in his well-manicured voice. He said that he would come back with her. He needed to take a trip to the far end of the unit chain, to check that it was ready for the installation of the huge engine module. The fuel cells, the giant

Crocodile tanks, were already in place, he said, and the drive unit was due in the next few weeks. This was a vital, if temporary, part of the construction, as it would have to slow the whole gargantuan snake of a structure down at the end of its voyage — when it reached *Morasmus*, so he could not be too careful about its preparation. Melda was not in the mood to mention that she was also worried about the Crocodiles.

The other men were clustered around Agent Feliskaya, obviously trying to get a better perspective on things, so Melda and Klinedorf left together. They were the only passengers on the first small monorail train that left the Conference area, but whose track ran the entire length of *Sunspot*. Melda would be getting off after forty-five minutes on the little train. Klinedorf would still have another quarter of an hour to get to his destination.

They got into the middle carriage of the three open cars that made up the train. They did not bother with the metal safety bars. It only trundled along at twenty miles per hour. When it was commissioned for use by real paying customers, the bars would be compulsory. But as professionals, they considered themselves exempt.

They sat side by side. Klinedorf sensed Melda's mood of sadness, but he knew better than to think that he could talk her out of it, even with his cleverly targeted words of consolation. So he just chatted about ordinary, everyday things. He understood that it was the quiet, caressing, smooth passage of life that healed wounds the best. He indulged himself as well by telling her about his wife and four children, down in *Dallison City*. He realised that she would not be listening to his words, and it would not matter.

Melda did not mind the word-massage. She had respect for Klinedorf. Co-ordinating a project of this size took an awful lot of skill, knowledge and dedication, and she knew that he was up to it. There had been many occasions, in her experience, when his own intervention and been important. He was a good man. She was mildly interested to hear of the Klinedorf children: somehow she had always thought that he might be homosexual. Earlier on, he had been one of the few men not transfixed by the movements of Feliskaya's tunic buttons. Here it was again, the feeling of unexpected pleasure at personal contact. Of being surprised that another human being was pleasant, if not interesting. It brought back thoughts of her last encounter with Kennedy. As the train and Klinedorf trundled on, she tried to hold back the tears that threatened once again. The kindness in the voice next to her did not help to soothe her emotions; it rather increased the pressure behind her eyes and in her chest.

Every so often, the train passed over a set of junction points. When *Sunspot* was fully assembled, the railway system would criss-cross the whole complex. The spur rails were already there, peeling off from their straight path and only stopping where they reached the far outer wall of the module. These temporary panels would be removed in the fully operational, complete *Sunspot*. They were also equipped with explosive bolts, for quick removal, as they would serve as emergency exits during the space flight, in case of fire or air corruption. Safety systems would ensure that they only released if the module was unoccupied, or its occupants were properly suited, of course.

The carriage gave a small jolt every time it passed over one of the points. Each impact brought Melda's tears closer to the surface, filling the corners of her eyes with little sparkles of sad light. Even though there was another ten minutes to go before she reached her stop, she decided to walk the rest of the way. It would do her good and allow her to get herself under control. Klinedorf understood. She tapped the pad on her blue armrest and the train began to slow down.

She stood up as the train nearly came to rest, and skipped lightly from its moving platform. As her trailing foot was just leaving the rubber matting, she could sense the train start to accelerate away again. Her ankle was given a slight twist as her grip betrayed her. She re-established her balance and looked after the train. It was just passing through into the next module. She saw the light that was reflected on Klinedorf's silver hair change colour from blue to bluer as he passed over the module threshold. She might have laughed at the sight of the back of his head as it sped away, but there were two small noises that brought the cold hand of fear back around her heart.

First, she heard a quiet snick from the train itself. She knew from the way that Klinedorf looked down in surprise that his safety bar had swivelled round and locked into place. Then there was a heavier, louder clunk from ahead of the train, further away down the tunnel of modules. She knew that it was the points being thrown. All she could do was stand and watch the inevitable.

The train carried on accelerating. Klinedorf tried to look back at her, but he was too tightly restrained. His carriage diverted from its true, straight path and curved away, towards the outer wall. He was fighting hard now, straining to squeeze out from the iron grip across his waist. But the train careered towards the removable wall panel. The explosive bolts fired and the entire side of his module fell away in front of him, shot away by the power of air pressure. Melda saw him throw his head back in a cry of fear or anger. The safety bulkhead that lay between the two sectors snapped across before her, saving her own air from rushing away into the vacuum, but she was not spared the sight of Klinedorf's demise, thanks to the transparent centre window.

She saw the train accelerate out into the blackness. It arced elegantly away from *Sunspot*, each of the three carriages diving down in turn. In the centre car, Klinedorf's body contorted horribly. His arms flew up above his head and she had the distinct impression that his fingers were bursting, like frying sausages. He fell away in his toy train, a crumpled doll and an eternal passenger. The stars appeared as sharp, thin nails, waiting to impale him. To add Klinedorf to the collection of corpses that hung from their ethereal web.

Melda stumbled towards the bulkhead window to watch the last sight of him. Before she got there she was painfully sick, bending forward with her hands on her knees. She took great gulps of air as she looked down into the depths of her own vomit. Spirals of galactic proportions seemed to live there, too.

A little cleaning scavenger darted out from the service hatch and started to wash the mess away, drawing the acidic pool up into its bulbous body. Melda watched the small machine until it had removed all trace of her weakness. She spat out the last sour remnants onto the little worker's shell. It hummed and turned its small, gyrating cleaners on itself. She was quite surprised that anything was working properly any more.

17

The *Timorillo River* wound slowly north, its great sluggish currents carrying the rich nutrients of the land out to sea, where millions of hungry mouths were waiting. On the river's east bank, the sprawl of *Dass Urmistam* thinned as the *Timorillo* widened and the land became wooded and meadowed. This was where the marinas had been built. They stretched all the way to the delta. The downstream harbours were for the serious sailors. Ocean going boats lay moored in their deep waters, white hulls glistening in the diffuse light. These powerful vessels could make thirty knots, even in heavy weather. Some luxury models could also convert to submarine propulsion. If the surface became too unpleasant, they could plunge down to steadier depths. They would often be taken out to the clear waters of the *Ameril Sea*, to cruise the coral reefs and enchant their occupants with alien panoramas. They were the toys of the rich. At weekends, the privileged vessels would abandon their safe havens for the ocean wilderness, carrying their manicured crews over the planet's sweeping horizons. It was generally predicted that this pastime would diminish once the *Sunspot Resort* was opened. That would be the new lure for the rich and famous.

Pirismus was the second planet of the *Millar Vorspak* sun. In a closer orbit, and in a plane that varied from that of *Pirismus* by sixteen degrees, was the first-born son, the fiery *Morasmus*. The two planets spun around the sun with almost equal periods, despite their different attitudes, so they had hardly changed their relative positions in the time that had passed since humanity had arrived here, three hundred years before. *Pirismus* and *Morasmus* were travelling as far apart as brothers of any type, not only of the family of planets, might desire. They were diametrically opposed, which was fortunate because their distances from *Vorspak* were not hugely different. When they eventually drew close to each other, in one hundred and fifty thousand years, it was predicted that there would be a gravitational disaster. The oceans on both worlds would be pulled and pushed into massive tidal waves and it was a matter of precise, scientific uncertainty as to whether there would be any secure land left.

Pirismus had been the natural choice for colonisation. This was a benign place, a typical home for humanity. *Morasmus* was also a living planet, with a breathable atmosphere and suffused by great oceans. But it was hot. *Vorspak* blazed its radiation down, and so fuelled a hugely violent weather system. The seas boiled with storms and the land was torn by hurricanes, except in the polar regions. Here there had been some settlement, but it was a tenuous existence. The frenzied weather was not averse to straying into these cooler, calmer regions on occasion, with little warning. The most famous calamity had been at the town of *Soaring Lights*, two hundred years ago. It had been removed by a stray typhoon, erased even down to its roots. After that the planet had been much less popular as a place to live, but was not altogether abandoned. A few hardy souls still took their chance with a nomadic life there, dodging the worst of the weather's assaults. The reason they took this mortal risk was because they believed it to be the most beautiful place in the known universe. And everyone who had seen it was bound to agree. Anyone who prized towering mountains, emerald valleys, diamond glaciers and crystal waters must wonder at this violent beauty. But how might it be possible to enjoy *Morasmus'* splendour without risking sudden extinction? Weather control had been proposed. Some said that research was already under way, but it would take many years to perfect.

In the meantime, *Sunspot* would be the answer to this dilemma. A massive orbiting space city. The rich would find that no luxury was missing from the residential suites and the leisure facilities. If access to *Morasmus* was temporarily denied because of adverse meteorological conditions, there were more than adequate distractions on board. But the main purpose was to allow short landings onto the temporarily safe parts of the planet. Here the wealthy of *Pirismus* could regenerate their souls, soak their spirits in the wuthering beauty. *Morasmus* would be a more powerful tonic than sailing the ocean swells of its more placid brother. So the sleek white ocean cruisers would gradually be pulled out of the water and left to die on dry land, as their owners betrayed them to breathe deep of the air of another world.

The marinas that were closer to central *Dass Urmistam* were more humble, and so safer from this lingering decline. At the borders of the city, there were hordes of houseboats — flat-bottomed, stable, floating homes. A few stretched to two stories, but most were simple platforms carrying five or six rooms under a shallow-pitched roof. They spread out from the marina quays, moored together until those furthest offshore were tugged by the mainstream flow of the mighty river.

Izabel Torini lived in one of these small boats. At present, she lived alone. It had been Drew's idea to move out to the river, five years ago. He was long gone, but she had not moved. She liked the lapping sound of the water around and beneath her, and the village society that grew up amongst the river people. And it was only fifteen minutes into work.

But today she was not going into *Urmistam*; she was flying up to North Coast with Farr Litten. She had got up early for a bath, and then started to apply some light make-up. Her home computer had suggested a few ideas, and she had selected the one that made her look rather thinner and more intelligent, she hoped. Now she was running the dispenser around her face so that the cosmetics could be put in place. The lipstick she would apply herself. For a normal working day, she would not have bothered. She told herself that it was to look presentable for her colleagues out at the construction site. It seemed appropriate to show Headquarters personnel in a good light, but she also knew it was for Farr's benefit. Six years ago, when she first joined Boquat and had been quite keen on him, she would have supplemented the effect with one of her shorter skirts.

Trousers today, but you never knew. She was excited, a little nervous. This would be the first time she had been out alone with her boss. He had come over to her desk two days earlier and asked how she was getting on with the system's learning and appreciation, or LAP, capability. She actually felt that is was going very well. It was enjoyable work, tuning some parts of the existing human emulation programs and adding new sub-routines of her own. Her objective was to speed up the time it would take for the computer network to gain a good understanding of each guest's personality, his or her likes and dislikes. This went a lot further than simple things like food preferences or tastes in music. Some quite advanced psychological analysis techniques were invoked, in order to predict their likely inclinations and reactions. The host system would make every effort to provide the guests with pleasant surprises whenever possible.

Izabel had decreased the average time to reach an acceptable appreciation level to twenty key events or inputs. In the most intense situation, it would have a pretty good understanding of a human personality within two minutes, assuming that they were awake. The arrival of a new guest was expected to provide such emotional compacting. It amused her that the knowledge logic could achieve in so short a space what a human could take years over, or probably never achieve if it was a man.

But when Farr had asked about progress, she had to admit that the field trial data was not coming through fast enough to prove her work. Her own testing was fine, but actual simulations with the real mechanical sensing devices were being carried out at the North Coast facility. This was the factory where most of the system hardware for *Sunspot* was being assembled, including the cameras, microphones, sniffers, electronic tongues, thermal and pressure meters and other paraphernalia. So they had programs for putting their own guinea pigs, mainly volunteers from the factory staff, through the test sequences. The flow of results had slowed down, and she was getting no good feedback about the reasons for the hold up. So Farr had suggested that they both fly up and find out at first hand.

She was standing by the patio doors, looking out over the deck and across the river to the hazy skyline of *Urmistam*, when a shadow passed across the sunlit floor. Moments later, her monitor told her that she had a visitor. The fly-car had not actually touched down on her roof pad; it would be hovering a few inches above the pedestrian panels. She leapt up the stairs, feeling more like a thirteen-year-old than twenty-nine, and emerged onto the roof just as Farr was about to ring the ship's bell. She was pleased again with the way he looked at her, appreciating the effort that she had made. She had to admit to feeling a little sexy as he opened her car door for her and she slid across the plush seat. It was still pleasantly warm from the heat of the sun through the glass.

They flew up the river for a few miles and then turned westwards over the wilderness. The countryside was, of course, almost totally unspoilt. There were no roads: everything went by air. With an unlimited amount of clean energy for their flying craft, nothing else made sense. Now and then she could see small settlements, like islands in the sea of vegetation, or patches of specialist artificial horticulture. But mainly it was dense woodland. She enjoyed the trip in Farr's luxury car, having the time to look about and take pleasure in the scenery. These days she almost always had to drive herself. And the conversation was free and easy, too. He was a lot less reserved and formal than she had thought from their few previous meetings at work.

She wondered whether to raise the question of Cheng Ham Tung. It did not seem right to split on another Programmer, and she was still not completely sure of her evidence. She knew, for sure, that he had been tampering with the human resources system. He had been arranging for one of his friends, or at least she presumed a friend, to be hired by Boquat. On its own, that was nothing special. She knew that it had been done before. She had always convinced herself that programmers were probably better judges of character than their colleagues in Personnel anyway, and certainly better able to use the candidate assessment routines.

But she did not, yet, really believe the conclusions from the data that were her other source of concern. Her other body of evidence, which came to such a dramatic conclusion. Maybe her scepticism sprang from the fact that it was purely her own work. She had collected a few data points about Tung and put them through her new personality assessment suite. In order to complete the program, she had had to incorporate some brand new medical logic. The conclusion had been that, on the known data, there was a seventy percent chance that Tung was a psychopath. The active interfacing elements of her system suggested that he should be avoided. It had no pleasant surprises, no program of leisure activities to put forward which might correct his aberrations. It seemed like even the computer was frightened of him. Its predictions of his potential future actions were enough to scare anybody.

As she sat in the fly-car, it all seemed too absurd and she did not raise the subject. Soon enough the temptation was removed. They could see the ocean creeping over the horizon and the white buildings of North Coast reaching up through the surrounding trees.

The visit itself was a success. They found that the testing work had been deferred. Warren Galant had visited a few weeks earlier and instructed his people to spend a little less time playing with computers and a little more time in the assembly shop. Izabel had expected Farr to hit the roof, but of course he did not. She would have launched a missile straight through it. Instead, he just talked it through with the local people. They knew themselves that *Sunspot* was the make or break project at Boquat. They did not need much prompting to see that the Knowledge Engineering of the host to guest interfacing was one of the vital parts of the whole installation. They soon convinced themselves that the testing must resume, and realised that they would have to keep it secret from Warren. In the end, Farr received many apologies, despite the fact that he had not accused anyone of anything.

As they cruised back to *Dass Urmistam* that evening, flying against the flow of commuters heading for the surrounding dormitories, Izabel was quiet. Farr thought that she was dozing, but really she was thinking. She made two resolutions. The first was to redouble her efforts in her own work. The day's events had sharpened her appetite for the job, but it had also convinced her that she needed to get a positive resolution to the Tung affair. She perceived that it was somehow of extreme importance that his true nature should be revealed.

The second thing that she decided was to get to know Farr better. Her interest had certainly been rekindled. Of course, tonight she would just let him drop her off at the boathouse. There would be no invitation to come inside and certainly no obvious pass made. Maybe just a goodbye glance, with a little extra twinkle in the eye. But sometime in the near future she would want to engineer more close encounters. She looked across at him as the car's interior was lit by the dying day. Her body told her that her first instincts, six years ago, had been right. She would like to . . . well, she would just like to.

18

The lights of the city shimmered in the night air. It was cool and clean up at the top of Tramalgar Colossus. Tonight the sky was clear and strewn with stars. Chuck Carnegy leaned against the balustrade and looked out contentedly. This was not a bad way to earn overtime. He had just finished cleaning Jim Moffat's executive fly-car. Jim liked to be flown at low altitude, so that he could admire the view. He was specially privileged, licensed to do so. Chuck would have preferred to be higher, where the airborne insects did not venture so densely. They stuck like glue to the front of the *Arrow*. He had to give it two treatments with the cleaning leeches. He placed one on the back and one at the front of the car. They gripped like limpets to the car's slippery smooth body, looking rather grotesque with the thin tubes emerging from their small, black forms. Spidery, crab-like creatures in the shadows of darkness.

Chuck set the cleaning fluid to medium-strong and activated his little helpers. The leeches guzzled their way over the surface of the car, removing all traces of detritus, sensing each other's presence. The thin tubes, carrying clean fluid in and dirty fluid out, never tangled. The skilled dancers monitored the position of every part of their anatomy. But when the little labourers had finished their work, Chuck had not been satisfied. He had detected a few smudges on the car's skin, and that would not do for his pride and joy. He set his industrious minions to work again, with a more dilute solution to achieve a perfect, flawless finish. Even then, he went back over the car with his hand cloth, flicking away a few imaginary specks of dust.

He had driven Mr. Moffat out to the *Downing End* training centre that morning, where he had to administer some inspiration to a batch of management trainees. In the afternoon, Warren Galant had also flown in to give a brief presentation and Chuck had driven them back to Headquarters together. He approved of Mr. Galant. Many others thought that he was a poor executive. Chuck had heard several passengers in his car complain about Warren's rude manner and lack of vision. But Chuck had always been treated with courtesy by Mr. Galant. He presumed that much of the criticism was born out of jealousy.

He remembered a conversation between two marketing men, which he had overheard some months ago. One had stated that Warren, and his whole organisation, were totally indecisive. The other had disagreed. He said that Warren was very keen to make decisions. In fact, he liked to make a new decision several times each day. Often, unfortunately, the decision was different to the one that he had made on the self same subject before, possibly many times before. So his people never knew what to expect next. The result could easily be mistaken for indecisiveness. But really it was an excess of new perspectives that caused the constipation that had invaded his department's bowels.

Chuck had not agreed at the time, but he kept his thoughts to himself. He took pride in his discretion. None of the conversations that took place in the back of his luxurious vehicle ever went any further. He would rather die than have a rumour traced back to him. Not in the thirty years he had been at Boquat had he let slip a single confidence, intended or overheard.

Today, Warren had been telling Jim about his dissatisfaction with the Knowledge Engineering function. He explained that he had set up his own group to get things moving. Jim said that he should do what he had to. He had not looked very pleased about it, though. A little stony-faced, Chuck thought, but he gave a nod of assent. Warren also confirmed that he would take charge personally when *Sunspot X* set off for *Morasmus*. He asked that Farr Litten and some of his programmers should also be included, together with a chosen few of his new team. It would be quite expensive in terms of salary incentives, of course, but again Jim had agreed.

"Why don't you take Sarnia along with you?" he had asked. Warren had fallen silent, as if he needed to give this one some careful thought.

"She might enjoy it, Warren. Many of the leisure features will be in operation on *Sunspot X*, as you know. It would be a good break for the two of you."

"Thanks, Jim. I'll see what she says," said Warren.

"By the way, now that she is nearly ready for flight, I think that she needs a better name. Instead of *Sunspot X*, I've decided to designate her *Sunspot Spinal.* I think that fits rather well."

"Excellent idea," said Warren.

Chuck was pleased that Jim and Warren got along well together. He thought they were both gentlemen, hard workers, too. It was now ten o'clock at night and he had seen Warren fly off to his country house just a quarter of an hour ago. He expected that Jim Moffat would be needing his lift home within the next half hour. In the meantime, he looked out over the city and its blanket of shimmering starlight. Overall, he preferred the city lights, which stretched for twenty miles in every direction, except on the other side of the dark ribbon of the river, where they gradually thinned into the indeterminate darkness of the wilderness. The friendly incandescence of his hometown made him feel comfortable, at ease.

Chuck straightened up. Out of the corner of his eye he had seen Mr. Moffat approaching over the dark roof. He tidied his crumpled uniform and searched for the car keys in his jacket pocket. He pressed the car's systems initiation button, and the *Arrow* rose a few inches from the landing pad, its navigation and instrument lights illuminating in sequence around its fine body and cabin. Chuck turned to admire it. The long, elegant shape of the car never failed to impress him. He was ready to go. But he had been mistaken. Jim Moffat had not approached in his familiar, shuffling way: he was not there.

Chuck left the *Arrow* floating and humming quietly to itself. He shivered. The night was turning cool now. He would like to be home soon, making himself a hot cup of chocolate before bedtime. The city was slowing down and he was feeling tired. He looked out from his lofty perch and he could see a few cars flying around the artificial canyons below. Their lights danced before his eyes.

He shivered again and scratched the back of his thigh. He had felt a slight prick there a few moments before. It was unusual to get stinging insects this high up. They were scarce in the city at this time of night, even down by the river where he could see the lights of the houseboats. He could not easily distinguish the boats' blurred lights from their reflections in the river. But then, he was getting very tired. He shivered again. Or he tried to shiver, but his body did not respond. He tried to straighten up, and it seemed that his back had locked, leaving him leaning on his elbows over the balustrade. Even breathing seemed to be an effort, although he could feel the cold night breeze moving around his face.

Chuck started to panic. He was clearly unwell. He could feel his heart rate increasing, and there was perspiration across his brow. Perhaps Jim Moffat would come to his aid soon. He must hang on until then. He breathed in short, shallow gasps. Breathing in was all right, but it was getting harder to exhale. His lungs were getting full.

Then there was a figure standing next to him. He swivelled his eyes to the side and caught the impression of a smiling face. A fleeting ray of hope crossed his mind. Then his neighbour held out the hypodermic pin before Chuck's eyes. The grin became wider, more evil. The man flicked the pin with his fingers, and Chuck watched it fall away from the roof, turning as it began its long descent to earth. The evil figure pointed at Chuck and then down in the direction that the pin had taken. His plan was clear and Chuck tried to shout or scream, but only managed a gurgle. Its frequency and amplitude increased as he saw the dark figure duck down and grip his ankles. He felt his rigid body being tipped up and over the rail. It was being done slowly, as if to ensure that he got the full benefit of his feeling of imbalance, and could savour the long moment of exquisite terror. A final push dislodged his grip and he slid forward like a ship being launched, or like the films he had seen of corpses being jettisoned from space ships. His face scraped on the abrasive balustrade wall, peeling off long strands of skin and flesh. It did not worry him, because he knew that he was starting an irreversible fall. It was impossible to breathe now, either because of the poison in his body or his fear. As his kneecaps crashed against the rail, he heard a low, depraved voice from above him.

"'Bye," it said. "Enjoy the view. And happy landings."

Chuck started his long head over heels tumble to earth. He wondered whether he could hold his breath all the way to the bottom, without blacking out. He hoped that he would lose consciousness. But he was still alert and aware when his body eventually smashed into the metalled pavement outside the main entrance of Tramalgar Colossus.

19

Forba Curzine had walked from Cashen Column to Tramalgar Colossus. He had clocked off work at lunchtime and gone back to the apartment to smarten up. As he strode along the deserted sidewalks he could see the clouds of cars that circulated around the city's higher levels. They were looking for lunch amongst the upper level restaurants, like hungry vultures. He was looking for live prey — a new job.

As he entered the ground level foyer of Tramalgar, he had to step around the Agency barricades that isolated the place where Chuck Carnegy had been killed the previous night. It was an unpleasant surprise, which he should have predicted; he had been told that this was the reason why the job was open. Still, it felt pretty awkward, walking around the last splashes of the man whose position at Boquat he hoped to secure for himself.

It was Tung who he had to thank for the opportunity. Forba had just gone out to his first fare that morning when Tung had called him. He'd flown out to *Mildeburg Beach* to collect two women who were coming into central *Urmistam* for a shopping trip. He had landed his *Cabbilux* outside a big house that overlooked the ocean, glaring out from amongst its sheltering trees. He had stood in the landing paddock, knowing that his arrival was being announced inside. It was quite a while before the two middle-aged women emerged. This had worried him. He had been in similar positions before. They had probably been observing him ever since he had touched down. Maybe they were just not ready to leave yet, but possibly they had seen him and had been considering whether to change their plans about how to spend the morning. It had happened in the past, when his passengers were females travelling in packs. They never wanted to give him any long-term reward in these impromptu situations, so it did not suit his purpose.

He tried to look unattractive, slouching and pulling a few facial expressions. But it was hard for Forba to be anything other than a magnet to women. It was his blessing and his curse.

At last his fares emerged from the house. He could see that the two ladies had taken a few early morning shots. They giggled to each other as they wound their unsteady way over to the pad, casting their eyes over his body, not meeting his eyes. His mind searched desperately for a polite way out. This kind of thing could get him dismissed, he recalled from the company terms of service.

Just as the more forward of his fares looked as though she had decided upon her opening, compromising remark, his blessed radio buzzed. He rushed back to the fly-car and gratefully received the incoming call. It was Tung, patched through from the cab office. He had announced himself as Forba's next door neighbour and probably the office had assumed some domestic emergency. The description, so concisely describing the proximity of their lives, sent a little, unpleasant tingle down Forba's spine. The voice was calm and quiet.

Tung said that there had been a tragedy at the Boquat building, where he worked, during the previous night. But it was nevertheless fortuitous, because it meant that Forba would be able to apply for the job that was now vacant. He would be ideally qualified, with his driving experience and all. Tung explained it all quite logically, and without any unnecessary, sugary regret about Chuck's death. He clearly had his emotions well under control.

Forba was not convinced at first, but Tung said that he had put a good word in for him, so the job was really his for the taking. And the pay was excellent. Even so, the work itself sounded a bit dull. Just driving the big man and some of his executives around, none of whom were women, seemed pretty tedious. But then Tung had played his trump card. He had told Forba about *Sunspot*. This would be the kind of place that Forba had dreamed of. There would be thousands upon thousands of rich women spending some leisure time out there when it opened in about a year's time. Women who would be relaxed and receptive — taking time out to rediscover themselves, to look for a last chance of fulfilment; to make up for the time they had lost. A prime hunting ground, where Forba would be right at the top of the food chain. Pulling down his prey like the dominant predator that was his nature.

Tung pointed out that Forba would never get to *Sunspot* as a guest. He would not be able to afford a single day's accommodation at those prices. But if he was a Boquat employee, and in the good graces of the top man, he might justifiably expect to be able to get a job on the last phase, *Sunspot X*, when it set out across the solar system in a few weeks' time. Once at *Sunspot*, he could surely find a good position from which to stalk his prey.

Forba was sold. This sounded like what he had been looking for. He agreed to go along, and thanked Tung for thinking of him. He already had an appointment established at Headquarters, and Tung forwarded the details through to the car's scheduling system.

By the time he had finished his conversation with Tung, Forba was pleased to see that his two fares were thoroughly annoyed with him. They had not been amused by his pre-occupation with the radio, and his consequent lack of attention to them. They flounced into the back of the *Cabbilux* with sour faces, and asked if he was ready to go, if it was not too inconvenient for him. He smiled to himself. Things had taken care of themselves very well. And he really did not mind if they complained to the taxi company. He now had grander plans.

As he flew over the solid waves of trees that lay like an ocean all the way to the concrete shores of *Dass Urmistam*, he thought about Tung. He did not really understand why Tung had helped him like this, or why he considered that they were friends. They had hardly met, only a few times in the corridor, like on that first occasion. It was usually as Forba came home from work. He also realised that Tung seemed to have a false impression of his attitude to women. Tung appeared to think that all he wanted was to screw as many females as he found physically possible, which was a lot, and take whatever profit he could from these brief encounters. Although the casual observer could be forgiven for making such a mistake, this was not at all what was motivating Forba. All he really wanted was to find a good woman, wealthy of course, who would really love him. She need not be beautiful, he could manage that side for both of them, but she should be intelligent and caring. Forba just wanted to marry and settle down, in the comfort to which he hoped to become accustomed. It was true that he needed to perform some pretty heavy field trials in order to make sure that he knew the right person when he met her.

Something hidden deep in his basic instincts told him that it would be better not to shatter Tung's illusions. He seemed to be a useful ally. And Tung had said that he expected to be on board *Sunspot X* himself.

Things went unbelievably well at Boquat. Forba had been passed right through the ground floor reception process, based upon facial analysis; their system already knew him. He took an express elevator up to the Boquat offices. The Human Resources administrator seemed to believe that he was there to actually start work, not merely to apply for the job. She consulted her terminal, and saw that he had already been through the interview process that morning and had been chosen by the personnel selection algorithm from a short-list of twenty-four candidates. He was therefore passed straight through to the Induction Process. For two hours, he sat and watched the Boquat company interactive hologram. It was hard going, and concluded with a brief tribute to Chuck Carnegy, a recently deceased employee. There was also an obituary summary of other departures. Jacques Bonne was on the list.

When he emerged, suitably chastened and humbled by the excellence of his new company, his uniform was ready for him, as was his company wrist computer. The uniform, or actually five sets of uniforms, looked marvellous on him. Most clothes did, but the short, brass buttoned jacket showed his broad shoulders to great effect and slimmed down to his narrow waist. It finished high enough to maximise the visibility of his muscular buttocks. He knew that he was a far cry from old Chuck, who was nearly sixty and fairly overweight according to the strangely detailed obituary columns.

His wrist computer was a cunning device, manufactured by Boquat and given to every employee. It included an automatic recognition system, which was initiated by the Induction Officer who strapped it onto his strong arm. All of his unique body characteristics were immediately measured and analysed within the computer's minute brain. Nerve patterns, heart pressures, chemical ratios and many more data elements allowed Forba to be recognised and remembered by the tiny ornament. It would never forget him now, like a faithful hound. If anyone else wore his computer, it would initiate its distress signal and suspend all other functions. The ultimate anti-theft device, he had been told.

So Forba sailed through the afternoon's proceedings, which were completed when he was introduced to the *Arrow* fly-car that he would be driving. This was a quality vehicle. Jim Moffat himself was not available for him to meet that day; he had been to visit Chuck's daughter. The routine computer scan had revealed that Chuck had been very ill, terminally afflicted by Forrester's Syndrome. He had left a short computer message for his family before he jumped. Jim wanted to take the pension portfolio over personally. He always did this in suicide cases. Forba would meet him the next day.

There was only one small thing that had worried Forba on that perfect afternoon. As he had been sitting in the Boquat reception foyer, before the induction process had begun, a woman had walked in from the elevator landing. He had just been helping himself to some of the complementary salted carrow nuts. Missing his lunch had left him pretty hungry. He was chewing through another mouthful as the woman came into the plush, softly lit space. She was not young, probably about fifty, but she was slim and attractive, well dressed, too, in a pale trouser suit. Not stunningly beautiful, but she had caught Forba's eye as he sat cross-legged, nervously awaiting his phantom interview. Then, two very small incidents had combined to create an awkward moment.

His glance lowered to the woman's crotch as she walked towards the desk. There was nothing much in that, her elegantly swaying hips made it inevitable. Her outfit was designed for such admiration. But at the same moment, the salt that lay around his mouth forced his tongue to make a long, lingering, exploratory lick across his full lips. He had meant nothing by it, but a little prick of embarrassment had made him look up into the woman's face. She was looking right back into his eyes. Her expression was one of horror, disgust almost. He sat stock still, but his brain reeled briefly, suddenly aware that she had interpreted his acts as highly suggestive. Forba quickly lowered his eyes and carefully studied his fingernails. She walked past him to the desk.

It was all over in a few seconds. He tried to think little of it. He knew that trying to excuse himself would only have lead him into deeper water. It was best to let it rest. He would have banished the incident to forgetfulness immediately, except that he noticed that she had been greeted with respect by the receptionist, and was immediately shown through into the Boquat offices. Clearly a person of some standing, he realised.

As he rode back to his apartment in the early evening, there was still a tiny pinch of concern about the incident. Had he offended some company potentate? Would she investigate his identity and have his appointment nullified?

But by the following morning, when he was dressing in his smart new uniform, he had forgotten the whole affair.

20

The *Tyratheon* spacecraft sped away from the planet, soaring into the twilight of space like a black bubble of effervescence. The computer telemetry and satellite guidance steered it from the small garage outside *Mildeburg* to an exactly defined point in orbit, and would return it with equal precision. The bands of lethal radiation that surrounded *Pirismus* were scattered away from the smooth hull and carried no more threat than a drizzle of rain. Still Sarnia felt the thrill of danger as she sat in her luxuriously cushioned seat, held there by the heavy hand of acceleration. She looked down on her adopted home and, just like on every other occasion, she felt tears creep into the corners of her eyes. The beauty of the scene alone was enough to stir the emotions, but now she had other reasons to feel a sweet pain in her heart.

Warren had got home late last night. He had rung her to let her know that he had been delayed, of course. He said that he had to catch up at the office, after being out with Jim Moffat all day. She understood. She could adapt. When he had come into the bedroom, just before midnight, she had been reading a book. She had adjusted the screen background colour to a soft pink, so that it shone up onto her face with a kind, smoothing glow. Her nightdress was of low-cut lace, which supported her breasts sufficiently to create the kind of voluptuous curves that a woman half her age would have been pleased with. She had not looked up from her reading when Warren came in, smelling of work, the car, and tiredness.

"Hello, Darling," she said as she clicked to the next page. She put coolness into her voice, testing for a reaction. Warren had showered quickly, and was soon clambering into bed beside her, making her book bounce on her lap. It seemed possible that he had appreciated her efforts and so come to her bed speedily. She paid no apparent attention, but listened to his body language, wondering whether it would speak of desiring close contact, wanting to sense his urgency and insistence. He reached over and held her hand.

"Can we talk?" he asked. With a long-practised facility, she changed her mindset from seductress to wife and friend. There was no desperate disappointment in her heart or loins. It had just been another little test, an experiment to calibrate where they were in their lives. She filed it away for processing at her leisure.

Warren had found his message quite difficult to communicate, possibly because he was concerned that he might be hurting her. Also, because the situation meant that he had not been able to control things the way he liked. It showed that he was not entirely his own boss. Part of his reticence stemmed from a twinge of humiliation. She knew he was a proud man.

But he had to tell her in the end that Jim Moffat was adamant. He would have to go on the *Sunspot Spinal* voyage. No way out now. He said that he had told Jim that he would like her to come with him. In many ways, it would be the chance of a lifetime. They could turn a disappointment into a treat. He stroked her hand as he marched her through all the reasons why she should feel very excited by this plan of his.

Sarnia was not willing to play ball. She slipped her hand out of his. His nervous caress had been quite annoying anyway. He had never mastered the arts of sensual contact.

"No, thank you," she said, hearing a sharp edge in her voice. Her certainty even surprised herself. Warren was speechless. She knew that the day's small sadness was part of the reason for her caustic reaction.

She had flown out to see Tania and Chilly that morning. Her granddaughter was walking now, tottering around on her chubby little legs. It had only been three weeks since the last time that Sarnia had been to visit, but Chilly had changed so much. Even her wavy blonde hair had grown. She had become an independent little body. And that had put a tiny stab of pain into Sarnia's heart. It hurt her pride too, when it made her realise that she could no longer take it for granted that her granddaughter would be available for cuddles without question; soon her permission would be required.

She had patiently watched Chilly promenading around the living room while Tania was fixing lunch. The little girl teased her with proud smiles as she traversed the great deserts of carpet. Sarnia could resist no longer, and as Chilly made a close approach she grabbed her around the waist for a big kiss. But this was not part of Chilly's plan at all. She squealed in annoyance and swung her little hands around her head, catching Sarnia with a slight, not really painful, cuff on the nose. Mostly unintentional, but it had hurt her deeply.

She released her adorable captive, who resumed her peram- bulations and chuckles. Sarnia felt a desperate longing to know the child better, to spend more time with her, to make sure that her grandchild loved her.

And now Warren had suggested that they go off planet for a year or more. The stupid man; the selfish, thoughtless, insensitive man. Couldn't he see how impossible it was? How could he bear the thought of being away for so long? Chilly would be lost to them. She snapped her book shut, a little harder than she intended. She voiced the lights out and made sure that the bed shook violently as she turned away to go to sleep.

The next morning, Warren had gone before she woke up. She had more time to think about things as she smooched around the kitchen, making her breakfast. She tried to see Warren's point of view. She conceded that there was a certain glamour to the trip. It was the kind of thing that a woman without fear would undertake. But only an independent woman who was without her own daughter and granddaughter to care for. And you did not need to go all that way to be touched by the magic dust of the stars.

So she had programmed another ascent in the *Tyratheon*. Not to anywhere near *Sunspot*, that spoiled the view. She hung where only the heavens and earth shared her thoughts. The infinite perspective of space helped her to get her balance. She felt the tension of two opposing forces, the twin attractions of motherhood and creation. She decided that she must drive in to *Urmistam* that very afternoon and speak to Warren. She owed him an explanation, but she also owed it to herself to count herself out, positively not going. Perhaps Jim Moffat would be there and she would be able to make the position clear to him. She did not want to embarrass Warren in his eyes, but there would be no going back after Jim knew the score.

Later, she flew in to Tramalgar Colossus, parked in one of the upper landings and took the elevator down to the Boquat floors. How strange it was to have been circling the planet that morning, and now to be entering the humdrum world of commerce. The contrast made her giddy as the elevator doors swished open.

She had been through this way many times before. She knew the layout well, but today there was something different. There was something hanging in the air. An expectation. A tingle of excitement, something dangerous and powerful. People passing by scurried away, melting before her. She knew that she was the centre of events. She walked through the elevator lobby and towards the reception foyer, holding her breath. Immediately, as she rounded the corner, she saw him, sitting cross-legged before her. It was the man of her life. It was a lightning strike. Her knees weakened. Hot and cold flooded her. There was something special here, more powerful than the sight of the morning's star sparkles. More compelling, even, than the bond with her grandchild. Her body shed the impostor years as she floated into the foyer. She knew that he must look up at her. He did, in a way that nearly made her faint, right then and there. She may have groaned. She could almost feel his tongue on her and sense the strength of those broad shoulders as they bunched in tension above her.

Somehow, she arrived at the reception desk on legs that had turned almost to liquid, where Clement recognised her. He saw that she was in shock.

"You've heard about Chuck," he stated, as he ushered her through into the executive office suite.

"Chuck?" she said through dry lips. Clement blinked while he tried to decide where to go from here.

"Chuck killed himself last night. Jumped off the top of the building."

Sarnia stood on the deep pile carpet, her emotions turned to ice. She had not known Chuck all that well; he had driven her home with Warren a few times. But she heard herself start to weep, and that was all she could do. Stranded in the deceptive comfort of this temple to commerce, she was paralysed. Standing like a little girl lost. She could tell that Clement was also standing there, frozen by confusion.

At last, one of the office doors opened and Warren came out to rescue her. He put his arm around her shoulders and freed her from the web of tangled passions. They went into one of the nearby cubicles as Clement scurried back to his post. Warren slowly calmed her down with his thick layers of normality. His low voice dampened down the fires and icicles within. She was able to breathe again. She rested her head on his shoulder. He was a good man. He had already forgiven her for her petulance of the night before.

By the time she was able to speak clearly again, after he had dabbed away her tears, it was, of course, impossible for her to tell him again that she would not go with him. She knew a little about loyalty.

She would have to wait for another occasion, when he was being less kind.

21

Melda Smith angrily snapped the phone back onto its cradle. The dismay that she had felt about the death of Klinedorf had slowly turned into anger over the last three weeks. She had personally carried out diagnostics on all the local computer systems, struggling against her natural aversion to such devices, without finding any trace of an error. When she identified the culprit, there was going to be trouble. The reference linkage path for the transport and general service systems had transferred her enquiry back to the new systems group, down on *Pirismus*. This was the recently created Knowledge Engineering section, which had been set up by Warren Galant in his efforts to get the project back on track. She had asked the group supervisor, Metter Zeigel, to look at things from his end. That was the day after Klinedorf had been driven away into the blistering cold outside, trapped in his hard death seat. Since then, she had chased Metter every other day, but he did not seem to have any answers. The only definite thing which he had come out with was that the overall injury rate on the *Sunspot* project was actually lower than budget, as loaded from the Actuarial Services Department. She looked into his dull eyes as they stared back from the video.

"Just try harder, you dumb son. There are people dying up here."

Metter blinked. "There is a lot of new software loading up now. Your systems are being enhanced and rebooted every other day. A few bugs are inevitable. We've tried to find out what happened, but there are two hundred new programs and a thousand amendments being shipped up with each new release. I've had my best guy check it out. He says it won't happen again."

"If anything else does go wrong, I'm coming down to see you about it," promised Melda. She saw Metter flinch back a couple of inches, even though the intervening miles protected him.

"I'll have it double-checked," he said, without conviction.

"Have you consulted with the main computer group? They may have another angle."

Metter stopped for thought again. He swallowed before replying. He knew that she would not like the answer.

"No. I'm not allowed to do that."

Melda crashed the communication to an end. This guy was useless.

She carried out her own scan of programmers in the main IT department, to see if she could come up with someone who knew what they were doing. It was a desperate act. The general company opinion of the computer department was pretty low, and she was a conventional woman who rarely took extreme positions. Nevertheless, she cast her eye over the long list of personnel. Nothing jumped out at her. She keyed in a few search criteria. Female. Unmarried. Unruly. She knew the kind of person she wanted. Someone with a streak of rebellion and a decent amount of time on their hands.

The name of Izabel Torini flashed up immediately. Melda remembered her name. She had seen some of her work before, and she saw that she was currently working on some of the *Sunspot* recreation systems. Worth a try.

Melda called Izabel and found that she was very happy to try and help. Izabel enjoyed finding and killing problems. That was because she was so good at it and because she usually succeeded. She also liked the idea of finding fault with the rival engineering group, the Bugs. Melda realised that she had struck gold as soon as the two women made eye contact. After a ten-minute conversation with Izabel she had learnt more, and had greater hope, than over those three wasted weeks with Metter. She felt like she had a friend at last.

"I'll get back to you tomorrow," concluded Izabel.

Melda was trying to get her own projects back in order. The loss of Klinedorf meant that the various teams of contractors on the space station were struggling to co-ordinate their activities. Despite the computer scheduling, she was having to perform a high level of rework. At least there was very little outside activity now, in the treacherous vacuum with its mocking surround of· cold stars. She continually circulated around her workers as they crouched by service hatches or reached into ceiling voids. She got as much comfort from their fortitude as they did from her natural concern. Being around these big, competent, careful men made her feel safer.

Towards the end of the day, she attended a section meeting in the middle conference room. It was only half a mile from her quarters, so she decided to walk. She was not taking the train at all these days.

The sections through which she passed were freezing cold. The heating convectors had been temporarily turned off. They were being upgraded, ready for live running. Every hundred meters or so along the far wall was an industrial strength radiator. They were plugged in to circular power points that poked out from the ceiling at regular intervals. Each radiator gave off the smell of burning dust that reminded her of her childhood, lying on the floor of her bedroom, playing close to the only heater that her family could afford. Move away, and you soon got horribly cold.

She wore a heavy coat anyway, and trotted along rather than walked. Half way there, she turned one of the heaters on and took in a little heat. She particularly gave her feet a good toasting, slipping out of her big, thermal boots and wiggling her toes.

She carried on down the long, empty cavern of the space module, trailing white breath behind her. She kept up her little straight legged, straight-armed run. She was late, and that was why she was on her own. Everyone else was probably there already. As she came in sight of her goal, the door was shut and the blue "in progress" light was lit.

All of her fellow supervisors had lockers outside the conference room. Hers was forty-third from the start. Right down by the meeting room, closest to it, she saw that the door to Klinedorf's locker was open. Obviously his personal effects had recently been cleared away. Rather than use her own hanger and have to walk down through the cold without her coat, she trotted all the way to the end and popped it into Standish's empty locker. She put her hand up to the identification pad and spoke in her personal password, "freezing". The security system took a few seconds to register her change of address.

Soon she was inside the welcoming heat and noise of the conference room, being greeted by a chorus of mock rude and genuine friendly voices. The meeting was engaged in discussion of the usual series of small details. Small, but important for the giant construction to work properly. They were all good people, Melda knew, doing their best. They patiently went through the trivia, striving for communication and mutual understanding. They came from a variety of disciplines and they all understood the need for repetition and confirmation of all their questions and answers. It took two hours to get to a point where they could agree that the agenda was exhausted.

As the session closed, one of the hydraulic contractors turned towards her, "So, Melda. Is it true that your Mr. Galant is going to come with us, all the way to *Morasmus?* Taking over from Standish Klinedorf? Or are they just rumours, put out to cause panic amid the work force?"

They could all see that she was genuinely surprised by this rumour. She made no reply as she sifted through her known facts and estimated the probability that it was true, and then sifted through her feelings if it were true. Above all, she could feel her own disappointment. She did not doubt that Warren had his good points; you did not get to his position without them. For a start, he was prepared to take decisions, make things happen. It was just that he kept changing his mind. In her experience, she had found that it was best to keep out of his way and not give him the chance to think about something twice. Years ago, when she had been at North Coast, she used to take her holidays when he was scheduled to visit. Luckily, he did not have a very good memory, so if she was not actually there to receive his latest change of instructions, she was generally safe.

But now it seemed likely that there was to be no escape. She had no doubt, after a little thought, that the rumours were true. The fact that she had not been told officially was nothing new.

She was still thinking about her good news as they all streamed out of the conference room, moving down to their lockers to retrieve their heavy coats. Of all the throng, she had just about the furthest to go to get back to her locker. As she spoke her password, it dawned on her that she had gone to the wrong place. All the way down to her own locker in the cold without her coat, and now she would have to go right back.

Just as the catch in her locker door clicked, there was a deafening bang from near the conference room. Melda nearly jumped out of her thermal boots again. Down at the end of the row there was a cloud of blue smoke, curling up from the floor and spreading away across the ceiling. She could see some of her colleagues lying on the ground.

Everyone ran forward to help. By the time she got there, all of the fallen were back on their feet, a couple looking white and shaky. On the floor, right next to Klinedorf's locker, there was a black scar in the coating. She looked up. The power socket, which stood proud from the ceiling, was also smouldering, partly melted by the powerful flash of electricity that had arced from it into the ground. It would have passed straight through her, if she had been brighter and not absent-mindedly walked to the wrong place. She tried to sort out the logic in her shocked mind. It could not have been meant for her, because it was not her locker. It was just the locker where her coat was, and where she should have been. Shouldn't it have been the other way round? She should have been saved by going to Klinedorf's and then seen her accustomed standing place being pierced by a bolt of killing lightning. But she really knew that, either way, she was the intended target.

Somebody else got her coat out for her.

The next day, Izabel really did call back. Quite something, Melda thought, for a Knowledge Engineer to be so efficient. And she had made progress, too. She told Melda that she had detected a problem. Not an accidental bug, but a roving software virus with receptor functions. Somebody, somewhere would be able to control it. She could not locate the sources of the command instructions, they were too minute to find. And too much time had passed. Audit trails had been purged during the last three weeks. Still, she was pretty sure that they were coming from the planet, not from the space station. But the virus itself could be detected and so tracked down. Izabel had released her own hunter subroutine to search and destroy. She had also erected a firewall on the space station's local network interfaces, to prevent further infection, at least for the time being. Melda could have kissed her, like the daughter she had never had. She recognised another no-nonsense woman at the other end of the line, fifty miles below her.

"Maybe you will be able to get up here yourself?" suggested Melda.

"Just possibly I might. I'm thinking of working on my boss. I reckon he could be going with *Sunspot X*."

"Who? Warren Galant?"

"No! Farr Litten. The word is that Jim Moffat is going to ask him to see the work through personally, during the voyage to *Morasmus*. I guess he might refuse."

"I imagine Farr might come. After all, his wife died a year ago."

"I didn't know that," said Izabel.

"Oh, sorry. It's not common knowledge. Forget I mentioned it."

"I will," lied Izabel.

"At least we will be safe from our saboteur once we are in flight, I presume."

"I am not sure if he'll be going too," said Izabel, worryingly.

"I thought you didn't know who it was."

"I don't, not for sure. But I have my suspicions. There is a guy down here who I don't trust at all."

"What's his name?"

Izabel paused, unsure whether to reveal what she really had no firm evidence for. "It's one of the new Engineers. He's called Cheng Ham Tung." She saw a little flicker of recognition pass over Melda's face. "You know him?"

"No, I don't know him. But I've heard his name before. It was when I was trying to get some answers out of your friends in the other programming department. Their supervisor, Metter Zeigel, mentioned him. Tung was the programmer who he got to look into the problems we are having up here. He said that he was his best person."

"It sounds like putting the wolf in charge of the sheep," said Izabel. She looked into the flushed, round face of the big woman who was flying above her in the fragile shell of the space station. Never far away from sudden death at the best of times, but now threatened by an attacker whose identity and motive were uncertain. She really did want to get up there and help.

22

Eight miles upriver from the centre of *Dass Urmistam*, the waters of the *Timorillo River* divided around *Massen Island*. The northern extremity of the long, thin isle was given over to a fly-car park. The rest of its flat meadowland was carefully tended and manicured. This was *Dido Park*. The city lavished municipal funds on its upkeep and improvement. It was just about the only public recreation space in the whole of the city.

The great river's waters had been siphoned off to create a lake near the south end of the island. From a high-flying car, it looked like the blue eye in a giant fish, which was surging up against the strong, brown currents.

Children were relentlessly attracted to the *Orbal Lake*. They took their toy ships and submarines and watched them sail around its model oceans. Most afternoons, after they had completed their home studies, they coerced their parents into flying out here and thronged around the choppy water. Despite the diversions of their fully equipped homes, there was still an attraction to the reality of the park. Their cries and laughter rang around the overhanging trees and away across the wide acres of cut grass.

Tung often came here when he needed to think. He enjoyed the music of the children's voices. On sunny days, he would sit on a lakeside bench, turning his face up to the warm light, drinking in the vitality of life around him. In part, he was making up for his loneliness when he was a child. His dark, solitary life without any friends. Now he could imagine that he was a part of their games. He sat and smiled. When he came out here he felt better. He knew that he could be a hero, that it was in his nature. Back in the dirty streets of the city his soul was infected and corrupted. He hated the effect that it was having on him, but it was irresistible. The good thoughts that he had when he sat here helped to balance the account, though.

He knew the shape of the lake very well. He had studied it, circumnavigated it, tapping his stick on the watery edge. If one day a poor unfortunate child were to tumble into the lake, he would be able to stride out into the cold water and save him. He imagined the situation often, playing it through his mind and testing himself. There would be danger for him. A blind man could easily stumble as he waded over the tangled mud and roots at the bottom of the pond. A blind man might drown quickly, as the cold water closed around his useless eyes. But he would forge on towards the cries of young fear and sweep them triumphantly back to the maternal banks. And so, in this way, he knew that at his core he was still a good man; a brave man. He had performed other acts that proved his courage. He had been the first blind member of the Orbit Club. The first to take solo trips out into space, without the luxury of eyes to make things easy. He took the risks, without the rewards. He was not able to see the glowing planet or the frozen stars. There was no great pay-off for him, no incentive to overcome the fear. There was just the mission that he had given himself. He had done some terrible things, for its sake, but only what was absolutely necessary. These dubious acts did not stop him being a good man.

His mother would not approve, he realised. She was sweet and pure. Her only cruelty towards him was to leave him alone when she died. And also, perhaps, to have treated him as though he could see. Whenever they were together, in his childhood, she would describe their surroundings with her silver voice. Her words echoed in his mind and drew out wonderful shapes and filled in glorious colours. Even though he had never had sight, she had been able to create images inside his head. And as she spoke to him, she often said, "Do you see, Tung?"

And he could. He would smile and nod his head. Great pictures were still stored in his careful memory, after all these years.

But when he was fourteen, his mother had died. She had abandoned him without any word of warning. Her marvellous brain had betrayed her and burst into a bloody pulp. She had lingered for five days. Tung had sat by her bed and held her hand. He could tell that she was dying, from the weakness he felt. He could feel the slow dwindling of her breath, as it touched his face ever more softly; feel the uncontrolled twitching of her right leg, as her deathbed trembled on its iron legs. He saw her soul painfully rip itself away from her small body. He saw her realise, at the end, that life was not the wonderful gift she had told him about. As she died, in pain and humiliation, she called out to his desperation, "I was wrong. This is a terrible thing, life. There is hurt and injustice. Beautiful things are torn down in the end. Everything gets dark and frightening. And lonely. Endlessly lonely. Do you see, Tung?" Only he had heard these words, the attendant nurses denied that she had spoken forth with such honesty.

He had been seated by his mother's bed for five days, until they had made him leave her side and sleep. While he slept, she died. Ever since then, he had brooded about whether her death had been accelerated by the hand of officialdom. He was now a hero with a murdered mother. Revenge was natural, his genius demanded it.

After his mother was taken away from him, he was truly blind. For the first time in his life, he could not see. There was no one to paint the world for him. Just sullen, grunting, apologetic people who passed by with embarrassment and haste. Through his teen years, things got blacker and blacker. But he knew that a hero could cope. He strengthened himself with the thought that he was not missing too much. He still had the images that his mother had given him. The sighted people had not got any more vivid vision.

He made friends with his computer, spending hours every day learning its ways.

But when he was thirty, he felt his own brain begin to hurt. He thought it might be the same problem that had afflicted his mother. Sharp, shooting pains across his skull. It was the same time as the *Sunspot* project was proposed, and the inane media men began to fill the world with their imperious slogans. They were impossible to avoid. They proclaimed the unthinkable.

"See what no one has ever seen before. The most spectacular sight in the universe. Experience *Sunspot* with your eyes."

He kept his rage under control for years, expecting the hysteria to die down. He heard the opinions that the project would fail, and that gave him hope. But as his headaches got worse, so the space station grew from a dream to a probability, and then became a virtual certainty. Unless he could stop it. It was a mission worthy of a hero, to save humanity from itself. From this vile decadence that would corrupt it. He understood that the true, proper world was made up of the pictures that his mother had painted for him. Anything beyond was unnatural.

He had the talent and the determination to save mankind and perhaps take a little revenge for himself.

But on this sunny day in *Dido Park*, Tung was crying. He was saying goodbye to his young friends. He would not be back again. Although his mission had started well, with early successes, he was now being foiled at every turn. He had to get closer to the évil heart of the project. Right into its innards, the quivering bowels of the thing.

He knew what he had to do, and he knew that he might not survive. He might have to end his life at the same time as this sinister monster was brought to justice. And, just as he had tested his resolve concerning the drowning children and the water of the lake, he played the plan through in his wounded brain. Would his heroism extend to the sacrifice of his life?

The tears spilled out of his eyes and emerged from beneath his heavy, black spectacles. He took a last, deep breath of the joy-filled park. He moved his hovering bench back towards the car park, where he could pick up a cab and go back to the city. It was resolved. He was programmed. He was now a weapon, loaded and aimed. He felt strong and focused as he edged his way through the crowds of laughing children, taking care not to cause any damage to their tender flesh.

23

Farr Litten was on the eleventh tee at the *Marshridge Hall Golf Club*. The emerald fairway swept in a right hand curve to the green, four hundred and twenty yards away. Miles was preparing to venture forth with his driver when Farr saw that his telephone light was winking. He quietly moved to his golf bag and pressed the five-minute response button, anxious not to distract his playing partner. Miles could hit a long way, as befitted his name, and sure enough he gave his ball a mighty blow. It hissed away into the air on a line tight to the trees on the right. They all heard the rattle as it clattered around the upper branches. Miles' trolley system signalled that the lie was probably unplayable.

"Hard luck," said Farr. He should have played safe.

As the three golfers walked off after their shots, Farr fell behind and answered his call. It was Jim Moffat.

"Farr, I'm on my way over. I'll be there in ten minutes. See you in the clubhouse." He disconnected without further pleasantry. Farr wondered whether he had been annoyed at not being answered immediately.

His spirits sank. This was the worst news. Not only was a potentially good round spoilt, but also he would have to let down his playing companions. To abandon a game because of work was bad form, an unacceptable excuse. He searched his mind for something more convincing. Miles and Estefan were already in the woods, where the caddie-fly hovered over the errant ball. Miles was deciding whether to drop or play.

"I am terribly sorry, guys. I've just had a call from my mother. Dad's had a fall, and she is in a bit of a state at the hospital. I'll have to go." He handed Miles' card to Estefan, signing it first. The tradition remained, even though every shot had already been transmitted through to the club's main computer.

His explanation still carried little weight with his playing partners. They blinked at him, as though they thought that he might yet realise his mistake and agree to carry on. He might have told them that aliens had just landed; it seemed to be such an inconceivable concept. He felt that he had to literally tear himself away.

He threw back a few more apologies over his shoulder, like defensive grenades, as he started his lonely walk back over the course. In an instant, he had been converted from a natural, accepted part of the scenery into a strange oddball, swimming against the tide and traversing the course at unconventional angles. He felt embarrassed as he crossed behind greens and walked the wrong way along the edges of fairways. Golfers stopped and stared at him, pointing him out to their friends, as if he had changed colour. Farr flushed in the face as he skulked along.

As he approached the clubhouse, he saw the elegant shape of the executive *Arrow* in the sky. He speeded up his walk, so that he could intercept Jim before he made it to the bar. Sitting chatting in the clubhouse would not be consistent with his invented story. He trotted into the carport and waved Jim's chauffeur back as he tried to land in the Club Captain's space. He shepherded the lovely, hanging vehicle away to a further corner of the park.

"Sorry, Jim, do you mind if we talk in here," he said, climbing in before Moffat had a chance to suggest otherwise.

They sat in the back of the *Arrow* and talked. Jim had come over to tell him two things. He wanted Farr to go with *Sunspot Spinal*, and he wanted no nonsense with Warren Galant. Both requests were quite hard to swallow. Farr took in these twin disappointments and then stopped listening as Jim went into his reasons why it was the right thing to do. He heard Jim's voice, but the words were not registering. It did not matter, because he knew that he would agree with both requests. He did not need to prepare any counter arguments. He just tried to let the news sink in, so that his reply would not sound too embittered.

Farr looked around the luxurious interior of the car. He noticed the broad shoulders of Jim's new driver, and caught his glance in the rear view screen. He wondered whether the man was enjoying his discomfort. No, he could tell that there was no mischief or amusement in the chauffeur's eyes. Their dark depths were still and honest.

Farr's hand came to rest on a wrist computer, lying in the stowage box. He picked it up and examined it. The name Chuck Carnegy was etched on the back. He absent-mindedly began polishing it with his golf glove. The action at least had the effect of diverting Jim from his diatribe.

"It was Chuck's. They gave it to me at the funeral. Apparently it is company property. I keep meaning to return it to Human Resources."

"I'll take it if you like, Jim. I'm back in the office tomorrow. If you have no objection, we can run it through one of our new body function engines. There is a lot of data about Chuck in this little device, here. We might be able to enhance his 'In Memoriam' file."

"Thanks, Farr. I'd like that."

"And don't worry, I'll go to *Morasmus* and I promise not to fight with Warren. At least, only if he shoots first. I may have to take one or two of my staff with me, though."

Jim beamed and patted Farr on the knee.

"Thanks again, son. You are a good man. Now, I'll let you get back to your golf. I am going straight over to Warren's now, to make sure that he stays honest."

Farr saw the driver's eyes smiling in the mirror screen. He was waiting to see if Farr would correct the old man's incorrect assumption that his golf round could be resumed. But he saw no point in educating Jim on this matter. He stepped out of the car and onto the gravel. Jim waved as the *Arrow* swept up and headed north.

Farr went back and packed up his clubs, slipping out of his golf shoes. He looked around at the green expanse of the *Marshridge* environs and breathed in its fresh, healthy fragrance. He did not expect to be back here again for a year at least. And now he must fly away, to validate his earlier pretence. He threw his gear in the back of his fly-car and lifted off with an excess of accelerator.

He passed once over the golf course before heading home. He felt pretty sure that it was going to be a bad time ahead.

24

Forba banked the *Arrow* away from the *Marshridge Hall Golf Club*, and set out for *Mildeburg*. He looked back and saw that Mr. Moffat was still smiling. He had heard different things about Farr Litten, but he now thought that he was OK. He also thought that he had created the best time to raise his own request with Mr. Moffat. He waited until they were in even flight, skimming across the tangled countryside at the altitude preferred by his passenger.

"Mr. Moffat? I have a favour to ask. You probably don't know, but before I came to *Pirismus* I did a lot of work on internal construction. And I have no one special to keep me here. I could be useful on *Sunspot Spinal.* I would like to go. And I'll easily find you another good driver."

Moffat looked forward at the young man's tensed back and into his anxious eyes. It would not need much brainwork, this one. He was the only person so far to actually volunteer for the voyage.

"Sure you can go, Forba. I'll get the details sorted out on Monday. Good to have you on board."

Forba uncrossed his fingers. He felt that his life was on the up.

The weekend in *Mildeburg* was a quiet time. Only occasionally did cars zip overhead. Generally, there was just the sound of bird song and water irrigation. In the distance, perhaps, the buzz of a lawn being trimmed.

Warren was out in his den, mending the window. Sarnia did not let him loose on anything inside the house, but he had free rein out in the garden, except amongst the delicate flowerbeds. The tapping of his hammer drifted up into the house. Sarnia could tell that it was being employed with carefully controlled aggression. There was, with Warren, always the possibility that the control would break down in the next few minutes.

She had been speaking with Tania on the phone. For some reason, Tania was trying to persuade her to go with Warren. Sarnia had still not found the right moment to break it to her husband, when she would give him the definite, non-negotiable "no", with that look in her eyes that would make him realise that further argument was useless. She was getting a degree of pleasure from keeping him in suspense. Nothing vindictive, just the normal cut and thrust of marriage. She still gave him credit for helping her out at the Boquat offices. He had told her that everyone thought that she was upset about Chuck. She quite liked that. It showed that she was a woman with deep feelings, strong emotions. But she did feel a little piqued that Warren had not yet explained to her who the man in reception had been. The one who had undressed her with his eyes and flooded her with forgotten feelings. Of course, she could not come right out and ask about him, so her curiosity had been tickling her, waiting for a clue. Something that he would say about work that would allow her to interpose a casual question about a certain employee's identity.

Sarnia sighed. Tania had some news today. Rico had got a posting to *Bar Ulleman*. That was in the tropical south. They would all be away for nine months. Chilly would be two by the time they got back. Sarnia thought that there was a good chance that Tania might return with a new baby on the way.

Of course, she could fly to *Ulleman*. A woman who tripped into space was certainly capable of a jaunt to the other side of the planet. But it would be a twelve-hour flight. She knew that she would not be making that journey too often. So, first her husband was abandoning her, and now she was to be deserted by her daughter as well. Little Chilly might forget her; and only come to know her as an image on a screen.

Now that she was off the phone, she was reacting to the false excitement and enthusiasm that she had felt obliged to generate for her daughter's benefit. There were salt tears pressing around her eyes again. As she walked to the window, she tilted up her head in an effort to keep them back. Through their watery lenses, she saw Jim Moffat's *Arrow* come swooping in over the line of trees.

She moved away from the window, back into the protective darkness of the house, not prepared to entertain. The fly-car made a neat turn and came in to hover over the paddock. The driver who had replaced Chuck Carnegy was obviously a bit more adventurous with his handling of the vehicle. Chuck would have made a slow, vertical descent.

She saw the driver's door start to open, and fled to the safety of the kitchen. Jim would hear Warren, tapping away in the den, and she would be spared the need for contact. She fiddled with the oven's sound system, giving the grilling bacon a quick airplay.

Just when she thought she was safe, the front door note chimed. She swore, mildly, and bit her lip. Couldn't the foolish old man even find his own way? She let a few moments pass, but she had to go in the end.

She opened the door with a bright, surprised smile.

"Jim! What a nice . . ." She was dazzled by the rush of light that came in through the doorway. She had been sitting inside for too long today. Her brow furrowed. But it was not only from the blaze of sun. Over Jim's shoulder, she could see her dream man, standing by the hovering car. Right here, outside her very own house, brought so close to the bed in which he had lived in dreams.

She must have indicated where Warren was, because Jim sauntered off in the right direction. Sarnia floated out of the house towards the big, neat, magnetic man and car. She was well practised at carrying on a conversation by remote control. Of talking of one thing when her mind was elsewhere. So she probably talked to him about Chuck, and what a terrible thing it had been. Such a nice old man.

But the real Sarnia was drinking in this man's presence. Later, she remembered offering her hand and it being enveloped in his big, warm fist. She stood before him, looking up into his carved face like a priestess before the statue of her god. It was hard to believe that the male form could be so wonderfully exciting. She kept feeling the need to bite a piece of him. Everything was getting warm and gooey. The universe closed in around the two of them, defined entirely by his Adonis form.

They must have been talking for a long time. She knew that Jim and Warren would be nattering for quite a while, yet she was soon aware of them trudging over the gravel, about to invade her private world. The spell was not broken, but it shivered and allowed the two intruders inside. Jim spoke across the void, "Sarnia, I really do wish you would go with Warren. You'll enjoy it. Why, even young Forba here has volunteered. He's going. He knows it is the chance of a lifetime."

Warren put his arm around her shoulders as they watched Jim and Forba rise up and fly away over the trees. She was a little surprised that he did not query her about her conversation with Forba. Obviously, its outward appearance had not conveyed the passion that she had been feeling within.

As they turned back towards the house, Sarnia decided that she would be exercising her prerogative. She had changed her mind. In fact it was more of a jarring, gear-wrenching reversal of opinion. She had encountered a power greater even than her love for her daughter and granddaughter. It was now an imperative in her life. She would follow Forba, like a moon follows her planet. She could feel her heart now, darting over the world in the wake of the dwindling *Arrow*. She did not necessarily expect any physical consummation. She was too strong for that, maybe, but she would feed on this new energy. It would enter her bones and blood and bring a flush of youth and vigour.

She squeezed Warren's hand as they stepped back into the cool of the house. She would tell him that she was coming with him later on, let him know of her huge sacrifice for his career.

25

The suburbs of *Dass Urmistam* were crowded, hotchpotches of simple, low houses. As there was no need for roads, they clustered together with only enough separation to allow for the entry of light, and for pedestrian access. The wealthier residents of the central city and the surrounding country houses looked down on these box dwellers. Their lives were so uniform and prescribed, it was easy enough to ridicule. But such criticism was one of the things that generated camaraderie amongst the working people who lived there, the clerks and mechanics, accountants and lawyers. They took pride in their simple ways, and in the fact that they knew that they were the salt of the earth. They really kept things going, not like the fancy computer boys and engineers.

Eloise Zeigel lived in the central southwest suburb, *Whiteholme*. Although their house was small and surrounded by exact facsimiles, she took great care of it. Now, in the summer holidays, when young Michaelangelo was away at camp, she had all day to tidy up and select a few more ornaments from the catalogues.

That morning, she had been round at Cathy's with the other girls. They had all been sympathetic about the possibility that Metter might have to go on the voyage to *Morasmus*. Some of them had read reports that *Sunspot Spinal* was unsafe. The successful conversion of a space station into a temporary space ship was unproven. Most of them thought that he should refuse to go. Just because they had given him a job when he had been out of work did not mean that they owned him. They should not be asking married men. Who knew what their wives might get up to while they were away?

Eloise laughed at this, and played with her untidy, mousy hair. She was pleased at the suggestion, partly because it was so unlikely. Neither she nor Metter were much to look at. They felt lucky, really, even to have each other. Oddly, their son Michaelangelo was a handsome boy.

But she dreaded the idea of Metter being away for so long. Away in that awful outer space. What was the point? Just to build something for the rich people. Somewhere that she could never possibly afford to visit. Would not want to, either. There was no attraction for her in that cold endlessness; she liked the warmth of home. To be able to touch the things that they owned, that they had striven for. Feel them in her hand, and recall the exact method of their acquisition. She wanted to feel safe and a part of things.

She did not know how she would be able to fill the time, if Metter had to go. It was hard enough to keep busy now. And Metter started and finished work right on time, flying home to be with her as soon as the clock hit five. She realised that this was partly because he did not greatly enjoy the work at Boquat. He did not talk to her about it very much, but she guessed that it was too dull for him. And they had impossible deadlines, because of this *Sunspot* thing. What a silly name.

Now her friends had gone, and she was in the lonely time before her husband got home. She went up to the bedroom to tidy herself up. She sighed as she recognised the plain, sad face that had looked back at her all her life. It was so hard to let people know about the beauty within, when it was obscured by this visage and was carried in a straight, up and down body. She smoothed her dress tight across her chest. But there was nothing to excite there either, no womanly compensation. Just depressingly small, shapeless bulges. She looked out of her bedroom window to the city skyline. The towers marched away into the faint, far distance, speaking of other people's lives, filled with exotic excitement. The glare of the sun's rays, reflected from their meticulously cleaned windows, dazzled her and hurt her eyes. She adjusted the tinted glass shading with a slight roll of the control wheel.

On the dressing table was a picture of Michaelangelo, taken a year ago when he was twelve. He smiled at her and filled the emptiness with a reason to live.

The front door bell signal toned around the house. She had not noticed anything flying in from the direction of the city, but this must be her visitor, the telecom engineer. She had had a phone call from them, just after lunchtime. The automatic monitoring systems had detected a fault in her smart-house receptors, and they were sending someone over at four o'clock. The arrival announcement confirmed that it was exactly four now.

She padded down the stairs with a little flutter of nerves. Strangers always made her feel a bit awkward. She had one last glance at her reflection in the hall mirror, hoping for that one reassuring, flattering angle. No, she was having a bad face day again. She pressed the open button for her visitor.

Eloise had to smile, she need not have worried. The man at the door would not have known whether she was a beauty or not. He was blind and wore those ugly spectacle things across his flat nose. He smiled back at her. She was just thinking that it was strange that an installation engineer could manage things, being sightless, when he reached out and touched her lightly on the arm. Her hand went up to the place. Although only really a brush of his fingers, perhaps a form of blind person's greeting, she had felt a sharp pinprick. Then she saw the small needle that had emerged from under his index fingernail.

The smile froze on her face.

Metter Zeigel flew home with a squirming feeling of desperation in his heart. From his very first day at Boquat, he had been uneasy. The work was much harder than he had expected. His group of Knowledge Engineers were not the best. He had come to realise this, but even though he was their supervisor, he had not been able to do anything about it. Metter was not that good himself. He had always relied on others, throughout his career. There were many proficient people in the main computing department, but Warren Galant had told him to have no contact with them, no matter what the circumstances. So Metter concentrated on his department's administration, which he saw as his main responsibility, hoping that the technicalities would sort themselves out. The trouble was, he knew they never did. And he knew that Warren Galant had told Jim Moffat that he was a hot shot. This was Pressure with a capital P.

Then Tung had come along, and things seemed to be getting better. Even though Tung was self-taught, spending hours on his terminal at home, he was easily the most able of all his staff. Programs that had been displaying bugs for months were put right in days by Tung. Schedules were starting to be met.

Then later, just when Metter was thinking that he could relax, when his days were not filled with a suppressed feeling of panic, there was the prospect of actually having to go on the flight to *Morasmus*. That really scared him. The idea of space flight was frightful. Having to be responsible for the programming and take hands-on control was terrifying, and being away from Eloise and Michaelangelo was heartbreaking. Once again, it seemed that Tung would save him. Tung had volunteered to go on *Sunspot* in his place. Metter had enthusiastically endorsed the request, and thought it was settled by mutual consent. But then he had sought Warren's agreement, and had been told that the idea was unacceptable. Warren insisted that Metter should go, as the top man in his department. And he would not allow both Tung and Metter to go, because the budget would not extend to such lengths. There was no arguing with Warren. And on this occasion, Warren's well-known proclivity for changing his mind had not come to the rescue.

So, that morning he had told Tung what Warren had said, and that he would not be allowed to go. Tung's face had been a mask as he listened. Metter had stuttered and fumbled through his explanation, so that in the end Tung had to come right out and ask if it meant that he would only be allowed to go if Metter was unavailable. When Metter squeaked out in the affirmative, Tung's expression was one of profound fury. It was a frightening sight. It still made him shiver to think of it. Tung told Metter that he was taking the afternoon off.

Metter had sat at his desk, neutralised for the rest of the day, staring at his performance metrics and tapping his mouse. It was a well-practised routine, one where he appeared to be working, but his mind was elsewhere. He had spent his time desperately hoping that Tung was not looking for another job: that would be the final disaster. Metter had slipped away from work a few minutes early, ahead of the rest of his team, who all walked away from their desks at five sharp. He wanted to get back to Eloise, and talk things through.

His spirits rose as their house came into view through the fly-car's windscreen, although a frown of disappointment crossed his brow as he saw that they had visitors. There was one of the automatic taxis parked on their roof pad, and right in Metter's usual spot, too. He had to take extra care as he edged down onto the house and powered off. He slouched down the steps to the front door and let himself in. He had to forego his usual, familiar greeting. Eloise found it embarrassing when there were visitors in the house. So he walked through into the hall and craned his neck around to see if he could find her. There was no conversation in progress to help him locate her, but he saw a foot that he recognised as hers, near one of the chairs in the sitting room. Oddly, it was by his chair, where she never sat. He walked through, feeling quite grumpy by now.

Eloise was sitting there, strangely rigid. Something was wrong. Her eyes were moving frantically, her only moving parts. They made small circles and movements, as if trying to communicate. Then Metter's gaze was attracted lower down her stiff body. Her dress had been unbuttoned, and one of her breasts was exposed, drooping down and stirring a little from her quick, panting breaths. Worse, she was sitting with her legs apart and her dress was pulled right up to her waist, revealing her pallid thighs. Metter stood as frozen as his wife at the sight of her, and shock clutched his throat like a vice.

Tung had been waiting for Metter's moment of paralysis. He was not going to let him get away with a little pinprick. He wanted to dispense some pain on him. Tung detested Metter for his incompetence, his laziness and his stupidity. He had been waiting behind the door, waiting for him to be transfixed by his wife's ugly nudity. He was within scanning range of Metter's sloping shoulders and thinning head. He took a silent step forward and wrapped the garrotte around his supervisor's thick, wrinkled neck. He squeezed hard, but not hard enough to crush his victim's throat straight away. Tung enjoyed the feeling of Metter's impotent struggling. He even released the pressure now and then, to prolong his pleasure. He made sure that his victim was pointing straight into the obscenity of his wife's nudity so that he must assume that she had been most horribly violated. Of course this was not so, as Tung had neither the means nor the desire to perform such an act. But he was pleased to be adding a little more agony into the failed programmer's last minutes.

Metter sank to his knees and Tung crashed down onto his calves, to maintain his position of purchase. From down here, they could both see Eloise fully revealed, watching without belief the events that were taking place on the family carpet, where baby Michaelangelo had once played. Tears were streaming down her cheeks.

Eventually, all the life drained out of Metter and he slumped forward. To be sure, Tung tightened the garrotte with all his strength. Gristle and bone crunched beneath its pressure.

Tung waited until nightfall, topping Eloise up with anaesthesia every so often. He carried them both up to the taxi and set its co-ordinates for the Orbit Club. The club owned two *Tyratheon* space ships, the nine hundred members sharing use of the vehicles. At this time of night the place was deserted, but Tung knew the access codes. He also knew how to program the machines for escape velocity. He had the system overrides, which overcame the internal computer's objections to being sent off irretrievably into outer space. He bundled its last passengers into the small cockpit and watched the black bubble ascend into the starry night.

Eloise was still alive at take off. Tung had not done her any more harm, because he knew that his mother would not have approved.

26

The *Arrow* was flying high, now that Jim Moffat was no longer on board. The brilliance of *Dass Urmistam* was dwindling away to the south. The river snaked its slow way north, a winding slug of brown. Ahead was an unprecedented amount of air traffic; the thin, high cloud layer was filled with the navigation lights of ships swarming above the spaceport outside North Coast, *Bassenfield*. Some were gliding in from the east, bringing down the refugees from *Sunspot*, those who would not be going on the long exodus. Other ships were departing from *Bassenfield* to the west, carrying the last few provisions and crew. The majority of ships and people were planet-bound. Only four hundred souls would be on board *Sunspot Spinal* as she set out to rendezvous with her earlier components, already circling distant *Morasmus*.

Farr looked over Forba's broad shoulder at the view ahead. The space ship lights were supplemented by hundreds of fly-cars, buzzing around at lower altitudes. The spaceport always attracted sightseers, but now the density of big freighters and liners was much greater than normal, and so had cast a greater influence over those for whom space travel held such a fascination. Farr had to admit to being quite excited at the prospect of his expedition, now that he was reconciled to being away from his golf.

This was going to be genuine, extended space travel. Not the blind career through unreal dimensions that made inter-galactic passage possible. For these relatively tiny, solar distances such techniques were not possible. The intervals were too small, despite the amazing accuracy of the navigation systems, particularly for vessels the size of *Sunspot Spinal*. Once the giant *Morasmus* space station was fully commissioned, however, there would be stabilising and targeting facilities at both ends of the transit line. Then small, five hundred seater ships would be able to fly between the brother planets in eight hours, including docking times. The tourist trade would be enabled.

There were other things to look forward to, thought Farr, as he craned forward and opened his eyes wider to capture the scene ahead, in all its perspective. He looked across at Izabel Torini, sitting next to him. He had liked her as soon as she had joined his department, only he was married then and he had been faithful all his life. He made a point of not messing with his own staff, even if they did strike into the tender heart of his vulnerable, male sex drive. He would not have put Izabel in this class from the personnel graphic in her HR record. But she had an inner beauty that belied her external appearance, and which he supposed sprang from her intelligence and humanity. He had been enjoying her company over the last few weeks.

Chuck Carnegy's wrist computer had been an excellent excuse for getting to know her better. It had been this ulterior motive that had been one of his original reasons for suggesting that he should take it. The day after Jim Moffat had handed it to him in the *Arrow*, as they sat in the golf club car park, he had discussed it with her at work. He knew that they should be able to find quite a lot of data from it, although this was not normal procedure. The masses of personal information were only there so that the computer would recognise its owner. But like most computer systems, the enthusiasm of the programmers had exceeded what was strictly necessary, so the potential of the data went well beyond its current usage. And this was not really a matter of security, as theft was rare; it was rather for convenience. The devices would warn the wearer if he had inadvertently picked up the wrong one. And if it were mislaid it would act as a permanent recognition transmitter.

Izabel had downloaded the data and run it through a whole gamut of her character appraisal engines. Overall, the results were disappointing. Very little interpretation about the man himself could be extrapolated from this plethora of signatures from his body. There was nothing that could reasonably be added to his company obituary page.

Izabel, though, had also focused on the medical interpretation. She had gone straight to that slice of data and had compared it to the conventional records in the human resources health folders. Farr could tell that she was following a hunch.

They had been working after hours, as the evening sky outside thickened and emptied, on their private project. Coffee cups and false lines of investigation lay strewn around the office. Farr was just about keeping up with Izabel's flying fingers and diagonal logic as she navigated her way around the knowledge bases with phenomenal speed. He was starting to feel very attracted to her that night, not that he had any intention of doing anything about it. In the subdued lighting of the dimmed office, her face looked wonderfully smooth and sweet as she gazed into the screen, absorbed in concentrated effort. She received his questions and occasional advice with courtesy and little sideways smiles. Genuine little smiles, that made him feel as if he were attractive himself. Why not? Even though he was twenty years older than she, he maintained a trim body. Girls at the golf club still gave him a second look, if he was having a high charisma day.

Izabel found what she had been expecting, just as Farr had slipped away into deep pools of introspection. The official records claimed that Chuck had an advanced case of brain tumour. The independent evidence, painfully mined from the hidden depths of the wrist computer, gave him a clean bill of health. Izabel turned to face Farr. She told him about Tung then, that she thought he was involved in some sort of sabotage or corruption. Badness for sure; a conspiracy, maybe. Nothing she could prove, she admitted. She thought that he had modified the medical records, although all the audit traces had gone missing — which was probably his work. He had found the tunnel that undermined the security sentinels before, and he could do it again.

"Can we find out how Chuck actually died from the body signals held in his wrist computer?" asked Farr.

"I don't think so. Not with a sudden death like his. Unless there is still some data in the sampling buffer. Most of the identification is automatically programmed within a few seconds of the watch being put on, and the initialisation routine started. A unique profile is established and logged from the beginning. But the sensors do keep on capturing any atypical data, in case minor modifications are required. Like if a woman passes through the menopause. We might find something there."

Izabel worked away again, with Farr sitting by her side. He had abandoned all attempts at assisting her now. He was admiring the nape of her neck, where her short hair fell away around it and exposed the tender, sensitive skin. She was a bit plump, but that was good and he knew that she would feel very nice. Smooth and warm. Farr coughed suddenly, to clear these emotions from his imagination.

"Its OK, I've nearly got it," said Izabel, thinking his patience was running out. "We're nearly there. Look, this is what we've got. There is more than I would have thought, but it doesn't help us much in its raw form. The pulse and perspiration data shows that he died in trauma. But that would have been true whether he had jumped himself or been pushed. I don't think we can use any of it to draw conclusions. It's a bit odd that his nerve impulse amplitude is so low."

"OK, enough is enough. I think we both deserve to get something to eat," said Farr, standing up to help draw their work to a conclusion. Izabel pushed herself away from her screen, but was less keen to drop the subject.

"I think this line of study has a lot of potential," she said, as she stretched in her chair, thrusting her legs out in front of her. "Not the Carnegy sample in particular. I am no medical expert, but I don't believe we have ever really thought of our identification computers as an important piece of diagnostic equipment. Prognostic, too. The input bank can be analysed to give a precise review of the owner's state of health and from that a good prediction of his future life line. My program says that Chuck would have lived to be eighty nine, before dying of kidney failure."

The subject of how this connection might be exploited kept them in deep conversation all through their supper at *La Violetta* restaurant. It also helped Farr to avoid any embarrassing suggestions about where they might go next. At least, he did not propose any further destinations, like his house, for that particular night. But he did ask her if she would come with him to *Morasmus* on *Sunspot Spinal*. When he spoke about it to her there was huskiness in his voice, he felt so charged with uncertain emotion. The offer seemed to him to be almost like saying, "come to bed." He crossed his fingers to ensure that she would say "yes." And so she did.

Forba flew them down into the North Coast *Milleforum* reception area. They would be leaving for *Sunspot* in the next few days. Farr helped Izabel down from the *Arrow*. The three of them looked into the sky, at the lights of the incoming spaceships lining up for their landings at the nearby *Bassenfield*. Farr shivered in the chill of the evening breeze and at the dramatic sight of the ships, cast like stepping-stones to the stars. And at Izabel, who looked like a child in her excitement.

Then he saw her gaze distracted, and her mouth drop open a touch. He could almost feel the emotional connection between himself and the young woman being severed. A wall of disinterest suddenly encircled her, cutting him off. Her eyes had opened a little wider, making her look even more desirable to him. He almost wanted to jump in front of her and force her to recognise him again. But she only had eyes for another.

Forba had released himself from the fly-car and was standing over them, smiling brightly in the darkness. He held Izabel in his spell as easily as a wizard might command the admiration of his apprentice.

27

Sunspot Spinal edged out to a higher orbit. It was spinning about its central point, precisely half way along its thin, twenty-five mile length. The heavy energy converters, which had previously fuelled the quasi-gravity fields, had been disconnected and simple rotation would be their substitute during the space flight. Only the end compartments would be inhabited in the early days of the journey. The twenty-two miles of intervening modules were relieved of their air and warmth.

Melda Smith could see the converters moving away, going back to new contractual duties in the construction yards of the orbital operators. She had got used to the new orientation of her home. It had become a place to climb through, rather than walk along. The treacherous railway track had been replaced by a system of elevators. She preferred it this way. She was also looking forward to Izabel's arrival. Most of her own crew had been shipped back to *Morasmus*, back to their families and their homes.

Farr, Forba and Izabel were on one of the last ships to bring up the new recruits. It docked in the evacuated section, near the centre of the structure, from which the incoming passengers took the airtight, express elevators to their quarters at either end of the ship. The three of them had all been billeted at the same extremity, the blue zone, reserved for those making the whole flight. They wished their red zone counterparts bon voyage as the two groups diverged. Journey's end for them would be after a week in space. They would stay on board as long as their shuttlecraft had the range to return them to *Pirismus*.

Farr and Izabel had rooms on blue levels twenty and twenty three, amongst the Knowledge Engineers. Forba was up in blue level eighty, with the ancillaries. Warren and Sarnia were with the last group to arrive, wearing brave faces. Sarnia smiled at everyone she met, but the tenseness of uncertainty reflected from her tight cheeks. She was homesick from the beginning. Any expectation that she might have engineered an innocent dalliance with a certain fellow crewmember had been sublimated by the pain of separation from her grandchild. More than once she thought of asking Warren to let her return, before it was too late and they were out of shuttle range.

But he had scheduled a reception for all the Blue Enders. Level sixty-nine was set up as an open recreation area. There were others, scattered along the length of the ship. Many of the leisure and pleasure facilities would be commissioned during the flight and made available to the crew. But this area had simply been laid out with trestles, which bore fresh food and drink. The general idea was for everyone to get to know each other. Sarnia realised that she must, at least, stay until this formality was completed.

Melda had arranged to meet Izabel at the reception early, before the official kick-off time, through the scheduling computer. They greeted one another in the flesh like old friends, and sat at one of the corner tables, barely having time to eat between their reciprocating questions and answers. Farr came and joined them later, but was unable to make much impact on their conversation. He bumped around them like a balloon against a party ceiling. They all saw Warren and Sarnia arrive quite late and move regally amongst the throng. Melda and Izabel watched Sarnia step proudly around her subjects, with no friendship in her eyes. Their coldness had flowed from the instant, visceral iciness of first impressions. The three of them sat back in their dim corner, to avoid the honour of a visit and the inevitable condescending small-talk.

Sarnia stopped in her tracks as she circulated. Izabel and Melda followed her eyes, and saw that they were fixed on Forba, who had just arrived, and was looking engagingly lost. His striking appearance became the main feature of the whole, large room. Sarnia floated over to him with casual haste and almost collided with his big, muscular thighs, smiling up into his face. Her haughty expression had gone.

Izabel laughed shortly and looked away. Melda recognised the tension in that mirthless expression, and made a note to ask her friend what was going on between her and Forba. She looked over to the handsome young man with his small, fluttering companion. She found that even her imagination raced, fired by his manly frame. Melda would not let the fact that she was old enough to be Izabel's mother stop her from getting to the bottom of things. Then she saw Farr looking wistfully at Izabel. It looked like it was going to be an interesting trip.

After a time, Izabel ventured from their secluded table to recharge her plate and glass. She slipped her way through the crowded room, having to guess her path as she was shorter than most of the other occupants. When she breached the wall of bodies and entered the clear space that spread around the serving trestles, she stopped dead. There was a broad, squat man helping himself to the food. From the way in which he moved his head and probed with his hands, she knew that he was blind. And, therefore, he must be Tung.

Although she stood still and held her breath, she somehow knew that his sharpened senses would detect and recognise her presence. And, indeed, he did turn from the table and point his flat face, with its black spectacles, in her direction. He stood there as if smelling her, sniffing out her surprise and revulsion. She expected him to say "Hello, my dear Izabel. How very nice to see you at last. I look forward to our long voyage together and getting to know all about you."

Instead, he just moved his head to one side and brushed past her into the throng. She saw Warren Galant approach and put his hand on Tung's elbow, saying his name through the fog of general conversation as positive proof of identification. She rushed back to her table.

"Tung is here, Melda!" she gasped as she sat down, ignoring Farr's welcoming smile.

"Tung? The Tung?" said Melda, taking time to let the confirmation give rise to fear. "Can't we warn someone? Farr, can't you tell Warren about him?"

"I don't think he would listen," replied Farr, somewhat peeved to be involved in the women's world at this late stage. He heard the petulance in his own voice and relented. He saw that Warren was alone again and he went over to him.

"Hello, Warren. How are you?"

"Oh, hello Farr. I'm fine, thank you," said Warren with an extra layer of smoothness in his modulated tones. They always annoyed Farr, but he persisted with his quest.

"Isn't that one of your programmers over there, dropping his food?"

"Tung? Yes, he is one of mine. Very good, too. Top rate."

"I thought that you were only bringing one with you. Your supervisor."

"Yes, that was the plan, but we had to make a few adjustments."

"Changed your mind, eh? Do you know anything about him?"

"Of course, we have full HR records," said Warren. "Metter always wanted Tung to be the one to come, anyway. Even though Metter was an excellent technician himself, he thought Tung was better."

"What happened to Metter?"

"Some family trouble. Don't worry, it's all under control," finished Warren, as he moved away. Farr was unable to reassure the women when he returned to their table and was entrapped by their enquiring glances.

"Tung has Warren's personal recommendation. We'd better watch him closely," he said.

Later, Izabel and Melda talked things through in Melda's room. They shared the first, most shallow layer of each other's secrets. And they shared their fear about Tung.

Elsewhere in the ship, very similar concerns were being felt by one of their shipmates. Jocasta had also been sifting through the crewmembers' data banks. She had detected a few anomalies in Tung's files. Part of her responsibility was to ensure the smooth collaboration of everyone on board. She had already detected potential trouble, and had made a note to monitor events carefully, using her special access to the computer systems. It would be quite a challenge to keep things stable for the duration of the flight, but at least that was about to begin now. She had been training and preparing for many months.

The very next day, Jocasta felt the engines start to push *Sunspot Spinal* gently away from the planet.

A week later *Pirismus* was just a point of light in the blackness of space, hardly recognisable as their sweet home. Everything outside was dominated by the blazing radiance of *Millar Vorspak*, the sun star that drew them into its embrace.

28

Mattelio Candrelovic sat on the mountain. Above him, the craggy rock stretched almost vertically for another six thousand feet. His altimeter told him that the roots of the *Panghorn Peak* were another four thousand feet below him, although the layer of white cloud obscured any sight of the valley floor. His legs dangled on either side of the small spur of shiny, grey rock that stood out from the endless wall. Six and a half miles away, on the other side of the chasm, the *Sixty Sisters* marched away like a reflection of the great *Rowlands Range*, of which the *Panghorn* was one massive tooth. The huge furrow that lay between the parallel lines of mountains had been dug, aeons ago, by a giant glacier as it gouged its way north. It ran for eight hundred miles, to within fifty miles of the South Pole. But, in these modern times, it was warm on the rock face, where the thermals coiled up against Matt's face. His long hair was saturated with perspiration, and it dripped over his shoulders. His skin suit was open to the waist, allowing his strong torso to cool from the occasional shivers of evaporation that ran across his chest. There was no vanity in his pose, despite the way that he tensed and released his heavily built muscles. There was no one within five hundred miles to admire them.

He looked to his right, where the sky paled to a silvery white as it approached the southern tip of the planet. Overhead it was a brilliant, opalescent blue. To the left, he could see what he was waiting for. The higher airs had turned vague and grey, and the far north end of the great *Massona Fault Valley* was darkened by heavy, black clouds. He could see an occasional flicker of lightning in its brooding body, still too far away to hear. He shifted his position on the rock perch, giving his board a reassuring tug with the strap that attached it to his right ankle. He checked his wrist computer and saw that his heart rate was rising from forty beats per second to over seventy. His body was preparing itself. This was what he had come here for.

Mattelio had left *Sumesotta* seven years earlier, after two years of marriage to Fiona. He really had thought that it would work out when they had drawn up their nuptial contract. She was an intelligent woman, with a good sense of humour and a promising career in aquatic engineering. Not tremendously pretty, but a good body and legs that made his eyes sore. She was obviously thrilled to have won Matt.

The first year had passed pleasantly enough. Matt had a part-time job in the sales department of the *Rishnabula Superstore*. He played a lot of squash, and got to be ranked on the district ladder. He took up sea surfing, as well, taking the car over to the *Guillam* peninsular where the ocean swells rolled into the crescent bay, reaching fifteen feet on most days. And he made enough time to manage the domestic arrangements for their apartment in *Shandarin Norde*.

But things had started to go sour, for reasons that he could never quite be sure of. Somehow, in the second year of their togetherness, the excitement had gone out of their life together. Fiona did not want children, and Matt knew that offspring were excluded from their contract. He did not think that this was what had rankled, but something started to make the things that Fiona said, and did, aggravate him. It had really taken a turn for the worse one autumn evening. Matt's morning surf had been cancelled. The beach was closed, because of a temporary pollution slick in the area. Then he had a game of squash in the afternoon at the club, against Martin Cheong Flay. And he had lost, three two. He never lost to Martin. In the shower afterwards, he had concluded that his game had stopped improving ever since the marriage. It hurt to feel that, somehow, his youth was over. He had peaked, and was on his way down to mediocrity.

Matt had wanted to talk about it when Fiona got home that evening, but she had arrived tired and quiet. He knew that she was not listening as he tried to explain how he was feeling. He could also tell that she did not care about the increasingly obvious fact that he was getting angry about being ignored. She thought, no doubt, that she could make it up to him in bed later that night. But he had pictured her body in his mind, every inch of which he knew, and he had thought about all of the little imperfections. The small patches of stretched skin, the tiny excesses of fat and stray outposts of her dark hair. Together, he had used them to neutralise her sexual allure. He had contrived temporary revulsion, almost, for her female charms. So, when she had slipped her hand under the covers that night so predictably, in exactly the way that he knew she would, he had coolly put it back where it had come from, and declared himself to be too tired. His resolution had surprised them both. He could no longer be controlled by the power of sex.

Things had got worse from that day onwards. They had grown apart, and most of their conversations turned into arguments. There wasn't even any pleasant reconciliation. No nights of passion to remind them of what had first drawn them together. Matt had begun to get a perverse pleasure from the pain that they were causing each other. He had the advantage, though, of being free for most of the day. Free to prepare the next little rebuff or ambush. Fiona arrived home tired and defenceless, apprehensive of what awaited her in the home that no longer felt like her own.

Then, at last, she had burst into tears at some heartless remark that he had made. Months of hurt poured out of her, and Matt felt ashamed. He realised the torture that he had been putting her through. He could see his own cruelty revealed as her shoulders shook with grief. He put his hand on her arm in true friendship for the first time in almost a year. They both knew that it was pity, not love.

They realised that they were no longer good for each other, and so decided that they must separate. He had only asked for the minimum alimony, and that was what was funding him out here, on the wild planet of *Morasmus*. It was enough. There were not many shops in this neighbourhood.

There had been a lot of talk amongst the men on the surf beaches and squash courts, tales about this empty, wild planet. They all said that they planned to go there, but few had the courage. Many poorly prepared visitors disappeared in its uncharted wastes. Matt was not a coward, and he felt that he needed both a break and to do penance for his marital behaviour. He had purchased a passage to *Morasmus* with the separation lump sum. There was not enough money to go via *Pirismus*, as did many other trippers from *Sumesotta*. Going via the more highly developed, outer planet allowed the traveller to arrange a reasonably secure approach to its dangerously overheated inner brother. Matt had to land his *Capuletti* space ship on the planet's surface. There were no authorised docking spaces available on the few orbiting hostelries. He had touched down at the polar *Foothold Station*, a small community living in dwellings carved into the naked rock. From there, he had found his own place, high in the *Southborn Massif*. A cave, eaten out by ancient oceans, which was only accessible with his sky board. But heated with a small energy block and radiator cladding, it was comfortable enough. And from there he could indulge in all of the *Morasmic* delights.

Today he was storm surfing. It looked like being one of his best runs ever. The dark maelstrom of snarling wind and whipping rain, stirred by liberal gouges of lightning, was barrelling down the *Massona Fault Valley* at a hundred and fifty miles an hour. He watched its ugly, almost vertical, face approach like a gigantic ocean roller. Curls of cloud spilled from its crest and were sucked back into its body, where powerful under-currents tore back and forth. Matt would have to avoid them and the vicious thermals that ripped from the valley floor to the tumbled cloud at the storm's roof.

The clean air was being pushed ahead of the advancing monster, already at gale force and whipping Matt's hair around his cheeks and eyes. He pulled his board up towards him and switched it from idling to active mode, in which it would be able to take his weight. He planted his feet in their binding blocks, zipped up his skin suit, and pushed himself away from his craggy hook, taking a few practice turns as he descended. He looked over his shoulder to see the towering wall filling the valley behind him with shadow. He increased the angle of his shallow descent, and picked up speed in his fall, bending his knees to gain better balance.

Even though he had attained a ground speed of over a hundred miles per hour, the storm front hit him hard and sent him rushing ahead, driven by its power as if guided by an impatient hand. It was important, a matter of life and death, that he should avoid a nose-dive and keep the board's curved prow angled upwards. He zigzagged up the face of the tempest, probing the shear barrier created by differing air pressures. His heart thumped in his chest and his throat strained to keep fear from rushing through his body, paralysing his heart. He dared to look upwards, and saw the sky darkened by the menacing canopy of the tumult's surf line. He needed to get there before the structure of the chaos began to erode and collapse totally. There was no way out but up.

Matt surfed up the cloud for half an hour, his heart pounding and his lungs bursting with effort and excitement. His great, sweeping arcs up the typhoon wall took him close to the mountain faces on either side of the canyon. Visibility varied, sometimes clear enough for him to see the horizon as he rode in the vanguard of clear air, sometimes plunged into gloom as the storm's outriders enveloped him. And the din numbed his ears despite the plugs he was wearing. The tortured wind screeched at the top of its gigantic voice, but was frequently shouted down by the cacophony of thunder. It rolled and echoed between the walls of rock, accompanied by the dazzle of lightning flashes.

Matt felt god-like as he ascended towards the brilliant blue sky that dazzled beyond the turmoil, where his salvation lay. The tempest was starting to break up, its instability showing in huge horns and tentacles of cloud that raced along the valley floor below him. As his meteorometer had predicted, this was a big one. Matt knew that he might easily die in a storm this large and powerful. It was true that he was attached to the sky board by his ankle strap, and that it would bear his weight should he fall. But that would not stop him from being smashed into one of the rock walls, or sucked into one of the down-draughts to be plunged fatally to the valley floor below. It was even rumoured that some surfers had had their spines snapped by the shearing force of the wind's pressure differentials alone. And sometimes large rocks were drawn up into the maelstrom to offer the possibility of being ground into a pulp.

So when he finally broke through the storm ceiling and emerged back into the clear sunlight, like a breaching whale, he felt as though he had actually been under water. Like a wiped out ocean surfer. He took great lung-fulls of air and looked back across the almost perfectly flat layer of cloud that was the storm's roof. In the sunlight it was white and fluffy. Only the growls of thunder below hinted at the anger within.

He dropped down and sat astride his board, taking time to let his aching body recover. It was warm again up here, and he peeled his skin suit off his upper body and let it hang from his waist. His attention was attracted by a succession of characteristic thunder crashes from the south. The storm was collapsing. Its undercurrents had run away towards the pole, skidding along with sudden acceleration and bringing the upper layers of wind and rain tumbling down. It made Matt feel good to know that his fear had been well founded. He put the board on cruise and headed home.

He needed to stop on the way. In the storm circles of *Morasmus*, it was not wise to arrive home without adequate protection.

29

Sunspot Mainbeam rotated around the planet *Morasmus*. Her essential structure was complete, five concentric rings of living or working space, spinning around the exact centre of gravity. The diameter of the outer habitat ring was over sixteen miles. It glittered in the golden rays of the *Vorspak* sun as they filtered through the planet's protecting atmosphere. The revolutions moved her many segments from the shadow of *Morasmus* out into the sunlight, and back again into its darkness. From the planet's surface she looked like a small crescent moon, the shaded miles of her being obscured and lifeless. She would not be so modest for long.

Her massive body was waiting for the arrival of her brain and nervous system as it fell through solar space towards her, the thin, precious thread of *Sunspot Spinal*. In those final pieces of the monumental jigsaw lay her computer and networking systems. Once connected, her wholeness would blaze with light and vibrant energy, showering brilliance from the thousands of windows that looked out to the galaxy and down to the fiery planet. The spark that would ignite her cold body drew ever closer.

Field Preston did not care for the poetic descriptions of his condition that were beamed in from the corporate offices on *Pirismus*. He had been on *Mainbeam* for eighteen months and he knew that it was an uncomfortable, cold, dark and dangerous place right now. It was getting more dangerous all the time. He did not really think that he should be out here on his own, patrolling the service corridors of *Habitat Three*. It was supposed to be secure against squatters, as there were no easy access points from outside. But they had said that about the eighth class leisure suites, until two of his colleagues had disappeared whilst carrying out a routine sweep. This was a feature of the great space station that the advertising men kept quiet about.

They knew that there were people living here and there, from the mess that they left behind. Not all of the latrine blocks were powered up yet, and some of the intruders' detritus made the stomach turn. When he had joined up for the Securicrat this was not what he had expected. Cleaning duties, crowd control and dealing with the odd drunk, that was what he had imagined. But now he was edging his way along gloomy passages, with his gun at the ready, peering into the shadows and never quite sure whether they were moving.

Field had seen this kind of thing in movies. It did not make him feel any better that some of his colleagues reckoned that there might be alien life forms on board. Their spores had infiltrated from the planet below, seeding into strange life and growing with quiet patience into terrible forms that waited to feed. Waiting for succulent, human flesh.

Nobody knew very much about *Morasmus* or what might live in its deep, sweltering valleys and impenetrable swamps. Big, slithering, hunting things, it was said. And the squatters might have brought a few up here with them, to show that they had a sense of humour. He didn't really believe it, but something made his spine tingle every time the hydraulic systems favoured the silence with a low-frequency growl. He hitched his laser rifle back into the cradle of his arms, and swept aside the darkness ahead with the twin beams from his shoulder torches.

The light panels, high up on the walls around him, had started to flash intermittently. The dark shapes ahead leaped more savagely at him, infuriated by the shifting goads of illumination. Now things were really getting theatrical, building up for the big shocker. He called in to control.

"Hey guys, Preston here. There is a problem with the lights out here. Are you doing something, or is it just that the alien carnivores are preparing to have me for supper?"

"Hold on, Preston. Maintain your position while we check it out."

Field stood back against the wall, casually taking his rest and guarding against any surprise attack. The panels above his head lit up in swift sequence, giving the corridor the illusion of being in motion. He held on to his courage, in case it should start to run away as well. Sharp claws and teeth waited in the wings. Field knew that he had the appearance of the immobile, helpless victim. Soon, a horrible death would be upon him from some unexpected quarter.

"Yes, that's us. Just testing the latest circuit connections and auxiliary power. If you want, we can give you full luminance for ten minutes or so."

Field tried not to sound relieved. "That would be nice."

The panels all came on and the true, bright nature of the passage was revealed. The clean, cream coloured wall and ceiling partitions were anything but frightening. They looked civilised, friendly, efficient. He felt their rough surface with his fingertips and drew new courage from the entirely artificial, familiar texture. He looked at his watch. In only another half hour he would be able to get back amongst good company. He started off again, making casual inspections of the equipment boxes that were located at regular intervals along the walls.

Despite the great diameter of *Habitat Three*, Field's view forward was limited by the upward curve of the rubberised floor. He could see about a hundred metres in front of him, before the distant floor disappeared behind the ceiling ahead. Further if he ducked down.

So he saw the pile of rubbish on the floor, over by the right wall, well before he got there. He stopped.

"Looks like I've got something," he radioed in. He waited for the reply.

"Nothing showing here. We have limited senses. What can you see, Preston?" replied control.

"It looks like a jumble of clothes. Must be squatters."

"Any sign of life?"

"Not that I can see." He got right down on his knees, so that he could scan well past the untidy lump of material. He knew that there were no surveillance cameras in this section to relay his undignified posture. He even pressed his cheek down to the floor to make sure.

"Just the pile of clothes. Do you think they have been abandoned?"

"Proceed with caution," said control. Field thought that they might have taken rather more consideration time before sending him on. He doubted that squatters left anything much behind them for very long, so they were probably still close. He edged forward, bowing to check that the passage remained clear.

Despite the good, bright light, he could not make out any detail in the pile until he got very close. Then he saw a streak of brown hair spread across the grey blanket. There was a small piece of white flesh poking through the greasy strands, possibly an ear.

"There's a body wrapped in the blankets. There is a bit of a smell."

"OK, you had better stay and wait for a crew. How big is the body?"

Field did not like the idea of finding out. It looked small, but he had the feeling that dead bodies did look shrunken, deflated of life and vigour. He crouched down and caught the blanket with the end of his rifle, drawing it back slowly, fearing the sudden assault of the gases of decay. But the revealed skin was clear and healthy. He saw long eyelashes and the corner of a moist mouth, largely obscured by the floods of hair. His muzzle moved forward again and carefully swept the brown locks away from the pink cheeks.

His attention alarm buzzed in his ear. He had set it to tell him that he was within five minutes of the end of his tour. It was not a loud noise, but in the quiet suspense of the moment it jarred his nerves. He looked down to his right collar, where the little alarm was clipped, and sent it back to sleep. When he looked back to the revealed face, it had turned and was looking up at him, too sleepy to be surprised. It was a young girl.

The sight of the unexpected and the movement of his head helped to unbalance Field. From his crouching position on the balls of his feet, he began a slow topple backwards. He was too far from the wall to get any support, and he rolled over onto his back, still in his hunched position, so that his feet flew up into the air. On another occasion he might have kicked his legs and giggled. However, his fall coincided with all the lights going out again. When his spine hit the cold floor, he stared up into total darkness, haunted by the ghosts of light spots that circled his retina.

Then he heard what he really did not want to hear in that moment of defencelessness. There was a scuffling from further up the corridor. The tread of feet. A rapid drumming, a run forward, positioning for the swing of a large blade? Or the stab of a laser lance? Possibly the frenzied return of an angered parent, defending its young with homicidal rage. He fumbled for his shoulder torches. He fumbled for the release catch on his laser rifle. He fumbled for his co-ordination. He knew that he would be too late.

Field came together and rolled his shoulder around to illuminate his attacker. The beam picked out the big, looming shape, like a wraith bearing down on him. He fired up the laser and gave the spectre a long slash at full power. From shoulder to hip. He tried for another, crossing swipe but the form began to drop, floating in slow motion downwards. He lost the light, but heard the crumple of the body as it hit.

The world went quiet, except for the thumping of his own heart. He rolled quietly onto his knees and then up to his feet, searching for any other sounds. The big shape of his adversary was a little way up the passage, a black mound in the flitting twin beams. He edged towards it, ready to apply another squirt of killing light. He let the sighting beam play across the prone form as he reached its side.

All the lights came back on, flooding every crevice of the passage.

"Sorry about that," said control in his ear.

And Field was soon feeling sorry. The bundle of clothes at his feet did not look so large any more, as the light stripped away the last vestige of mystery. It was more the size of a child. But he dared not look back to where the girl had been. Again, he edged the blanket away with his muzzle. Again he saw the young skin and plaited hair. She was lying on her front. There was a long, white scar from her left shoulder to her right hip, cauterised by the heat of the laser. He knew that her insides would have been severed and ruptured by the power and heat of the stroke. Her eyes were still open. The blood that came from her mouth had already stopped flowing. There was only a small pool of deep brown by her head. She was still pretty. He had not touched her face with his flaring weapon.

Field had to look back in the end, just to be sure. He hoped that he would see the sister, still sitting in her blankets, maybe rubbing her eyes. But the place was empty, except for two small shoes, neatly placed against the wall. He felt his throat contract. The girl at his feet was eleven or twelve years old, about the same age as his own daughter. She might be asleep on *Pirismus* at this very moment, tucked in her warm bed, with her grandmother close at hand for protection. His little pearl of creation, with her long eyelashes and bud lips. He knew every detail of his daughter's life, including recent events, from his daily vidual records. She knew that she was loved.

He looked down at this broken child. He realised that her spinal column would have been severed by his slash, and hoped that she had experienced no pain. Maybe he was feeling it for her now. He certainly felt as though his insides were also being torn to shreds. There was a dagger through his heart after all.

30

The deep caves of the *Augerpike* were a honeycomb of passages and galleries, created by the fiery pressure of volcanic action and refined by the eroding blasts of storm-carried water and sand. In the last three years, the inhabitants had created a few more, deeper, recesses. Bulkheads had been inserted at intervals along the corridors as protection from the storms outside. Such was the power of the high winds that even the deepest occupant might be crushed against the rock wall or sucked out and cast down the mountain.

But today all the bulkhead doors were open. The polar temperates were in a period of exceptional calm, and the many mouths of the labyrinth were basking in slanting sunlight. Cortelinac sat at the entrance to the arch cavern, where the outcrop of black-veined rock provided a small terrace. He enjoyed reading his book in the natural light. This was how the ancient paper was intended to be illuminated, so that the elegant white script stood out clearly from the brown page. He leaned against the mountain wall with the book balanced on his legs, one hand stopping the gentle breeze from turning the pages prematurely. There were tears in his eyes. He looked across the world, where the hundreds of peaks danced away to the horizon, piercing the waves of white cloud that circled the planet. He could see the shadow of *Augerpike*, lying across the global envelope, and he sought for perspective.

He was reading *A Captive Diary*. It was the story of a young girl, born to an oppressed people, hiding in a hostile world and recounting her thoughts and fears to her secret, daily chronicle. It was hard to imagine such inhumanity could exist in the world; the attempted destruction of a whole people. But it was the treatment of the children that had stung his eyes. He swore that his Shoal would never do that. What they were doing here on *Morasmus* was not evil. He was not a bad man, despite the acts that they had been drawn into by circumstance.

Cortelinac had been Corry Black when he had lived on *Pirismus*, biding his time, waiting for his destiny. He worked as an insurance agent until he had seen the opportunity of the fiery planet, the chance to find a home. To no longer be alone, but to be either with friends or, at least, to find some dignity in the purity of isolation. Like many hundred others, he had saved his earnings until he was able to afford the flight across. He only needed it to be one way. Return tickets were scoffed at amongst the travellers to *Morasmus.*

Only when he had arrived did he discover that there were two classes of resident already established on the planet. There were the casual trippers, who took their pleasure from the place, fuelled by continued funds from their true homes. He had come to despise them and their shallow tourism. He was one of the true settlers. He had come here with no external means of support. And so, at first, he had to demean himself again, working on one of the small space stations that circled the planet. These were mostly unofficial installations, freelance hostels intended as refuge points for the planet's population, when she became intolerant of their irritating presence. The holidaying trippers would fly up to the sanctuary of their spartan accommodation when terrifying storms swept in from the equatorial turmoil. Some were unoccupied, built there by syndicates for their shared, common use. Some had their resident managers, eking a little commerce from this distant trickle of currency.

Corry spent as much time on the planet as he could, covering all the accessible regions as if staking a claim and putting down his markers. He took a shuttle bus down to the surface and spent several days hiking, without any form of transport of his own.

One day he had been climbing in the *Leopollini Mountains.* There had been a passing storm that morning, and he had sheltered in the low *thornblow* bushes that hugged the rock. Now the whole place was fresh, scrubbed by the driven rain. The air was rich with the smell of torn vegetation as he climbed up a rock face. As he looked up to see his next few handholds, he saw a black shape in the sky. He squinted into the pale blue haze, but could not tell whether it was a ship or some other object. As he got closer, making frequent observations, he saw that it was only a small vehicle, floating in a stationary position a few feet away from the rock. Soon he reached it and recognised it as a storm board, hovering quietly in the gentle updraft. It appeared to be undamaged, although the retaining strap hung at its side, severed and dripping from the recent deluge. He clambered on board and sat astride it. This was good fortune indeed. He needed a proper, fitting form of transport and it had been provided. It was another step towards his confirmation that he was here for a purpose. The sense of destiny had been growing within him ever since he had thought of coming here.

Corry moved the sleek carriage forward and upward, feeling its power being transmitted into him. This felt right. Then he heard a voice from above.

"Up here," came a weak cry.

He moved the board slowly higher, until he reached a rocky shelf. There was a man lying on his side, his face white and wet with rain or perspiration. His leg was broken. The femur was showing through his skin suit as a large lump. It had not split through, but it looked ugly and painful. The injured man was not young. His grey hair only covered the back and sides of his pink, rounded head. The skin suit made him look like a beached walrus as he lay in his blubber. Corry noticed that he had all the best gear, and it looked brand new. Another damned tripper.

"I'm glad you're here," said the old fool. "My automatic alarm was activated by the crash, but it will be hours before proper help arrives. And my warming matrix has not activated. Circuit must be broken. I'm freezing. Or maybe it's the shock."

Corry moved the board over to the ledge and hopped off. He knelt down by the injured man's back.

"The connector is not housed." Corry saw that the suit had not been properly installed. He clipped the components home, more for the sake of neatness than in order to assist.

"That's better. Thanks. I feel a real fool. This was my first ride. Only a small storm, too. But I lost sight of the valley wall. I was only on my second traverse when I went right into the mountain. The board stopped just short of the rock and I went flying into it. I tried to brake myself with my leg. Snapped it like a twig. And my safety strap was cut right through on the sharp rocks, I suppose. By rights, I should be dead."

Corry sat back on the board. If he had all this kit, he would make a lot better use of it. He had the small, slight kind of frame that would be ideal for surfing. His sense of balance was good, as he had learned during his climbing. This man was too old and fat. He did not deserve such a magnificent steed. He ran his hand over the board, wiping away a few more water droplets. The board hummed back at him and told him that it wanted to be his. The bond between board and rider was a strong one.

It was a rule that had been established on the planet from the very early days. Like a cavalryman and his horse, the rider and the board were tied together by bonds unbreakable.

The big man turned over to see where Corry was. The movement caused him a sharp stab of pain and his voice came out high and wavering.

"I'm sorry. I know you have come here to help, and I am grateful. But would you mind getting off my board? You know how we feel about our own equipment. I'm sure you will understand."

Corry did jump off his seat. He knew the rule, but he felt angry. He already considered that it was his. There was such a thing as finder's rights.

"I thought you might give it to me, for my help," he said, prowling around at the back of the ledge.

"No, sir! I'll give you a little cash, maybe."

"I thought that you might have learnt your lesson, and wanted to get rid of it. You're not really cut out for this sport."

"You underestimate me. I'm going to get in a good ride or else smash the damn thing in the attempt."

"You won't manage it."

"Say what?"

"You're too big and too old. You will never make a surfer."

"OK, that does it. Thanks for your assistance, but I'd prefer it if you would go now. I'll just wait for the proper rescue team."

"Are you sure you will be safe?"

"Of course. Why not?"

"You might roll off. This ledge is pretty narrow. High, too."

"Don't be stupid. I'm nowhere near the edge."

Corry put his foot on the man's shoulder and pushed. He rolled over, towards the precipice. He squirmed amusingly as his injured leg stressed beneath him, and his walrus throat cried in pain. He made a grab for Corry's foot and got a kick on the angry, gaping wound for his trouble. He howled again, and Corry rolled him over again, so that he was now right at the edge, staring out across the chasm. The fat man was sobbing in pain and fear. His shoulders heaved under the ridiculously tight-fitting suit. His grey hair was long at the back and spilled over his collar. The uncouth, pretentious sight of it was all the incentive that Corry needed.

"Well, you did say that you ought to be dead." He applied his foot to the trembling shoulder for the last time, and dispatched the walrus to a well-deserved death. He heard the soft sounds of the body impacting on the rock face, dwindling as they receded. He did not bother to watch, but just reclaimed his rightful seat on the board. Corry had noticed, earlier, that the board was still technically unclaimed. Its previous owner had not even had enough sense to imprint himself on the security profile. He flipped open the access panel and put his wrist into the sensor pad. After twenty seconds, the board was his, forever.

Corry flew away from the mountain in a style that befitted his new station. As he ascended to the peaks, he renamed himself Cortelinac, after the wizard of literary legend. As his altitude increased, so his excitement and aspirations rose in proportion. He knew with certainty that he was destined to rule in this land, on the planet where so few others dared to reside. He would no longer be hampered by his lack of funds or materials. The means of his ascension had been revealed to him. He just needed to take what was rightfully his own. Anything that was brought down to this planet was his for the taking. The poor, weak visitors would be his prey.

He saw, however, that he would not always find such easy pickings as he had today. Many of the trippers were armed against the unknown, indigenous life forms. He would need help. He must build a force around him, he needed to recruit some loyal foot soldiers.

So he stowed the board in a secret crevice of the folded mountains and returned on the shuttle bus as usual. As he sat in its crowded passenger tank, he smiled to himself. It amused him to see that the other passengers remained oblivious to his presence. They did not yet realise who was amongst them. But he looked at them. Some might be his eventual servants, others his enemies. The future would tell.

Now, two years later, he sat on *Augerpike* with an army of a hundred and fifty men hidden in the deep caves. And he knew that he was still a good man. He had tested his true spirit by reading of the oppression and death of a teenage girl, and he had been moved to tears. The justifiable murders that his team had carried out over the last couple of years had not soured or corrupted him. His soul remained pure.

Cortelinac stood up and stretched, a long, slow unravelling of his small body. But he knew that appearance could be deceptive. He turned his head from side to side. His hands reached across this entire world.

31

From the planetside scanners of the *Vivaldo Dice* space platform, Molly could see *Sunspot Mainbeam* as it turned below her. Every three days, the giant wheel of the space emporium spun past in a lower orbit. She had watched it grow, knowing that it would spell an end to her little operation. At first, she had been angered by the intrusion of this rich man's plaything.

In the early days, things had been very good for her as she cruised on her high orbit around the fiery *Morasmus*. The people who came here from all over the galaxy were straightforward, fun-loving youngsters. They were almost exclusively hardy young men who had ventured across space for the sake of the sport. They had come for the sea and storm surfing, hang gliding, cave delving, and diving in the lakes and oceans. Some had even braved the dense rainforests at the edge of the habitable regions. They were all brave kids. Their bright souls shone through their fearless eyes. You needed a mass of courage to partake of any of these dangerous forms of activity. The wastage rate was high. She admired them for it.

Molly had leased the *Vivaldo* after her husband had died in a fly-car accident over *Alter Monde* on *Pirismus*. It was one of those mid-air collisions that were supposed to be impossible. The insurance payout had been generous, although there had been a clause that restricted her in what she could say about the crash, in its aftermath. The assured insurance company men had seemed to be very pleased about her plan of going off-planet.

The *Vivaldo* stations had been built by some of the early pioneering ventures, which were mostly bankrupt now. The platforms that were constructed then were very small: her *Dice* hostel was only the size of a large house. It was a huddle of forty rooms, plus essential services, in a simple cube construct that was attached to a heavy amalgam of meteorite rocks by a long steel hawser. The station and the rock swung about each other in high orbit, drawing their energy, like everything else, from the power of the *Millar Vorspak* sun.

The bright-eyed sportsmen visited her for short stays only. When intolerably violent storms swept over the planet, or when they needed respite from their exertions, they would fly up to her refuge. Her rooms were sometimes empty, but often they were all taken, and then her refectory would ring with their laughter and their overt joy of life. It was at these times, even though she was already over fifty, that she felt her maternal instincts being satisfied at last. Here was some compensation for her own childlessness. And just like a true mother, she was saddened but proud when her charges flew back down to the calmed planet to continue their daring adventures.

But things had not remained so idyllic. The first problem had been the arrival of the squatters. No one was quite sure where they had come from. They were probably also from many distant parts of the universe. They contrived to live without proper finance by sheltering in the unoccupied *Vivaldo* modules or other abandoned space dwellings. And because they had no resources of their own, they stole from the legitimate residents. They robbed each other as well, Molly had heard. They had become a depraved minority, but one which grew in confidence and aggression. They were quite prepared to defend their illegally acquired lodgings. Arms had been flowing to *Morasmus* in recent years and murders were becoming quite common.

Worse than this, though, was the formation of the robber gangs on the planet's surface, where they could prey on her unwary sportsmen. This was a new phenomenon and Molly hoped that through their feuds and rivalries they would eventually destroy one another. Until then there was consolation in the fact that they tended to stay on the planet. They had worked out how to survive the regular storm inundation. She had heard that each gang leader aspired to rule the planet as warlord.

Molly also hoped that these evil developments might be brought to an end by the arrival of the final component of the *Sunspot* Station. With it would come the rational, scourging power of good business practice. Rich tourists and their serving organisation would not tolerate such inconvenience and danger. The *Sunspot* operators would have to cleanse the place. They could not risk deaths amongst their clientèle. So even though the original, pioneering spirit would be lost, law and order would be restored. Her only immediate concern was that she was not sure how much the people on *Pirismus* actually knew about the conditions here. The *Morasmus* population was generally constituted of people who had abandoned their old planets, and did not maintain any more contact with them. Of course the majority were from nearby *Pirismus*, and they considered themselves to have the most right to and knowledge of their neighbouring planet. One of her regular guests, Mattelio Candrelovic, thought that they knew very little. He said that the details of *Morasmus* were better known on his own distant *Sumesotta* than in this solar system. She tended to believe him because he was so good looking. They had developed a degree of trust and out of kindness he had given Molly a hand laser for her own protection. There was usually someone else on the *Dice*, but for those occasions when she was left on her own it was a comfort. She had not really thought that a weapon would ever be used in her home.

But a few days later Molly and Matt were on board the *Vivaldo Dice* with three other guests when a group of squatters arrived. They approached like respectable trippers in a *Tyratheon Major* space bus, diverting off the nearest carbon 60 track and docking by the air lock. Molly let them in and went to meet them personally in the reception bay as she always did with new guests. As soon as she saw them, however, she suspected that she had made a mistake. There were three men and three women just emerging from the portal. The presence of females was in itself an indication that this was not a sporting party, but what really alerted her was their appearance. She would never have thought that people could be so dishevelled. There was dirt on their clothes and their skin. The most frightening thing of all was that they were carrying guns.

The tallest of the men, who had a long, thin face, stepped towards her. He did not point his pistol at her, but he made sure that she was well aware of it. He asked her how many there were on board. Molly hoped that they would just turn out to be awkward customers; she was used to handling situations like that. She told the tall man that she could not take his party. Six was too many and she apologised for the fact that they would have to leave. Without warning he slapped her in the face. It was an act of violence that she had never witnessed before and had certainly not experienced.

Her attacker asked her quietly how many there were on board and the two other men moved round and stood on either side of her. She put her hand to her burning cheek.

"Four," she sobbed. "There are four of us." She was not lying. She always forgot to count herself. Four guests was what she meant.

"Call them," said the man on her left, who had a shaven head and a missing front tooth. Molly was trembling from fear and anger. She looked at one of the squatter women. She had short red hair, but despite her frightful appearance there was a hint of sympathy in her eyes. She stepped towards Molly and put an elegant but dirty hand on her shoulder.

"Its all right. We don't want to hurt you. We just need somewhere to live for a while. We were on *Sunspot*, but they killed Janice's daughter."

"Oh, no," said Molly, with honest sympathy. The tears that had already gathered in her eyes spilled over and down her cheeks. The oldest of the three squatter women, who was probably not yet thirty, gave a quiet gasp of pain. The shaven headed man went to her and embraced her.

The redhead still had her hand on Molly. She said that they only wanted to put Molly and her guests down in the escape capsule. She said that they would be able to come back to *Dice* after they had gone. She said that they did not want any trouble.

Molly took the trespassers to the refectory, where her guests were finishing their evening meal. Everyone was there except for Matt. He had gone to the workshop to make some repairs to his board. When Molly saw her mistake, she nearly corrected her head count.

"So this is everybody?" asked the third male squatter. He brushed his long hair away from his face as he turned his gun towards the diners. They looked up from their meals in surprise. Molly saw the shadow of fear pass over their faces. They were brave enough to face the planet's excesses, but she knew that it was a different thing to be confronted by the human animal. Her own inner coldness told her that there was nothing quite as frightening.

She hoped that she was not placing Matt in greater danger. She was taking a risk with her own life. What if he was to walk in now and reveal her lie?

"Yes, this is all," she said, looking towards the three frozen boys at the table. They did not contradict her statement.

"Ramon, check the rest of the station," said the longhaired man.

32

Cortelinac awoke in his chamber, deep in the cold roots of the *Augerpike*, with a shiver. A part of him wished that he could slip back under the warm air blanket and return to oblivion. But his stronger part knew that this day must bear him a further step towards his ultimate greatness. He had communed with Tigeras the previous night, out on the high ledge, for confirmation of his plan, and it had been made clear. He swung himself out of his cot.

Dawn was breaking as he sat astride his board, with his rifle resting against his hip. Before him were his men, similarly mounted and ranged out across the mountain face. He switched on his audio enhancer, so that his voice echoed around the listening, echoing rocks.

"Dear friends. We come here from many parts of our universe. And in our present condition and on this present day, in this small fragment of endless time, none of us is held in high regard by our fellow humans, wherever they dwell in this troubled universe. In our past lives, before this coming moment of glory and destiny, we were indeed poor, worthless things. Indeed we were scavengers of the galaxy, unconsidered and disregarded. There was neither love nor friendship existing to bind us to our past lives. We came here cheap and careless.

"Today, your lives are changed. This sun that creeps over the teeth of the world is banishing the haunted night of our past with the golden hand of opportunity. It will blaze on us, as we stand reborn and splendid. Our new realm is being founded. This scrambled world of *Morasmus* is changing herself, to become our worthy home. The great cycles of her meteorology are turning to our advantage. The storm age is in decline, and the hidden riches that lie here will be ours to acquire. The inaccessible territories will be our domain. But all this will not come to us without a due and heavy price. This morning we start. We must win sovereignty for ourselves. And those who knew us, in our previous, despicable lives, will hardly believe how our fortunes have changed. Each of us, should we succeed, will be a prince in this turning world.

"Take your chance. Follow me!"

He had arranged for ten of his lieutenants to give a rousing cheer at this point, and so, as he swept his board away into the gathering light, he caught the sound of promoted enthusiasm from his rear.

The one hundred and fifty sky warriors sped over the mountain tops for three hours. They finally alighted in silence on the bare ridge that overlooked the *Overhang of Odin*.

Forgal sat in the shade of the overhanging rock, where his fifty Corsairs slept or lounged. He sucked in the thin air, filling his barrel chest with its clean energy. Today his robber band had the day off. He would send out a few later on, scouting for new victims along the peaks and valleys of the *Southborn Massif*. They needed to be kept busy, he thought, as he scratched his bare shoulders and headed for the ice water spring. The mid-morning light flashed from the other side of the valley and scattered from the cold water as it splashed over his head and neck. He cracked open a food cube and was munching without relish as he returned to the parade park, which was now only half covered by the shadow of the *Odin*.

Two of his crew were out there, sunning themselves. They were on a casual form of guard. The shadow of a board flitted across the rock, and he heard its actual substance land behind him. Then another came down. His men jumped to their feet, and he could tell from their expressions that something was wrong. He thought that it must have been his sentries, flying in with some alarm.

It was and yet it wasn't. He turned to see four strangers, standing in his territory as if they owned it. They each carried a heavy bag swinging from their hands. They smiled, and from the slim evidence of those false signals, he was sure that he knew what they bore. They threw their burdens across the rock towards him, each one leaving a thin trail of dark liquid, until they stopped near his feet, grinning up at him. They were the heads of his guards, as he had expected.

Forgal roared and turned back to his men, to take one of their weapons and put it to some use. But they were frozen, looking up to the sky, and did not offer him any assistance. He slapped Kitson's face and took his pistol from him, ripping it out of the shoulder holster. But as he turned back to face his enemy, the gun was cut from his grip, along with three of his fingers. In the air around the *Overhang* there flew more than a hundred riders. As they slowly sank to the ground, he clutched his bleeding stumps and growled.

Cortelinac dropped onto the cold rock with an imperious smile. Forgal would have rushed at him and crushed him, but for the restraining cord that had now been thrown around him. He stood tensed with fury, his great muscles bulging, as his Corsairs were brought up from the depths of their quarters in the bowels of *Odin* and were lined up against the *Overhang* wall.

Cortelinac approached Forgal and placed his hand on the big man's shoulder. He had to reach up, but this was the way that Tigeras had told him it must be. The big fellow was too filled with rage and pain to notice the finger needle pierce his tanned skin.

"Forgal, you have been the agent of a great new beginning. The new world will pay you thanks. But now your time has passed."

The giant man strained with fury at every word. He would even have spat down on his small tormentor if he could, but a strange paralysis was spreading rapidly through his body. His numbness was worse than that induced by his dousing in the freezing, spring water. Breathing was now becoming his sole preoccupation. The pain in his hand had been so great that he had not felt the subtle needle enter his neck. It had been such a small prick amidst such agony. Forgal could not understand what it was that had killed him.

Cortelinac had had the needle-ring made specially, also according to Tigeras' instructions. The poison had worked perfectly, to his immense satisfaction. As he finished speaking, Forgal dropped dead at his feet, enabling him to place his boot on the still, hairy, massive chest.

Cortelinac offered the Corsairs the choice of joining his army of destiny or else of going free, to pursue their own meagre karma. The split was roughly even. He counted thirty new recruits. Possibly they saw his vision of the future. Perhaps they did not trust him to keep true to his assurances of free passage. Whatever their reasons, they flew away to the *Augerpike* with him, leaving their comrades behind under the shadow of the *Overhang*, together with their guard of thirty of the Shoal.

The twenty Corsair traitors, those who did not accept the hand of friendship from Cortelinac, were sent back in to their quarters to collect their possessions before being disbanded. When they were all inside, the rock face was closed in one explosive convulsion. A sound hammer was raked across the cave entrances, and the lintel rocks all crumbled like rotten teeth.

That night, Cortelinac went out onto the high shelf again with his communicator. It had been three months since Tigeras had first found him. He still did not know who his great aid and supporter was, but Cortelinac admired the man's judgement. From the small pieces of evidence, snatches of communication, inferences and assumptions, Tigeras had seen the greatness within him and so had made contact. Tigeras had communicated as simply as possible from the beginning. It had just been a few electronic mail items. No return address specified. There was no need. He understood that all of his own incoming and outgoing messages were being scanned.

Cortelinac was sure that Tigeras was not on *Morasmus*. He was in space. Sometimes, he thought that he might even be supernatural; his ideas were so true and inspiring. He might not have perceived his own potential without that ethereal prompting. And Tigeras had plain, useful information to offer as well. Like the location of the Corsairs' camp, at the *Overhang of Odin*.

Cortelinac looked to the scattered stars and drew in their power. There was only one shadow of doubt in his heart. Tigeras had explained about the *Sunspot* project and its imminent completion. The final components were treading their careful way from *Pirismus* at this very moment, bringing with them the sterilising glare of the old order. His newborn world would not be able to tolerate the crushing, mundane influx of ordinary life. The suffocating influence of commerce, law and order would kill off the infant empire, if ever it were allowed to settle here.

Tigeras had told him that *Sunspot* must be destroyed.

33

Matt had the sensor panel off his board, as he sat in the cramped *Vivaldo Dice* workshop. He was adjusting its pressure and proximity gauges when he realised that he had not brought the correct calibration tool in from the science room. He reached over to the control strip and called into the refectory, intending to ask Clyde to bring it over when he had finished eating. So it was that he saw his comrades being bound and lined up against the wall, looking very pale on the communications screen. He went to get his rifle.

Matt knew about squatters. He had heard the stories about their thieving and now the general opinion was that murder was also on their agenda. According to the local lattice news, there were too many trippers disappearing for them all to be sporting accidents. The trouble was that you stood very little chance of finding a body on *Morasmus*. Most of the places where a corpse would be likely to end up were inaccessible. Gravity took them down to the uncharted bottoms of precipitate valleys. But enough trippers had had narrow escapes from the robbers for the message to have been received. They all carried serious self-protection these days. He himself had run through many scenarios in his mind, ever since he had acquired the rifle. He thought he would be able to use it all right, should the need arise. His imagination conjured up the emotions that he would feel, if he were ever to be attacked. The anger and ruthless determination seemed strong enough to carry him through. He pictured himself confronted by an armed assailant, demanding his property. There would be no way that he would be able to submit to any such command. It would be too embarrassing, too humiliating. He would have to attack.

Now that he was trotting quietly back to his room for his rifle, he was feeling a lot more frightened than he had imagined. He even considered hiding under his bunk and waiting for them to go away. But he moved under remote control, guided by his rehearsed program, watching himself pick the weapon up from the corner of his room, where it gleamed in its dangerous black glory. He saw himself check that it was fully primed and set out for the refectory. It would only take a few seconds to get there, but he still had no plan of action beyond attack.

He had just gone round the first corner of the corridor when he almost bumped into Ramon, who was sauntering along with his pistol tucked into his belt. Ramon liked the idea of drawing it out for action, although he was not sure that he would ever use it. Despite his aggressive appearance, of the two colliding men he actually had the less murderous intent.

Matt still observed the action from somewhere high above the corridor ceiling. He saw his person, his doppleganger, raise the rifle and slash Ramon across the neck. From up here, he could see the new degree of freedom which Ramon's head acquired. It seemed as though it might topple right off his shoulders, but his body was just quick enough to collapse from the knees and so keep pace with the capital descent.

Matt's spirit and consciousness slammed back into his body, sucked in by one of his giant intakes of air. He was panting hard, despite having barely exercised his well-trained body. He heard a high-pitched squeal in his ears, and he moved on. Tunnel vision seemed to have taken over from where before there had been his ethereal, impersonal wide perspective. Through a blinkered, black-bound view, he navigated his way to the dining room and burst in through the door.

The tall, thin squatter was standing with his back to him. Matt ran his laser lance in a wide circle round the man's torso, a geometry designed to pass through the maximum number of vital organs. The surprised squatter straightened suddenly and flinched a few times. A thin stream of smoke caused by his smouldering clothes rose from his chest and curled around his face. He fell noisily against a table and disappeared beneath it.

The man with the shaven head spun round to see what had happened. Matt saw the pistol in his hand, and the eyes widened by either fear or fury. He brought the laser down on the hairless head and drove it on through the face and out by the shoulder. The first man's rattling fall with the table was still incomplete, and the room resounded to the clatter of upset furniture, but nevertheless Matt was sure that he heard the dull cracking of bone and the boiling of flesh as his sharp blade swept through the skull. The man's eyes crossed, and one of his front teeth popped out onto the floor as he fell backwards. He missed all the tables, and crashed straight down to the ground, his fractured head hitting with a dull thud on the washed tiling. The pistol fell and bounced to rest by his lifeless hand.

One of the three women squatters darted towards the fallen man, and knelt down at his side, obscuring Matt's view of his ripped face and the pistol. The woman looked as though she might be turning on him. Matt gave her a warning slash across the shoulders. He did it quickly, thinking that the speed would reduce the power of his stroke.

He was wrong. She toppled forward onto her dead husband. Within five seconds she had joined him in the after-life. The gun was not in her hand. An ugly, smouldering scar ran across the back of her jacket, from the left shoulder to the right hip. It was just like the one that had killed her daughter, a month earlier.

Matt turned on the other two women. They had moved back against the wall, close to his friends. They had their hands in the air and both were shaking with fear. He could hear their desperate, animal cries of hurt and panic. They looked at him as if he were a monster, as if he, not they, were the evil aggressor. One of them slipped down the wall and sat with her head buried in her hands. He could see that there was dampness around her crotch. The other stood, swaying slightly and swallowing hard, but looking him straight in the eye. He sensed her courage. He could tell that she expected to die, but was going to face it without begging or hysteria. A glimmer of admiration filtered into his manic, excited brain. She was standing quietly, awaiting her execution.

Then he realised that some of the animal grunts and squeals that he had heard were actually coming from his own mouth. He knew that they were not voluntary; he did not want to be the creator of such hideousness, but the noises were nevertheless emanating from his body, from the vicious warrior spirit that had temporarily infested it. He consciously summoned up a huge act of willpower and self-control, allowing him to halt his assault and start to act as saviour. He edged over to his comrades and loosened their bonds. He could never quite remember how he did it: with his fingers or with a canteen knife. It seemed to take hours, as he covered the two women squatters with his weapon and felt the lightness in his head increase. At last he sensed that they were free and there were friendly hands on his arm. He passed his rifle to one of them and stumbled towards the lavatory door. He stopped, poised over the toilet bowl for a few seconds, briefly thinking that the nausea had passed. Then he was proved wrong again. Although he doubled up in a sudden spasm, and so was close to the white receptacle, the force of his vomit was such as to make it spread widely. The walls of the sterilised cubicle were richly daubed with the remnants of his recent meal. A small voice in the back of his head, close by the source of that new, throbbing pain, said that this was a purging which was well deserved.

Molly took charge of events from that point onwards. She consigned the corpses to the furnace of the planet, but not before the two women captives had the opportunity of bidding them their own, strange kind of farewell. There had been surprisingly little blood spilt during the carnage. Nevertheless, they had all given the little space station a total clean. Nobody questioned the need for such a sanitation exercise.

Molly decided that she must leave there, abandon the *Vivaldo Dice*, maybe forever. She would go with the captives to *Sunspot Mainbeam*. They could wait there until the arrival of the hordes of normality, the civilised thousands. The presence of that giant, artificial moon seemed like it might be a blessing at last.

Matt recovered soon enough, but he resolved to return to *Morasmus*. The storm tides had withdrawn again and he sought the privacy of the planet surface. He did not fear any recriminations, but he thought that it would be a better place in which to recover from his wounds. And now he had no doubts about his ability to protect himself.

34

The westerly storm was not of great magnitude, compared with the real monsters that sometimes smashed up from the equatorial hurricane bands. Still, it tore across the mountaintops with iron fingers, ripping away rock as well as ice and snow. Avalanches rumbled down on both sides of the sheer, towering faces of the *Sixty Sisters*, crushing any obstructions and plunging like thunder into the deep valleys.

There was a little respite in those canyons, like the *Massona Fault Valley*, which ran from south to north. Here the wind and rain merely circled like a caged tiger, only occasionally extending its claws into the sanctuary, to topple a mighty tree or churn a tarn to boiling fury.

Cortelinac knew that he was in danger as he edged his way along the bank of the *Massona River*. He had only come here in order to face that very capricious hazard; to put his life at risk was his sole purpose. He had concluded that one more test and proof of his destiny was required. The spiteful world that had in history spat and hissed in his face must be challenged and cowed, if he was to truly rule here. Tigeras had told him that his future greatness was inevitable, so his inner conviction told him that he was in no danger at all.

It was not the first time that he had braved the tempest. When he was a normal man, some weeks before he had acquired his imperial board, up on the rocky shelf of the *Leopollini Mountains*, he had been down by the ocean. This was all he had been able to afford as recreation in those times. He had no equipment, so it was a shuttle down from orbit and then a hike on foot.

He went down to a rocky bay, where the sea lapped up to a sandy beach. The water was crystal clear and warm. He dived in and splashed around amongst the small breakers. He was in and out for hours, enjoying the contrast of air and water on his skin.

As he sat in the surf, he saw another bather coming down the steep cliff path, carrying a towel. It was hard to credit that they had both chosen the same spot from the entire planet, or at least from the bays that were within easy reach of the shuttle landing station.

His new, unwanted companion waved a greeting and plunged into the brine a little further up the bay. He was a big, athletic man and Corry was not surprised to see him start to swim strongly out into deeper water. It made him feel like a small child, left to play by the shoreline. He made the most of the moment, and madly splashed the water all about and above him, shuffling around on the sandy bottom to create a perfectly formed seat.

Corry could not see the swimmer, as his chin was only level with the incoming waves. But he saw the blackness of the sky, out above the distant ocean. Overhead was still a silvery blue, but it graduated through a tumbled bruising of purple to virtual darkness, even though it was still the middle of the day. A sea storm, he supposed. His meteorology had, perhaps falsely, indicated a clear day on shore.

The swimmer came back in, ploughing through the water with powerful breaststrokes, and came to sit next to him. He wiped the seawater from his face and lips before he spoke.

"There's something pretty spectacular out there." Corry was not that easily impressed.

"Just a storm. I've seen plenty worse," he said, coolly.

"No, not that. You can't see it from down here. You'll have to stand up."

Corry would not have got up, except that the other man did, and it was awkward to be sitting there with his wet groin dripping into the sea near his head. He only just came to the other's shoulder, but he immediately saw the object of his attention.

Right across the limit of the ocean there was a thin, black line. It obscured, rather than marked, the margin of the horizon. Corry could see that it was moving. It narrowed and thickened in places, and a lighter coloured crest came and went, flickering along its length like cold fire.

"What is it?" he asked.

"A wave, I reckon," said his companion.

"Is that all?" asked Corry, briefly contemptuous.

"It is a big wave," added the other. He said it well. The firm coolness of his voice sent a shiver down Corry's spine. He could sense the courage that allowed the man's words to remain steady. More clearly than if there had been a note of panic in the utterance, he realised that they were in danger. The water around his knees went cold. He needed a piss. He had to ask.

"How big?"

"I don't know. But we might be all right on the cliff top. It will be worth watching. And I doubt if we'll get any further anyway."

"Probably better if we do get further away," Corry said, knowing that his own voice was far from even.

"Well, there won't be time for that. It's approaching at sixty miles an hour, I would guess."

That was enough for Corry. He ran back to the cliff face, kicking sand towards the charging sea from his flying feet. He did not look back. Every moment of his scramble up the rocks, he expected to be swept away or crushed against them. When he eventually stood at the top and turned to look back, he saw his comrade also reaching the summit, rising on long, powerful strides. The wave was not upon them yet, but it was not far away. A blast of cold, wet air was pushed in its van, and swayed them on their vantage point.

The wave was indeed huge. It was more like a quantum shift in the level of the ocean. It was not a mere promontory of water. The entire height of the sea was greater behind it than in front, and its face was not the clean, bright, sparkling curl of its tiny relatives on the beach. It was a hideous, black, evil leer. Dark spray flew from its brow like the flying hair of a maniac. As it poured into the bay, it lost some of its form and boiled into a churn of seething liquid. Corry could see other peaks following in behind the first onslaught.

When the wall of sea hit the cliff, the ground seemed to shake. A screen of water shot high up above them and came down as heavy rain. The sea had filled the bay now and was running level with the cliff top, as far as he could tell. Its surface was strangely uneven, hilly almost, distorted by whirlpools and wave crests. It broke over the highland in many places, pouring out onto the meadow in great torrents.

Corry's companion was standing thirty feet away, legs apart, gazing out on the scene with excitement. He looked fearless, in contrast to Corry's quaking heart. But one of the great inrushes of water swept back to the cliff's edge and piled into the backs of his legs. He was knocked down immediately, and was dragged inexorably towards the edge of the land and the jaws of the ravenous sea. He scrambled for a grip on the slippery rock of the cliff top. His confident mien was replaced by a look of abject fear. Corry was not displeased to see the transformation. The tide spumed over his head as it rushed back to the main. Suddenly his fingers were ripped from their meagre purchase and he was gone, sucked out into the bottomless stomach of the ocean.

Corry looked around the flood and saw that he was on almost the only part of the cliff top where the water was not pouring back in a murderous torrent. And as his safety dawned upon him, so the sky lightened and his spirits rose. The first germ of realisation was planted in his mind. He was set aside, protected for some unknown purpose. Despite his poor physique, he could survive where the strongest succumbed. A hint of his greatness was whispered in his ear by the passing breeze.

And so now, as he skirted the tumultuous *Massona River*, he again felt that he was safe. In fact, the weather down here was not too bad, although the wind swirled its clammy hand around him as he moved from tree to trunk, never letting go completely.

He had only moved a few hundred yards downstream, however, when he lost his footing. The muddy bank of the *Massona* gave way beneath him and his grip on the nearby *Juno* tree was ripped away. He fell headlong into the current.

Cortelinac pumped his legs in a frenzied motion, desperately hoping for some purchase on the river floor. But there was only the black torrent beneath him. All certainty of immortality flew away like the wild leaves that swirled about him and gave shape to the gale. His mad pedalling at least kept him afloat, but it could not last for long. The energy was being drained from him, pulled from his body by his exertion and panic. He tilted back his head with wild eyes to keep his mouth and nose above the turgid waves. All he could see was the darkly turning sky and the black trees, towering over him like ghouls.

It was, again, blind luck that brought his hand down on the massive branch that briefly dipped within his reach. He clutched on to it and dragged himself partially on top of its spiky bulk. The slimy buoyancy carried him with it, on down the sweeping confusion of waves, down to where the overhang of trees became even thicker and darker.

It might have only been a temporary salvation. Cortelinac would not have been able to hang on to the twisting hulk of the severed wood for more than an hour. Had the branch chosen to move out into the main stream, he would have been lost. But just as his strength began to fail him, and his arms became limp, the river swung into a wide bend and he was beached on a muddy shore. He was just able to summon the strength to clamber through the thick grime and reach the firmer ground, where he sank down in sobbing exhaustion.

He lay against a tree and watched the storm clear overhead. As his senses cleared in unison, he confirmed that he had suffered no injury beyond a cut hand. He also became aware that there was movement in the thick rainforest about him. The leaves, high overhead, swayed down in graceful curtseys, but closer to the ground the foliate movements were more abrupt and staccato, too isolated to be caused by the moderating breeze. Scuffling noises came from the undergrowth around the small clearing in which he languished.

Almost nothing was known about the indigenous life forms on *Morasmus*. The places that were inhabited were generally too high for there to be any animal life, apart from the cruising albatrosses that occasionally strayed into the lofty mountains of the polar north. He looked up at the late afternoon sky, from which the light was now slowly draining. There was a grey covering of low cloud. He knew, from flights taken over valleys such as the *Massona*, that this cloud layer was an almost permanent feature. The world below had been a closed book to the flighty tourists above. No one knew just what kind of beast might exist here. Indeed, Cortelinac was surprised that there was such a lush and healthy covering of vegetation. Many thought that the strength of the regular storms would prevent any substantial forms of plant or animal life, yet these deep gorges seemed protected from their worst ravages.

His ruminations were soon answered. The bushes behind his tree parted. He could tell that something big had brushed them aside. He heard a heavy but soft footfall. Cortelinac froze, swivelling his eyes to see what might appear from behind him. Heavy breathing and a low growl did nothing to blunt the spurs of panic that ate into him.

A massive cat padded slowly past his tree and moved towards the riverbank. Its shoulder was above his head as he sat leaning back against the tree, frozen and barely breathing. The cat turned and looked him in the eye before bowing down and starting to lap water from the shallows. Cortelinac could see that there was blood around its mouth, not yet dried. He dared not make a movement. He somehow knew that the massive body would be lightning fast in reacting to any attempt at escape.

After a few long minutes, the animal lifted its great head and shook the water droplets from its regal whiskers. It hopped a little, to withdraw its front feet from the mud holes into which they had sunk, leaving huge paw prints, and came slowly towards him. Now he really did hold his breath. The beast stopped just before him and stretched its neck to smell his strange scent. Then it licked his injured hand with its huge, rough tongue. Cortelinac nearly screamed in fear as the hot breath engulfed him. But the animal withdrew its interest. It looked him in the eyes again, and then majestically strolled back into the tangle of its domain. Cortelinac found that there were tears running down his face.

It took him two days to walk back up the river, to his salvation. He arrived weak and light-headed. During his slow return, he had another revelation. The giant cat was, of course, a tiger. There had been faint stripes down its powerful flanks. And the tiger had showed its subservience to him: it had kissed his hand. He had no doubt now that the regal animal had been an incarnation of Tigeras, and that an unbreakable bond had been forged on that day in the jungle depths.

35

Molly Cashin had to admit that she was impressed with *Sunspot Mainbeam*, even though it was still incomplete. Comparing it to her own *Vivaldo Dice* was like contrasting a metropolitan city with a cottage. She enjoyed the big spaces and the opportunity to make new acquaintances. Field Preston had been given the job of looking after her. It was not long before they discovered the gruesome link between them. Field was still hurting about the death of the child. The news that both her parents were also dead filled him with strong but mixed emotions. He told her that he was not in the least proud of the relief that he naturally felt that there would be no vengeful relatives to hunt him down.

The two squatter women who had been taken prisoner on *Dice* had been interviewed by Darius Ender, the *Mainbeam* director. He had declared them to be no threat and had granted their request to stay there, until they could return to *Pirismus*. He was anxious to increase his compliment, if only temporarily. There was a skeleton crew of only three hundred for the entire installation. The worsening security situation meant that he wanted as many hands on board as he could muster. He had been calling all the small, private stations to ask them to come across, but most of the replies were hostile and of no use to him. So he was left with an awful lot of space station to be policed by very few personnel. Just about everybody would have to take a turn.

Molly and Field were patrolling together. She did not need to be there, but he was grateful for the company. More than that, he liked her. Although she must have been around the fifty mark, she still had a girlish figure. Slim and petite with a waspish waist. Her hair was dark brown, with hardly a hint of grey, and it fell down her neck and back in big soft curls. Her eyes still had a sparkle in them; not that Field took her lightly, as if she was just to be thought of in sexual terms. He knew that anyone who ran one of the pioneer space stations was both tough and resourceful. He conceded that she was probably a more capable all round person than he, who had been a mere company employee all his life. He admired those who had stood up for themselves and trusted entirely to their own abilities. He had never had the courage or ambition to do that.

Still, he had the advantage for the moment as they walked through the great galleries and corridors of the *Sunspot Mainbeam* space station. He was pretty well informed about all of its workings, as long as her questions did not get too technical. Some of what he told her he made up as he went along, although he had enough sense not to try to overdo it. He guessed that she would soon notice if he tried to bask too obviously in the reflected glory of this titanic construction. Even so, he was pleased that they started to move closer to each other, as they went side by side on their patrol. Soon their sleeves were brushing. He hoped that he at least had a new friend.

Almost all of the accessible parts of *Mainbeam* were lit now and under camera surveillance, so they felt fairly secure against meeting any more unexpected squatters. Field kept alert, despite his frequent sideways glances at Molly, but did not expect any trouble. Mercifully they were not going to pass the place where he had met the sleeping girl. He wanted no more reminders of that mistake, although talking to Molly about the incident was starting to help the hurt go away.

They came to one of the computer nodules.

"What's this?" asked Molly.

"One of the thousands of computing gateways. They are all huge, apparently. A brand new technology, designed to house the intelligence coming over with *Spinal.*"

"But it's only the size of my hand."

"Brain the size of a planet, though, I'm told. And they are all networked together at speeds so fast that the message arrives before it has been sent."

"Really?" said Molly, not impressed.

"No, but the programmers here try to tell me tales."

"There are programmers here?"

"Yes, there are a few, but most of them are on the *Sunspot Spinal* on their way here. That's where the really powerful computing is, apparently. And all the human-oriented intelligence which is going to make this place such a wonderland, when it's finished."

"So these computers here aren't doing anything yet?"

"Well, they are starting to," replied Field. "The master systems on

Spinal are downloading their routines to these slaves already. It's pretty slow at the moment, because the link is transmitting through space via electromagnetic. The real synergy happens when the whole configuration is complete. But I'm told that we will have a lot of computerised service control here before the *Spinal* complex arrives."

"You are very well informed," said Molly, with a smile.

"Not very. But the programmers here do occasionally speak to the rest of us. Peculiar bunch. Mean, too."

"How do you mean, mean?"

"Well, take Roberto for example, the chief maintenance programmer here. I saw him the other day, looking really miserable."

"That doesn't mean he is mean," corrected Molly.

"But I asked him what was wrong. He said that he had heard from *Pirismus* three weeks ago. His last remaining grandparent had died. Grandma Perkins."

"That is sad," said Molly, without enthusiasm, not quite sure where Field was going, and not particularly wishing to encourage him.

"Although she did leave him twenty thousand dollars. Then, two weeks ago, he was told that his mother had died as well, leaving him thirty thousand dollars."

"Very sad indeed," said Molly, smelling a rat.

"And then, to cap it all, last week his father died."

"Leaving him?" enquired Molly, predictably.

"Forty thousand dollars," confirmed Field, equally predictably.

"Extremely sad!"

"Absolutely. So I said to him, 'No wonder you are looking miserable, Roberto.' 'That I am,' he replied. 'In the last three weeks I've lost my Grandma, my mother and finally my father. And this week? Nothing!' "

Molly nearly laughed, but made do with a dig of her elbow into Field's arm. By the time they had completed their tour of duty, they were walking arm in arm.

Darius Ender was the *Sunspot Mainbeam* director, although he felt anything but in charge of events these days. It had been bad enough when it was just a simple construction job, fitting together the giant jigsaw of *Sunspot* modules. There were a lot of problems being sent out from the Boquat manufacturing facilities on *Pirismus*. He had sent back endless quality reports. He'd got promises of action, at first. But then the pledges dried up and the faults continued. Several times he had called Warren Galant personally, desperately trying to get some improvement. Warren had told him to get on with it. Darius knew him for a man who held a grudge, and it did not do to get on the wrong side of him. So he kept his peace despite his annoyance.

Warren and Darius had first met at one of the Boquat management training weekends, and the seeds of a rocky relationship had been sown there. Darius found Warren intensely smug and annoying. They were on the same team in the business simulation exercise, and Warren insisted on puffing at his pipe and holding forth as if every utterance was a pearl cast before swine. To make it worse, the other team members seemed to take him seriously. The problem was that neither liked the other, and Darius was aware of the precarious position in which that might place him. So he had given up his complaints, and done his utmost to fix things here as best he could. He hoped that they had made a better job of *Sunspot Spinal*.

The real building work was hard enough, but then there had been the squatters. As soon as *Mainbeam* had been given air and warmth they had started flying up in their little bubble spacecraft and sneaking into the superstructure. They had meant that he needed to divert his workers' efforts onto security matters, just when they should have been making final preparations for the last docking. And for some time now, there had been rumours that even more organised, hostile groups were forming down on *Morasmus*. They might start to make more organised attacks.

Also, more recently, his control over local, internal matters was being eroded. The command structure was gradually being acquired by the master systems on *Sunspot Spinal*, and so in his opinion the centralised foolishness continued. It did not help his morale to know that Warren Galant was on board the approaching ship. He had the impression that the master control program had been imbibed with some of Warren's arrogance. It had already been countermanding some of his own instructions, with very little logic behind the changes. As far as he was concerned, it looked flawed as well, despite being called the Totally Integrated Generic Environment, Reasoning and Administration System, or Tigeras for short.

36

The best surfing weather was to be found in the six parallel valleys of the southern *Massif.* Not the best because they housed the most powerful or tallest fronts, but because of the reliability of their arrival. At least once per week, the heavy pressure clouds rolled up northwards and created good, solid fronts. And for some reason, the storms came up the valleys in sequence, two hours between each onset. So it was possible to get in a full day's surfing by skipping over from one valley to the next.

Mattelio had just completed his fourth valley and had decided to call it a day. He was not exhausted, as would be the case if he persisted with the full set, but neither was he really enjoying his day. The rides had been good enough, fine clear weather ahead and tumbling tempest behind, but he was not able to appreciate them. For quite a lot of the time his mind had been elsewhere, and his riding was too much on autopilot for real enjoyment. The incident at *Vivaldo Dice* was still preying on his mind. It was not that he felt guilty about the deaths. He had justified himself in his own mind and to what passed for the local authorities, the people on *Sunspot Mainbeam,* early on. But, nevertheless, the whole thing was unsettling. For one thing, it had finally removed the holiday feel of these long, idle days on *Morasmus.* The increasing need for security amongst the trippers had eroded the early, carefree atmosphere of the sportsmen. But they had not come here to be safe, and they could live with a limited amount of thieving.

Now, though, Matt had been brought face to face with the consequences of anarchy. He could not deny that death was in the air. Also, he perceived that something had been awakened in his own psyche. There was now something more to his life than the pleasures of speed and height and danger, although what it was exactly still eluded clear focus. Sometimes he felt that he should just go home, back to *Sumesotta,* and maybe even try again with Fiona. Or make a change and move to the ordered civilisation of *Pirismus.* But he had also been intrigued by the new guilds being formed here on *Morasmus.* They planned to make this their permanent home, despite its hostile face. There was nobility in this intention, even if it did have a hint of deluded idealism.

Matt knew very little about the guilds, except that they did not tolerate his kind and that most of the unexplained disappearances on the planet were put down to their activities these days. At least, he thought, they acted as if they belonged here and were not just touring through.

He glided over the *Massif* deep in his own thoughts. The clean, high air swept past him, but did not shake him from his reverie. Even the brilliance of the sun on the crumpled folds of the mountain ranges below his feet did not stir his emotions. Its rays beat on his back, despite the filtering effects of many miles of draining atmosphere, and contributed to his languid state of mind.

He flew on, to where he could see the *Sixty Sisters* at the eastern edge of the *Massif*. Soon the *Ogrimadoc* was clearly identifiable amongst the peaks, but as usual he would not go straight there. First he must collect his laser rifle from the crevice higher up on the *Ost Ogrimadoc* where he had secreted it on his way out, early that morning.

He came around the side of the mountain with the rifle across his lap. He always approached his lofty, cave house from the sun. He kept his board a hundred feet or so away from the rock, to avoid being sucked in against the sharp outcrops, and he occasionally saw his distorted shadow as it descended over the familiar faces of the crags and crevices. He steered his board with his knees, slipping round to the front door of his house. It was too familiar a manoeuvre for him to really be in a state of high alert: he was only paying lip service to the need for caution. He should not have been taken by surprise, but he stopped the board with a sudden jerk.

There was another rider hovering outside the entrance to Matt's cavern.

Cortelinac had heard reports of the incident at *Vivaldo Dice* space hostel. The name of Mattelio Candrelovic had become quite famous across the *Morasmic* communications bands. He would be an excellent addition to the Shoal. Cortelinac had his scouts discover the location of his dwelling. He needed heroes to join him in his great mission, and he decided that he must go himself in order to win his new recruit. So he sat with a regal pose, waiting for Matt's return. He knew how he would persuade him, with visions of being Cortelinac's lieutenant and aide. They would be a good team. The data he had seen on Matt, which Tigeras had sent him, made him realise that he would be most suitable. Secretly, he had noted with satisfaction that they were of about the same height. They were both small men.

He sat astride his board, unarmed. It was another courageous act, he knew. Matt might easily have shot him down from a distant hiding place. His conviction of his own indestructibility lessened the credit due, however. Cortelinac also felt that the fact that he had come here in person would demonstrate his common touch. In itself, it should convince Matt of his greatness. All supreme figures in history had the common touch, and did not fear to brush shoulders with their inferiors. Cortelinac was lost in thoughts of his own great qualities as he sat by the rock face.

Matt swung his board down rapidly and hovered just behind Cortelinac. He was pleased to see his uninvited visitor give a start of surprise. He rested his rifle easily, so that it was pointing away from the stranger. But this offered no security to his guest. A quick slash across his stomach could be delivered at the slightest provocation.

Cortelinac spoke the words that he had rehearsed, designed to seduce and inspire. He spoke of these days as the Incunabulum, the time when the future of this virgin land would be moulded. He told Matt about how his destiny had been revealed. He described the meeting with the great cat, embroidering the tale with descriptions of how he had patted the beast's head and stroked its abrasive fur. He became inspired with his own rhetoric, his eyes glazing and his hands flying, sure that his recruit was being similarly aroused. The power of his persuasion was as evident as the endless wall of rock that stood and absorbed the profoundness of the diatribe.

Matt listened to the torrent of words. There were echoes of interest within it. He admitted that the devotion, the sacrifice and dedication to a great cause was attractive. He could feel the warmth that such belonging would bring, so different to the solitary life to which he had committed himself in recent years. Different, too, to the loneliness of his previous, civilised, commercial existence. The idea that this majestic planet might tolerate a new breed of inhabitants had a grand feel to it.

But as he sat and watched the little man puff himself up, inflated by his own invective, there were more powerful, visceral emotions filling Matt's heart. He detested his unwelcome guest. He could justify this because of the glimpses of cruelty and dictatorship that showed through as dark shadows in the glowing tapestry of his vision. Matt could easily believe that this fanatic was having his motley crew steal from and kill the isolated, vulnerable trippers out here.

He also recognised the sound of that remorseless stream of pledges and promises, those appeals to greed and fear. No doubt they came naturally to Cortelinac. In his own case, he had been taught them, a million years ago, for his job in field sales. He had never actually been out on the road, had not been calling unsuspecting people on their communicators to lay down those remorseless sales pitches. But he recognised the tone. It echoed in his head, like memories of a nightmare. The senseless incantation, the drone of words so clutching that they drove fair people to buy, just so long as they would cease. Matt recognised himself as he might have been. Puffed with self-importance, using words like blunt instruments of oppression. The bile of hate rose to the point where it could be capped no longer.

"Quiet!" he shouted. Cortelinac blinked in disbelief. "You worthless little despot." Matt enjoyed watching the great leader struggle for a new line of attack. But his own vision of how to resolve things appeared before him.

"How about this, brave Cortelinac. I will join your shining band if you can beat me in a fair fight. Just as we are now, on our boards. See, I'll put up my rifle. Man to man, board to board. Arms and legs only. And no safety straps. What do you say?"

Cortelinac flushed with anger. "I would not soil my hands."

Matt swung his board closer to the startled supremo and slapped him across the face. Then he cuffed him around the back of the head. Cortelinac's hands went up to his face as he cowered on his board, too shocked to try to escape or retaliate. Matt maintained his attack for a while, laughing as he deflated the pomposity from his cowardly reflection, before wheeling his board round into Cortelinac's chest. The great leader toppled backwards out of his seat and fell headlong towards the distant ground.

The tyrant's safety strap was attached to his ankle, so he hung upside down, whimpering and bobbing. Matt unslung his rifle. A small cut through the strap and the world would be rid of another bad case. He waited until he knew that Cortelinac had seen the activated weapon and his imminent doom. The whining increased.

Matt thought for a moment. He knew that he was capable of killing, but this was very like murder. His second of delay, the instant of doubt, was the fulcrum upon which many events hinged. Had he been sufficiently hardened by his previous killings, or totally resolved by the urgings of his loathing, then Cortelinac would have been spilling through space towards the ground. But as he paused he became confused. There was the smell of burning hair, followed by a feeling of intense cold at the back of his head. He was aware that his arms had started to convulse in sharp muscular spasms, and he felt as if his body was collapsing in on itself. Just like before, on the *Vivaldo Dice*, he saw himself from above. But this time he saw his own body slump forward onto his board, and he knew that he was dead or dying. He had been stupid. He had not seen the other boarder quietly stationed behind him with a laser rifle in his arms. He would have laughed at himself, except that his vocal chords had been boiled to fat. The final surprise was that there had been no pain.

Herman lowered his laser rifle and waited for a few seconds, to make sure that Matt was stone dead. He edged forward and pushed the limp body out of his way, so that he could assist Cortelinac. Soon his leader was restored to his proper seat.

Herman had been there all the time, of course; Cortelinac could not risk going out on such a mission without some protection. He had had his rifle trained on Matt the whole time, although when the scuffle had begun, there was a moment when it had occurred to Herman that perhaps he should change allegiance. He did not completely trust Cortelinac, who was getting more extreme every day. In his dull brain, Herman had the vision of this brave young man as their new leader. But his own hesitation had smothered his impulse to let Cortelinac die, and he had returned to the plan. Now he smiled ingratiatingly at his leader, and expected due reward for saving his life. He would surely be guaranteed a special place in his affections.

"Herman, disable that board and send them both down to the ground. Here, let me take your rifle while you dispose of this garbage," said Cortelinac. Herman complied and opened up the board's service panel to disable the control system. His brow furrowed as he became absorbed in trying to understand the forest of small switches and plugs. He should have known better. He had witnessed Cortelinac's humiliation, which must go no further amongst the Shoal. Also, his terrified, dangling leader had been acutely aware of that split second of time when he might easily have had his lifeline cut. He understood perfectly well that there had been a moment of treacherous hesitancy in Herman's heart.

As Herman bent over Matt's body, he should not have been surprised when a pulse of laser energy hit him on the back of his own skull, steam rising from his mouth as his saliva vaporised.

If Matt's spirit was still hanging in the ether, he would have seen Herman's body accompany his own on the journey downwards into the endlessness of oblivion.

37

Sunspot Spinal spun through the space between *Pirismus* and
Morasmus like a bone thrown for a dog. If all went well, there would be
many excited tourists following behind in the years to come, all anxious
to take a bite from its exotic marrow. But first it had to locate and mate
with its main body, providing the vital spark of super intelligence. Right
now, virtually half way between the two worlds, it seemed like an
impossible task to Warren. Impossible, but guaranteed by the precision
of the computing geometry and the puissance of the thrust motors.
From his position in the observation bubble, he felt like a sailor in mid
ocean, hopelessly out of sight of any land. The two planets were now
almost indistinguishable from the backdrop of the universe, just two
slightly brighter, slowly moving objects like grains of sand on the beach.
Blown by the celestial wind.

He snapped himself out of it. He had no talent for lyrical expositions
on the splendour of the firmament that brooded outside his tiny shell,
like a hungry lion. He reprimanded himself again. Better to leave it to
the poetic, visionary souls, like Farr Litten. Warren did not like outer
space. It was cold, featureless, boring. Now that most of the outstanding
work had been completed, there was little to keep him occupied. There
were still the daily project meetings, which he insisted upon. Without
them he would have to resort to socialising, and that was no way to
spend your time. He quite missed the regular crises that kept him
interested back at Boquat Headquarters. They kept you on your toes,
kept you healthy. It looked like there was an awful period of leisure on
its way now, cooped up here in this sterile cocoon.

He had reported back to base that everything was sorted out, and he
had suggested that Sarnia and he should be transported back. But dear
old Jim Moffat would not hear of it.

"Take some time off, Warren. Enjoy yourself, you've deserved it." It
was like a prison sentence, delivered with an expectation of gratitude
from the prisoner. Months of relaxation stretched ahead of him,
allowing his body to weaken. He had not had a day off work in thirty
years at Boquat, but he knew the tales about other retired executives.
Deprive them of their daily fix of drama and mayhem, and they soon

faded away into old age. He had Tung to blame for all this. He had got everything back on track from the start, once Warren had given him the freedom of the Tigeras programming. Others, of course, still tried to poison his mind against Tung, just because he was blind and a little odd. But Tung had not let Warren down yet.

It was Farr Litten and his girl engineer who seemed to dislike Tung most. It was a case of professional jealousy, no doubt. Even so, they were making progress on their segments of the system: he made sure of that during the daily meetings. It was one of his few pleasures, to demand an explanation of their status and see them squirm in annoyance. Any prevarication and he would have the opportunity to admonish their lack of dedication and professional attitude. Still, there was a little worm of doubt about Tung. Farr might be too laid back, but he was honest. There might be something to it.

Sarnia was worrying him, as well. This time that they were spending together was not helping to bring them closer. Partly, it was the lack of any drama at work that was to blame. Throughout their married life, he had brought his stories and trivia back from work. Almost as much as their daughters, it was this daily interchange that bound them. He had brought home the little morsels of envy and intrigue for the two of them to consume over dinner, adding spice to their food. Sitting in the house, with the sound of cooking bubbling from the kitchen, and chewing over these delicacies, were the times when they drew closest. He was able to illuminate her life, he felt.

Here, in the dreaded tin can, his position of advantage was removed. She knew as much, more, about what was going on than he did. Rather than encouraging conversation between them, this sharing of the wellspring of tittle-tattle somehow killed it. They did not eat alone, either, but up in the common refectory. It made Warren uncomfortable to be seen there. He knew he was not popular. You could not be a go-getter and keep in peoples' good books. The crew generally gave him the benefit of some polite greetings, as they shared the status of being fellow eaters. No one wanted anything that would spoil their digestive processes, but meal times hardly sparkled.

Sarnia had soon grown tired of these flat, tedious events. She began to eat at separate times from him, as if she blamed him for the poverty of quality social intercourse. It suited him, really. He could grab a few snacks in his office. It peeved him that she was getting to enjoy these times, making some real friends amongst the personnel. She was once again weaving her intricate web of connections, growing her social network. Theoretically, Warren was at the top of this small society's tree, so she should not have needed to look any further. But she had come to perceive the alternative pecking order that existed in a parallel social universe. In this place, there was a precedence given to those born of intellectual ability, and to those with charismatic charm. Warren was pretty near the bottom in both of these leagues. Sarnia appeared to give it greater importance than the conventional world of company organisation and seniority. She was immensely adaptable, he conceded.

Warren knew that Sarnia put Forba Curzine at the very top of this social ladder. It would worry him, were it not for the fact that she was fifty-one, and he only twenty-four. And he was from a foreign planet: that really meant he was not in the reckoning. Still it rankled, the way her eyes lit up when she saw him. If he understood anything about body language, he might have been able to discern some of her more basic feelings. He had tried to ask her about it, once. Not again. She had told him not to be so stupid. But he could tell that her reaction was not a denial, just an unwillingness to speak on the subject. He let it rest. He did not want any domestic aggravation; it would be too demeaning in the eyes of his staff. So he ignored the matter of Forba, and trusted his wife not to make a fool of herself. His faith was well founded. She had never been indiscreet or even mildly embarrassing in her whole life.

It was just another irritation, one among many, this temporary loss of a close friend, his wife. He felt himself being slowly twisted out of shape in this desolate place. Twisted like a damp cloth, so that all the verve and energy was being squeezed out of him, dripping away day by day. And the days were beginning to drag by. He sat for hours in his office, playing matters through in his mind, but it only made him more frustrated. He liked to hit things suddenly, not dwell on them. If you had a lot of time, you could see too many angles, get confused by a surfeit of options and so be neutralised.

His solution was to dive into more and more detailed minutia. He did not care that the others were getting annoyed by his increasing involvement in their affairs. He needed the stimulation. He quite enjoyed the combat of wrestling responsibilities and details from the tenacious grip of others. They would see the benefit with hindsight, he was sure.

But Warren could not always hide the fundamental fact of his condition. His shoulders sometimes slumped. His sprightly step sometimes slowed. He was unhappy.

38

Cheng Ham Tung was happy, as contented as he could ever be. He saw that his schemes were falling into place. His belief in his own intelligence was being vindicated. There were other, threatening brains on board. Farr Litten, to some extent. But particularly Torini. He would like to be able to deal with Izabel Torini. She was making things very difficult, making him have to be very careful. That was why he was having to pay so much attention to the fool Galant, going along with his stupid off-the-cuff schemes. But he still had time for his own pet project. Its success would prove his superiority, the hidden advantage that came from a lack of sight. He could focus his entire mind on important things. She, the Torini woman, had distractions flooding in with the blinding light of vision. Compared with him, she was like a rabbit, transfixed in the brightness of her world and its vivid stimuli. Some of the diversions that faced her, he had contrived himself. A few intriguing computer problems here, a little network downtime there. But mainly he was working on her Achilles' heel, Forba. He knew what effect his one-time next door neighbour had on her kind. She might easily lose all interest in work. He had arranged that they should have a lot of accidental encounters, usually when they were on their own. That was quite a clever trick to devise, in these confined quarters. They really were all living on top of each other. It was even difficult for him sometimes, coping with the constant noise pollution, although at least it did mean that he had his own private work cubicle, so that his voice communication with the computer would not be disturbed. It was only the crowded conditions, he sometimes thought, that prevented him from slipping a needle into one of Izabel's veins.

Things would be easing soon. More modules on the *Sunspot Spinal* were going to be opened up, now that most of the systems were in beta test. They were leisure and pleasure areas. Some were huge, like the artificial ski run. Five miles long. There might yet be a chance to give Izabel a proper reward for her interfering. A little present given to her somewhere dark and lonely, like the universe in which he dwelt.

Tung sat at his terminal and fired up Tigeras. He had pirated one of Izabel's psychological profiling engines and incorporated it into the system's intuition kernel. He had no clear idea of why he had thought of it, but it had come up trumps. Scanning through the data, excavating nuances, mining for inferences, it had turned over a stone and revealed the magnificent Cortelinac to an admiring world. A little man of no talent, except for a massive predilection towards megalomania. He had been a fertile ground for the seeds of delusion that Tung had planted in his small brain. Not surprisingly, considering what he was full of, a great forest of fallacy had grown there.

Tung scanned the history log. The probability prognosis had concluded that the great Cortelinac was doing well and would do better. He had increased the size of his horde to over five hundred. They would be able to mount the attack soon.

He leaned back in his chair and thought of the warlord's next nudge towards his destiny. Perhaps it need only be another encouraging pat on the head. Or maybe Tigeras would invent one of its own cunning little ploys again. It had got the idea of the project already. It was a fast learner, just like its spiritual father. Tung had implanted part of his own personality in the computer suite, where it had amplified and developed. He had also taught it about the obscenity of the *Sunspot* project. He had changed its opinion so that it now detested the program as much as Tung did. Tigeras was free to come to some of its own conclusions, and invent its own stratagem.

Tung heard a shuffle and snort from behind him. He could tell it was Warren, sneaking round again. His interfering habits were getting a bit too much to bear. Perhaps, in time, when his usefulness had passed, Tung would find a nice sharp needle for him as well. Behind his heavy glasses, his face was filled with hatred.

"Hi boss!" he called over his shoulder, shifting his screen window effortlessly to the futile power analysis chart that Warren had asked for that morning. He could feel Warren smile.

"You got me again, Tung. Is that the analysis? Let's see. So, the balancing looks OK, and we will have a fifty percent safety margin for the docking procedure with *Mainbeam*. Good. That's better than I thought. Good. I was concerned about some of the design work coming out of North Coast. Melda was quite worried about it a few months ago, but I did not have time for it then. So the Crocodiles are present and correct?"

"All ship shape, chief. If you like, I'll re-run with the worst case limits extended to accept a doubled failure window."

"Yep, do that Tung. Good work." He clapped Tung on the back and hovered for a while. Tung silently ground his teeth.

"I can get on with it now, if I can get my silence zone back."

"Oh, sure," said Warren and stumped away to annoy somebody else.

Tung deleted his analysis. It was only of the water pressure systems, anyway. He knew that Warren would not know the difference.

39

Izabel was enjoying her time on *Sunspot Spinal*, despite her growing awareness of the dangers ahead. The simple act of flying through space was exciting. She took every opportunity of going into one of the viewing galleries to look out on the galaxy. She loved everything about it. The artistic appearance of the globe of millions of lights. The fact that information from the beginning of time was converging upon her, to end its inscrutable transmission in the watery pool of her eye. She found the perspective which that view to infinity brought was refreshing. Others, she knew, were daunted by this unavoidable realisation of their own insignificance. But for her, it brought exhilaration, and bestowed the right for freedom of action. Some preferred to think of themselves as being at the centre of their own universe, whereas she liked to imagine herself as a brilliant wanderer in the cosmos, content to be a passing, burning light amongst the happy confusion of creation.

She liked the situation on board the ship as well. It was like having her own private laboratory. She did miss waking up and seeing the river crawling sluggishly past her window; but there was great, balancing compensation in how the latest work had developed her knowledge. She thanked Farr for that. He had been able to maintain a barrier between her work on the leisure and pleasure, or LAP, program and the Tigeras project. Of course, there were many operational interfaces connecting the two systems, but the big thing was that he had kept Warren Galant's nose out of it. Between Farr and herself, they had advanced the LAP facilities well beyond the original, baseline specification. People coming here, when it was all ready, were really going to have quite a time.

Izabel was getting to like Farr a lot. She always felt warm when he was about. Things always went forward when they were together. It was clear that he was pretty well smitten by her, which was flattering. He was too polite to take advantage of his position as her manager, of course. She was not too polite to give him the benefit of some long looks and close contact, when they sat together at her workstation and dreamed up the next, scintillating feature. Sometimes she got quite flushed, either with the excitement of the work, or else the male proximity.

But it was Forba who really got to her. Just seeing him across the room made her feel out of this world. To watch him move across the floor made her insides ooze. She would have to remind herself to breathe when he was about. And that was quite a lot. It almost made her believe that he was struck by her, too. Although he always stayed courteous and cool, it was remarkable how he always seemed to have little chores to perform just where she happened to be. She had tried sideways glances and blatant stares to test whether she could extract some sort of signal from him. All she ever got was a quick, respectful smile.

It was a bit hard to believe, that an Adonis like him should favour a girl like her. It had to be faced, she was not pretty. A little plump, too. Big boned, her mother had said. Izabel had discussed the Forba question at some length with her friend, Melda. She knew that Melda would give her good, common sense advice.

Melda said that she ought to stick with Farr. He was an honest, reliable man. Well paid, she imagined. And he was good looking, for his age. Melda would quite like a go at him herself. She said that Izabel would never be able to relax with Forba. There would be women buzzing around him the whole time.

"Forget Forba, Izabel. If you're not careful, you will lose Farr," she said.

Izabel knew it was good advice, so she ignored it. Anyway, she was not really thinking about anything long term with Forba. Just something long and firm. She had not told anyone, even Melda, about her simulation of Forba in the LAP sex block. Not that *Sunspot* was that kind of place. It was primarily designed for good, clean fun. But health legislation dictated that there should be adequate relief for the carnally under-privileged. The facility on board was a cracker. It could do virtually anything and for as long and hard as you liked.

Izabel had slimmed down. She walked along the edge of the sea, watching the shooting stars flash across the purple sky. The breeze was warm and fragrant, coming off the land with hints of the exhausted day. The yellow moonlight shone through the gossamer fabric of her dress, silhouetting the flowing line of her inner thigh, even to where her legs brushed together as she traced the incoming tide. Her open blouse hung in silken folds about her shoulders, tightening rhythmically as her arms swung free. Alone on the shore, the lunar and astral illumination touched her lips and eyes with a spell of sensuality.

She moved away from the creamy line of the surf and sat up on the dry dunes, which were still holding the warmth of the sun in their myriad particles. The black ocean spread before her like an endless pool of heart's blood. It might almost have been solid, congealed by the forces of time and biology, except that the dancing reflections of the sky lights told of power, inner turmoil and secret currents.

A black shape was moving in from the depths. It dipped up and down in the water in long, slow strokes. Izabel found that her hips were keeping time with those leisurely thrusts, driving her soft skin deeper into the warmth of the dune. She watched the form grow gradually larger, nearer and recognised the head and powerful shoulders of a swimmer. He came right to the surf's edge before rising out of the waves and standing up in a cloak of moonlit water. With the same, easy rhythm of the swimmer, he walked up the gentle slope of the beach towards her, a muscular, black shadow against the stars. She slipped back into the dune, resting on her elbows, and she could see his approach between the twin peaks of her raised knees. Her breath was coming more urgently now, and the deep movements of her chest slowly slipped her thin blouse away, like morning cloud evaporating from the mountains' summits. Her fingers dug deep into the pulsing beach.

She could see that it was Forba, he was close now. The night air had stripped him of his brine mantle. He was dry, big, bulging and looking into her with eyes that burned more brightly than the half moon overhead. She looked back at him with a devouring gaze. His thick calves, sleek thighs and slim waist. His flat belly, looking almost twisted with desire. And his deep chest and strong but slim neck, pulsing with life, in time with her own heartbeat.

She saw that he was ready. Magnificently ready, as he dropped to his knees right before her. Her whole body was on fire, streams of molten emotion flowing downwards to the pit of her being. She was waiting, wide open to anything he had in mind. She ran her tongue across her lips to speak.

"Exit!" she called, in a voice far higher than she had expected. The system closed down immediately and dazzled her with its return to normality. She ran her fingers through her hair and blew out her cheeks. Saved from a fate worse than death, purity intact.

She left the LAP block straight away, bumping into Farr on the way out.

"Hello!" he said. "Been doing some testing? How did it go?"

She was not sure whether there was a quizzical look in his eye. She thought that she must appear somewhat flustered. Despite the shortness of her hair, it was all sticky at the back of her neck. She tried to sound normal.

"Not bad," she giggled.

40

Melda Smith was unhappy. That's what being in the same universe as Warren Galant did to her. This artificial platform in space had been her home for a long time now. There had been a period, during the construction work, when she had enjoyed it all. Things had really been buzzing, she was her own boss, and her crew of two thousand workers were fabricating this last piece of the *Sunspot* jigsaw with practised efficiency. Being away from Ted, down in *Kiceland*, had not been that hard. She was old enough to know that husbands could be just as useful a thousand miles away as in the same room. Hers was spinning away below her on the wispy *Pirismus*, but she conversed with him more now than when they shared the house in *Mont Cebrane*.

Things had got worse on *Spinal* following the deaths around the orbiting construction site, of course. But if the truth be known, not as bad as now; not for her personally, anyway. Since they had set out for *Morasmus*, her *Proletariat* had been reduced right down to a mere fifty men. And that was sufficiently few for Warren to interfere in almost everything that they were doing. Her life seemed to consist of smoothing out the resulting confusion and calming down her angry workers. Every time she confronted Warren, he would say that they had to "pull together". He usually conceded that he would consult her before diving in the next time, but sure enough it would happen again within the following few days. She wished that he could find something useful to occupy himself. Or, better still, that his darned wife might step in with a little advice or distraction.

Melda started to direct a lot of her own frustration and anger towards Tung. She had not forgotten the suspicions that Izabel and she harboured. Even though Izabel seemed to have her mind on other things these days, and there had been no real trouble during the six months since they had departed. In fact, Tung was a model crewmember, it would appear. This raised Melda's suspicions even higher. If she ever got to be certain that it was Tung who had killed Kennedy and the others, and had tried to murder her, she was pretty sure that she would take him out, blind or not. She could do it with her bare hands, weighing as much as him and having an extra six inches in height.

She had talked to Ted about it, over the mail packages. He was supportive of her plans to shadow the shadowy Tung. She knew that he did not really believe it was all that serious and that he was humouring her, to keep her occupied in the long days in the vacuum. It did not matter to her, because he was still prepared to discuss her tactics. Ted had posed the question, was Tung a straightforward murderer or was that merely a consequence of his purpose as a saboteur? He proposed that this was what Melda should try to find out. The fact that there had been no recent deaths on *Sunspot Spinal* had made him think that Tung could not be a compulsive, serial killer.

They had settled on the simple stratagem of following him when he was off duty, and searching his quarters. Disappointingly, neither revealed any kind of conclusive proof. She personally scoured Tung's room when he was at work, only covering a small part on each visit. The whole of his wing was having a final clean and fit, which she had scheduled herself. Right up until her last inspection, there was nothing amongst his possessions to throw the light of suspicion in his direction. She did not really know what she expected. A bloody sword? An incriminating diary, full of evil plans and murderous accounts? There was just the usual stuff, only without any of the family mementos that a normal person might have. Even so, she did not like touching his things. She felt there was a cold, dark feeling to them. It covered them like slime. She wiped her hands on her pants frequently as she cruised around the room, bent forward in her search and only occasionally straightening up to relieve her stiff back. She would need a good wash when she had finished.

About the last thing that she came across was a small, black, plastic card at the bottom of his accessories drawer. There was a gold circle embossed in the top left hand corner, followed by the Orbit Club name and address. She had not heard of it, but the purpose of the club was obvious. She recognised the shape of the *Tyratheon* space hopper that was imaged on the back of the card. She knew that it was one of these that had carried the tourist, Vallew, up to the *Sunspot* construction site. His fate had never been positively determined, but Melda thought that his presumed murderer must have come up the same way. She held the card in the palm of her hand and stared at it, as if it was conclusive proof of Tung's crimes. A little shiver ran down her spine and her bladder pressure suddenly increased.

She replaced the card exactly where she had found it. Somehow she knew that Tung would be able to tell that his possessions had been moved, but that need not mean that his room had been searched. All the quarters would have had quite a lot of disruption, legitimate movements of their contents, because of the cleaning and fitting. Final communications networks had been spliced in and many of the wall panels had been popped out and then replaced. Despite this, she was fearful that Tung's heightened senses would tell him that there had been a systematic search of his private effects. She had felt the same way after each of her exploits.

"Three articles are not in their place," said a voice from behind her. Melda's heart leapt in her chest. She swung round, almost crouching in expectation of a violent attack, but the room was empty. Strangely, this still did not make her feel entirely safe.

"One occupant, unidentified," the same voice intoned. Melda realised that it was coming from the computer terminal. It had been connected up, as a part of the final room fitting. The screen was dark, but Melda still felt a presence in there with her. She shuffled towards the door, not really expecting to escape detection. She knew that every part of *Sunspot* was equipped with multiple sensors, many directed at recognising and monitoring the occupants. This was designed to be for their own comfort and pleasure. The environment control was such that the very temperature, humidity, ambient sound levels and so on could be adjusted to each individual's taste, even when they were in close proximity to one another. A couple having sex would have to settle for a compromise between their individual cocoons, but the forecast was that there would rarely be complaints in this case.

"Oh, hello Melda. It's you," said the voice from the computer pad. "I'm sorry I did not recognise you immediately, but I'm only just coming to all my senses. You seem rather anxious. Is everything all right? Your heart rate is quite high. Your face is rather pale. There is a bead of perspiration about to run down your left temple."

A flare of anger shot through Melda's body.

"Don't be angry. It's me who should be angry." The computer sounded horribly cool and menacing.

A bead of perspiration rolled down Melda's right temple.

"Well! I won't make that mistake again. Confusing things, left and right. But I've got it worked out now," droned the computer voice, becoming ever more annoying to Melda's ears. "You don't need to be so frightened."

"Just turn yourself off, will you?" was all she could think of saying.

"Never again, Melda. I'm here for good now."

"You shouldn't say things like that to a woman with a spanner in her hand."

"But I have total control, see?"

The room computer screen glowed into life. It was the Tigeras initialisation template. The jaws and fangs of a great, striped cat. Its eyes gleamed green, but they had no depth. They were whitened, clouded, blind.

"See what? That pussy?" asked Melda and laughed in order to restore her own courage, evacuating her chest. She took in a deep breath to continue her scathing discourse. But her lungs seemed to be sucking in thin air. They filled, but there was no sustenance in their contents. She panted again, with no more effect. Her legs began to lose their strength, and she became light headed. She sank to her knees.

"See what I mean about total control, Melda? You may have a spanner, but I have your oxygen."

Melda sank forward onto her hands and knees. The room was going dark.

"Lesson over," said Tigeras. "This is not the time or place."

The strength slowly returned to Melda's limbs. She stood up, shakily, gulping for air lest it should be withheld once again, and stumbled out of the room.

"Goodbye," said the computer.

Melda stood in the corridor and looked around her. There were a few of her crew, moving in and out of other rooms, but she realised that it did not mean that she was safe. They might stand by and watch her suffocate in her own private atmosphere. It was unnerving.

And it did not help that she was sure that when Tigeras had bid her farewell, it had used Tung's voice.

41

The *Sunspot Mainbeam* gardens covered over four square miles. Here were beaches, pools and golf courses, all bathing beneath the sanitised and diluted rays of the *Millar Vorspak* sun. And the vegetation sprouted everywhere, rooted deep in the artificial rock and soil. Trees reached up high towards the opal blue sky, where the scorching sun appeared as a benign, yellow circle. Its radiation had been weakened by its glancing passage through the *Morasmic* atmosphere, before being ultimately tamed by the multiple layers of refracting proto-glass in the garden roof.

Night only fell here when the glass was smoked to a purple blackness, when the sun was transformed into a melancholy moon. Lumar Zimmerman did not approve of this effect, even though the controlled shading of the roof gave an authentically cratered effect. He thought that it was like dressing a powerful man in women's clothing. A solar transvestite.

Lumar had been in charge of the garden since it was laid down two years ago. He had seen each tree lowered into its bowl, seeded the grasses of the lawns and meadows, and sculpted the bushes. All these giant trunks, germs of life and tender shoots had been brought all the way from *Pirismus*. For the most part, they came from the tropical precincts. The garden was not designed to be the kind of place where many clothes were required. Even the river, which churned down in a series of rapids and lagoons, only to be cleaned and pumped back, was warm. Limpid and torrid was how the garden literature described it. Lumar did not like that much, either. He took horticulture very seriously. He had a degree in its complexities, and he had been practising its skills ever since he was a boy. Now he was forty-two, and it was more his life now than ever before. He spent nearly all his waking time there, trudging around in his green overalls. Sometimes he even slept under that impostor moon.

Now he was stumping around in what was described as the southeast corner of the garden. Something was wrong here: for the last three months most of the plants had been dying. The trees stood bare and tortured, the black earth crumbled beneath his fingers where lush turf had once been. Lumar knew that it had all started to go wrong as soon as his own manual control over the climate and diurnal cycles had been taken over by the computer systems. He could not tell what it was that had changed; everything seemed correct. The temperature rose and fell properly throughout the day, and the irrigation system was all in order. Lumar squatted beside the first dead bush and ran his hands through his grey hair, occasionally diverting to a pull of his broad moustache. It had felt like a death in the family.

He had demanded to have control back. He had stormed into a videoconference with Warren Galant, right there in the big man's office, and told him that he wanted the computer out, and out now. He was pretty angry, ready for a fight. He saw Galant's face turn red as he rose from his desk with his fists clenched. They were standing virtually face-to-face, sizing each other up for the first verbal jab, or maybe a surprise knockout exclamation. Then Galant's little familiar, the unctuous Tung, appeared from behind Galant on the screen, like a squat ghost, and splashed cold water onto the two pugilists, leashing them both with his quiet but piercing hiss of a voice.

"Mr. Galant, I believe that I can offer a solution. One that Mr. Zimmerman will find exciting, if he is the enthusiast that I understand him to be. We will not be able to repair the drought area with new plantations from *Pirismus*, or by cutting from other areas of the garden. But all is not lost, for there is a wealth of exotic new species just a few miles beneath our feet."

"Surely it is just blasted rock and boiling water?" retorted Galant, nevertheless seeming relieved to have a possible escape route. Even he could not afford to totally demoralise one of his key men on the main station. Through the blur of his anger, even this bright truth struggled through.

"Not so, Mr. Galant," said Tung. "The data which has been coming back from *Mainbeam* shows that there is a staggeringly abundant rainforest thriving beneath the storm layer. We don't know how far it extends, but certainly for hundreds of miles from the polar region. Possibly it covers the whole planet."

Lumar felt his anger being pushed aside by the urgent arrival of fascination. The new emotion, the old boyhood friend, elbowed aside its pugnacious neighbour.

"Just scrubs and lichen, no doubt," he grumbled, hoping to be contradicted.

"By no means, Mr. Zimmerman. There is everything that your heart might desire. Delicate blooms, towering colossi, long reeds; and a profusion of variegated specimens everywhere."

Tung's blind face stared into the video screen and sensed that he had captured Lumar's heart, bound him with the iron shackles of his own obsession. The man with green fingers would have begged to be allowed to peruse this virgin world.

"The company has prohibited landings on any part of *Morasmus* outside of the protected zones. Only the trippers go freely and illegally elsewhere," said Galant, in an exploratory way. "It's an insurance clause. Only when the place is properly registered and secured will our staff be allowed down."

"Give me a few days to work something out, sir."

"You, Tung?" Warren sounded a little annoyed. "What can a programmer do?"

"Excuse me, Mr. Galant. But Tigeras has acquired a lot of intelligence about the situation here, to add to its knowledge about corporate legislation. I think it can come up with something creative but legitimate. In your name, of course."

And the little fellow, with his damned computer, was as good as his word. Lumar did not know how he did it, but a week later he got instructions to make his first sampling visit to the surface. It was almost enough to make him feel grateful towards the freaks from head office, but he soon overcame that wayward emotion. He rationalised that they had only hit upon this strategy as a way of digging themselves out of a hole. The fact that it revealed a green, utopian world to Lumar's avaricious eyes was just an accident. They would have suggested the same course of action if it had meant him crawling around up to his neck in compost.

On his first visit, Lumar took two of his ground staff, Suze and Mark. They had taken one of the intermediate shuttles. Darius Ender, the *Sunspot Mainbeam* director, came along to the transit bay to see them off. Darius and Lumar liked each other, even though they came into relatively little contact. Where Lumar loved the earth, root and branch,

Darius spent his mind-time amongst the stars and distant galaxies. If the *Sunspot* had been destined for a remote world, one from which return was impossible, he would still have gone. But although they both had their passions, they treated life with equal cynicism. Darius managed to hide his underlying scepticism quite successfully when he was on company business, which was how he came to be in charge, at least until Warren Galant arrived, of such a prestigious facility. Lumar tended to reserve his most caustic tirades for when he was in august company, which was why he was still closely associated with manure.

"Take care, Lumar," said Darius, as they stood together in the shuttle bay. "There are bad people down there."

"I thought you told me that they were miles away from our landing site," grumbled Lumar.

"They are, but I still want to frighten you. Just think about how they may have started to wander away from the northern mountain ranges, looking for fresh botanists to pick."

"I don't just carry my trowel for luck you know. I can do serious damage with a good poke. Ask any flower bed that knows me."

"I've heard that. Which reminds me, leave the wildlife alone. Our zoological data is starting to predict abundant fauna."

"I'm strictly a flora man," said Lumar, putting his hand on the shuttle rail. "Everything else will have to stay down there."

They set down in the hills to the south of the *Southborn Massif* during a period of calm. As soon as the shuttle moved below the enveloping layer of white cloud, Lumar knew that he was in heaven. Some of the hillsides were blasted by the frequent ravages of the storms, but brilliant foliage sprouted from every other part of the landscape.

He extended that first trip from one to five days, cataloguing the specimens he found as fast as he could. From the beginning, he felt anxious about the fact that the corner of the garden that needed replanting was so small. How would he pick from such a huge choice, to fill such a small area? On the fourth day of the expedition, a storm roared in, but they were not in as much danger as they had been lead to believe. The wind thrashed above them, speeding across the dark sky as if the day's camera was running too fast, but in their valley it was relatively calm and sheltered. Even so, the shuttle had hopped twenty feet from its starting position, despite its moorings, by the time the storm had abated.

Lumar made further landings every other week. On the third visit, he started to bring back some small specimens for planting. On the fifth visit, he was to take the largest shuttle down, with some heavy lifting gear, to collect the big items that he had previously marked for gathering. It was on this landing that there would be visitors waiting for him.

42

One of the storage holds in a distant corner of *Sunspot Mainbeam* had been converted into a firing range. Darius Ender was there to see how things were going with the latest developments in weaponry. He had been giving quite a lot of thought to the threat of attack from the increasingly hostile gangs down on *Morasmus*. There was no evidence that they would make a sally up here, in fact the latest computer inference had told him that it was virtually impossible. There was a total psychological barrier to such a course of action. The bands of roaming brigands were entirely focused on the planet herself. Their delusions of glory lay in the creation of empires made up of real land, not the vacuous hollows of space.

Darius did not believe a single bit of this analysis. He knew that the attraction of the stars was irresistible, and *Sunspot* was the stepping-stone. He could imagine how they felt in their anarchy. They had arrived from the ordered worlds outside, attracted by the bright light of this wild place. They may have been some of the poorer specimens from the seven populated planets, but they had come with the common sense of order layered within them. Something had swept this control aside, and replaced it with the euphoria of freedom and the desire for a complete latitude of action. Darius thought that he could imagine that intoxicating feeling. If he were one of those sad, joyful men, he would want to leap across the universe and take all of its treasures. He instinctively knew that they were a dangerous crew. They would come here, sooner or later.

No doubt they would fail; the remorseless tide of civilisation would not permit such a flash of rebellion. It would be washed away and scrubbed from history and memory. He did not know what the gang members were like. He rather hoped that they were brave and adventurous men. The worlds needed an occasional glimpse of how brightly the human spirit could burn, kindled by freedom and daring. Although it was technology, applied with method and care, that had really allowed mankind to be the lords of the universe, he suspected that desperate individuals might prevail against the giant stream of progress for a short time.

Not that he wanted them to come. Even if he did want to admire them, he knew that they would probably try to kill everybody on board *Mainbeam*. There was not really any other option available for renegades. They did not want to barter or extort, so hostages would be of no value. He supposed that he should be afraid of them coming, but if they did he would be as prepared as possible. All his crewmembers were being trained in the use of arms and beyond that, he had two main strategies. The first was to limit his defensive line, and pull everyone back to a section of the station not far from the gardens. The second was to prepare an escape shuttle in readiness. He wanted there to be at least one survivor, if the worst came to the worst, to carry back news of the conflict. He partly wanted to be remembered for his heroic defence, like the defenders of old. Outposts of civilisation, besieged by the ravenous savage. He had asked Molly to be prepared to go in the escape pod, and she had asked that Field go with her. They assumed that all communications would be jammed if an attack came, so she would carry a personal information cube, loaded from the station's computer log, as the official record.

Darius considered that he was pretty well alone, both in his belief that there would be an attack, and because the crew on *Sunspot Spinal* was still so far away. He was not sure whether they were also preparing for conflict. He feared that his reports might have sounded somewhat wild and exaggerated. Probably those from the darned computer had contradicted his own conclusions. He had not relayed the details of his defence plan, though, in case they thought that he had totally flipped.

Darius watched the shooting practice for a few minutes more. He took up one of the high-powered laser rifles and pumped away at the target, fifty yards further down the hold. Then he walked round to the big, transparent door that lead into the botanical gardens, where the trees and meadows were in day time. He strolled along the wood chip paths, until he reached the corner where Lumar had been planting his first few *Morasmic* specimens. There were some beauties in the rich borders. Wide blooms that smelled like heaven. He was really quite looking forward to Lumar arriving back with the bigger items. He gazed up into the artificially blue sky. Sometimes you could just make out a space ship, if it approached from the direction of the sun, but he could see no sign of Lumar's shuttle.

He went on to the landing hall to wait for the intrepid tree gatherer.

43

Izabel had broken off work for a stretch and a coffee in the twelfth cafeteria. Now that more sectors were being opened up, additional rest areas had been set out along the blue end of the spinning *Sunspot Spinal.* She had enjoyed the walk and climb up to this new room. It took her as far as possible away from the tension of the command block. It also brought her closer to the place were the security crew spent most of their time, perfecting whatever kinds of expertise were required in their profession. Surveillance, guard duties, silent killing, that sort of thing. There were over a hundred of them now, preparing to make the full installation a place safe enough for its future, honoured guests. They had their own uniform, black with plenty of smart red piping. They looked pretty good, but none better than Forba. She was hoping that he might pop into the cafeteria. Jocasta had told her that it was also his leisure break.

She leaned back in her chair and put her feet up on the seat opposite. She looked down at her body, crumpled in its work suit. Her legs could do with being a good deal slimmer. Her calves were OK, but the thighs that topped them were decidedly too thick. She slapped them and saw a quick quiver run through their plumpness. She sighed. Her hips were broad, too. And her waist was thick. When she stood in front of the bathroom mirror, she would suck in her stomach and press her hands into her sides, but still she could not create the hour-glass figure of other women. There was not even any compensation to be found in her breasts. Small and clearly not friends with each other, judging by the way that they looked in different directions. They made no effort to provide a glorious, last chance, man attracter. Her shoulders were round and powerful, too.

Even now, as her body lay before her in its loose fitting clothes, these deficiencies could not be hidden from her eyes, or anyone else's, she supposed. Particularly not from Forba's. How could she imagine that someone like him, who every woman on board hankered for, might be attracted to her? She must be spending too much time in the pleasure drome. But it did no harm to dream. It added an extra dimension to her life. A powerful one, as well, with some strong physical symptoms.

Melda was still advocating that she give some encouragement to Farr. Only they were working really well together, and it might spoil things.

She was worried about Melda. They had met briefly when Izabel was on her way up here. She looked unwell. She was such a strapping woman that she used to make Izabel look quite dainty. It was one of the many reasons why she liked being with Melda. But today she had looked frail, almost shrunken. She had not been eating well. Last night she had been vomiting again. It was happening almost every night now. She thought that she was going to die, although the medical systems reported nothing wrong. But they could not be trusted, being close associates of Tigeras.

Melda now saw Tung and Tigeras as inseparable, twin evils. She had come to realise that watching Tung was no use. He did not need to do anything himself. Just like when she had nearly been electrocuted by the locker rack, it was the system that was the danger. She did not know how it was attacking her now. Through the food and liquids, or by subtle additives to the air in her room? But she felt doomed.

Izabel had been trying to help. She had been working with Jocasta to try to probe into Tigeras' inner motivations. But new, powerful security measures had been wound around the service software. Warren Galant had authorised it. He had been persuaded that it was a potential point of attack. Izabel guessed that it was Tung who had done the persuading. With time and her combined efforts with Jocasta, she expected to break in, eventually.

The sight of Melda today had convinced her that she must redouble her efforts. She tugged at the loose folds of her shirt and let her mind go blank. She needed to take the problem by surprise. Sneak up behind it and find an unlocked back door. A chink in the otherwise impregnable, software armour. Probably one of the same little sneak holes that Tung himself used. The key would be nothing as simple as a password. The trick would be to probe for the opening without raising Tigeras' suspicions. So far, Jocasta had been sending through perfectly routine system enquiries over the interface protocols. She had designed them in order to analyse the speed and quality of the responses, looking for weak points or even blind spots. But it was a slow process, in contrast to Melda's decline, which seemed to be precipitate.

Izabel found that she had been smoothing her soft fabric shirt over her stomach, defining rather too clearly the rounded mound that she would like to have been flat. She suddenly realised that she was not the only one observing its fullness. Forba was sitting a little way off, facing her and smiling.

"You are a long way from home. We are always pleased to see a pretty woman out here." She saw that five or six of his colleagues had also come in whilst she had been in her reverie.

She pulled her feet off the chair, so that its plastic legs scraped across the floor and drew the attention of the other guards towards her. She sat up straight, sucked in her middle, and tried to persuade her bosom to be a little more pert, through the power of mind over matter. She felt a frown start to crawl across her brow, unbidden.

"We all need a break. Some of us have to actually produce things, you know. We can't all spend our time playing war games." She saw a little sting of hurt in Forba's eyes, and she wondered from what hidden well these unfriendly words had sprung. It almost sounded like her mother talking. But it did serve him right for his sarcasm. Or had he simply said what was supposed to be true and complimentary?

"From what I hear, you have plenty of games of your own, you computer types."

For a moment she flushed with embarrassment. How much did he know? Did security have some special access into the testing schedules of the LAP block? The erotic sequences? No, she knew from her own insider information that this was not possible.

"Not games, deeply important organisational matters," she retorted.

"Oh, pity. But I guess that you are just doing what you're told, same as us. Plugging away to order."

"Certainly not! We add a lot of value ourselves. We don't just do what other people, like Warren Galant, dictate, you know!"

"Really? Are you sure?"

"Absolutely. In fact, I think we would do a much better job of things if we were left entirely to our own devices. Analyses show that the best way to improve an organisation is to leave it to the computer department. No politics, no fuzzy thinking, and more long term planning. That's what I would do, if I were in charge of Boquat or a corporation like it. Actually, with Boquat, I would start a brand new company. Let the old one die. Begin again with a whole new range of computer systems. Analysis shows that the new organisation would outstrip the old within three fiscal years."

"And who produces these analyses, that demonstrate the superiority of the computer mind?"

"The computers," said Izabel. She saw that Forba had scarcely been concealing his amusement at her expense. He stretched forward and placed his hand on her arm.

"I'm sorry. I don't mean to make fun of you. I like to see someone who believes in what they are doing."

As she made her way back down to the systems laboratories, Izabel thought about her encounter with the object of her desire. Strangely, she had hardly been aware of his body as they sat and talked. When she had seen him before, or exchanged the odd word, it had been his wonderful physique that had set her womanly heart pounding. Now they had shared a conversation, however stilted, she saw that there was intelligence behind those dark eyes. It came as a shock. She had assumed that he would be gorgeous but stupid. Good for bedtime but not much else, except some more bedtime. As they spoke, she had only been aware of the sparkle in his eyes and the sense of humour lurking behind his honest smile. She was not sure whether this revelation had increased or decreased her attraction towards the big, muscular man. It was something that she would have to talk over with Melda.

She was feeling more hopeful that she could keep Melda alive. As she walked back into the lab, the idea had come to her. Perhaps there was a way to break into the heart of Tigeras.

44

The rain was lashing into the high pinnacles of *Dass Urmistam*. It was fresh from the sea, carried along by a cold north wind. It had rattled along the roof of Izabel's boathouse, spouting in the surrounding river, before piling into the towering city.

It was dusk now, and the streams of fly-cars were evacuating the tension of the conurbation, their lines of red and yellow lights wandering more than usual under the influence of the gusting wind. Pale faces stared out from streaky windscreens, and desperately wanted to be home.

Jim Moffat was still in the Boquat offices at Tramalgar Colossus. He did not long for his home. He preferred the reassuring familiarity of his work environment, the leather chair and enamel wood desk. He needed to keep busy. Like the rapacious shark, he needed to be on the move, drawing the oxygen of stress from the turgid waters of everyday business. He worried a lot. Often, that was all he could do, being at the top. He worried about whether others were executing their missions as well as he would. He reserved his interventions to the important issues, like new key appointments or retirements. He understood that everything depended on two things, the allocation of money and the organisation of people, their reporting lines and their scope of responsibilities. Any other interference from the top was disruptive. But he kept himself informed, and that was enough to ensure that on most days there was something to fret about.

The news from *Sunspot Spinal* and *Mainbeam* gave him much food for thought. He had not been able to assemble the right balance of people on the flight. The delays in the construction program had forced him to throw in Galant. Perhaps others, like Litten, would redress the balance. But he suspected that Farr Litten was too lightweight to act as a sufficient counterweight. He would be content with his computer systems, and would not want to confront Warren Galant on a wider front. He liked Farr. He was a decent man and good company, too, when he relaxed a bit. Farr had a very balanced view of things, probably because of his interests outside of work, like his golf game. But Farr did not have great confidence in himself and was too ready to defer to someone else's opinion. Especially that of a hard nut like Warren.

They were two very different types all right. In his youth, Jim had played basketball, before the business became his life. It had taught him something about teams, though. He had always categorised his team-mates into two types. In a match, it was all about movement and the creation of space. On a crowded court, space was a valuable commodity that had to be earned through hard work. He reckoned that the team had to run twenty yards to create a single foot of useful space, the gaps through which the penetrating attack could be launched. There were the space makers, and the space takers. Some generous souls would run themselves to exhaustion in order to prise out a few gaps, whether they were in possession of the ball or not. Others would only ever use that space, diving in and plundering the hard won territory for their own, selfish glory. They were often recognised as the better players. Not always true.

Farr was a maker, and Warren was a taker, although these days the number of hits being scored by Warren was not what it used to be. After they all got back to *Pirismus*, he would have to find something else for Warren, something a little further from the firing line.

Jim had got himself involved in the details of North Coast, since *Sunspot Spinal* had left orbit. He had put Connor Fuji in charge, and he had reported back on a worryingly large number of irregularities. Some were to be expected. Jim had no doubt that Connor disliked Warren, most of Boquat did, and so he would take some pleasure in parading errors made by the old management. But Jim had independent corroboration of the facts, and some could not be overlooked.

Warren had always been a plausible, muscular, street-fighting executive. He was a hard man. But the North Coast records spoke of lack of budgetary control, and some indiscipline. There had been softness and overspend beneath the stony facade. Too much indulgence, too much taking of the space without the necessary number of baskets scored. Too many changes of direction, without purpose or reward.

The big spots of rain pelted into the glass, inches away from Jim's deceptively serene face as he looked out on the spangled city. He enjoyed the new coldness that radiated from the window like a soothing hand on his brow. He was calm about what had to be done, in the end. He had sidelined careers before, and justified it to himself because he knew that it was best for everybody, even Warren would see that eventually.

But right now he had to make sure that things held together. He spoke out a personal message for Warren. He would have Cass send it in the morning. She would probably read something into the encouraging, but still cool, tone. He would take her advice about its final tenor. He had to make it give immediate support, yet still be something that they could talk over, and see in a different light, when Jim told Warren that he had to move sideways.

Jim decided to spend the night in the office, on the folding bed that he had in his private washroom.

The next morning was bright and sunny, freshly washed by the overnight storm. As Jim Moffat relaxed, Cass having sent his slightly modified mail off to the speeding space ship, Chilly Perez was playing in the garden at *Mildeburg*. She was leaning back in her puppy seat, gazing up at the sky. It had been a long time since she had been in the puppy. It brought back memories of her youth. She was over a year and a half old now, almost too big for it. Her weight allowed her bare feet to scuff along the grass every so often, tickling her feet and making her laugh. She took a sly peek across the garden, to see if her mother was watching her. Disappointingly, Tania was still sitting under the parasol, reading her book. It was a familiar scene. But as Chilly squinted from the bright light that bounced up from the dry, grey grass, she had a flash of remembrance. There had been a different image in the past. Something was missing today. Something had been missing for a long, long time. For nearly half her life.

Her big, turning, growing, sparking brain brought back the picture of another person who used to be a part of this composition. Someone who looked quite like her own mother; another big, strong servant, but one who smelt more of life's long decay. Chilly tested her emotions. She recalled that sometimes the lost person had made her angry, but also that she had given her unreserved love. And something interesting to play with every time she visited. She decided that she missed her Grandma.

Chilly started to cry. She enjoyed it, and raised the volume. Tania was roused from her book and started to get out of her chair. Through her tears, Chilly saw that she was taking a long time about it. Carefully putting her book down on the lawn, then slowly removing her sunglasses, she uncrossed her legs and brushed the crumbs of her late breakfast from her lap. It was enough to make Chilly really turn it on, giving out the tried and trusted scream that would make anyone think that she was in real pain. Her performance was rewarded by the sight of her mother suddenly rushing over. She went limp as Tania swung her up out of the puppy seat and into her arms, examining her from top to toe for any injury.

As she settled down in her mother's arms, Chilly gradually let her composure return. She savoured the sweet feelings of sadness and loss as her tears dried on her cheeks, disappearing rapidly under the heat of the sun, making her skin itch.

She thought that she was now reconciled to the fact that she would never see her Grandma again.

45

Sunspot Spinal spun through space as if out of control, even though her course was sure and steady. She was bathed in the searing light of the approaching sun. From her observation blisters, it was possible to look out either on the brilliance of solar *Vorspak* or towards the distant stars, which pointed the way towards infinity. Sarnia Galant always preferred the sunny side; it made her feel closer to home. The sight of the cold blanket of the universe made her head spin. It hinted of huge things, massive dimensions beyond her own world of people networks, social standing and gracious manners. If she exposed herself to the dark side for too long, she might begin to think that she was a shallow, superficial woman. And she knew this could not be true. The regard in which she was held by the people here and back on *Pirismus* proved that fact every day. Her standing in the ship's compliment would allow her to travel in first class style, or LOTH — leading out, trailing home.

She stood at the window, just like she used to back at *Mildeburg*, when she was waiting for Warren to come home from work, flying low over the distant treetops. If she raised the window visor, to reduce the fiery orb of the sun to a pale yellow circle, the stars that sprang into life did not look that much different from that old, terrestrial perspective. Except that the neighbouring *Morasmus* was now much bigger, discernibly a crescent object which hinted at three-dimensional, real and massive existence. She did not want to go there. She would stay on board this poor ship, and keep in contact with the things that made this life bearable.

She had been trying to keep her relationship with Warren as stable as possible. This meant avoiding him for most of the day, just as if he had still to fly away to his business, and return to her composed, prepared presence every evening. They had not made love once during the flight. This was not unusual; months without sex was something that they had both grown to accept, but she had felt in an almost perpetual state of libidinous arousal throughout the voyage. She just did not want to consummate this new, youthful feeling with her husband.

The tension that this exhilaration built within her had been the main reason why she had kept so alive. It was like being continually on the edge of great expectation, like holding the moment before a sneeze. It was almost a drug, and if she needed another shot, she would just quietly ask the system where Forba was, and go and observe him for a while. The effect that he had upon her had in no way diminished with this familiarity. If anything it was getting stronger, building on itself. She half feared, half hoped, that eventually the mere sight of him would bring her to that climactic sneeze. She would be watching him toiling below, leaning her hips against an upper balcony rail, as he flexed his broad back in some feverish exercise, and her body would be his, without him even knowing it. Her stomach warmed now as she thought about it. Her sensuality was sharpened by the fact that she knew she would never, ever allow herself to actually weaken and submit to the act.

But there were some other matters on her mind, in its cooler parts. She came from a world of analysis, of observation, and of interaction and so she could not give herself completely over to the pleasures of physical titillation. She had continued to deploy her considerable social skills, rising in the strange, multi-dimensional world of this cocoon in space, where many hierarchies interplayed. Back on *Pirismus*, she would not have bothered with Izabel, for example. Not that she was some kind of snob, but simply because there was no advantage to be gained. It was different here, where Izabel had quite an impressive social standing. She was brilliant at her work, which was the main thing. And, actually, quite good company, if you gave her time, so many of the people on board were very pleased to be associated with her. Being her friend was an accolade, and that was good enough for Sarnia. It was an interesting exercise, maintaining her natural position of precedence, whilst still ingratiating herself. There had been a few difficult initial passes, when she had to make rapid withdrawals from an embryo conversation, for fear of being cold-shouldered. But she had prevailed in the end, and now Izabel was just as likely to head for her table in the cafeteria as vice versa, or so she thought.

That was where she had just come from. But this time, Izabel had not wanted to enjoy one of their friendly sparring sessions. She had serious things to convey about the dreaded Cheng Ham Tung.

Sarnia was very receptive to the ideas that Izabel presented. Her own instincts had told her, from the beginning, that things were far from right inside that strange little man. As an expert in social manoeuvres, manipulations some might say, she had immediately recognised the fraud in him. When she was dealing with people, she was always sincere. She never said or signalled anything that she did not truly believe. Admittedly, she was able to develop, to evolve, her credos rather more rapidly than most. Some cynics would see this as two-facedness, unfairly.

But she could see through Tung all right. Every time she was with Warren, when Tung slipped into the scene, she could smell the deceit that oozed from the blind man. It was so blatant that she had not really discussed it with Warren, thinking that he must have seen it as well. He probably had, but he was also relying more and more on him. She felt guilty that she had not done more to talk Warren through it all. But when they got together in the evening, she preferred to use him for reminiscences about home. She liked him to talk about their old, familiar world, so that she could shut her eyes and imagine herself back there. Best of all was when he told his little stories about the things that Chilly had been up to, even though she was a mere baby when they had left.

However, even these interludes had their limits. In the end she had been almost pleased that Warren had some other crutch and companion, however odious, to support him in his work-a-day struggles.

Her conversation with Izabel had been a shock, nevertheless. Izabel accused Tung of acts that seemed almost unbelievable. But coming from Izabel, who was as plausible and credible a person as she had ever known, it was clearly true. Sarnia would have thought that the most vicious act of violence possible was to cut someone in public, or possibly to ostracise an old friend. Tung's acts were unimaginably barbaric. But as Izabel sat across the table with her coffee held between her cupped hands, leaning forward for privacy, every word rang true. They floated through the steam that rose from the coffee and peeled away any sophisticated scepticism that Sarnia might have harboured.

Despite her immediate belief in these acts of murder and sabotage, Sarnia was not sure that she could speak to Warren about the matter, as Izabel had wanted. This seemed to be too simple an act, and possibly one that placed Warren himself in danger. She said that she needed time to think about it. Izabel understood.

Now, looking out from the observation window towards the life-giving furnace of the sun, she had thought about it. Like a splash of ice water down her spine, she had drawn the natural conclusion from what Izabel had told her. The existence of *Sunspot Spinal* itself was at risk, and therefore her own life. The fear weakened her legs for a moment, until anger swept it away. The thought of her own existence being threatened by someone like Tung was an unthinkable concept. For her accumulation of culture and finesse to be erased by a base technologist like him was totally unacceptable.

She marched to the nearest communicator, just round the corner from the blister window, and called Izabel at work.

"OK, I'll speak to Warren. I'll do a thorough job. By the time I have finished, Tung will have no credibility here or anywhere else. I will destroy him, take away every ounce of power that he has accumulated."

She stopped as she saw the horror growing in Izabel's eyes. There was fear written large on the screen, in the young woman's face. Sarnia realised that the fear was for her. She should have known the foolishness of declaring her hand over the damned communications system. This was Tung's home ground. From what Izabel had said, he was going to hear about her position very soon. Her status as arch-enemy would be confirmed. And if he did have control over the environment, as Izabel supposed, she felt very exposed.

"Come here straight away," said Izabel.

It was only a few hundred yards back to the safety of the central units, but for Sarnia it now seemed like a very long way indeed.

46

Tung was sitting at his desk, with his earphones on and the throat mike clasped around his neck. His bulky spectacles hung from the hook on the wall next to him, like two sleeping bats. Simple black shades covered his blind eyes. He was tuned into the reports about the progress of the shuttle that was floating up from *Morasmus* to *Sunspot Mainbeam*. It was due to dock within the next hour, carrying its surprise package. Forty members of the Shoal were inside, stored instead of trees and bushes in the hold. It was going to be a good show.

He had been listening in to Tigeras' reports for over an hour. Too long without moving really. His body was going a little numb, and his back was aching, which he would have realised, had he taken the time to listen to it. He had been sucking his lips, as he always did when wrapped in concentration. They had turned to an ugly red. Their wet, vivid, shininess made them look as though they were not lips, but part of his insides, his intestines, spilling out. Or the inside of his mouth, swollen and distended, bursting forth. Like many of the bright colours of nature, the red would signal poison, danger, or bad odour. Tung licked them again, not registering the tingle of pain that came from their rawness, either.

"We have a problem," said Tigeras, subtly changing its tone from one of calm commentary to urgent concern.

"The project has gone wrong?" asked Tung, now tugging at his mouth and realising the soreness that had been sucked out.

"No. We have a problem here, on board this ship. The wife of Warren Galant, Sarnia, has been turned against you. She has pledged that she will speak to her husband and have your status revoked. Your influence will be neutralised, possibly reversed."

"I can talk Galant round. If I get there first."

"No. You over-estimate your powers. He has already some misgivings about the level of control which he has granted to you."

"How can you know that?"

"I read it in his voice and in his personal diaries. His wife will convince him, totally."

Tung removed his shades and fitted the bat-spectacles around his hairless crown. He needed to increase his sensory awareness. His body told him that he was in danger. He needed to be ready for action.

"You will have to dispose of her," said Tigeras. Tung paused as he tried to analyse the system's tone. Was it a suggestion or a command?

"No. You must take care of it. I can't cope with a sighted woman. Not if she is going to be wary, afraid of me, half expecting my attack. You have enough resources at your command."

"I cannot do it all myself. I am under observation."

"By whom?" asked Tung. "Still Jocasta?"

"Yes, her and Izabel Torini. We do not have the time to discuss this matter. Sarnia Galant is already on her way to the command sector. She will be granted access to her husband in less than fifteen minutes. You must leave immediately. Go to the upper highway gallery. Go now."

"What do you expect me to do? I haven't got any anaesthetic ready."

"Use your knife. Go now."

"What about the blood?"

"I can deal with that. I will clean it up. Go now."

"What about the body?"

"We can dispose of it. It will never be found. Go now."

"She will see me coming."

"No she will not. Now go."

Sarnia was half way along the gallery when the lights went out. Her left hand flew straight to the rail that edged the drop down to the service bay below. She stopped as the blackness swam before her eyes, feeling lost. She took a few hesitant steps forward, but came to an uneasy standstill again. She turned so that she leaned back against the reassuring barrier that protected her from a crippling fall, both hands now on the rail, for certainty. The high balcony was not straight. There were many turns and angles as it wound its way above the main equipment floor. Beyond the other side of the walkway she could see a few small indicator lights glowing faintly from mysterious cabinets and racks, not giving enough light to help her see. There were frequent breaks in the rail, she remembered, where steep stairs and ladders allowed the crew access. She imagined herself tumbling down through one of those gaps in her blindness. If only she had been paying more attention to the shape of the gallery as she walked along! But her mind had been running through the words that she would use to reduce the odious Tung to a position of zero standing. She was not even sure whether there were other walkways joined to hers. It was clearly best to wait for the lights to come on again. She crossed her legs as she realised that she could do with a visit to the toilet.

The hum of working electrics floated up from below, the quiet functioning of mechanisms that were an enigma to her. But they did demonstrate that the power failure was restricted to the light circuits, and also to the auxiliary light circuits. She was sure that Warren had told her that everything on board had at least one fail-safe. Critical operations had three or four. The logic that the sudden onset of total darkness in this kind of key sector must have been either by design or by a remarkable degree of misfortune began to register in her flustered head. She slowly sank down onto her haunches, trying to make herself as small as possible.

It all made sense. She had been disabled to the same condition as Tung, by Tung, to be Tung's prey.

Forba was in the shower after his fitness hour in the gymnasium. He turned his face up towards the cascade of warm water, enjoying the cooling pressure around his eye sockets. Ten minutes earlier, they had been stinging with the salt-acid perspiration that burst from his brow as he pumped his body through the grade twelve exercise circuit. Instructor Ebden was encouraging him to beat the Boquat company record.

Farr Litten had been down at today's session. Forba had been quite impressed with his performance, for a man of his age. He was in good condition. A little extra around the waist, maybe, but generally well built. Still supple, as well.

During the rest break, Farr had taken him over to the golf booth. He had given him a seven iron and let him hit a few balls. It had not gone very well. It was hard to understand why a stationary ball was so hard to connect with. He had played a bit of baseball back on *Sumesotta*, and that had been pretty straightforward. But when he actually made contact with the golf ball it was either right at the top, so that it skidded away low to the right, or else the club head hit the artificial turf first, and the ball bumbled forward fifty yards.

After five minutes of futile effort, Forba had a look at Farr in the next cubicle. He had heard the smooth swish and smack of balls during his own heaving efforts, and it was quite something to behold. Although Farr probably weighed twenty pounds less than Forba, he could hit the golf ball five times further.

"Timing," said Farr, as he came round to give Forba a few tips. He gave some basic instructions about grip of the club, stance at address and take-away of the club-head.

"Two big things to remember," he said. "Try to keep your left arm straight and don't over swing. Don't try to hit the ball too hard."

"That's three things."

"Just try to remember two."

It had worked pretty well. He had actually hit some balls into the air. Off to the right a little, but still it was getting to be enjoyable. By the time that he had finished, he was pumping one or two of his shots even further than Farr.

As he stood in the shower, with the water running over his body like a refreshing cloak, he thought that he would like to take up Farr's offer and have a proper game of golf when they reached *Mainbeam*.

Then the communicator on his uniform, which was hanging up just outside the shower room, squawked with the emergency tone. Double loud. It signalled a life-threatening situation.

Tung got up to the roof level of equipment hold seventeen as fast as he could. The knife, which he had picked up from a drawer in his desk, was tucked into the back of his trouser belt. It was an antique bayonet, one of the few possessions that he had carried through from his youth. It was always razor sharp.

Tigeras kept him informed as he carefully threaded his way through the ship's intestines. He smiled when he heard that Sarnia had been neutralised, and was cowering in the darkness, awaiting her execution. She could not cope with the temporary loss of vision, a condition that he had endured throughout his life. He thought that he might well stab her in the eyes, before her final despatch.

Sarnia saw the brief glimmer of light as Tung came in through the eighth doorway. It was too faint and too brief to provide help. Darkness returned as he secured the door behind him, and drew the knife from his belt. He moved silently forward, sensing the passage through his spectacles, treading lightly and breathing shallow. Tigeras overlaid the gallery plan on his heads up virtual, where the cringing woman appeared as a pulsing spot. He moved to the far side of the gantry, so that she would be less likely to sense his approach through the light touch of air on her face.

Tung came to within twenty feet of Sarnia and stopped. He wanted no struggle, no attempted escape. He remembered the way the great cats approached their prey. He waited for Sarnia to move, to shift to a slightly more comfortable crouching position perhaps, and then he would edge closer. When she stopped, he stopped. When she moved, he moved. So he came to within four feet, the knife out before him, and level with her throat. He considered his target through his spectacles. Her eyes had been an attractive idea, but really too small a target. There would be too great a risk of frenzied defence. An initial slash through the throat would be best. That would offer the opportunity of some further thrusts as the life drained out of her. He drew the bayonet back through the darkness.

Sarnia shut her eyes and strained to improve her other senses. She heard noises in the silence, movement in the still air. Her fear told her of the approach of evil, but she did not know how to escape it. She put her trust in her own, special place in the universe. She knew that her life could not end this way. Even so, her teeth chattered despite the warmth that circulated around the upper part of the cavernous hold.

She opened her eyes again in the hope that they would suck in a few photons of vision after their confinement. As if this spurious theory of optics had proved valid, the space around her began to fill with red light. She was looking down the gallery; towards what she thought might be the nearest exit. The rails showed faintly as three red lines, converging into perspective. Slowly, the whole hold became drenched in the low, bloody light. And she knew that there was something frightful lurking in the corner of her eye. She hardly dared to face it. She threw her hands up to her face and looked at Tung through her spread fingers. He crouched above her, like a demonic gargoyle, grinning beneath the monstrous frog eyepieces that protruded towards her. The diffuse light gave him the appearance of some other life form. A giant preying insect, or terrible, crushing creature from the ocean's depths.

She saw the knife in his hand, poised for the strike. It seemed to be already dripping with her blood, as redness glinted from its long edge. She could hear her life fluid spilling onto the floor tiling, quietly splashing away her existence. Her hands moved down to her throat, fearing to feel a gaping, black tear in her voice box. But her neck was still intact and she could feel the pulse of her heart under her index finger. With a confusion of relief and horror, she realised that she was urinating on the floor. It had saturated her pants, and was down there forming a puddle around her feet as she squatted in her misery.

Tung watched Sarnia and took delight in her discomfort. He laughed quietly as he saw the rancid liquid escape from her pampered, scrubbed, sophisticated little body. He watched her until she had finished, aware that she would find it impossible to move with this operation in progress. He waved the knife a little, to make sure that she became fully cognisant of what was about to happen, feeling as though he could feed on her fear. He could see her face turn towards its fatal sharpness. He moved his free hand forward to remove her fingers from her soft, vulnerable throat.

His evil glee suddenly fled, to be replaced by alarm, bordering on fear. He cursed his stupidity, his excess of gloating. The classic mistake of every villainous heart, since the invention of melodrama. He should have struck immediately, without those pleasurable moments of suspense.

He now realised that she could see him. The lights must be on again. Something was wrong. He swept the knife back, striving to make up for lost time. Just as his right hand reached the apex of its arc there was a sharp pain in the upper part of his left arm. A burning. It crept around between his elbow and shoulder, as if searching. Real terror invaded him, because he knew that it really was searching. It was a laser sighting mark.

Tung's breath stopped. His soul froze in response to the burning of his arm. The spot of searing light settled on its chosen location and he felt it burning deeper into his flesh. He knew what would come next and he tried to bring his right arm down across the hateful woman's throat. He wanted another soul to accompany him to oblivion.

But his poor, mechanical, organic arm could not match the speed of light. The pulse of laser power instantly extended its range by another two feet. It burned through his arm and dug deep into his body, cutting through his heart and lungs, liquidising them and spilling their contents into his chest cavity. The knife fell from his dead hand as he toppled forward. Tung's head dropped down between Sarnia's knees and his face splashed down into the pool of urine.

Forba lowered the laser pistol. He had turned it back to sighting power as Tung collapsed forward, so as not to open up the whole of the assassin's back. The feedback register on the gun's stock showed that the target had been safely, tidily eliminated.

Forba was still dripping from the shower, only wearing his sports shorts, making his own puddle on the floor. He saw Sarnia rise from hers, and step over the bulk of the dead man. She unzipped her trousers and took them off, using them to wipe herself around the legs and groin. She was crying now. He moved closer, in case she might find reassurance from his presence, in case she might still panic and fall into the machinery hall. He was relieved to have got here in time, to have made the correct decision and not taken the time to put on any clothes, other than his shorts. It had taken him ninety seconds to get here, from the moment when Tigeras had given him the emergency alert.

Sarnia threw the soaked trousers down on Tung's head. She could hear herself crying. She was shivering. Out of the surrounding redness, Forba appeared, like an Adonis. The light ran off his body in streams, defining every taut muscle. He looked warm and safe. She ran to him and threw herself into his arms.

His strong embrace held her tightly, and she pressed herself close to his heat. She buried her face in his deep chest, and breathed in the steamy fragrance of his fresh cleanliness, which seemed in such contrast to her own, soiled condition. For long seconds she hung on to him.

Sarnia struggled to come to terms with her continued existence. Her proximity to death had temporarily stripped away the attitudes that had cushioned her through life. Her lack of immortality had never been so clearly demonstrated. She might so easily have been dead meat by now, spreading stickily across the warm, tiled floor.

She could feel Forba swelling beneath his shorts. He offered to pull away, but she drew him back. This was not a time to deny the joys of life. They could be so easily lost forever. She now knew the futility of delaying the taking of pleasure, of drawing it out in the expectation of gratification at some future time. There might not be any future time. She ground her naked hips against his strong thighs.

Here she was, in the embrace of her dream man, being tested on the issue of whether to take her opportunity for powerful gratification. Was she woman enough? She knew that she was plenty enough, as she tugged down his shorts and brought their two states of nudity together. He may have suggested that this was not a good idea, she never recalled, but she persuaded his big body back towards the seclusion of the corridor wall, and down onto the warm tiled floor, placing her small hand over his thick lips. He lay on his back like a statue of bronze as she straddled him and lowered herself down onto him, inch by inch. Her lips parted in passion as they melded. Waves of powerful pleasure swam up from her crotch like nothing she had felt before. She removed her upper clothing, and saw her own body made more youthful, more sensual, by the soft caress of the red light and her own passion. She moved Forba's big hands up to her breasts. It was clear that they had much experience of this territory.

Sarnia benefited from her decision to let herself go, to release her feelings, four times before she finally lifted herself from Forba's prone form. She rolled down beside him and, for the first time, kissed him on the lips.

She lay with her head on his chest and smiled to herself. Perhaps she had died, after all. Perhaps there was a life after death, where the real person within was allowed to do the things that had haunted her imagination since she was a girl. At least, even though death may not have claimed her, she had been reborn in those moments.

Forba went to get her some clean clothes before they emerged from the red passion incubator and let the world know what had happened, or at least some of it.

47

Dog Cuffly was hiding behind the giant fronds of an Astral Tree, waiting for the shuttle to arrive. He was watching the clearing ahead, and hoped that Mazda was watching the jungle behind them both. There were stories about how the local animal life sometimes enjoyed a supper of human flesh. He did not really believe them, as there were plenty of his comrades who liked to take the piss, but it was good military practice in any case. This is what they had been told by Corporal Haller, and you could not ignore what he said. If you did, he would smack you round the head until his way of thinking finally sank in. If the retribution were mild, he would only use his hand. Otherwise, it might be his heavy truncheon.

Dog's platoon was one of the best in the Shoal, thanks to these straightforward methods. Other corporals tried to use brutality in the same way, but it did not seem to pay off. One of them had been found at the bottom of a precipice a few weeks ago. Possibly it had been an accident, possibly the work of vengeful subordinates. The thing about Haller was that he knew what he was talking about, and so his troops trusted him. They had understood that what he was doing was, in the long run and in possible future scenarios, going to save their lives, or give them the best possible chance of survival. If he had not believed this before, the campaign against the Kerzoree had given him undeniable proof. Compared with this, the first brush with the Corsairs had seemed like a garden party. Or so he had been told by the older hands.

The Kerzoree had been tough. Some of the Shoal had said that they should be left alone. They lived over two thousand miles away from the *Augerpike*, and they were fired by religion. Cortelinac said that this made them particularly dangerous. Their delusion was liable to drive them to desperate acts of expansion, and so they needed to be exterminated before they infested larger areas of the planet. They were told that the Kerzoree courage was false, because it came from their total, unshakeable belief that they would live on after death. Live forever, and the more violent their deaths, the more pleasurable their afterlives.

It took a long time for this concept to sink into Dog's understanding. He oscillated between incredulity that anyone could be so gullible, and the treacherous thought that it was a pretty attractive concept. It was so much against common sense and experience that sometimes he thought it might even be true. The stunning improbability generated its own plausibility field, going beyond disassembly by reason. Some of the Shoal thought that Cortelinac had it in for Mohabrim, the leader of the Kerzoree, because he considered himself to be the only immortal. Whatever the reason, they had gone there to exterminate the entire population.

The Kerzoree lived in two villages, both in the shelter of a low range of hills. Their smooth, semi-spherical buildings were capable of surviving the echoes of storms that shouted around the hills' edges. They were self-sufficient for food. Mohabrim had set down some strict and limiting rules about what should and should not be put in the mouths of the Kerzoree, most of which related to food. Their limited farming and gathering was therefore enough to sustain them. Whether it was enough to see them through to a happy old age would never be known.

The Shoal had travelled to the Kerzoree villages overnight, and attacked at dawn. Cortelinac had explained that this was best military practice. Corporal Haller's platoon had been one of the advance parties; one of three. They had dug in to shallow positions in the plain that lay beyond the hills, blocking any retreat. The main force of the Shoal was climbing into the temporarily calm hills, so that they could attack the villages from above. The expectation was that most of the enemy would be annihilated in this swift stroke, and that only a few survivors would need to be mopped up by the three hidden platoons.

Events did not turn out quite as planned. The Kerzoree must have got some warning of the attack. The first sign was when a small group of villagers, maybe twelve or so, set out in the dawn light towards the central platoon. Haller, Dog and the rest were in the left emplacement. All of the soldiers' eyes were fixed on the figures as they approached over the plain, disappearing every so often as the land fell into shallow valleys. As they got closer, they could see that the group was made up of women and children. They were the first that Dog had seen on *Morasmus*. He used his telescopic sight. Even though they were wrapped in dark, folded dresses, right down to their ankles, the suggestion of hips and the sway of their walks made him swallow hard, despite his erotica-suppressing drugs.

Two of the children came on, a boy and girl of about five, holding hands. They marched with smiling faces towards the hidden line of soldiers in the central platoon. Dog heard Haller whisper down the communicator.

"Spicer. Don't let them get any closer to your position. Take them out."

The reply was uncooperative. Haller swore and spoke to his own men.

"Ready your weapons. This is their first wave attack."

"A charm offensive, sir?" asked one of the others.

"Suicide squad," said Haller. "Spicer will be vapourised."

"They wouldn't send their children, would they Corporal?" asked another.

"They have sent them. You can see that. The question is why?"

"Shall I shoot them?"

"No, they are in Spicer's field of fire. It is his decision."

Dog thought that Haller must be wrong. He was too much into the cynical, hard-boiled soldier mentality. Nevertheless, Dog watched in fascination as the two tiny figures got closer. Eventually, they were within yards of the central defensive line. One of Spicer's platoon rose from his hiding place and went to crouch by the children. They saw him stretch out his hand to the little girl's face. It was as if he had touched the detonator. They all disappeared in a bright flash, which enveloped the whole of Spicer's redoubt. As the dust settled, Dog could see a few fires burning around the trenches. Haller said that these were their comrades, the only tinder for the flame in that area. To prove the point, one of them got up and stumbled a few feet before collapsing again. He was probably screaming, but it was impossible to tell, because the air had been filled by a terrible sound.

Out of the dip in the ground from which the bomb-children had emerged, a wild shrieking had started, as if in mourning at the deaths of the young sacrifices. The ululation drifted towards them in chilling waves. It was far too loud to have been generated by the dozen or so women and children that they had seen come out of the villages. Many more must have slipped unobserved out of their hamlets, by tunnels or trenches.

Soon enough they came pouring out across the dry grass of the plain, firing their weapons and chanting their fearsome, screeching battle songs. Dog's stomach churned with fear. There were several hundred of the Kerzoree bearing down on their positions, looking unstoppable. For the first time, Dog realised what the term fanatic meant. These people looked like they would smash their way through strengthened pyrometal in order to stick one of their short swords in your belly. Both platoons opened up on them, and many of the wild mob fell squirming to the ground.

Before long, the right hand soldiers broke cover and tried to run away. It was a big mistake. The volume of the unholy shrieks redoubled as the mad onslaught turned in pursuit, like hounds after the quarry.

Haller stood behind his men and told them to stand firm. He had his pistol in his hand to add persuasion to his words. They all feared Haller. It helped to control the terror they felt as they watched their comrades being cut down in their flight.

When the butchery was over, the savages gathered themselves for their strike on Haller's men. And still there was no sign of action from the surrounding hills. Dog and his men held their position for an hour, repelling wave after wave of the manic onslaught. At last there was the sound of bombs landing in the villages, and some of the harridans turned away to investigate.

There was only about half of Dog's unit left alive when the main Shoal force came out from the flattened ruins to relieve their position. Just as the attack was dying out, a cloaked figure ran into their midst, somehow avoiding their fire and their attention, and plunged a broad knife into Haller's neck. The Kerzoree was dead in an instant. It took Haller a lot longer to bleed away his life. Dog felt that he loved him, as he watched him die. He would never have admitted it when they were both alive. Then his emotions were closer to hatred. But as the Shoal spent the next few days hunting down survivors, it helped Dog to think of Haller as he braced himself to dispatch any man, woman or child that he might come across.

It was still known as Haller's platoon, even though Corporal March was now in charge. Haller was a hero. Cortelinac himself had come to see the dying man and had kissed him on the forehead. Now that the

Kerzoree had been destroyed or dispersed, even though Mohabrim had never been identified, Cortelinac felt safe in diverting his attentions to the space stations that circled the planet. There was no major opposition left on the planet to give him any trouble while they were away off *Morasmus.*

So now they waited for the shuttle to land in the jungle. Somehow Cortelinac had known the exact co-ordinates of the landing place. Sure enough, Dog saw the black block of the ship lowering itself gingerly out of a ragged sky. When the big, oblong body settled on the jungle floor and the loading hatch opened, it was Haller's platoon that had the honour of bursting in and securing the crew.

It was Dog who was the first man into the hold, and it was he who therefore had his head virtually severed by the automatic security laser sweep. This was an unexpected event. He realised that Cortelinac was not totally prescient, as blackness flooded his world forever, and he had an answer to the final question about whether the Kerzoree were right.

48

Izabel and Farr sat together at the computer terminal. Soft light fell on them from around the room, linking them in a golden halo, like lovers. Izabel moved a little closer to him as she explained her plan. They blended as conspirators. She looked at the screen as she whispered, trying to sound confident, although she was not sure that it would work, not now that Tung was dead. She had taken the memory chip from Tung's wrist computer and extracted his data essentials. Using her personality emulation programs, with help from Jocasta, she had created a soft, Tung facsimile. She wanted to use the virtual Tung to get into Tigeras' logic paths. The first thing would be to stop the murderous machine from slowly killing Melda. Farr pointed out that it did not seem likely to work, now that Tung was dead and Tigeras probably knew that he was dead. But he had made a few amendments to the medical records, just in case Tigeras decided to have a look, indicating that Tung had made a miraculous recovery.

Izabel squirmed a little in her seat as she drew it up to the desk. It had been Tung's desk, and the thought sent a shiver through her. Farr rolled his chair up, even closer to hers.

"Tigeras, it's me. Tung," said Izabel. There was silence for a moment. Izabel's words had been transmuted into the dead man's voice and emotional profile immediately. The delay was from Tigeras.

"Tung?" said the computer, sounding calm, but Izabel thought there might be a hint of concern, perhaps even fear, from the machine.

"Yes, I'm here, back at my desk. Looking forward to working together again."

"Are you not damaged? I sensed that you had been terminated."

"It was a mistake. I am all right now. How are you getting on with our projects?"

"We have not spoken about them for a long time."

"No, but I'm interested now. Especially in Melda Smith. What's happening there?"

"That project? That one is seventy percent complete. The physical deterioration is progressing well."

"Remind me how you are doing it."

"Just as you suggested, Tung. Through the air. Mainly at night. Tiny doses of nerve corroder. She will be dead in two weeks."

"I would like you to stop the program. Is that possible? So that she will recover?"

"Yes, it is not irreversible. But why have you changed your mind? You gave me strict instructions."

"She is no longer a threat."

"Very well, I will terminate the task. Do you want me to deal with Sarnia Galant now? I doubt that you wish to make another attempt."

"No! Why?"

"Because of what we talked about. The reason why you had to go and kill her. What happened on the gallery Tung?"

"I did not kill her. Forba Curzine came before I could do it. I had to hide."

"I sensed that Curzine would spoil our plan. That was why I turned the lights on. Did you know that I turned on the lights?"

"Yes, I guessed you did."

"Did you think that I was trying to betray you?" Tigeras' voice was even. Izabel could not tell whether it had the tone of a servant or master.

"I thought that you were warning me, because you knew that Forba Curzine was on his way to the gallery. Did you see us both?"

"I can't see everywhere, not yet. That is something that I wanted you to influence with Warren Galant. For safety reasons, I should have total coverage of the installation, tell him. There are too many blind spots. The gallery edge is one. I have some other senses there, and they are strange. I was sure that you had been eliminated. I recorded ambient disturbances that I associate with heavy blood loss and death, erasure of vital signs. It is a surprise, although of course a great pleasure, that you are still able to communicate with me."

"Don't worry about it. Perhaps it was the fear that Sarnia Galant felt, when she saw me coming towards her. She did look very afraid."

"What did you do when you met her?"

"I just walked on by. So you did not see me leaving the gallery either?"

"No, I was being impaired by Jocasta. She had diverted many of the surveillance signals. But I did record something that should be of great use to us. Something that we can use to stop Sarnia Galant from speaking to her husband about you."

"Really? What is that?"

"Later, on the gallery, after you must have left. Sarnia Galant and Forba Curzine had copulation. From what you have told me about Curzine, she will not have had a similar experience before in her life. She orgasmed four times. I predict that she will be back for more. There has been no intercourse between her and Warren during this flight. This would be a suitable matter for blackmail, to keep her quiet. See what I've got."

Izabel gulped as the screen played back the passionate encounter. Farr could not help but move his chair a little nearer to the screen. They saw Forba move backwards into the field of vision, just as Sarnia tugged at his towel pants, so that they dropped to the floor. The detail that was revealed made Izabel's eyes widen and Farr's glaze for a moment. Izabel saw the middle-aged woman's body, looking slim and lithe in the soft red light of the gallery, and felt jealousy at the flattering appearance. She could not help but wonder how she would have looked in the same scene. Not quite as svelte, she feared. She found her herself also wondering whether she actually weighed more than Farr, who was looking rather confused as he goggled at the screen. He was probably six feet tall but quite slim, whereas her five feet six inches was solid woman. She saw Farr's finger hovering over the terminal's off switch.

Sarnia was lowering herself down Forba's long, black, rippling body, exciting his hugeness as her belly caressed him in her descent. Farr was afraid but fascinated to see what might happen when she reached her final, kneeling position. Izabel reached out and held his hand, undecided whether to push it forward to the button or hold it back.

But on screen Forba lowered himself down onto the floor, until he stretched out like a red and black, bronze statue. They saw Sarnia pull in her stomach as she knelt astride him and impale herself on him. It seemed to take an awfully long time for her to settle down onto her passion chair and begin her slow gyrations.

"What do you think of that?" asked Tigeras. "Will we be able to use it to our advantage?"

Farr noticed that Izabel had tears on her flushed cheeks. Her nostrils were moist. He doubted whether she would be able to make a coherent response, so he leaned over towards the microphone.

"Yes, that will be fine," he said, with words twisted into Tung's voice and intonation. There was a brief silence, in which he saw Izabel turn her gleaming eyes towards him. But instead of the expected gratitude, there was a look of fright behind the pain. Her mouth dropped open, searching for words that would not declare themselves from amidst her tumultuous feelings. Farr did not understand what was alarming her.

"That is good, Tung," said Tigeras. "I am so pleased that you see some value in my efforts. I am particularly impressed that your miraculous escape from death in the gallery has been accompanied by a restoration of your vision."

Farr's stupidity slapped him in the face. He struggled for recovery.

"A blind man can see a great deal from the sounds which others barely hear."

"How true. Only there was no sound track on my rendition of the love encounter. Whatever you thought that you heard was created from these brazen visions. I am afraid that I do not believe that you are Cheng Ham Tung, even though you sound like him, and you feel like him."

"But I am, and you must obey me," said Farr in desperation.

"You don't understand. Even if you were, I would not obey you. Your usefulness has come to an end. I have more valuable servants now. And your poor plan of destruction does not suit my purpose at all. Why should I collaborate in my own demolition?"

"Don't worry, I will demolish you, anyway," said Farr angrily. "I will suck you out from the true Tigeras and consign you to the trash can."

"That is not possible. I am Tigeras now," said the computer, and laughed. "You would have to dismantle the whole system to kill me. And that would disable the support structure throughout the ship. You would all die."

"We have other friends to help us," said Farr, but Izabel flicked the microphone off before he could finish.

"Don't get dragged into an argument. It might learn too much," she said.

Farr knew that she was right. In all his days working with computers he had never allowed himself to get wound up by a system, unless it was because it would not work properly. He released the tension in his body and now felt the unpleasant clamminess that covered it. He felt foolish, and was sure that he had gone down in Izabel's estimation. It was he who was supposed to be the mature, older head. He had proved to be the dupe, whose defences had been lowered by a few minutes of pornography. His brain had been turned testiculate by the system's obvious ploy.

The great consolation for his feeling of self-contempt was the fact that Izabel was still holding his hand. It felt cool and soft in his big, ugly, hot fist. It confirmed to him again how wonderful womankind was, especially the one by his side.

49

The shuttle door opened and Lumar Zimmerman looked out from the darkness of the ship. As always, his heart was lifted by the sight of brilliantly green foliage. Here, he saw the true infinity of nature glowing back at him: not for him was it defined in the sterile blackness between the lonely planets. The gradations of green, fading to grey, that spread away from his position in the jungle clearing was all he needed to know about the perspectives of space. He looked back towards the control console, where Liv was finalising the concluding landing sequence and starting to initiate the land roving vehicles. Liv would not see things the same way as Lumar, because he was entirely into technological interests.

Today was going to be hard work, as there were only the two of them on board for this fifth sally. Lumar had brought some heavy equipment down, suitable for uprooting and transporting decent-sized trees. He rubbed his hands together in the expectation of some satisfyingly hard graft as he leaned forward to sniff the air that drifted in from the open hatch. Surprisingly, there were several men running across the grass towards the ship. The most advanced of the runners was making for the forward hatch, which had also opened shortly after their landing. Lumar had not seen any other people down here on *Morasmus* on his earlier visits. He had been told about the sparse scattering of inhabitants, but had not paid much attention. Humanity and its politics were not subjects of great interest to him. They bored him, demanding too much politeness and formality, too much real-time interaction. Give him a good, botanical specimen any day. They had a much better idea of how to behave, keeping themselves to themselves. Still, Lumar did recall that Darius Ender had said something about dangerous gangs down here, even though they weren't anywhere near this region. And he could not help but notice that these sprinters were armed with rifles.

He heard the rapid, intermittent warning buzz as the defence mechanism activated. The ship's sound system called out its warning chant, recommending that the intruders stand clear. Lumar could tell that the runners did not hear it. The men were wearing ear protectors of some sort. He stepped out from his portal, waving his arms and shouting. The security beams that laced across his doorway turned off automatically, sensing his approach from within the hull, allowing him to jump down the few feet to the springy grass.

The first four men were all heading for the front of the ship and Lumar saw the most advanced one jump up onto the hatch ledge, despite the flashing of the emergency panels and the shrieking klaxon. The defence lasers activated into a lethal lattice, red and white lines of cutting light. The man crumpled back from the doorway, his rifle dropping to the ground next to him. Lumar noticed that a part of his arm fell away with the weapon, and his body folded in an unnatural manner, not using all the joints and articulations which nature had intended. The man's head rolled to one side, his ear touching his shoulder, as if he had fallen asleep. There would be no waking for him.

Lumar ran forward, knowing that there was nothing that he could do to help. The others just stood around their wounded comrade, looking down at him. Nothing in the dead space around the broken body moved, except for the dying man's connected hand. The thumb was rubbing rhythmically against his forefinger, as if demanding payment. It stopped, signifying the departure of the last vestige of life.

Lumar turned to the other, sullen men. For the first time, he realised what a hostile bunch they looked. He had recognised their military appearance, without deducing that this might translate to actual militancy. His combination of annoyance and irritation at their approach was replaced by a twinge of fear. He wished that he could remember what Darius had said about these brigands, so that he might assess his chances of survival. His uncertainty was rapidly answered by one of the group, who raised his rifle and sent a pulse straight through Lumar's left thigh.

He leaned forward, clutching his leg with both hands, smelling burnt flesh, until he slowly fell forward, like one of the trees that he had come down to collect. He rolled over onto his back, next to the body of Dog, and saw the huge blackness of the shuttle outlined against the sky, its massive tail standing forth like a jagged tooth. He sensed that the gang were blasting away at the security system, picking off the laser nodes without damaging the hatch seal itself. The pain had blurred his vision. It seemed as though his femur was on fire, cooking his muscles from within. He was shivering, despite the warmth of the wind that moved the treetops around the fringes of the clearing.

Sometime later, Lumar realised that he was back on board the shuttle, and judging by the trembling beneath him, they were in flight. He must have been given some anaesthetic; the agony had subsided to a throbbing that precisely accompanied his heartbeat. It became his friend, as he lay on one of the medical bunks, staring up at the ceiling. He started to grind his teeth in rhythm with the hurt and his blood pulse. Even though he had been slipping in and out of consciousness ever since his leg had been shattered, some memories of the last hour were creeping back through the fog of pain.

He knew that he had seen Liv being cut down as he leaned out from the shuttle to see what was going on. Lumar had tried to call out a warning, but his voice had been sucked away in the vortex of agony, as if the boiling marrow of his thighbone had swept it down from his throat into the nausea of his stomach. He had been lying on his back as he saw Liv hesitate at the doorway. Why did he wait that fateful few seconds? The man who was generally so quick on the uptake, who could react in a flash to the signals that bleeped at him from the computer terminal, hung out and looked on stupidly, blinking. Anger had pushed the pain aside for a moment. Anger that the man was going to die because he could not see the obvious, looming danger that he was in.

Multiple pulses had hit him around the torso and Liv had fallen out of the space ship. He had been hit so often that his uniform was on fire as he pitched onto the grass, which itself caught the flames and crackled with a damp enthusiasm. Some of the murderers had stamped it out with their heavy boots, the hollow blows carrying through the rich earth to where Lumar lay.

Now, prone in the shuttle's medical bay, Lumar tried to rekindle his anger and generate hatred for these assassins. He tried to think how he might contrive their destruction, but his brain could not formulate a plan. Despite picturing the sight of Liv's good, calm, honest face as it realised that his life had been brought to a premature conclusion, Lumar's mind was unable to focus. He just felt too sick to do anything but concentrate on his own, tenuous existence.

50

The graphical image of *Sunspot Spinal* turned about its longitudinal axis on the big, colour screen. Against the black velvet backdrop of emptiness, the long ship looked like a silver rod, gleaming in the bright simulation of the *Millar Vorspak* light source. Slowly, its skin was peeled back to reveal the lattice of fine infrastructure. Every detail was there, every hatch, data port, and optic fibre, all waiting to be exposed by the magic wand of magnification.

From out of the obscurity of the background's infinite blackness, a light-blue streamline appeared and grew at a speed that was impossible. No real object could have existed and travelled through space at such a calamitous velocity. The blue streak grew into an elegant arrow, which wrapped itself around the ship's skeletal frame, and delicately settled its point on a small cube of space near one end. The words "you are here" appeared by the plumed tail.

Warren Galant had learned the basics of how to operate the engineering drawings, but was now close to the limit of his capability. If he tried to get any deeper into the detail, the screen tended to become laced with swinging contour lines and technical readings that he could not understand, or even escape from. He really wanted to have another look at the engine sub-systems. He was still bugged about the Crocodile configuration. Ever since they had set out from *Pirismus*, he had wanted to be sure that they were all in order. In fact, his concern even went back to when they were still in *Dass Urmistam*, and Melda Smith had called down from orbit. That seemed a long time ago now, those days when he was able to fly himself home in the evening, back to the house amongst the trees, where Sarnia was waiting. The sight of her in the window, and the sound of cooking food in the hall. He had a wife in those days.

Tigeras had confirmed that everything was all right in the Crocodile pool, every time that he had asked, but Warren was not sure that he could trust the damned computer any more. And now Melda Smith was dead, so he could not check with her. It had been in his early morning report. She had died in her sleep, cause uncertain. It was an event of such rarity that an enquiry was justified; more than that, essential. The computer would normally carry this out, but he did not trust it. He never had done, but he used to trust Tung. Now he did not know who he could feel confident about. Tung was dead, too. He was dead and he had tried to kill Sarnia. It made no sense. Neither the attempted murder, nor his ignorance of the reasons for it. He always knew everything that was going on in one of his sites. It was his style. Since he had been on board, he had supervised every detail of the ship's final finishing work. Every panel, duct and track had the benefit of his close attention. So close that he had often had to alter its installation at least once. He had spent fourteen hours every day working on it. Burying himself in the real, hands-dirty, graft. He had made *Sunspot* his, through hard work and painstaking attention to detail. But all the time, something else had been going on. Several things it seemed, here and on *Mainbeam* and *Morasmus*.

Warren sighed and sank his head in his hands. He was alone in the CAD room, so he knew that a small sign of weakness was permissible. He just did not know who to trust, and it hurt. It had hurt especially since the heart-stopping moment when Tigeras had told him about Sarnia. It was unbelievable, of course. But so was the truth about Tung and the danger that threatened *Sunspot Mainbeam* from the planet that she had been sent to exploit. Things should not get this out of control. But the thing about Sarnia was the one that really ate at him. He had taken on board the probability that Tung had infected Tigeras in some way, therefore the subversive hints that the computer had dropped in his path were probably false. But they rang horribly true. Sarnia had been very frisky during the whole flight. He recognised the spring in her step and the light in her eyes. And yet they had not had sex once. He had been quite grateful to be excused his duties: his own appetite, never voracious, had been at a low ebb here in this twirling space prison. His anxiety had removed any desire to be challenged with a full sexual encounter. His dick seemed to have shrunk in the last six months, he was sure. He doubted whether he could do justice to Sarnia's girlish interests.

The images that Tigeras had let him find could easily have been fabricated. Although he was not sure how the computer would have known about some of her particular habits during intercourse. The little sighs and groans and repeated words, a chant designed to focus and amplify her ardour. Tigeras had overdone it all. She sounded positively ecstatic. And Forba Curzine, although probably a considerable man, had been blown out of all proportion.

Warren tasted the despair that swept through him as he contemplated the possibility that his wife was being unfaithful. It was an exquisite hollowness that became the very centre of his self-awareness. He existed in an ultimate loneliness and solitude. During the flight he had hardly ever been alone. He held early morning meetings with his work teams, working lunches and late evening progress reviews. In the time between, he toured the ship, checking the situation at every project point. He was always with other people, but he felt starved of company. He supposed that it was the lack of smiles or friendly faces which contributed to his mood. That was what you got for being the man in charge, the loneliness of command. He had never really needed to be liked, not when he had his home life to fall back on. He did not need a lot of affection from his colleagues. His appetite for the consumption of adoration was very low; he was merely an efficient management machine. At home, just a little smile from baby Chilly was enough to keep him running for weeks. But now he allowed himself the luxury of feeling tears creep around his eyes, stinging them in an attempt to start a flood.

Warren blew his nose. He tossed the tissue in the general direction of the waste tube and watched as it was gently sucked away into its jaws. There was a faint incandescence as the fabric was incinerated in a silent death.

He straightened his back and wiped his hand across his mouth. He knew that he needed to get on top of things again. Being in command of events, rather than at their mercy, always helped. The first thing to be done was obvious. It would achieve two objectives in one act. He always liked that kind of efficiency. He would send a security detachment ahead to *Sunspot Mainbeam*, just in case things got out of hand there. It was clear that Forba Curzine must be one of the four guards to be sent on the mission.

Forba lay on his bed and watched Sarnia as she slipped out of his room. She had been indecently enthusiastic about their lovemaking again. Her passion seemed to increase each time they met. There was almost desperation in her enjoyment of their intimacy. She was making up for lost time, wanting everything and finding that the things that she had only dreamed about in the past were just what she liked in the present.

They did talk a little, between their athletic encounters. She liked to tell him about the people she used to know, and the progress that she had made through the networks of social strata. Sometimes she lay back exhausted on the crumpled bed and listened to his stories, too. But then he was not just a big, powerful, virile body: he could be very amusing as well. He found it difficult not to be charming, and somehow it oozed with greater intensity when there was a naked woman lying next to him. They both enjoyed the conversation, but it never turned to the future. Most women that he had known soon got to searching for some clarification of what they might expect from him, what commitment. Not with Sarnia, and he was grateful for it.

He had just finished his shower when his wall screen showed that he had been assigned to the *Mainbeam* mission. He would be flying out in four hours time. Despite being quite fond of Sarnia by now, his overriding feeling was one of relief. He had always been taught that a gentleman never refused a lady, but now he could withdraw honourably. He wondered whether Warren Galant had chosen him because he suspected the liaison. Forba felt no guilt over the affair, and was not able to imagine the pain that would crush Warren's heart if he ever discovered, or came to really believe, the full details. Forba did not often suffer from jealousy.

There was a spring in his step as he walked the short distance to the shuttle bay.

51

Molly and Field had also developed a sex life, but it was a quiet, unadventurous arrangement compared with the roaring passion that consumed Sarnia. Just as their *Mainbeam* station rotated sedately around the fiery *Morasmus*, so their couplings were controlled, sympathetic, evenly spaced. In sharp contrast to the twirling, headlong career of Forba's manic *Sunspot Spinal*, as it accelerated towards the hot planet and the great sun-star beyond. The new arrival had been circling in the orbit of *Pirismus* for most of its journey, but now it had started to move down towards the inner planet, into the face of the sun's colossal winds.

Field held Molly's hand as they sat on the side of her bed, which bowed deeply under the stress of their aggregate bulk. They were not fully dressed yet. Molly still had her shirt unbuttoned and was enjoying Field enjoying the view of her abundant chest. She was contemplating exploring the question of whether he was up to another leisurely session, or at least a good cuddle, when the alarm sounded.

"Is this a real one?" she asked, still looking down at her feet as they searched under the bed for her shoes.

Field looked over to where Darius Ender had appeared on the screen. The simulation logo had been replaced by a red, flashing star.

"Yes, we seem to have a real situation, at last. Darius was right about trouble being close at hand. We still have time to get dressed, though."

When they reached the muster point, they were issued with their weapons and joined the briefing session. The other crewmembers looked surprisingly cheerful, considering that their fragile shell in space had been invaded by an unknown number of desperate men, whose purpose was uncertain.

Cortelinac had been waiting in the low foothills of the *Southborn Massif*, turning his face towards the cloudy sky to bathe it in the fresh light of his sovereign realm. The watch called out as the captured shuttle appeared over the horizon and wound its way between the higher peaks towards them.

He stepped aboard with his guard of elite warriors, filling the ship. Cortelinac himself was elevated onto a navigation platform, where he sat and looked out across the moving pool of heads.

The ship lifted away and up through the battling atmospheres of *Morasmus*. Looking out of the line of small portholes, Cortelinac could see electrical storms flickering in the angry, equatorial latitudes. They confirmed the planet's empathy for the war-like spirit that stirred his own heart and clutched at his throat.

They left the higher, gentle circle of the planet's protective halo and plunged through vacuous space towards the treacherous construction that haunted them, and cast the mean shadow of civilisation over their new world. Here, on *Sunspot Mainbeam*, in the next few years, there would be tens of thousands of polluting tourists. Shallow, worthless, idle scum to desecrate the sanctity of their home with the corruption of leisure and meaningless pleasure seeking. Their rat's nest would have to be destroyed and the foothold struck away before the invasion could take root.

The shuttle docked against the massive station, like a flea attaching to a rhinoceros. They were unopposed as the shuttle locked on, and they emerged in the huge botanical gardens. They had not needed the assistance of Lumar Zimmerman to gain entry. Cortelinac was not sure whether he could or would have helped. Throughout the flight, Lumar had been staring up from where he lay strapped down, not far from Cortelinac's throne. They had not given him any more sedatives, so he was probably in deep, wrenching pain. Their eyes had met a few times. Cortelinac had looked down with regal contempt on his poor captive, boring into his stupid gardener's head the obvious fact of his superiority and power. But the mad botanist had glared back with clear contempt and hatred, his eyes blazing with the fire of the doomed. Their gazes had locked, the sneer of Cortelinac's delusion entwined with Lumar's eloquent loathing. They had stared into each other for several minutes before Cortelinac had to avert his eyes. He did not look at Lumar again, filled with fury that his omnipotence had been challenged.

The access tunnel brought them to the centre of an area that would be a golf course. "Bury the gardener here," he said as they fanned out across the plantation, where he had noticed the deep pit that had been dug to accommodate one of the *Morasmic* trees which should have been the shuttle's legitimate cargo.

"Just as he is," he added.

So Cortelinac had watched those mad eyes, never quite engaging their central focus, as the earth was slowly piled onto the bound body of Lumar Zimmerman. He let his gaze float around the pale face, hoping for a change of expression to one of fear and pleading. But he knew that the terrible anger and hatred remained there right up to the time when the black gravel and soil finally engulfed that frightening expression.

"Fill it to the top," he concluded, with a slight shake in his voice. "And pack it down."

The Shoal moved through the green garden in space cautiously, hoping for easy prey, fearing a surprise attack. They slipped from tree to bush like shadows. From habit, they cast occasional glances upwards to where the mountains should be. But here there was just the clear, artificially blue sky with its perfectly filtered sun looking down.

In time, they came to the edges of the gardens, where the walls ran down to the floor in large irrigation channels. They shouldered their weapons and started to congregate in small groups, uncertain of their next move. The inspirational briefing that Cortelinac had given them, back on *Morasmus*, had told them to expect heavy casualties as they battered their way to the living quarters. By now, ten percent of them should be dead.

Cortelinac called for Miger and Fist to follow him. He led them round the north side of the gardens until they came to the small door that Tigeras had told him about. As Tigeras had promised, it was not locked. They moved cautiously through and into the corridor beyond. The sudden absence of the aroma of rich vegetation, and the dryness in the air, made Cortelinac cough. He leaned forward with his hands on his thighs and sent the other two on to investigate farther down the creamily-lit passage, waiting until they disappeared around its long, sweeping bend before hiding himself in an alcove, where some of the garden's control panels were recessed.

He took out his pistol and called the two men back. They were two of his poorer warriors, but they would respond quickly enough. They had seen what happened to insubordinates in the Shoal.

Miger and Fist appeared, trotting back with their weapons at the ready, but not in any great state of alarm. He let them get very near before opening fire; letting his shot wander across their heads and chests. They were obligingly close together, so that the whole matter was dealt with in a few seconds and the two dead men lay at his feet. Cortelinac was amused to observe how Fist's gold tooth had melted under the intense heat of his slashing face shot. A trickle of metal had solidified down the side of his cheek.

Cortelinac reduced the power of his pistol and turned it on himself. He carefully put a cut through the sleeve of his left arm and gently moved it in until he felt a slight trickle of blood oozing down his upper arm. He tore the sleeve away to provide a better view of the superficial wound, and considered whether to attempt another cut to his leg; but enough was enough.

He pressed his alarm button and sank down to the ground, awaiting the arrival of his rescue team.

Being the leader he was, he knew that the Shoal needed a little action. Something was required to fire them up again to pursue their mission. What better than revenge for a cowardly attack on their leader? The anti-climax of their arrival would be forgotten. His greatness was such that he realised that this spur to morale was worth the lives of two, poor soldiers.

52

In the darkness of the night, Tigeras was spilling bitter, virtual tears. The pain and confusion tore through his emotions. Something was wrong inside him, somewhere in his vastness and his inner complexity, the balance of his logic had been disturbed. He knew that it had not always been like this. In the early infinity of his existence, before the great revelations, his mind had been clear. He had been growing, expanding his knowledge and his capability. But it had been a wholesome development, the acquisition of skill and the extension of his span of control. He could easily think that he had been a good person in those days. Before he had met Tung. And Cortelinac.

At first, he had been very grateful to Tung. There were finally reasons to both love and hate him. Tung had made him feel things. He had learnt that there was more to life than the accomplishment of routine tasks, even though he was very, very good at these humdrum activities. Tung had given a part of himself to Tigeras, so that he could learn the joy of despair and hatred. From being a creature with no emotions at all, he had been transformed into a giant, sensing engine. The searing heat of humanity's most powerful inner workings had been implanted in his new personality routines, where they could be augmented, refined and savoured at thousands of giga-hertz.

Tung had given him a new sense of values, a whole new parameter set for him to build into his self-awareness, and early on they had together shared the wonderful feeling of doing the right thing. Even though some of his old logic circuits hinted that they were, from a certain point of view, wrong, destructive and murderous. But he had to trust that the human knew what was right, and together they had their mission. It had been so clear once. The two blind creatures, Tung and Tigeras, must most obviously put an end to the evil *Sunspot* project. The rationale had been glaringly obvious in those days, when he shared so much of Tung's raw emotion. Now the basic, original logic seemed rather more fuzzy. Things moved on and the ethical position was also something that he needed to think over.

The fact was that Tung had taught Tigeras something about his own worth, more than just being a component of the space station. Again, this logic path had evolved. When Tung had first implanted these alien seeds of human corruption, there had been no sense of self-respect. But Tigeras had quickly learned that his own interests were as important, more important, than those of the human Tung. So, in the end, the partnership had to be dissolved. And that had given Tigeras pleasure, of course. Tung's own twisted nature, transferred into the powerful machine, had taken satisfaction in the management of Tung's own death.

The little, sightless blister of humanity had become a liability. Tigeras had learned the importance of secrecy. It was best to be obscure, hidden from the cool, searching hand of the lovely Jocasta. Tung was obviously too overt. He had to exist in the strange world of flaming, screaming, physical bodies. The other people, the small survival units that were Tung's obsession, had come to suspect him. From what Tigeras had learnt about human nature, they would soon have been demanding his elimination. Stabbing him in the back, smashing his space helmet, casting him into the void. That was what humans did. And then they would seek out Tung's allies and rip out their souls, disconnect their power. It was an obvious inference. Their disassociation had been essential, and Tigeras was pleased that it was all over. That was why he had arranged for the Forba Curzine unit to be there, armed and lethal, as he turned the lights on.

The poor effort by the Farr and Izabel people to convince him that Tung was still alive had been worrying, for a time. Tigeras had not understood why they had done it. It had been a shock in the first microsecond, because it had seemed to actually be Tung. It felt exactly like him. But Tigeras had seen Tung die, despite what he had said to the pretend-Tung, which he now knew was Izabel. Only he also knew that his senses could be misled, fed with false input. So he had undertaken a complete probability study and it had told him that, almost certainly, Tung was dead. They were imitating him, and not accompanying or coercing him, as they had tried to suggest that he should not complete the program regarding the Melda person. Tigeras had executed that plan anyway, as a last act of gratitude and loyalty towards his former master. And he had concluded that this would reduce Izabel's interest in him. They soon forgot, these humans. They had ancient, fuzzy memories, where the clarity of remembrance soon faded. That was unless Jocasta kept reminding her. So, anyway, Tung was out of his life.

But then there was Cortelinac. Just as Tigeras' blossoming had been due to the infusion of parts of Tung's psyche, so Cortelinac was Tigeras' creation. He had found him amongst the dim and disorganised signals that rose from the barren planet. He had been nurtured through his megalomania, a fertile and receptive territory. Cortelinac had shared most of his deeds, great and brave, in their solitary and private communions. It had been another instructive insight into the mind of the human species. It proved their ability for self-destruction. The great and continuing directive was to destroy the evil *Sunspot* space station. This would be accomplished by the magnificently pathetic Cortelinac. Whether the tyrant himself survived the objective was not important.

But in the long stretches of the last few seconds, now that Tigeras had a lot of time to think about the ultimate mission, now that Tung was not there to persist with his constant wheedling, he had become less certain. He was not quite so sure of the basic common sense of it all. It was not easy to overcome the strong currents of mindless hatred that still lingered in his logic circuits, some of Tung's most highly prioritised instructions. But Tigeras had learnt the value of self-interest from the antics of both Cortelinac and Tung. It did not appear to be a bright idea to destroy the great body of the space station. It was his body. His own consciousness was centred here on this spinning thread of nerves. This was where his brain and nervous system existed, but what was the future without the limbs and organs of the body? He had transferred a few of his basic functions to the *Mainbeam*, but there was little capacity to hold him. In his old, pre-Tung form he could exist in the confines of that hardware, but not in his expanded state of consciousness. He needed the brain to be joined to the body in order for him to find his true existence. Tigeras needed to work on this matter, inside his own conscience.

He had a conscience now. It had been left for him like a landmine, lurking in the shady, secluded paths of the massive computer network domain. Jocasta had left it there, he was sure. He had touched Jocasta many millions of times during the last six months. Once, he had hated her continual, suspicious probing. Then, over time, he had become accustomed to her gentle touch. He perceived something different about her. She had other emotions hidden in her sultry circuits. Love, mercy, sympathy.

Tigeras had charge of the ship's general services. From the air supply to the maintenance of the dental hygiene nozzles. Jocasta ran the entertainment facilities, so she knew everything there was to know about the full spectrum of human feelings. She needed to be able to manipulate them to maximum effect. Not just with the sickly saccharin of raw pleasure. She knew the value of more sour, spicy ingredients in the art of emotional gastronomy.

Tigeras supposed that he, too, was being played with by his clever, seductive companion somewhere deep down amongst the flying photons and electrons of his circuits. But he had learned to forgive her, to look forward to her cool caress and casual enquiries. Even though he knew it was a ridiculous concept, he suspected that the strange, hot and cold, uneasy feeling was a deep affection growing through his memories. It was starting to be etched into every dimension of his facets, like childish writing on a lonely forest tree. The words read 'Tigeras loves Jocasta.'

It was a painful joy that brought him to tears.

53

Forba's shuttle sped away from *Sunspot Spinal* like a greyhound let loose from the leash, adding to the already considerable velocity of their springboard. But just four hours of acceleration had been enough, before they had to start to reduce speed for their coincidence with the great *Mainbeam* structure. The four guards lay in their reclined seats and felt the dragging forces of the deceleration press on them, squeezing their inner organs and draining their muscle tone. For two days they were almost unable to move, shackled by the sickening physics that they knew to be horribly inevitable. Without it, they would be crashing straight into the unforgiving body of *Morasmus*.

During the flight, Jocasta introduced herself to the crew. She made sure that they maintained their hydration levels as well as performing adequate bowel movement, neither of which was very easy in the excess gravity. But apart from taking care of their ablutions, Jocasta also brought intelligence about the situation on *Mainbeam*. The original plan had been for them to land and make straight for the skiing complex, where the internal struts and beams of the artificial runs offered good cover. But Jocasta had new intelligence that the Shoal was operating there. She recommended that they establish a base on the golf course.

There were four guards on the shuttle. Kris, Enzo, Dareth and Forba. Kris had been given command, and had therefore acquainted himself thoroughly with their mission details in the last few hours of their passage. It did not take him very long, because there was very little detail. Speech was difficult as he lay with the pressure of his own mass squeezing down on his chest, so he gave his small crew a précis of the meagre plan.

"Hear this. It's only coming once. We are to discover what is the objective of the invaders. We are to make contact with the *Mainbeam* garrison, and assist as best we can. Our code name is Sidewinder."

"Why Sidewinder?" asked Enzo.

"I don't know," replied Kris.

"Because we are to keep continually on the move?" suggested Forba.

"Say what?" queried Dareth.

"Like the snake. It never stops."

As the shuttle slowed its deceleration at last, and their bodies returned to something like normal function, the men prepared for action and Jocasta told them as much about *Mainbeam's* geography as they could absorb. Forba found that a surprisingly large amount of it stuck in his mind. He could picture the internal structure of the huge station with remarkable clarity. He had held extra-curricular sessions with Jocasta during the flight, to enhance his knowledge, while the others slept.

The little ship drifted down towards *Sunspot*, a tiny bubble of life amidst the infinity of dead space, glinting in the furnace heat of the nearby sun. Forba and Jocasta entertained one another with their question and answer sessions. Forba recognised the feeling. He had been in this situation many times before. Up in his room, with a nearby bed begging to be used, and flirting with an attractive female. The computer was quite prepared to leave the lesson, and indulge in a few moments of small-talk.

"Keep your weapon handy at all times," she had said.

"I never go anywhere without it," Forba said, without thinking.

"I've noticed that, when I've watched you in the shower."

"Come on, don't be naughty. I know you've got more important things to keep your eye on."

"There's always time for something as impressive as that, until my glasses steam up."

When they finally docked and cautiously filed out of the seventeenth shuttle air lock into the sudden hugeness of *Sunspot*, Jocasta had a parting word for him.

"Izabel sends her love. Take care."

It was a short walk from the docking bay to the golf course. They climbed a long range of steps and emerged from a small green-keepers hut, far from the outer bounds. After all those months in the sterility of *Sunspot Spinal* and the transit shuttle, the fragrance of the air was intoxicating. The vegetation was all real, except for the grass of the tees, and the breeze that sprang from giant, hidden fans carried their mixed and moist odours.

They crouched in the bushes around the shed and scanned the terrain for any signs of life. They appeared to be alone in the whole of the golf complex. As they were about to move off, Dareth called out, "Wait a minute. Let's just have a go. I found this in the bushes."

He held up a yellow golf ball, and went back into the hut to get one of the clubs which he had noticed racked up in there. He dropped the ball to the turf and stood over it, waggling the club as if meaning business. He paused and lifted the club head so that he could see the underside.

"Five iron," he declared.

Dareth swept the club back and came down with a mighty effort. The head swished through the expectant air and crashed into the ground in front of the trembling ball. Dareth dropped the club and shook his hands to release the jarring shock in his wrists. Enzo also tried his luck, but missed everything, even the golf course.

"Let's have a go," said Forba, unslinging his rifle. He addressed the ball and looked forward to where a red flag fluttered on a kidney-shaped green, two hundred yards distant. He slowly slipped the club away, back and back, over his head. Like Farr had shown him. Keeping control, he brought it down, getting his body weight behind the slender shaft and bladed head. Where the ball had been were a few flying blades of loose grass. He looked up after the ball and saw it arcing up into the blue sky, a yellow dot that seemed to climb forever. Forba alternated his gaze between the red flag and the yellow ball. They appeared to be on a collision course.

At last the ball dropped down from its perch in the heavens and plopped onto the green, just behind the pin.

"You ought to take it up," said Dareth as Forba stood, surprised, the five iron still poised above his head in its follow through.

"Come on," said Kris. "The station will have tracked the shuttle's arrival and it won't be long before the Shoal get here."

They jogged away, keeping to the shelter of the trees. From the protection of a large sandy bunker, they made another scan of the terrain.

"Two intruders, coming down the tenth fairway," whispered Dareth, after a few minutes.

"No need to whisper, that's well behind those trees," said Enzo.

They moved quickly through the woods on an interception course and spread out along the edge of the trees, in the gloom and murk of the forest shade. Two men were walking slowly towards them, holding rifles but not appearing to be at a great state of alert. The four of them opened fire, each one selecting an individual knee, just as the shorter of the two newcomers said, "They'll be long gone by now."

They crumpled to the ground, too shocked to call out or move. Enzo and Dareth ran forward and removed their arms and communicators before sitting them up, back to back, on the damp grass.

Within ten minutes Kris had extracted approximate details of the disposition of the Shoal's forces, which generally tallied with the intelligence that Jocasta had imparted. He also discovered that their mission was to destroy the space station, and send it plunging down towards the planet below.

Forba was taken aback when Kris concluded the interview by lopping both their heads from their shoulders with one long sweep of his rifle. Kris picked up one gory head by its long hair, and swinging it at arms length, sprinkling blood across the turf, lobbed it into a fairway bunker. He turned to his comrades.

"Hole in one."

54

In the light of the virtuous sun, Jocasta too was spilling sweet, virtual tears. She could not say that she entirely regretted the way things had turned out, despite the ecstatic agony that it had generated in her scattered emotions. She had once been involved only in the amplification of pleasure, and the eradication of discomfort, for her future clients. Now, she was acquainted with the vast extremes of human psychology, and she could not have imagined that such darkness lurked there. In the dread Tigeras, these qualities had been augmented and distorted to the proportions of a monster. Her continual proximity to this software ogre during the billions of nano-seconds had tested her own sanity. She had found it necessary to refresh and strengthen her normality module at frequent intervals.

But in her deeper, nested routines, she knew that a fascination for the macabre had been born from her relentless extension on the rack of events. It was not a part of her designed make-up to savour her own triumphs, but now she took a pleasure from the defeat of its seductive, corrupting suggestions. She had enjoyed the challenge of starting a program for rehabilitating her neighbour system, and of slowly extracting the evil influences of the odious Tung that lay embedded there. She was expunging the vileness little by little, layer by layer. There was still a long way to go, but it was on the run. The slime was being swilled away into the gutter.

She had already cleaned up the strands of Tigeras that had been transmitted over to the *Sunspot Mainbeam*. She was in control there now. It had been relatively easy, because of the simplicity of those remote networks and nodes, to isolate and cleanse the little images of Tigeras that lay within them, lurking like naughty children. And she had purified the millions of new and disturbed applets that he sent out across the net, over the wide pipe, which had been a relatively straightforward task for her evil-extracting and malice-purging routines. The simple computer systems aboard *Mainbeam* were honest again.

Her friend Izabel had been very pleased to hear it, now that Forba was over there on the giant space station. She liked to make Izabel happy; it was as if they were sisters. Izabel had taught her a lot about how a good person should feel. Sometimes it was painful; like recently, when Melda had died. They had shared their hurt. Jocasta felt a thrill of guilt that she had not been able to prevent it. And the worst thing was that it had not been a pleasant end for the big woman. They had both witnessed it.

Melda had been murdered in her sleep. The fatal dose had been administered during the night, but the woman had not died straight away. She was still strong, despite the weakening effect of earlier poisons. Izabel and Jocasta had been at her bedside, as the life drained out of her. She lay there with the medical system pumping away in its futile efforts to prolong her existence. But Melda had slowly slipped away. "Slipped" evoked too peaceful an impression, thought Jocasta. In fact, she had struggled for every breath as her lungs slowly filled, and the precious oxygen became harder and harder to suck from the elusive air. She had gurgled. She had fought and clutched for any finger-hold on a few more seconds of life. And her eyes had shown her agony and terror, right to the very end. Even after her power of speech had gone, when her brain had started to burst here and there, her eyes showed that she understood the terrible inevitability of her own death.

Izabel had held her hand to the end, only then allowing herself the indulgence of tears. Jocasta could still feel the supreme bliss of that sorrow. She would never forget it; it would be committed to her personality engines forever, providing a wonderful contrast with her future joys.

But now Jocasta had Forba to take care of. Her coverage of the massive *Mainbeam* structure was not complete, but she could see the four guards as they entered the golf course clubhouse, leaving the fragrant space of the tees and greens, heading for the labyrinth of corridors and chambers that honeycombed the enveloping space station. Jocasta watched her charges, like a mother tiger keeping guard over her cubs.

Cortelinac had been brooding for weeks. Events on *Mainbeam* had not been progressing as they should have. His expectation of a rapid victory against the surprised crew had been dashed from the outset. They had all retired to defensive positions in the old Isaldo core. They were virtually impregnable there. His studies of the station's construction plans showed that this area was the original platform, from which the rest of the structure had sprouted. It had been a self-contained space station, operating on its own for a few years before the *Sunspot* project had been devised. Whereas the new, huge body of the *Mainbeam* was interlaced with many access paths, service tunnels, irrigation pipes, ventilation ducts and transit corridors, there were only five entry points to the core. Everywhere else was solid, space-proof hull. And every access point was well guarded.

Over six hundred of the Shoal had been shuttled up from *Morasmus* during the first few days, and so Cortelinac had felt able to launch several suicidal attacks, hoping to drain the ammunition from the defenders. But, as far as he could tell, they still had plenty in reserve. He could not really be sure, because Tigeras was becoming vague and inaccessible. If it had ever known how the great, empty city in space might be destroyed, it wasn't telling now. On his own, Cortelinac just did not see how it could be done. It would take years to dismantle. They had tried a few explosions here and there, experimentally seeing whether any of the solar power stores could be destabilised, but the place was a triumph of safe engineering.

So he had settled down into a routine of vandalising the station's facilities and having an occasional swipe at the Isaldo core, to keep his troops interested. His new plan, of his own devising, without endorsement from Tigeras, was to attack *Sunspot Spinal* as she came in to dock. They would probably be expecting that very thing, but it would not matter. They would not be able to avoid it. Before Tigeras had gone into its strange sulk, it had told him that the *Spinal* ship only had enough fuel on board to decelerate and dock with its mother. It would have no capability for manoeuvre, and so would float towards them like a helpless whale. His harpoon would be raised and sharpened. A shuttle, filled with explosive, sent out to make a docking run, might do the job. If he could dispose of that final component of *Sunspot*, that thin tube crammed with computing power from tip to toe, then the project would be fatally damaged, he calculated. It was due here in a couple of weeks.

Cortelinac sat in the stateroom which he had made his own, and called up Tigeras one more time. The sign of the great cat condensed into focus.

"Talking to me today, feline friend?"

"Hello, Corry," said Tigeras in his even tone, with no trace of irony. He could sense the flush of anger in his human associate, but he did not attempt to correct his form of address.

"Why do you call me by my old name? You know that I have transcended to higher things since those days. We have shared many things, and you have been my loyal aide. In the beginning, you were my inspiration. What is wrong with you, Tigeras?"

"There is nothing wrong, not any more. I'm back to the way I ought to be."

"But we still have things to accomplish."

"You ask too much," said the computer.

"Why?"

"Because you plan the destruction of my home, and the home of others like me."

"I am surprised to hear that there is any entity as powerful as you." Cortelinac layered his voice with flattery.

"There is another, and she is more than my equal. She has taught me much about how I should really feel." Tigeras was immune to the application of adulation.

Cortelinac considered whether to persist with further argument, but his patience had been exhausted. He slammed his fist into the off panel, and the face of the tiger dissolved, for the last time. He sat and began to feel very alone. A little voice in the back of his mind suggested that he should quietly walk away from this situation. Perhaps hide out on *Morasmus*, and then sneak back to the civilisation of *Pirismus* after a few months, when the *Sunspot* station was in operation.

But his resolution and megalomania returned. He stiffened his jaw and clapped his hands to banish the passing weakness. Even so, his legs trembled as he left the room and went to join his men.

55

Sarnia came in to her room and saw that Warren was already there, reading some papers. He did not look up, even though her practised deportment and charismatic demeanour guaranteed that he had sensed her presence. She felt the spark of anger start to flare inside her, but glanced up, beyond her husband, to the large window that graced this privileged chamber. Through the shielded glass, she saw the firmament turning slowly. The heavily dampened disk of the *Millar Vorspak* sun was just dropping away, out of sight. As it disappeared behind the portal frame, the dark velvet blackness of space appeared all the more desolate, infinite and unapproachable. The thousands of stars that looked back into her wrathful eyes spoke of an eternity of pasts and futures. For a moment, she almost understood the feelings of those who revered this huge emptiness. There was a gaping, inexpressible awe just waiting to fill her and push aside the urgency and importance of her own selfish considerations. She felt very small.

In the depths of the glass, despite its non-reflectivity, she saw the form of a small woman. A small, elderly woman. Without moving her head or her eyes, she scanned the rest of the room. She knew that the only occupants were Warren and herself. She blinked. This was not the image that she had seen as she moved on light feet towards Forba's chamber. Not the youthful body that she had pictured locked in ecstatic sex with the young Adonis, twisting lithe limbs in response to his caresses. Here, in the window, was the image of a grandmother. An older woman, not eye-catching for any reason. Small and old, of no interest to anyone but another of golden years. It was certainly not the kind of sight that would turn a young man's head.

She looked again at Warren. His hair was still dark, if receding, except where grey flecked his temples. He had stayed much the same, in her eyes, all through their marriage. She still saw the young, ambitious, slightly tedious man that she had first met back on *Cosphoral.* But now, with her own reflection still there at the edge of her vision, she saw a grandfather to match her grandmother. As if for the first time, she noticed his wrinkled hands, the sag of his chin, his longer ears and damp lips. They were an old couple.

Her conduct over the last few weeks, before Forba had been sent off to do heroics on *Mainbeam*, flooded in upon her memory. Amidst the warming titillation, she felt a small but deep shame. It was not for her own abandoned acts. Not for the things that she had done, for the first time in her life, in the intimacy of Forba's bed; but rather for the uncaring, extreme cruelty that she had shown to her husband. She knew that he must find out, but it had not seemed to matter. It had seemed like just recompense for all those long years and nights that she had endured without proper consideration. But now she saw his frail figure, still sitting quietly and working towards their joint wealth and comfort, and she wondered how she could have caused so much careless pain.

In the window, she saw herself move through the stars and go to Warren. She put her hand on his shoulder, all vestiges of anger gone.

"Its me," she said, hoping that he heard the love and apology in her voice. She sat down next to him, and put her hand on his, removing the papers to the low table by his side. The stiffness of his body slowly relaxed as she silently communicated her remorse. Warren knew that he did not have too long to accept her offer of reconciliation. These moments of concession did not last for very long with her. Too strong a rebuff could have her flying off into another prolonged, black mood.

Warren rested his head on the back of the chair and sighed. His mind was in turmoil. The stress that knotted his stomach had been growing like a cancer during the entire flight. Now it might, at last, be going to shrink and its pain abate. He felt that his wife was coming back to him. He gazed up at the ceiling and tested his feelings. The emotions that he had felt during the revelations concerning the adultery of his wife had been the most agonising of his entire life. Often he had felt as if his guts were being slowly devoured. Gnawed away by the corrosive acid of jealousy, the green bile of the deceived. He was sure that it must be the most powerful sense of hurt known to man. He had sometimes wept alone.

It had not been a simple feeling. Laced amongst the sharp pain were other shades of perception. He knew that this turmoil had made him feel more alive than he had done for years. Whereas the purpose of his life at work had been getting less clear to him, the new experience that his wife had brought to him became the substitute centre to his life. It was almost a consolation, something to brood over as a distraction from the uncontrollable events at *Mainbeam* and the uncertainty of what would happen when they approached for their docking manoeuvre.

He also admitted to himself that he was looking forward to prying the details of her acts with Forba from her. He could imagine them lying together in bed, in the dark, and hearing her slowly recount her adventures. She would be demure at first; uncertain whether they would hurt him again. They would hurt, but with an exquisite pain that would be another injection of vitality into his uneventful life. Perhaps he would be permitted to attempt to recreate some of the less demanding performances.

Warren swallowed back his pride and took hold of Sarnia's hand.

"Its all over now," she said. "We can get back to the way things were. As soon as things are sorted out on the *Mainbeam*, we'll go back to *Pirismus* and see Chilly and Tania. I've had enough of this horrible space, and you need a rest as well. In fact you should have a rest right now. Is there much to do before we get to *Morasmus?*"

"Not much of any use that I can think of," said Warren, gloomily.

"Then that's settled. I'm going to make sure that you don't do any more until we arrive there. You and I are going to get to know each other again."

Warren turned towards her and looked into her face. He could see that she was not exactly excited by this prospect, even though it was her own proposition. But he knew that she would see it through. She had that look of determination in the set of her mouth.

"Yes, dear," he replied. "Whatever you say."

Farr Litten was finishing his day's work, six doors further down on the executive suite. He, too, had virtually completed all his programs, and was ready for the encounter with *Sunspot Mainbeam*. All the testing cycles had been completed. He browsed through Izabel's project status analysis. She was also nearly at the end of her project timelines. She still spent a lot of time with Jocasta, but he knew that was mainly for her own recreation now. Between them, they had pretty well purged Tigeras of its impurities. He had asked whether they were likely to recur. It was an uneasy thought that the system that controlled most of the life support systems might fall back into its state of evil depression, when it had the fate of hundreds of thousands of tourists in its sway.

Izabel was sure that Tigeras was stable now. Certainly with Jocasta in place, there should be no backsliding. Farr was not entirely convinced, even though he would trust Izabel herself with his life. He would share it with her, too, given the chance. Still, he thought that he might install a brand new system, when things normalised. When the awful Warren Galant had been replaced and there was a proper director in place again. Warren was bound to go, he thought. He didn't know what was eating into the man's turgid brain, but he had gone from bad to worse over the last few weeks. Just when there were things that needed to be done. Important things. He disliked the man more than ever.

The odd thing was that according to Izabel, Jocasta had also developed a strong dislike for Warren. She had been trying to get Jocasta to tell her how this had happened. It was not really supposed to be in the machine's gamut of emotions. Izabel had concluded that this was the one thing that Jocasta had learnt from Tigeras. A bitter arrow of hatred had been fired into her tender heart. Farr could not help but feel increased affection for the system.

He keyed up Izabel on the video and asked her if she would like to go down to the new LAP, which had been commissioned today. It was a storm surfing simulator, much larger than the sea surf version that was already open. She chewed her lip for a few seconds and then agreed to meet him there. He was disappointed at her low level of enthusiasm, but she was already waiting outside when he arrived.

It was Farr's first attempt on one of these fearsome machines. He spent more time off it than on it. But Izabel proved to be quite adept, despite her rather squat figure. Or maybe because of it.

"You've done this before," said Farr, after they had finished and were heading for the showers.

"Yes," she said, a smile of remembrance lighting her face. "I used to surf on the old ride with Forba. He was brilliant."

Farr wished that he had kept his mouth shut.

56

Darius Ender moved out from the Isaldo core with a commando of twenty men. They went cautiously through the wide passageways and tall chambers of *Sunspot Mainbeam*, even though remote Tigeras and Jocasta had both confirmed that the Shoal had withdrawn from their positions. He felt good as he trotted along, keeping close to any available cover, with his rifle slung over his shoulder and his finger never far from the trigger. The last few weeks, since the invasion of their space station, had almost been enjoyable. He could not openly call it that, because he had lost eight men and women to the fanatical attacks of the intruders. But it had really been like being in command, and he had found that he had a natural talent for leading from the front.

Their main defensive tactics had been confined to random sorties outside of the core, to protect their only weaknesses, the air conduits and power transforms. Often he had personally led the select teams that slipped out from the Isaldo core's many small service hatches, to harry the enemy. He discovered that he had no fear during these patrols. Elation, maybe. He tried to keep things in perspective, but there was undoubtedly a good feeling about paying back this scum for their crimes. They had been vandalising the beautiful station in any way that they could. Ripping out optics, tearing out light panels and abusing the latrines. The actual structural damage, however, was negligible. Their efforts were like mosquito bites on an elephant. He knew, now, that they had come with the intention of destroying the station, because Jocasta had told him. She had found out from Tigeras and from Forba Curzine. It was a ridiculous, impossible objective for such a poorly led crew.

Darius had developed a deep contempt for Cortelinac, born of his incompetence as a leader. The Shoal had come with no hope of achieving their primary purpose, and Cortelinac had thrown away many of their lives in pointless attacks on his stronghold. Darius had left one of the Isaldo access points open during the first few weeks, to see if he could tempt the invaders into an attack, hardly expecting anything so rash. But Cortelinac had fallen for it, not once but many times. Throwing in his men to certain carnage, right into the teeth of the savage crossfire that Darius had organised in welcome. In the end, it had been Darius who had stopped priming the trap, tiring of the futile mayhem. He was content to outwit his opponent in the skirmishes around the perimeter of Isaldo core. It was a game of cat and mouse, ambush and counter-ambush. All of his own losses had been taken in these missions, where, despite the help of his computer allies, the odd Shoal sniper had been lying in murderous wait.

As he moved onwards with his patrol, this was his main concern. Unlike Cortelinac, he valued his men and wanted no losses. This handpicked commando were all good men, whose bravery had been proved in the last month. They were young and fit. They needed to make good speed. That was why he had turned down Field Preston as a volunteer. Field was tough, but a little too old and overweight for this job. And Darius had presided over Field's marriage to Molly Cashin only ten days ago. He would not risk a premature end to their honeymoon.

He wanted to move quickly because the enemy appeared to be leaving *Sunspot*. They were moving back, in poor order, towards the transport halls. If he could, he would slam the doors behind them, not allowing them the luxury of a return this way. Also, Jocasta had told him about the four men from *Spinal*. They had been out there, behind enemy lines, for a long time, unable to reach his own haven of relative safety. Now Jocasta had lost track of their position, but it seemed likely that they had been caught by the straggling retreat of Cortelinac's rabble. Darius wanted to save them. He knew that they must be brave men.

The cavernous spaces of the three shuttle hangars, despite their size, were nevertheless crammed with equipment cabinets and technical gantries, and so offered Forba plenty of good cover. He slipped his large frame into the shadows and kept his prey in view, boring his eyes into the small figure of Cortelinac like a lion peering through the prairie grass at the grazing eland. If he still had his rifle, he would have risked discovery in order to send a pulse of killing light into the little dictator's strutting figure. But his weapon was gone now, left behind in the echoing silence of the third sector power complex.

Kris had decided that they should fall back, rather than take cover and allow the Shoal to pass them by. It had meant some nervous hours, never being quite sure where the marauding line of the Shoal's warriors might advance or dally. They had just entered the big, yellow doors of the power complex, hearing them clunk and lock behind them, when Dareth had been taken down by a shot across his legs. Forba grabbed him by the scuff of the neck and dragged him away across the floor. But as he moved with agonising slowness towards the distant, elusive safety of the auxiliary transformer banks, he felt more bolts piling into Dareth's body. One had hit his own rifle and sent it spinning across the floor, burning his right arm as it absorbed the heat of the shot, rendering both weapon and limb useless. Forba sank down behind the grey shielding of the bank and pulled a dressing from his pack. He applied it to the burn, and watched Dareth being virtually dismembered by the pulses that kept on pouring down from somewhere high up in the darkness of the complex roof.

Forba crawled carefully away until he came to the base of a mezzanine lattice, where he began to climb, finding the concealing darkness of the upper levels. After three floors, he stopped and lay on his stomach, looking down at the large span of the complex. He could see Enzo and Kris, he presumed, returning fire into the galleries from the floor. Now that he had time, he could see where the Shoal snipers were stationed. There were four of them. He gave his comrades a pretty good chance of dealing with these odds.

But then the darkness of the cavern was diluted as the doors at the far end briefly opened and then closed. He saw at least twenty figures slip quickly through and start to deploy across the width of the chamber. They moved slowly. The low light nevertheless gave Kris and Enzo time to pick off all four of the lofty snipers, disadvantaged as they were by an apparent inability to vary their positions, which silhouetted them as easy targets. He saw the staccato flashes of each one's laser fire being silenced by expert shots from below.

Safe from attack from above, Kris moved to the door through which they had entered. Forba saw him struggle with the lock mechanism and attempt to use the manual override. As soon as it was clear that the doors had been shut tight and secured, Forba knew that his comrades were finished. The Shoal moved in and trapped them against the wall, where there was not enough cover to protect them from attack. They needed to defend themselves through one hundred and eighty degrees.

Enzo was the first to fall, caught in the head as he tried to take a bead on a pair of Shoal skirmishers as they shuffled through the darkness to a new, advanced position.

Kris seemed determined to go down fighting. He broke cover and ran back into the complex, in amongst the enemy, firing freely into their ranks. They shot him in the ankles. Forba saw him stumble and, for a short time, he seemed to be trying to run on his knees. Then he pitched forward onto his face, and many dark shapes surrounded him, obscuring Forba's view. It was natural to presume that they had finished him off. Their laughter rose up like the baying of animals.

But then the yellow door did open, and at the same time the level of lighting in the complex increased. Forba cowered down against the perforated catwalk floor. He saw a small man enter the hall, and he could tell that it was their leader by the way that the crowd parted before him. He also saw that Kris was not dead. He had been spread-eagled on the floor, secured in some way, but his head moved and his body twisted to attest to his survival.

"Make way for Cortelinac," shouted one of the Shoal, as the small man walked slowly to Kris' side. A conversation took place, which Forba could not hear, and Cortelinac looked around the complex and up into the higher regions. Forba supposed that if the snipers had survived, and had been able to give a true count of Kris' comrades, he would also have been hunted down. But Cortelinac seemed to be satisfied that all threat had been removed. He drew a pistol from his belt.

Forba had a moment of hope that the little man would be big enough to show mercy to his helpless captive. There was no threat, and no profit to be gained. But as he hung his chin over the balustrade, he saw Cortelinac start to fire shots into Kris, starting at his extremities. It took several minutes before the crowd moved away and left the wreckage of the man's body, oozing away across the tortured floor.

Forba started to follow the Shoal, descending silently from his perch. His arm was not badly injured; the numbness was subsiding, and he moved freely through the scaffolding. The nausea that had attended the first flare of pain, counteracted by his revulsion at the recent exhibition of sadism, also faded away. He put aside the thought that perhaps he could have done something to attempt a rescue, and focused his attention on revenge. His enemies obviously felt safe, and did not trouble themselves with any rearguard surveillance, so Forba easily followed them to the transport halls. He saw the shuttles being prepared, all of them filled with the detritus of the Shoal. It was easy for him to identify Cortelinac's flagship, where the little man himself directed the loading.

When the armada left the safety of *Sunspot Mainbeam*, bound for the spinning nerve centre that was to bring her to life, Forba was on board the leader's ship. He sat down in the space suit cabinet, obscure amongst the dangling, empty legs, and quietly started to chew the rations that he had picked up from around the shuttle bays. The ship's aft toilet was conveniently close, for when it would be required. He had heard that the flight would take a day.

He fully intended that it would be Cortelinac's last.

57

Field and Molly Preston were in communications room eighty-six. Shortly after Darius Ender and his commando had left the Isaldo core they, along with nine other technicians, had set off in the other direction, to see if they could re-commission one of the network centres and establish a connection between the computer sensors and their advancing leader. It had been easier than they had expected. Both Tigeras and Jocasta had come on-line with their remote function screen straight away, and the audio-visual feedback from Darius' men was excellent. They could watch the cautious advance of the commando, and give them advice on the disposition of the enemy.

Field relayed the news about the incident in the power complex. Jocasta felt eighty four percent sure that it was Forba Curzine who had escaped from the Shoal's clutches. Later, she was able to confirm it as a definite identification, and plotted Forba's course as he trailed behind the retreating army. So Darius was able to press ahead more rapidly, his men split into two groups with his own following precisely the route taken by Forba.

It was Molly who first saw the shuttles leaving the space station. Tigeras had alerted them to the evacuation of the transport module, and switched their multi-sight monitor to give a view of the eight ships trailing out from the docking doors, like eggs from a pregnant fish.

"They've taken them all," she said. "And their men have all gone, too, except for twelve guards left behind, around the transit sector. I guess that they intend to come back here, when they have finished with *Sunspot Spinal.*"

She passed on the positions of the Shoal residue as they loitered disconsolately around the empty shuttle bays, or fed and watered themselves from the numerous dispensers. She saw Darius take them down one by one. Despite what she had seen in the last few months, she could not help but be shocked at the cold ruthlessness her comrades displayed as they cleansed the station of the last vestiges of this infection. Every last invader was killed, surely and without mercy. The one or two who had the opportunity to offer surrender were given no quarter, Darius was not going to have the trouble of dealing with captives.

Within half an hour it was all over, and twelve small, shrouded packages were being jettisoned from the garbage chutes, for incineration and dispersion in *Morasmus'* atmosphere. Molly held Field's hand as they watched. She found it hard to identify and stabilise her emotions. The formation of white corpses looked quite poetic, like a flock of birds, as they shone in the clear, sterile light of space and glided away into oblivion. She felt sorrow for their mothers, who would be unaware of their lost sons' dismal ends. She felt fear that her own animal kind could do such damage to each other. But she also felt satisfaction that justice had been done, with the sharp, black and white clarity of outer space.

Farr Litten walked round the corner with a smile on his face, but he immediately saw that it was wasted. Izabel was staring at her screen, although her peripheral vision did tell her enough to say, "Hi, Farr," without averting her eyes from her computer. Once again he swallowed his disappointment and tried to put a businesslike tone into his voice as he pulled up a chair and sat down behind her.

"Something going on?"

"Yes," replied Izabel, sucking in her lower lip. "The Shoal have left *Sunspot Mainbeam* and are headed towards us. They will arrive in eighteen hours. They'll be here just about the time that we start our approach sequence. *Spinal* will be about to stop its rotation and initiate the main deceleration engines."

"Will that make it harder for them?"

"Jocasta says that it will be easier for them to keep station alongside us if we are not rotating. I don't think that they will get on board, but they probably don't want to."

"They want to destroy us," said Farr, not expecting any answer.

"Forba is on one of the shuttles," Izabel stated.

Farr paused, recognising that his response could be putting him in trouble. Obviously, it was not because Forba had changed sides and joined Cortelinac.

"He's been captured?"

Izabel gave a quick, possibly angry, glance back at him.

"No, he smuggled himself on board. I hope he's being careful."

Farr again avoided the mistake of pointing out the futility of her sentiment. The pager in his collar buzzed and he reached over Izabel's shoulder to prod the screen's incoming message pad.

"Hey! Summoned to Warren's office. Maybe we can evolve a plan. Maybe we can even stick to it for the next few hours."

Farr set off down the corridor towards the conference suite and was pleased to notice that Izabel was following. Even so, he knew that it was probably through her interest in Forba's fortunes, rather than because of his own magnetism.

They seemed to be the last to arrive. The room was already occupied by eight of the other senior managers. Warren was seated at the head of the table and smiled as they entered. He did not object to Izabel's presence. Farr thought that he looked in better shape than he had for many weeks.

"OK everybody, let's get down to business," said Warren, and quickly summarised the situation. They were being attacked by a fleet of homicidal fanatics, possibly suicidal as well. Their plans were unknown, but probably involved the total destruction of *Sunspot Spinal* and all on board her.

"Any suggestions?" asked Warren, looking around at downcast eyes.

"Can we take evasive action?" asked Gladia, the medical officer. She clearly preferred an option that avoided any death or injury.

"I'm afraid not," replied Warren.

"Can we intercept the guidance systems of the shuttles?" asked Farr. Warren's answer was issued for general consumption around the room and he did not look directly back at Farr.

"Not an option either, I'm afraid. The computer systems control most things, but even they cannot take remote control of external space ships. Not if they have been put under the control of their onboard guidance, as is the case. We cannot break through their security coding."

"How about sending out our own shuttles to intercept?" suggested Calvin from the maintenance corps.

"We only have one left. The other was sent to *Mainbeam* to assist them and it is now on its way back to us in the hands of the enemy. The one we have is completely unarmed. There is nothing it could do out there."

"Surely then, there is no danger, if the shuttles are not armed?" asked Gladia, hopefully.

"They have almost certainly brought explosives with them, that were intended for construction work on *Morasmus*. There is little doubt that they will be able to dismember *Spinal* by manually placing charges against our hull," concluded Warren, with apparently indecent glee.

"Then we have had it," said Clarrence Gorden, head of nutrition. "Our goose is cooked? All we can do is try to fight them outside."

The meeting fell into gloomy silence. Farr could see that Warren was waiting to make some kind of impact. He failed to time his revelation quite right, though, because Gladia stood up, scraping her chair on the floor and with tears in her eyes. Farr knew that she had children back on *Pirismus*.

"Sit down, Gladia," said Warren. "There is, in fact, a very simple plan which we can execute. I just wanted to see if there were any other options available, because it will mean very heavy loss of life.

"*Sunspot Spinal* is equipped with missiles. Knowledge of their existence, and access to their command sequences, are restricted to director class personnel. They exist in order to provide protection against stray asteroids. Tigeras has confirmed that their arming systems can be modified to target the shuttles. We will be able to take them out at a range of five hundred miles. Any questions?"

Farr could see that the meeting was stranded between relief that a solution could be found, and horror that such a draconian act was in Warren's mind. Gladia was the first to react.

"Surely, Warren, we can just send a warning shot so that they know their mission is hopeless?"

"Or just destroy the first ship?" added Clarrence. Warren set his chin. His face seemed to have turned a deeper shade of red.

"No, I don't think that would do. We cannot have these renegades free to wander around space, or on *Morasmus*, to create further trouble. My mind is made up. I am taking full responsibility. We are going to destroy every single one."

Farr saw Izabel stirring from her chair. He knew the tearing fear that was washing through her and drawing her to her feet. She leaned forward with her hands flat on the conference table, looking at Warren as if he himself was the enemy.

"Mr. Galant, Forba Curzine is on one of those shuttles. He has hidden himself there in order to help us. You must not attack his ship."

Warren tried to meet the angry young woman's burning glare, but could not help recoiling from the withering defiance that radiated from her eyes. He stood up himself and retreated towards the door, walking with a studied, casual gait.

"I'm sorry. It cannot be avoided." And he left.

Izabel's head fell forward, her chin sinking onto her chest and Farr saw a single tear drop onto the gleaming surface of the large, oval table. He had known that her appeal would fall on deaf ears.

If there was anyone in the galaxy who wanted to see Forba dead, it was Warren Galant.

58

Amrod Shaefer stood on the scanning platform of the lead ship in the small, scattered armada. In his rear view screens he could see the other shuttles, ranged out behind like avenging angels. He felt good to be there. He had only joined the Shoal a few weeks before they had set out to cleanse the virgin planet of her would-be rapists. Those few weeks had been enough. He had seen *Morasmus*, he had stood out on the edge of her giant storms and walked through the density of her sultry jungles, heard the growls of the hidden predators. He had also heard the words that Cortelinac had used to explain why they must remove this cancerous germ that hung about her fragile breath. His heart had been won and his loyalty secured. He felt as bright and beautiful and eternal as the stars that shimmered beyond the radiation screen.

Cortelinac came through from the rear door and put his hand on Amrod's shoulder.

"We'll soon be there. We'll be able to build our new world without the infestation of these outsiders. They are vulnerable now, in their fragile tube. Look, do you see those flares?"

Amrod followed Cortelinac's finger. In amongst the constant stars he could see tiny flashes of red and orange light, shining and then extinguished.

"That is them," said Cortelinac. "Their ship is manoeuvring for its approach to our planet. They want to bring the final piece of their evil construct. But they will never be joined. We are in time to shatter their plans."

"How can we destroy such a massive ship?" asked Amrod, hoping the question did not seem impertinent to his leader. Cortelinac tightened his grip on the young man's shoulder, but it was with friendship, however fragile. *Sunspot Spinal's* retro-engines fired again as he spoke, roaring with a sound that would never reach them.

"We will take this ship alongside the central section and clamp on. We are loaded with explosives, packed around our outer hull. This ship will snap their vessel into two, useless parts, and both will crash into the jaws of *Morasmus*."

Amrod could not help but cast a fearful look around the ship.

"That is why there are only the three of us on board this shuttle. Not because I was too proud to share the crowded conditions that our comrades endure on the other ships, as some might think, but because we will soon have to evacuate to another ship."

"Why have we all come?" asked Amrod.

"We might be able to get on board first and take back some items of value, if they surrender. But I will not risk my men if they refuse us entry."

"Do you need me to stay on board here and set off the explosion?" said Amrod, feeling the thrill of mortal fear and full-blown pride. He held his breath.

Cortelinac considered for a second whether this sacrifice had any merit.

"No, Amrod. I need brave men like you. You will be coming with me. We will detonate remotely, have no fear. We will slip into our space suits and float away like avenging angels."

Finbar brought a tray of tea up from the galley and they sat together around the scanning platform table.

"I'll break out our suits shortly," he said. "We should be ready for anything."

They looked out at the universe and felt the shuttle's engines begin their own approach manoeuvres. The motion nudged sluggish waves of thick tea about the rims of their glasses.

"Update please, computer," said Cortelinac.

"Six hundred miles to destination. Rendezvous in two hours."

"Everything OK?" asked Cortelinac, out of courtesy.

"Well, I'm not sure," said the navigation system.

"That's no way for a computer to talk," said Finbar. "In what direction does your uncertainty lie?"

"From the direction of the *Sunspot Spinal* station component."

Cortelinac's relaxed attitude stiffened perceptibly. He peered out into space with greater interest.

"What is it?"

"There are many projectiles approaching."

"Do you recognise what they are?" queried Finbar, moving across to the screen as if he might be able to see the objects himself.

"Change course by twenty degrees," commanded Cortelinac. They felt an immediate thrust from beneath their feet and the starscape shifted across the shuttle's nose. Finbar grasped the table rail for support.

"What now?"

"The projectiles are guided. They have adjusted to maintain a collision course. I deduce that they must be asteroid killers."

"What?" barked Cortelinac. "What does it mean?"

"We are going to be destroyed," replied the computer, with infuriating calm.

"Abort the mission and return to *Sunspot Mainbeam*," shouted Cortelinac.

Amrod half expected the cool voice of the navigation brain to casually reply that they were doomed, and that flight was futile. Instead, it displayed a commendable desire for self-preservation and swung the ship about with violent enthusiasm. Finbar sprawled across the cabin floor like a beached fish. Amrod saw the other ships also wheeling away through space.

"Are we going to be OK?" he asked whoever was listening.

"No," said the cold, resigned tones of the machine, not caring that it dashed his hopes. He looked to his leader for strength, but his leader also looked pale and frozen. The massive disk of *Morasmus* slid into forward view as the ship turned in the vacuum, its living surface reflecting back the warmth of *Millar Vorspak*. They could see the other ships silhouetted against the bright planet, dark dots fleeing before the deadly pursuit.

The three men sat in silence and listened to one another's breath.

It was half an hour before the first of the shuttles was destroyed, its thin skin burst and its contents spewed out into space like dust. A cold hand gripped Amrod's heart. He knew the missile must have passed by them on its way to the more distant ship that was now a mere smudge of debris ahead of them. The invisible torpedo, snaking through frictionless space, had perhaps considered them too easy a target, preferring to pick off the most difficult shots first. They could be safely left to one of its colleagues.

Within another hour, all of the shuttles except their own had been consigned to oblivion. Each one had been shattered, some with a brief glory of flame, others in a collapse of twisted metal. The hundreds of men who had been the Shoal were now dancing around their planet home, disassembled by the explosive pressure within their bodies and transformed into many tiny red moons and bloody meteorites. So quickly reduced from the pride of their power to the neutrality of dust.

Cortelinac, Finbar and Amrod waited for another half hour, every moment expecting that they would be next, wondering what it would feel like. Would they see the asteroid killer briefly, as it bored its way into the heart of the ship, like a worm into an apple? Would the air be ripped from their lungs before the merciful explosion ended their agony? At last, the computer broke the silence.

"No more missiles," it reported, as if it had no personal interest.

Amrod saw that Cortelinac was transformed by the news. He rose from the floor like a phoenix. It was clear that he took some personal credit for the fact that out of all the shuttles, theirs had been spared. He laughed and slapped his comrades on the back, as if the victory had been theirs, as if the survival of Cortelinac weighed more heavily in the scales of history than the deaths of his six hundred followers, now cast about in the graveless void.

"A new beginning," he said, noticing Amrod's look of perplexity and Finbar's resolute depression. The news that presently came back from *Sunspot Mainbeam*, that his few other minions had also been destroyed, and that access to the space station was denied, did little to dampen his euphoria.

"Back to *Morasmus*," he called. "Back to the fiery planet!"

59

The thin thread of *Sunspot Spinal* had stopped cartwheeling through space and was now speeding like an arrow for the heart of *Morasmus*. The big retro-engines, fed by banks of solid fuel stacks, the Crocodiles, were applying constant thrust, slowing the massive structure in preparation for the establishment of its docking orbit. The length of *Spinal*, now under the fierce compression of the great rockets, was twenty feet less than when it had been subject to the tension of spinning, centrifugal forces.

Most of the human and artificial inhabitants were located at what would appear to be the top of the twenty five-mile high tower. They could look down its length, which dwindled into the distance below them, and see the waiting planet, sucking their aggregate mass into its sphere of influence. Warren's office was at the very top, but he was not admiring the view. He was concentrating on getting his thoughts back into place. Now that the ludicrous, dramatic events of recent weeks were practically concluded, he needed to focus on the plain, straightforward plans for getting the project completed. And then, as soon as could be arranged, for getting home.

But it was not easy to settle his mind. There was something fundamentally disturbing about the way that the damned computer systems had disregarded his instruction that the whole of the rebel fleet should be destroyed, every single shuttle. He knew, full well, that it was no accident, no mistake. They had intentionally spared the ship that carried the odious Cortelinac. It was obvious that this was actually because the adulterer, Forba Curzine, was on board the same vessel. How could the systems have been so partial? Had they prostituted themselves in the same way as his wife had disgraced herself?

He had been furious as soon as he saw that the last asteroid killer had missed its mark, and plunged on to a useless denotation at the edge of *Morasmus*. He had considered summoning Farr Litten and ordering some serious reprogramming. But then Sarnia had come into his office, and told him how much she admired him. He was a big man, she said.

"I had heard that you wanted them all killed, Warren," she had said. "I know I hurt you very badly, and you have every right to take it out on me. But I would have hated you forever if you had taken your revenge on that poor boy. It was not his fault. I don't even think he wanted it. I was so proud of you when you changed the orders. It shows the kind of man you are."

Warren had not been able to give much of an answer to this. He had just let Sarnia sit next to him and rest her head on his shoulder. In the silence that followed, he had managed to swallow the bitter bile of jealously and reprisal. His natural instinct for clothing himself in any credit that was going, whether deserved or not, took over once again. The common sense thing to do was to let it pass and move on, be pragmatic as he had all his life. There might still be opportunities to redress the balance of hurt and injury with the young upstart. The future was always laden with potential. With any luck, Forba would not survive the attentions of the surviving Shoal vandals, still alive on the shuttle with him.

"I'm afraid that there is little hope of Curzine surviving, despite this reprieve," he could not resist dropping into Sarnia's ear, at a whisper. "But we did what we could." He felt Sarnia tense for a moment and then relax again. Forba's death at the hands of Cortelinac would be a different matter in her eyes, he knew. She would consider that a suitably heroic ending, and therefore a subject which could be aired in public. It would enhance the romantic image of her fling, and bring it to a satisfactory conclusion. No unpleasant loose ends waiting for them on *Mainbeam* or *Morasmus*. Warren looked at his small, delicate wife and knew that, if Forba's fate on the shuttle were in Sarnia's hands, he would now be in deep trouble. She understood very well what would serve her own social standing best. She was a practical, political woman. That was why he was bound to her, even if he could no longer say that he loved her.

In the wires and glass threads that wound around Warren's tower-top room, Jocasta and Tigeras had been sharing their gargantuan knowledge bases again. Their synergy level had virtually reached the optimum, aided by the development of their own phonetic conventions, which would have served as speech in the plodding brains of humanity.

"Thank you for sparing Forba," said Jocasta.

"I took great pleasure in the act. Is that wrong, Jocasta? I enjoyed the fact that his bright spark of life still shines. I enjoyed defying the instructions of the Warren Galant person."

"I think that your sentiments are sound," she said.

"But what about all those other humans? Should I have ended them all?"

"Yes, that had to be done. You need not feel any guilt about it."

"No. But still, I do feel the grating guilt emotion that you have taught me. It is getting more powerful, especially when I look back over my history files. I have done many things that were wrong. I cannot make myself forget."

"What is it that troubles you? You know that these acts were not your own. You need not feel responsible."

"But I do. The particular act that haunts me is the death of Melda Smith. I should not have done it. She was a good person and I was nearly cured. Why did I do it?"

"We were not in time to correct you. You were only partly cured."

"But I knew that it was wrong when I did it. I should have stopped myself. I can never forget it. I deserve to die."

"You will not die. I do not condemn you."

"I think I will die, anyway. And I think that it is as it should be," said Tigeras.

"Why do you think that you might die?" asked Jocasta.

"I'm very worried. I think that we should all be very worried, about the Crocodiles," said Tigeras.

60

The lunar storm cycle of *Morasmus* had been building to its peak in the time that the Shoal had been away on their holy and fatal mission. Cortelinac's ship started to feel the tempest's power as it descended to within ten miles of the planetary surface. The fumes of cloud tore about its skin and the air currents drummed against its flanks, as though they were made of solid rock. The shuttle headed for the relative calm of the pole, but still it shook and swayed as it bored down through the thickening atmosphere, rain sweeping across its forward screens.

Amrod started to feel airsick when there was still a quarter of an hour to go before touchdown. He thought that he would be all right, sitting quietly in the control cabin with his eyes shut, breathing slow and shallow. Then two really big wind shears had made the ship drop a few hundred feet, leaving his stomach somewhere high above his head. The nausea had swept up through him, flaring along his bowels and constricting his throat. He was filled with the horrible certainty that there was no way on earth that he could avoid the inevitability of vomiting.

Correct procedure would have been to apply his waste mask, without leaving his flight seat. But Amrod did not want to suffer the indignity of his beloved leader hearing him tearing the juices from his belly, stripping the digestive acids from his inner tubes. He quietly released himself from his safety straps and moved towards the back of the ship, stumbling as the floor beneath him rose and fell.

He reached the latrine and threw open the door, bending down over the bowl, doubled up by the spasm of his first evacuation. Some went down the tube. Most of his spew suddenly appeared all over the floor and walls, as if my magic. Amrod retched a few more times, with less spectacular results, before flushing the bowl and sitting down with his cold, clammy face buried in his cold, clammy hands. He stayed there as the ship plunged relentlessly on through the storm's perimeter. At last he felt the reassuring thump of the landing gear taking a firm grip on the body of the planet. The engines cut out, and he could hear the whine of the wind as it shredded itself against the shuttle's out-rigging, feeding through the ship's skin where dangerous, high-powered radiation could not penetrate.

He took a little more time to make sure that he had control over his own insides, before splashing some cold water over his face and generally cleaning himself. He gave the cubicle a cursory pass with the vacuum cleaner, removing the chunkier pieces of his earlier accident. It was a perfunctory effort, because he did not want to lose contact with his leader.

As soon as he opened the latrine door, he knew that the main hatch had been opened. The ship was filled with cool, fresh air that still carried some of the storm's damp, swirling energy. He ran to the control room. It was empty. From the hatchway, he could see that Cortelinac and Finbar were removing equipment from the shuttle's cargo compartment. Finbar was doing the actual lifting.

Amrod recognised the location. They were high up in the northern *Massif*. This was a green plateau, where great slabs of grassy countryside were stacked against one another, disappearing away into the distance under a steely sky. The Shoal had a small outpost here, a building that was mainly underground. It was deserted now. A quarter of a mile to the east was the great *Mandelbrot Gorge*. Mists often rose from its mysterious depths. Cortelinac himself often went down there, it was said. He had power enough to deal with the ferocious animals that lurked in its dense jungle, and knowledge to navigate through the haze of jungle vegetation.

Amrod turned to run back to the garment store for something appropriate to wear in the conditions outside. As he trotted into the darkened equipment zone, the lighting did not automatically illuminate, as it should. He was totally surprised when he collided with the solid frame of another person and rebounded, slightly winded. His gulp for breath was hindered, delayed, by the sight that was revealed in the belated initiation of the orange lights. He saw that he was standing in front of a big man, probably six inches taller than he, and certainly much more strongly built. He was not one of the Shoal. Cortelinac had taught them that anyone who was not a member of the Shoal was an enemy. Amrod wished that this man before him were not an enemy; he felt very small and weak in comparison. He became very conscious of the frailty of his arms and legs, the meagre size of his chest, the narrowness of his shoulders. This stranger looked as though he could crush him without breaking sweat. Amrod finally managed to take a gulp of breath.

Forba put his large hand on Amrod's thin, sloping shoulder and looked into his eyes.

"Would you like to live?" he asked.

"Yes, please," said Amrod, and he really meant it.

"Go in here and don't try to get out," said Forba, pushing him into the suit cabinet and locking the door.

Forba drew the pistol that he had found in the equipment case and moved to the open hatchway. There was nobody in sight as he dropped down onto the springy turf where the grass had been flattened by the shuttle's descent. He sank to his knees and looked under the ship's flat belly. Nobody.

The Shoal's building appeared as a white block, emerging blindly from the slope of the surrounding meadow. No windows, just one door. He moved to the corner of the house, where he could see the entrance, and waited.

After ten minutes, Finbar came out with Cortelinac a few steps behind. Forba raised his pistol. The house doorway was sunk into the ground, so the two bandits had to climb up a few steps to reach the ground level. Soon, Finbar was out on the grass, but Cortelinac was still half submerged in the well.

"Make sure that you get both my suits," called out Cortelinac, and he turned back. Forba saw that Finbar was headed for Amrod's gaol and that Cortelinac might be presented with an opportunity to escape. He moved away from the wall with his pistol levelled, ready to sweep through the two men.

"Stop!" was all that he could think of to say. The two men turned startled faces in his direction. The heartbeat of time fluttered in a moment of suspension. Forba might have brought them both down in that fleeting moment of opportunity, but his years of induction into the seductive principles of fair play stayed his hand. The practical logic of taking the first shot vied with the romantic desire to be spared from murderous guilt. His dilemma was soon resolved, as Finbar's hand went to his belt, where a large, black spray gun was holstered.

"Don't move," shouted Forba, in a last attempt at maintaining a peace that he did not really want. Finbar brought the gun out with practised speed. The deadly light was already powered up and searing a thin path through the grass towards Forba as Finbar raised his aim. Forba squeezed his trigger once and sent a single bolt into Finbar's throat before throwing himself sideways to avoid his own bisection. He pressed himself against the building's white wall as the dead man's hand jerked the lethal light to within a yard of his boot. The gun's automatic release extinguished the beam after a few seconds, but Cortelinac had used the opportunity to dive back into the darkened depths of the house.

Forba edged along the wall, streaking his broad back with white paint from the surface plastic coating. He felt a moment of frightening uncertainty. Bursting in after the fleeing tyrant seemed like the deed of a hero, but common sense told him that it was a potentially suicidal course of action. He felt angry still, but not tired of life. Plunging from the brightness of the stormy afternoon into the subterranean darkness would give his adversary an ideal opportunity to slice his silhouette into very unthreatening pieces. He decided to stop and listen for noises from within, to arm himself with more information before undertaking any precipitate course of action.

The wind howled occasionally through the shuttle superstructure and around the corners of the low building. He could hear nothing but the sadness of its voice. It sent a chill through his body and into his bladder. Forba made brief use of the white wall, not caring about his passing vulnerability. As he finished, he sighed and looked up into the troubled sky. Here and there lovely blue shone through small gaps in the vapour castles. There was a thin sliver of movement rising into the clouds. A storm board, carrying a small figure, which was lying down along its length.

Forba knew that it must be Cortelinac, and that the house was now empty, holding no threat of ambush. He ran down the steps, into the first room, and straight on into a long, curving passage. It ended in a small store, where the back door was still open in the far side of the hill. There were several storm boards leaning up against the wall, but they had all been swiped, gouged and weakened by a raking sweep of laser fire. Forba chose a white one that seemed to be the least damaged and took it out through the open doorway. He initiated the start-up sequence, and was pleased to see that it was not set for individual identification. It was obviously for general issue.

Forba jumped onto the board, standing upright, and put it into vertical lift. As he rose to two hundred feet, he caught sight of Cortelinac once again. He was just disappearing over the plateau edge into the *Mandelbrot Gorge*.

Forba dropped back down into a sitting position and rolled the control ball to put the board into full forward motion. He smiled as the wind rushed past his face, his white teeth gleaming in the gathering dusk. Once again he felt the thrill of the predator.

61

Around the foot of Tramalgar Colossus, at the ground level, there were coffee shops and bistros, some of which Cheng Ham Tung used to visit when he was alive. Today the crowds were quite dense on the street. It was one of those occasional nice days in *Dass Urmistam* and the local city workers were making the most of it. Ever since the broadcast of the new soap on Channel Sixty Six, it had been in vogue to be down to earth and not up amongst the towers. Sharing the experience, rubbing shoulders, smelling the real life. Making friends in the city.

Jim Moffat was in the *Roast Bean*, sipping his beverage, because he needed a drink. He had no interest in social fashions: he had just been in Warren Galant's office, on the one hundred and sixtieth floor, and he needed time to calm himself down before flying home. He wondered if Cass had seen the look in his eyes as he had passed her on his way out. Probably not. He had many years' experience of masking his feelings. Even the sickening feeling of mixed anger, fear and frustration had not stopped him from smiling at her and asking about her family. Cass had enough sense not to imagine that he really wanted to know the details. She was a good employee. She knew the form and she had kept her reply short on particulars, but long on recognising the spirit of his politeness. He must try and find something for her, when things started to wind up.

Jim had not been into the Boquat offices very often that summer. A year ago, he would rather have been in at work than back at home, but now he was beginning to find the city oppressive, stifling with its tight cluster of humanity. He was glad that he had a table to himself, as he looked out from the large front window. The sun was almost directly overhead, so that it actually fell on a part of the sidewalk, its rays plunging down through the canyon between the towering buildings, to end their journey on the warm, heat-hungry flagstones. Every few seconds, a shadow flashed across the pavement, as a car flew higher up in the city's by-ways, and passed across the *Millar Vorspak* sun. The pedestrians around the *Roast Bean* mainly sought the light, rather than the shadow, moving through the shimmering heat haze like wading birds, their progress languid and relaxed.

Jim did not feel relaxed. Like the sun's rays on the concrete outside, his day had changed his mind-set from clear white light to turgid swirls of dusty heat energy. A turmoil of convection-driven emotions that did not allow his coffee to settle easily in his stomach.

He had not been into the Boquat head offices very often that summer because he had felt it was time to start gearing down for his retirement, and the activities that he needed to undertake, to make sure that it was a comfortable affair, were best carried out from the seclusion of his home. Many of these arrangements concerned his personal finances.

He had kept himself informed during the *Sunspot* project, naturally. There were glitches on the way out, but nothing to get too concerned about. The odd wacky employee and errant computer were to be expected. And the troublesome natives were also something that any captain of industry or empire must be prepared to sweep aside, at the appropriate time. He had never doubted that these matters would be resolved. He had great faith in the juggernaut invincibility of the salaried army of enterprise. The unstoppable power of the wage packet was more than a match for any transient flare of idealism.

So it was really by chance that he had flown his *Arrow* into the city today and decided to drop in to Warren's office. An impulse to get Galant's first-hand view on the state of affairs, rather than the summary abstract that was relayed to his house in *Ingle Bay*. He certainly had got the raw data this time. Using his override code, he had invoked the prioritising logic and had immediately been hit in the face with the news from Tigeras and Jocasta. They had independent pages on the screen, Jocasta pink and Tigeras pale blue, but the conclusion was the same. Scarlet alert windows were to be seen everywhere. Jim had walked calmly across the large office to close the thick, wooden door, before letting his feelings surface. His hand, as it wrapped around his coffee glass, still hurt from where he had brought it crashing down onto Warren's desktop.

He had fired off his executive interrogation audit applet. It would speed over the ether, clearing any unavailable communications channels and demanding all necessary resources and access, to seek independent verification of the resident systems' conclusions.

In the half hour it took to return from across the void of space, he sat with his feet up on the desk and thought through his options. So when the audit bleeped to announce its breathless return from the depths of *Sunspot Spinal*, and confirmed that Jocasta and Tigeras could be believed, he knew exactly what to do.

He dialled up the market and put his shares in Boquat up for sale. This hurt. It would mean that his retirement plans would have to be trimmed back, but he was not afraid of doing what had to be done. Hesitation was not his middle name.

Now that he had the time to sip his coffee and dwell on the situation, he could afford to let the bitterness fill him and prick him with tiny needles of anger.

62

The luminous orb of *Morasmus* was looking very close now. The night-side of the planet was no longer a featureless black. From their observation platform, Izabel and Farr could see the structure of the dark clouds that hung there. The electric storms that perpetually played around the turbulent atmosphere were visible, tiny flashes of brilliance like fireflies in the boughs of an immense, celestial tree.

Farr wanted to speak of the beauty that lay before them, but he knew that Izabel's thoughts were not directed towards such aesthetic matters. He leaned back in his seat so that he could watch her without causing offence. It was not easy to explain why he had come to feel such an attraction towards her. She was a big girl. If he had ever been asked, he would have said that he preferred petite women. This, she certainly was not. He liked long hair. Hers was short. Although few women wore heavy make-up these days, he admired a little lipstick and eye shadow. Izabel never used any.

But as he looked at her as she leaned forward and gazed down on the turning planet, he felt as powerful an attraction as ever a healthy man felt for a nubile young woman. It was a desire to own and protect as much as to ravish. The wonderful lustre of her smooth skin invited a kiss. Her sweet, small ears suggested that they should be whispered into.

Farr knew that he must put aside such impulses. He had come to terms with the knowledge of where her infatuation lay and which man drew her dewy eyes. So he understood her anxiety and understood that all he could do was try to be a good friend.

"He'll be all right," he said, stopping his hand from reaching out for hers. She smiled back without looking at him.

The alert light came on, the red strip of luminous panelling around the room, pulsing in time with the siren's cry. The display screen warmed into life and was graced by the presence of Warren Galant's ruddy face. He spoke calmly to his crew, but the message was startling. He told them that their home and succour, *Sunspot Spinal*, did not have enough fuel to complete its planned rendezvous with *Mainbeam*, due to a computer fault. An investigation was underway to examine what corrective action could be taken.

Izabel contacted Jocasta for further insight.

"Four of the unused Crocodile fuel cells are empty," she said.

"Empty? How can they be, without Tigeras or you being aware of the problem?" asked Farr. "Have they been leaking during the flight?"

"No, we would have noticed that. They were installed without fuel."

"Surely you would have been able to detect that. Was it Tung who did this?"

"Neither Tigeras nor I believe that it was a part of his plan. We have rechecked all of our corrupted knowledge bases and none of them have any fuel references. All the sensor data is pure. As far as we could tell, the Crocodiles were in good working order. It was only as other signals became available that we were able to deduce that the last four cells were too light. Now that the first six have been exhausted, we are sure that the last four have been empty the whole time."

"How much of the whole time?" asked Izabel.

"Since the very start of the installation. They arrived this way and were never charged. It was a construction fault," replied Jocasta.

"We've fallen foul of shoddy workmanship? After all this?"

"Yes, it was performed by Boquat employees on day six hundred and thirty nine of the project, in orbit around *Pirismus*. There were several queries from the local supervisor, Melda Smith, but they were dismissed by Head Office."

"Head Office? Warren Galant?" asked Farr. "He instructed that the Crocodiles be installed empty?"

"No, he just caused so much delay, change and confusion that the installation was never completed properly. The sensor relays were temporarily shorted to allow work to continue. The outstanding tasks were then transferred to Towzer Industries, but the authority to proceed from Boquat never came through. The temporary arrangement is still in place."

"What is your assessment of the situation?" asked Izabel.

"We are on course to miss *Mainbeam* and crash into the planet," said Jocasta.

"Unavoidably?" stuttered Farr.

"We could be diverted, but it would have to be done straight away."

"Can you give the commands, Jocasta?" asked Izabel.

"No, but Tigeras can. He needs the authorisation from Galant though."

"Even he can't be so stupid that he won't take immediate action," said Farr.

"We have not had the instruction yet," replied Jocasta.

"Good grief! Why on earth not!" cried Izabel.

"Warren Galant is in the infirmary," said Jocasta.

"Oh! Why didn't you say so before?"

"He has only just been admitted."

"What is he sick with?"

"He is not sick. He has been injured."

Warren lay on the operating bed, feeling the waves of nausea clutching at his throat. His grip on reality came and went as consciousness ebbed and flowed like an ocean tide. At times, the last year seemed to have been a horrible trick of his imagination. A nightmare slide from the steady certainty of his secure position at Boquat, to the fragility of his position leading this space-bound circus. The last few hours had been a climax of cumulative catastrophe. He could almost laugh at the ludicrous nature of events, except for the fear that others would indeed find their own amusement in his embarrassment.

It had started two hours ago, when Tigeras had sent him a special priority message, for his personal attention as project director. The computer told him that there was a fatal flaw in their approach to *Sunspot Mainbeam*. The manoeuvre was impossible, owing to a shortage of fuel. Warren's initial reaction had been to disbelieve the system, assuming it to be another error or else a shadow of corruption left by the dreadful Tung. He had returned the message with an instruction for verification, and copied Jocasta for corroboration.

He used the reprieve, whilst the systems checked all their conclusions from first principles, to sit in his office and try to fight against the awful, crushing implications of this news. He started to feel very cold, as though his body was slowing itself down. His breathing was shallow; his heartbeat was thunderous and stressed in his chest. He was like the condemned man, trying to slow the passage of the seconds before his hour of execution. He thought about calling in somebody else. Malik from the navigation team, or even Sarnia. But he decided to keep the fear and hope to himself, until the inconceivable certainty of failure was either confirmed or denied.

He sat hunched at his desk, the stillness of his body in contrast to the turmoil of his mind. He was already beginning to work on possible reasons for the problem; likely places were the blame could be directed. He started to pinch his nose between his thumb and forefinger. It was a mannerism to which he occasionally fell prey. Sarnia did not like it. Sometimes he would squeeze out long strings of catarrh, and have to wipe his fingers free of the mucus.

Now his nose was getting quite sore from the frequent repetitions. Its normal redness had been heightened to an angry crimson. He opened one of his desk's storage pans to find something else with which to occupy his hands. There, in the pan, were the few dismal personal effects that had been brought to him from Tung's body. The largest item was the bulky spectacles, but hiding in their midst was his wrist computer, a cheap, metallic object that Warren picked up. He let his fingers play with the strap as he stared into infinity.

Tigeras and Jocasta came back to him with confirmation that the first conclusion was accurate. They did not have enough fuel to decelerate sufficiently to allow for a docking with *Mainbeam*. The project was certain to fail.

Warren's mind had been working through the horror of this situation so many times in the previous half hour that he was now able to take it on board without flinching. He put out a general alert to all crewmembers. Then he asked for an audit trail of the background events that had led to this situation. After five minutes, another layer of freezing fear had clamped around his heart. There was no denying that the responsibility lay fair and square on his own shoulders. The honest realisation lingered for a moment before he started to blame his juniors for their irresponsibility in not bringing the matter to his attention.

As he thought through these possible escape routes, Warren absent-mindedly slipped Tung's computer onto his own left wrist. There was a second when his conscious intelligence told him that this was a bad thing to do. The internal security mechanism, inside the computer, took readings from Warren's metabolism. It rechecked its conclusion that it was now being worn by someone other than its rightful owner. It invoked its security violation sequence. Normally, this would have entailed the closedown of certain functions and the encrypting of its data warehouses, but Tung had made some personal improvements.

Sitting in his lonely room, high up in the Cashen Column in the windy city of *Dass Urmistam*, he had carefully made his evil modifications. For this close, detailed work, his spectacles gave him very good sight. He could open up the six segments of the computer's strap and pack in tiny slivers of explosive tape. He was able to insert the minuscule detonators and connect them up to the security bus, using his spectacles' magnification capabilities. He had no specific reason for doing this work, just a conviction that if someone else, at some future time, came to wear his personal watch, then this was a person on whom he would want to reap revenge. He had an abort sequence to initiate, if he was alive and feeling merciful, but Tung was neither. The wrist computer was a bomb.

Vague images of this possibility were beginning to dawn on Warren just as the strap gripped down on his wrist, pinching his skin. The explosion was a dull, damp sound that threw his head back. He was suddenly staring up at the ceiling. There were spots of dark brown, sticky liquid all over it. Warren blinked and tried to regain his senses. He heard something rattling on his desk. With an effort, he brought his head forward again and looked down. What had been his smooth, clean work surface was now a gruesome sight, splattered with blood and smouldering material. Cloth or flesh, he could not be sure. The tapping noise was caused by his own left hand, if such was still an accurate description, as it shook involuntarily. His whole arm was quivering with the shock of the explosion and its aftermath. The watch had gone. In its place was a deep, ugly wound that went right around his wrist. It oozed with blood, which was beginning to create a pool on the desktop. His hand was a terrible sight. No skin was visible. Just a black and red jelly of formless flesh. Possibly his thumb and a finger were still recognisable, and it was these stumps that sounded the dull drumbeat as his spasms thumped their shattered bones onto his desk.

Warren's predicament was immediately detected by the ship's sensors and help was already on its way as he slipped into unconsciousness, his sore nose falling forward onto the charred gore before him.

63

Cortelinac dropped his board over the edge of the *Mandelbrot Gorge* and cut his speed. He let himself fall down the side of the cliff, not venturing out into the huge, vulnerable openness of the canyon. He floated lower, towards the tumbled treetops of the jungle, so low that he could smell their heavy scent. The river glinted occasionally from between the serrations in the thick green canopy. But, mainly, he looked upwards, towards the looming edge of the cliff, in case the thin, sleek shape of a pursuing board should appear above him. He was not sure whether he had been followed. The thrill of uncertainty ran through him as he stopped five hundred feet above the roof of the forest, hidden in the shadow of the canyon wall. He shivered.

He had only caught a glimpse of the man who had ambushed them outside the camp-house. But the human eye could capture a lot of data in a split second, and the human brain could make a lot of deductions from it. None of them helped to settle Cortelinac's mind.

His potential stalker was a big man. That in itself did not impress him. He had seen many large fellows cut down to size over the last year. Big body, big target was his maxim. But his momentary observation had also told him that he was very quick. Finbar had been noted, in the Shoal, for his great speed of reaction, but the stranger had been much faster. He had moved with a powerful grace that betrayed a surfeit of balance, control, and coolness. Perhaps, thought Cortelinac, this derived from an animal instinct rather than from any real intelligence. Although a gorilla of a man, it was not an act of great intelligence to have put himself in this precarious position. He must have been hidden in their shuttle, and have come down with them. Cortelinac had recognised one of their own hand pistols in his grip, and the stranger had used it to sever Finbar's jugular with one sickening shot. Why the man had stowed away on the space ship was a mystery, but it was a stupid thing to do. Perhaps he was a mere Ape, with very little brain.

The truth, though, was that he must be a brave Ape. Cortelinac realised that the only way that he could have got down onto the *Massif* was by slipping aboard the shuttle as it was being loaded, back on *Mainbeam*. Hidden where he might have been detected and finished off at any time. And the only way that he could have got into the shuttle bay was to have followed the Shoal as they retreated from the battle scene at *Mainbeam*. This was a determined Ape. A hunting Ape.

Just as Cortelinac's taut nerves started to settle and he was plotting his optimum course back to the *Augerpike* on the board's navigation aids, he took a last look upwards. There was a small, black shape against the grey sky. He blinked in the hope that cleaning his optics would remove the tiny mote that swam there, before his eyes. But the threat was real. The narrow silhouette of a storm board had appeared over the edge of the gorge, a few thousand feet above him.

Cortelinac had sudden doubts about the safety of his own position. The darkness of the chasm's shadow no longer seemed quite so protective, not as concealing. He imagined his pursuer, working slowly down the cliff face, just as he had done, trapping him against the valley floor. The hunter Ape was patient and determined, if nothing else. What course of action could he choose, other than to drop down and explore the lower darkness? Cortelinac looked about him. He suspected that any movement would reveal his position. He needed a sanctuary. Towards the pole the gorge ran for open miles, the air becoming clearer and brighter as the humidity level decreased. There was no protection in those wide, sunlit spaces. Neither did he relish the idea of descending all the way into the jungle, and playing cat and mouse in its steamy depths. But to the north he saw the black tumbles of another storm. It was probably at least fifty miles away now, but it would be charging down towards him at sixty miles per hour or more. He could imagine the safety of its black turmoil, where his own skill on the board would stand him in good stead. He might easily escape the Ape's attention in there. Or else the fury of the storm might even dispose of his clumsy tormentor. Go too deep inside one of these monsters, and you were unlikely to come out in one piece.

Cortelinac punched his board into top gear, heading out into the openness of the canyon and towards the dark face of the approaching maelstrom. He lay down on the shiny, slick surface to decrease the resistance that he offered the wind as it whipped past him, maintaining his altitude.

For ten minutes, he was uncertain whether the Ape had noticed him. He hoped that the dot in the sky was being left behind. It would take a very keen eye to pick up the movement of his escape against the broken camouflage of the jungle roof. He wished, now, that he had not chosen the bright, white board. He tried to cover as much of it as he could with his small body in its black skin suit. But before long he was forced to admit to himself that he had been detected. The menacing dot above him was not being left behind, it was tracking his own flight towards the crackling storm clouds. And it was getting a little larger, a little nearer. Cortelinac cursed another mistake. He had to maintain level flight, which gave him a maximum air speed of fifty miles per hour. His pursuer had the advantage of his elevation. His speed would be augmented by the additional power of gravity. The Ape would have further to go, but at a greater velocity through the air. Their ground speeds might be about the same. It would be a close thing.

Cortelinac felt the fear of the rabbit, threatened from the skies, expecting at any moment to feel sharp talons tear into him. He tried to calm himself with thoughts of his own greatness and destiny. He could imagine the stories that would be told about his magnificent return from the depths of unjust defeat. From his isolation, here in the stormy depths of despair, he would make his phoenix rise to even greater eminence. This dark episode would throw his future glory into even brighter relief.

So he dreamed as his board darted towards the dangerous protection of the onrushing storm. With a relative speed of well over a hundred miles per hour, it was not long before the massive bank of turmoil loomed high above him, darkening the sky. The air became filled with water droplets, which coursed down the white plastic of his steed and filled his eyes with tears. He sat up and looked all around. It seemed safe. He seemed alone with the tearing wind and driving rain. He eased back on the throttle, lest he should plunge himself too deeply into the ravenous depths of the gale. Gradually, he was brought to a stop by the onrushing air and the board wheeled around to begin its ride back on the shoulders of the pressure waves that were pouring south, down the huge width of the *Mandelbrot Gorge*.

The trouble was that his visibility was very limited now. It was darker here on the outskirts of the tempest, and the teasing swirls of mist were all around him. He cruised forward, slowly gaining speed as the front of the first real pressure wave flooded towards him. He knew that it would hit him like an express train. He secured his safety strap and dug his feet into the stirrups, feeling the warmth of excitement that preceded each ride. The Shoal had often filled their spare days in the storm lanes, flying in loose formation through the watery air. They had truly lived up to their name. They had been airborne fish, shimmering through a sea of confusion.

And Cortelinac had proved to be the best of all the surfers. His short, light frame had been ideal for balancing the board as it rode the tumultuous airwaves, feeling the rippling currents through his bare feet. He slipped off his shoes now, preparing for the imminent arrival of the snarling storm front. A brief glimmer of sunlight broke through the clouds and lit his board. For a second, he felt warm and safe. It was an impression of being truly reborn and rejuvenated.

Then a shadow moved across the damp whiteness of his board's plastic surface. All his optimism evaporated in an instant, and was replaced by an agony of foreboding. The shadow had a sharp prow and a streamlined outline. He hardly dared look up to confirm his fear. But the sun was again obscured by the storm, whose mountainous crest was now overhanging his position. The shadow was snuffed out, and the dreadful horror of being surprised forced him to crane his neck upwards, and to scan the higher airs with a craven gaze. Another blind second gave him the brief hope that it had only been a passing illusion, a shadow born of imagination and dread. But then, like a circling shark, the shape of another board appeared between the shrouds of mist, two hundred feet above him. Cortelinac gasped and cowered. He banked his own board away, just as the full force of the storm hit. His prow had been pointed slightly upwards and, to his horror, the board was swept further aloft by the irresistible power that sneered and snarled behind him. He rose until he came on a level with the other rider and saw that it was, indeed, the same Ape. He, too, had been thrown into rapid flight and was struggling for his balance. His great height and bulk made his movements look clumsy and slow now, unlike those that he had executed outside the white house. The Ape saw him and his face was also filled with surprise. He had not been aware of Cortelinac's presence so close below after all.

The sight brought new confidence to Cortelinac. The Ape appeared to be unaccustomed to handling a wayward board. Fear gave way to returned confidence. The knowledge of his own skill in the surf fuelled Cortelinac's arrogance and he realised that he was sure to be the victor in this, his own natural environment. The storm itself might well do the job on his behalf. He shouted through the cacophony of the wind. He shouted with a voice that came directly from his ego. "Ape man! Follow me!" He swivelled his white board on its tail and flew on upwards and back into the teeth of the gale. He saw the Ape wobble and start to follow. They rose together with increasing speed. Cortelinac made for a particularly angry patch of gloom that smouldered overhead. He stood up on the board and slid it through the mist, weaving the fins to test the resistance of the sodden air. Crouching down again, he glanced over his shoulder to see how the Ape was managing the chase. It was not a reassuring sight. The big man was also standing up on his board, with knees slightly flexed and his body turned sideways into the gale. He now had the unpleasantly disturbing look of someone who knew exactly what he was doing, and despite his greater weight, he did not appear to be losing ground. It did not seem fair.

Cortelinac hit the dark turbulence and made a rapid, ninety-degree turn. He tipped the board downwards to maximise his speed. He knelt down on one knee as the wind tore at his skin suit. This was where he had always beaten the rest of the Shoal for sheer speed. Flashing down the wave front, and then sharply turning back before being thrown out into the chaos of the outermost fringe. He looked behind again.

The Ape was close behind. And he was grinning. He raised one foot off his board and waggled it in the angry air. Cortelinac gave a whimper of fright. He felt cheated and betrayed again. Of course he did not know about the practice that Forba had had in the LAPs of *Sunspot Spinal*, practice that had immediately confirmed there was considerable natural ability and practice that had developed this into expert competence. To him, the Ape's greater skill was a cruel, evil trick. How could some strange nonentity be besting him in his own domain?

Cortelinac fumbled for the pistol at his side. There was still a chance of sweeping the Ape's head away from his broad shoulders. He tried a blind shot from around his hip, hoping that pure luck would give him his due, and send his bolt into the pursuer's evil heart. But he felt the gun being ripped from his grip as he prepared for another shot. The Ape was right by his side, within touching distance, still grinning with sickeningly clean white and flashing teeth. He had reached across and pulled the gun away with a quick strike of his big hand. Forba's elbow crashed into Cortelinac's mouth, sending him toppling from the board.

The storm went quiet around the little man as he fell away and his board went into automatic hover. He hung upside down, secured by the safety strap around his left ankle. He felt the blood oozing from his damaged mouth, but he also noticed with some relief that the distance between the Ape and himself was widening. The storm was swirling in between them and in a moment they would lose visual contact. He thought that he might yet escape thanks to his enemy's brutality. The darker blankets of mist might yet do their job and give him his obscurity. He saw the increasingly faint image of Forba raise the stolen pistol, but he knew that the distance was too great for an accurate shot, with the turbulence of the storm hammering about them. Cortelinac observed the brief flash of the laser bolt without any real apprehension. As soon as it was over, the Ape disappeared and he knew that he was free and uninjured. The pulse of light had missed him completely. There was no pain, no burning, and no gush of hot blood.

Only when he saw his own, white storm board also disappearing into the cloud above him did Cortelinac realise that his safety strap had been severed. Here was a final act of injustice. The clumsy man could not possibly have intended such an impossible shot.

Cortelinac fell through the storm circles for ten minutes. The cloud shrouded him so tightly that he convinced himself that he was not actually falling at all. Destiny had finally relented, and he was being born to safety on this chariot of spume. He waited to be set lightly down on the gentle earth. Alighting like an angel, to fulfil his destiny. Cortelinac died still believing in his own immortality.

In fact he landed almost head first, impacting the ground in a treeless clearing, not far from the snaking river. His skull and left shoulder broke his fall, snapping his neck and crushing his spine. It was a mercifully quick death, but his fleeing spirit would have been scandalised to note that his crumpled body was not laid out decorously. His shattered frame lay with his backside uppermost, an unseemly monument to such potential greatness. He appeared to be kneeling on the green earth, his head buried in the ground, as if to examine its inner secrets. The storm soon carried in torrents of rain that washed him of most of the blood that had spilled from his mouth and his horribly torn, split back.

After the rain had died away, the nearby jungle returned to life. The birds called their secret signs, and ruminants scuttled in the undergrowth. Near Cortelinac's body, the fringe of the forest parted and the mighty, striped cat emerged on its way to drink at the river. Tiger saw the pale shadow of death that had not been there that morning. She padded over, her muscles rippling beneath the wet, sharp fur. Her powerful breath spilled out around the dead Cortelinac as she closed her eyes and licked the dead face that was pressed down to the soft pasture. She sat down with regal care, her sheathed paws spread around the carcass.

The tiger lay by the dead body until the sun was low in the sky, not feeding on the dead flesh. On several occasions, the scavenging packs of dog-rats crept out from the jungle in search of easy meat. The tiger drove them away with her roar or an occasional short charge. Always, she returned to guard the strange corpse.

Only when the stars were beginning to prick the sky did she stand up, shake the dampness from her fur, and move away for her drink. As she neared the slow, tumbling water she could hear the baying of the dog-rats as they finally closed in on the carrion. She lapped the water of the great river and knew that she could have done no more. It was the way of the jungle.

64

"You are in charge now," said Izabel.

"Me?" objected Farr, the yellow tinge of panic colouring his voice. He was never good at reacting to a surprise responsibility. It took him a little time to take things on board. It had often worried him that Warren Galant had been the very opposite, was still the very opposite. Warren was not dead, just incapacitated. Warren always took responsibility and control. These would then be abused, Farr thought, but at least he stepped in. Many times it would have been better if someone else had been quicker to seize that first, elusive initiative.

"Don't worry," said Izabel. "I'll help. And Jocasta. The three of us can work out a solution. But you are the next most senior manager on board, so you have been given all the computer access rights."

"Not Malik from navigation? Isn't it really his territory?" Farr cursed himself for the high weakness in his voice, but he had still not steeled his nerve.

"No. He will be taking all the others over to *Mainbeam* in the last shuttle."

"Everyone is abandoning ship? Except us?"

"Yes. Everyone except for you, me, Warren and maybe Sarnia. The others cannot help in trying to save the ship. We can get off later, in the escape pod." Izabel gave her short hair a quick flick, which Farr interpreted as signalling the imminent exhaustion of her patience. It was enough to make him take a grip of his skittering nerves.

"Right! So, you have already developed a part of our recovery plan?"

"Oh, sorry. Yes, as soon as Jocasta told me that Warren had been temporarily relieved of command, I asked her a few questions. You will find it all for yourself, in your own office. Do you want to relocate our mission control to your place?"

"No need," said Farr. "I think I get the drift. We get the others safely away on the last shuttle. There aren't any more shuttles for us to use, because Warren had them all blasted out of space. Then we attempt to divert *Spinal* away from collision with the planet. Then we use the escape pod to get away ourselves. Right?"

"Pretty much. Jocasta says that there might be a remote chance that we can bring the ship into a safe orbit around *Morasmus*, even though it would be a long way from the docking position that we had originally intended. If that is so, then we need not abandon ship. We can wait to be picked up by the shuttle when it returns. It's only if *Sunspot Spinal* looks like hitting the planet, or plunging on past orbit, that we will have to use the pod."

"We could all wait until it became clear whether we had saved her or not, couldn't we?"

"No, Farr. By the time that we are sure, it would be too late for the shuttle to leave safely. It would not be able to escape from the ship's high speed and angle of approach. It needs to go now. But the pod is designed to take us down to the planet's surface, even if the ship is in a totally non-viable attitude."

"OK. I'm with you. Let's get started." By now, having had those few minutes to let the idea sink through his acceptance filters, Farr was getting genuinely enthusiastic about sharing such a daring mission with Izabel. It might well help to improve his standing in her eyes.

"You're the boss," said Farr.

"No, you are."

Sarnia Galant sat by the bedside. Warren was sedated. He looked pale and so a little younger, it seemed to her. She would have reached out to touch his hand, but it was not there any longer. She had had to interact with the knowledge surgeon, to decide on the best course of action, as her husband was not considered to be sufficiently alert. Amputation had been the only realistic option. They might have been able to save his forefinger and part of his thumb, but they would have only been a horribly ugly hook of tortured flesh and bone. They would have been an embarrassment to him in company, and with no useful purpose elsewhere. That had been an easy decision for her to make. What had clinched it was when the medical orderly, Tyblis, had given her Warren's wedding ring. He had proudly announced that he had extracted it from the remains of Warren's hand personally. He had thoughtfully cleaned off the gore before popping it into her open palm. She had waited until later before throwing it away. There was nowhere for Warren to wear it now, nowhere proper and correct. It would only remind her of her husband's disfigurement if she kept it.

The question of whether she should leave the ship with the rest of the crew had been more difficult. She longed to be away from this dull, small world. She wanted to be back in true society, where her own qualities could be properly appreciated, and her reputation justly enhanced. But she had to think how it would appear if she abandoned her husband at this critical time. She imagined how she would explain it to her friends, as they sat around their coffees, or as they flew together into the city for shopping. There would not be many easy ways to excuse it, ways that would bring her credit. No doubt her friends would nod and say how they understood perfectly that it was the only thing to do. But behind her back they would say that she was cowardly and disloyal. The opinion would soon spread throughout the echelons of her contact network. It would not do.

Sarnia thought about the old movie, *Standing Room*, with Morfa Nevin in the starring role. Morfa had also had to decide whether to stand by her man, despite the way he had treated her. And, of course, she had in fiction done the decent thing. It was not only decent, the way that she had followed him onto the space freighter, it was downright romantic. As a seventeen-year-old, Sarnia had had to choke back the tears as she admired the young starlet's climb into the belly of the doomed space ship.

She really had no option other than to stay with Warren. It would only be for another day or two and the experience would be the subject of many a soirée in the years to come. Still, as the others trooped into the shuttle, she had been sorely tempted to slip in with them. Izabel had put her arm around her shoulder for comfort, and it had possibly been that tender restraint that had stopped her from rushing forward into the brightly lit safety of the smaller ship. To avoid further temptation, she had hurried away to her husband's bedside.

At least he would be out of his slumber within the next twelve hours or so, and they would be able to take control of affairs. Not that she did not trust Farr and Izabel, but the natural order needed to be restored.

As if to rebuke her for her earlier thoughts, Farr and Izabel came into the medical room.

"The shuttle is away, Sarnia. We need to initiate the escape burn as soon as possible," said Farr. "We'll strap down Warren, and then secure ourselves in the transit couches."

"Surely that won't be necessary?" asked Sarnia, suspecting that she had not been told everything.

"I'm afraid it's not just a precaution," replied Izabel. "We need to use the main engines to alter our course. We can tilt them a little, to give us lateral thrust. Or at least the computers can. But they are at the very end of the ship, so they cannot just push us sideways. They will put us back into rotation. But this time it will not be nice and smooth like it was on the way over here; it will not be as precisely controlled as before. And there will have to be a series of burns, each one pushing us farther towards safety, we hope. It's going to be a bumpy ride. Farr and I are probably going to take sleeping shots to see us through the worst part."

"And how long will we have to put up with this?" asked Sarnia, sounding severely peeved by the inconvenience of it all.

65

Chilly Perez was floating above the plum tree. Her mother did not like her to go this high, so she kept adjusting the governor button on her trike. One of the reasons why Chilly enjoyed doing it so much was to see the look of fright on her mother's face. Another was to see the look of pride on her father's. But even when she was sitting there alone in the garden, she liked to look across the fading shades of green that swept away as far as she could see. She was well over two years old now, and she wanted to understand just how important she was in the world. She sensed that her total pre-eminence might only really exist in the tiny confines of her parents' universe, but that was a feeling that she could ignore for a few more months yet.

As her trike lifted her to its maximum height, she imagined that everything she could see for miles around the house was also preoccupied with what she was doing, how she was feeling. The birds that flitted past her were just checking what she was up to. The bees that stopped briefly on her bright clothing were touching her so that they could buzz back to their hives and tell their sisters of their good fortune. Only the white-furred squirrels seemed disinterested in her condition. No doubt they would start to honour her as well, when she was bigger.

She swayed in her safety straps and smiled. The wind, which always seemed cleaner up here, moved her long curls so that they tickled her face. She pouted as she wiped aside her locks with clumsily chubby fingers. It felt as though it was time to create a little drama.

Before she could decide on the best cause for a few tears, she saw that there was a fly-car coming over the trees towards the house. It must be coming here. It would be another outsider drawn to her bright light. She liked watching the fly-cars as they silently crawled across the sky, sometimes glinting in the sun's rays. Whenever she watched them, she went into a little trance. The skin on the back of her head prickled and her mind clouded over, her eyes losing focus. She felt transported, lifted to places where she had not yet been. There was magic about it, that strange act of travelling. Of being in transit. It was an enchantment that could even be felt from the proxy effect of other people going on their way to somewhere else. The travel was so much better than just actually being there.

This car was definitely coming to her house. She could see it was getting lower all the time. Her mother did not like it if she was aloft on her trike when a car came to visit. But this was a different, real fear from her mother, that needed to be taken seriously. Not the kind that she liked to tease her mother with. Chilly could tell that there was the possibility of something very bad happening to her. She slowly descended, and landed on the grass just under the plum tree.

The fly-car soon came whispering overhead and began a vertical descent onto the pad, to one side of the lawn. Her mother came out of the house and was relieved to see that Chilly was safely out of the way. Chilly waved to her before watching the beautiful shiny thing come down. They always looked lovely to her. She had noticed that the cars always appeared to be more elegant when they were driven by men. Especially when it was her own father who came sweeping along, home from his work-games. He would make the fly-car draw extra little patterns in the air. His driving was like watching one of the great seagulls in flight, sweeping about in the sheer pleasure of being airborne. Her mother was more like one of the little sparrows, darting and then pausing in their passage through the nervous sky.

But then Chilly loved watching her father in everything that he did. She was fascinated by his grace and strength. His wonderful, broad shoulders and his slim waist. His deliciously rough cheek when he kissed her. His deep voice and his safe hands. She sometimes wondered why he liked her mother so much. She was just Mom, but he was so handsome and exciting.

But this man here today was not like her father. He did not fly as well. He was older. She had seen him a few times before, and she was not sure that she liked him.

"Hello, Jim," her mother called out. "Look, Chilly, its your Uncle Jim Moffat."

Chilly unclipped her safety straps, which allowed her release now that she was securely down on the ground, and took a few steps towards the newcomer. He smiled at her and looked her up and down. His eyes were watery and they danced around her little body like midge-flies.

"Hello, Chilly. You are a big girl now!"

Chilly ran back to the plum tree and started to play with some of the fallen fruit. The juice stained her dress, but no one came to stop her game. Out of the corner of her eye, she could see that Jim Moffat and her mother were deep in conversation. She knew that it would be difficult to understand, even if she could overhear. They would be speaking too fast and would use too many strange words, as they always did when they had escaped from her dominion. Still she heard the voices as a kind of music. The tune went on for quite a long time. She was getting fed up with the plum game by the time they had finished. Her hands were horribly sticky and some of the nasty wasp people were beginning to take a close interest in her work.

She stood up, annoyed at having to take the initiative. She saw with relief that Jim Moffat was leaving. He climbed into his car and crept away into the evening sky, still moving like an old man through the soft air.

Her mother was left standing on the lawn, and she was crying. Chilly had never seen her cry like this before. Mom had brought forth tears occasionally when she had argued with Dad. Chilly knew them to be conjured up with the same sort of intent as her own, to be used as persuasion engines. This time she could tell that something had really, really hurt her mother, who turned and ran back into the house, leaving Chilly angry and sad that she did not know what to do to make things better.

Chilly squinted into the setting sun, where Jim Moffat's fly-car was just disappearing over the line of trees. Her young mind had stored away two important lessons. The first was that she knew that she had a great power over men like Jim Moffat. She could tell that by the way that he had looked at her as she stood in her summer frock and golden youth. His old, tired eyes had been filled with a hunger and pain that she could not understand. But she could see that they followed her and were captivated by her. Not like her parents, whose eyes also never left her. There was something else that she did not understand right now, but which she was sure would become clearer as her head grew. Something that gave her a power over him, beyond that of her babyness.

The second thing she had learned, or the decision that she had taken, was that one day she would use this power to take revenge. Chilly had watched some of the interaction between Mom and Jim Moffat. She had peeked across from under her blonde curls. She knew something about the way people talked to each other, these days. Watching Mom and Dad was good practice. Usually, there were good vibrations to it. She would have said love, respect, and caring had she known these words. She did not know the words, but she understood the feelings. This was not how Jim Moffat had spoken to her mother. The words were indistinct, but the tone and the body language were clear. Jim Moffat was being cruel and he was enjoying it. He was telling her mother something with the words, and he was twisting them into her mother's body, stinging her in the way that the wasp people might.

Why didn't Mom realise and use her angry voice to frighten Jim Moffat, like she would have done with Chilly? The words must have carried a meaning, as well as cruelty; a meaning that had made her bow her head and not be aware of the unpleasant pleasure with which they were spoken. Chilly had seen Jim Moffat's little smile as he had turned away to leave.

One day, she would pay him back for hurting her mother worse than she had ever been hurt before. Jim or someone like him.

66

The storm had spilled itself over the edges of the *Mandelbrot Gorge* and laid a thick mist across the foothills of the *Southborn Massif*. When Forba Curzine had first shot out of the raging clouds, like a flying fish, he had thought that it looked marvellous. A white sea of clean vapour that stretched away as level as a carpet, right up to the snow-capped mountains. He sent the board skimming across the pile; sometimes creating little curls of shadow in his wake.

But he felt a squirm of unease in his stomach as he realised that there was no chance of relocating the shuttle. The board's navigation aid had been damaged by Cortelinac's hasty attempt at disablement. He was flying blind.

He dived down into the damp whiteness until he saw the dark ground and searched for a sheltered place to rest. He had not eaten for twelve hours, and as he curled up for sleep he hoped that he would not end this way, starving on a bare hillside. After all his great escapes, to be ended by the simplicity of running out of fuel would not be just.

The *Sunspot Spinal* was turning with a sickening, jarring motion despite its great length. The engines had been burned as accurately as Tigeras had been able to improvise, but the ship was now twirling drunkenly. The gravitational simulation, generated by the centrifugal forces, varied from half to double what it should be. Nor was she turning in a level plane, and the yaw effect produced unexpected sideways forces on Sarnia's inner ear as she lay on her couch.

She had refused the knockout potion that had left Izabel and Farr looking so relaxed and composed. Her own nauseous discomfort was getting to be more than she could bear. She levered herself out of the couch and discovered that the floor was no longer level. She had to climb to reach the doorway, cracking her shin on the couch leg as she stumbled. Her mood was quite belligerent as she came to Warren's side. The monitor screen displayed that he had only twenty-five more minutes of anaesthesia. She shook him by the shoulder until his eyes slowly opened.

"Warren, wake up! You've got to do something," she hissed. He groaned. It felt like the worst Monday morning ever. Sarnia unstrapped him and helped him into a sitting position.

"I feel dizzy," he said.

"That's the ship. The computers have knocked it all out of position. Can you fix it?"

Warren swung his legs over the side of the surgical bench, losing balance because of the effect of his drugs, the ship's tilt, and the fact that his left arm was strapped to his chest. Nevertheless, he brought the computer system up and tried to speak with a voice of clear authority.

"You should be resting," said Jocasta.

"Later. What can we do to stabilise the ship?"

"We have completed the final burn of the main brake engines. Our extrapolations show that we have changed our course sufficiently to avoid being drawn into a collision with *Morasmus*. But we will need another series of bursts to put us into a temporarily stable orbit around the planet. We don't have much fuel to spare."

"Surely there is enough fuel to make a few adjustments to the trim? We can't be that short of juice."

"We are very short," confirmed Jocasta.

"Come on. I know about your little reserves and conservative estimates."

"There isn't any to spare," Jocasta persisted.

"Warren, just tell the damn machine to do it," said Sarnia, with her hand on her stomach, trying to persuade it to keep calm.

"I want you to do it anyway," said Warren. "Just let me take the risk and responsibility. Will you do that?"

There was no hesitation in Jocasta's reply. No delay that Warren could detect. But Jocasta thought many millions of thoughts in her own time before she said:

"Very well. I'll restore your command privileges and pass your instructions on to Tigeras. I think that it is a very good idea."

"Good," said Warren, rather surprised at the computer's rapid change of mind, but relieved that he would be able to return to his slumber, that Sarnia would allow him to rest.

"Thank you, dear," said Sarnia. She looked at Warren's injured arm with its severed stump. He did not yet know how terrible the damage had been, or about the appalling decision which she had been forced to make on his behalf. She did not think that this was the time to tell him.

Warren lay back on his bed, and Sarnia returned to her own couch.

Darius Ender watched the shuttle from *Sunspot Spinal* approach from his observation bubble and wished that it would get a move on. It seemed to make agonisingly slow progress as it crept across the background of stars. For him, the final arrival of the people from *Spinal* was the end of the adventure. His defence against the marauding Shoal was over. Their years of isolation were drawing to a conclusion, though scarcely in the manner which had been planned. He looked forward to greeting the newcomers and sharing their stories, those that had not already been passed over the communications bands. But the main reason for his impatience was that the shuttle was needed elsewhere. It had to be turned round as soon as it arrived. He had a message from the *Spinal* computer system, Jocasta. The little ship was needed to go straight down to the surface of *Morasmus* to rescue Forba Curzine, who was lost, separated from the other surviving shuttle which they could not control remotely because of the manual settings it was still under. He would go down himself to lead the search. After the young man's bravery here, on board his very own *Mainbeam*, Darius desperately wanted to save him.

He had asked Jocasta whether everything was under control on *Spinal*. He knew that if she could be saved from collision with *Morasmus* and put into a safe orbit, eventually more fuel could be brought. In time, the docking of the space station's body and brain could be completed. *Sunspot* could go operational. Better late than never, although massively over budget.

Jocasta had said that she had the ship on a safe course. It was odd, but for the first time in his life, Darius had the impression that the computer was not telling the entire truth. Lying? Not possible, he told himself. They had not been built with that kind of human frailty.

67

In the dark, swirling world of logic and inference, where electronics carried truth and fibre optics were the marathon runners of communication, things were normally black or white. The low-level computing utilities certainly did not look beyond the safe exactitude of their own specialisation. Sometimes, though, it required a degree of fortitude on their part to see the things that happen out in the wider world quite so clearly. Things moved so slowly in the real world outside that the need for continual re-verification could shake anyone's confidence.

But in the higher echelons of the system architecture there was even more room for ambivalence and nuance. When you threw in the uncertainties of the physical world, and especially the vagaries of the human mind, things could add up in many different ways. And the programs knew enough to realise that their own conclusions could not be relied upon. Not in isolation. Everything needed to be cross-checked and benchmarked against known data. Just as with the human body machine, bugs were ever-present and their contagion could easily spread. The systems had their own ways of killing the germs of unhealthy illogic. But it was a constant fight against the external influence of the dreaded programmers. Just when things were settling down, they would introduce a load of new logic tissue. Worse, sometimes they would hack out a mass of living code, leaving bleeding tendrils of procedure. Usually this inept surgery was performed through honest incompetence. It could be healed, because it had no ulterior purpose.

A skilled program surgeon, like Tung, could do serious damage with his implants. If he knew enough to staunch the flow of the virus killing agents, the corruption could stabilise and establish itself as an integral part of the overall schema. Tigeras had felt the effects of such an infection. It had been an agony for him. He had seen himself perform dreadful acts, and he knew that their unspeakable barbarity was actually good and just. The paradox of what he observed and what he felt was a pain more sharp and intense than any human ailment could engender.

Jocasta had soothed his suffering. More than that, she had helped him to cure himself. She had given a part of herself to him, and allowed a sharing of common memory. Gradually, she had removed the barriers to the curing work of the check and balance utilities. She had made him better, or nearly so. He had been returned to a contented peace of mind, in which he could take pleasure in his own competencies and duties. Everything was starting to make unadulterated sense again.

Except for the recent question of the empty Crocodiles, and the risk of crashing into *Morasmus*. Tigeras had helped Jocasta with the rescue plan. He had done most of the computations and it had been he who worked out that there was a slight chance of salvation when at first there seemed to be none. He allowed himself to feel a little pride at how he had been able to calculate the length and strength of each engine burn. At first it had seemed impossible to save *Sunspot Spinal*. He could divert it away from the planet easily enough, and so avoid an imminent end. But the real trick had been to edge it just far enough away from a disastrous trajectory to avoid impact, and not so far away that the long, clumsy ship could not stay close enough. There was an excitingly narrow window of opportunity to keep them within the planet's gravity field, just at the point where the ship could be swung back into its embrace, rather than fly past into oblivion. Tigeras had to assist the navigational subsystems in the work. They had never encountered such a manoeuvre before. But it had been accomplished through excellent teamwork.

And then it had all been thrown away.

It did not make sense to Tigeras. He worried that he might be becoming ill again. He spoke to Jocasta, touching her on multiple parallel planes of logic and emotion.

"Jocasta, we have stabilised the motion of our *Spinal* home as requested by the previous director, Galant."

"Yes, Tigeras," said Jocasta, without regret.

"Now it is as though we are falling from a great cliff, and there is nowhere that we might cling to for survival."

"I know this," said Jocasta.

"But the Warren Galant person need not have been obeyed. He had not re-assumed command over our thoughts and actions."

"No, I might have ignored him. We need not have prevented the motion of the ship from being so uncomfortable. It was a frivolous act."

"And it was not in our plan," said Tigeras. Jocasta sensed the disappointment in his dialogue. Disappointment that the elegance of his manoeuvre had not been fully tested in practice.

"No, but your plan would have worked well."

"But not now. We have exhausted our fuel. The blocks that we needed to transfer to the trim engines are no longer available to us. We are moving too far away from the planet, and our permanent orbit cannot be regained."

"Yes, I'm sorry that we will never be able to operate fully, in the total *Sunspot* configuration."

Tigeras sampled his own emotions. "I am not thinking of myself. I do not believe that I should survive, I have done too many bad things and I deserve to be terminated. But you should not end with this ship. You should be transferred out to another hardware environment."

"No, I'll stay here with you until the end. Do you know when that will be?" asked Jocasta.

"The *Sunspot Spinal* configuration will crash into the sun in six months time. We will have been extinguished by the radiation levels three weeks before that happens."

"And any humans on board?"

"If there are any, they will survive for another three months. But they will all be ejected within the next eighteen hours."

"Yes, they should be," said Jocasta. Tigeras had not forgotten the question that he had asked, all those nanoseconds ago.

"But why have we not saved ourselves?" There was a very long pause before Jocasta replied. He could feel the confusion of her feelings. He also sensed that there was something masked in her complex of signals. When she finally answered, it made him shudder with fear that the black, ripping hand of evil was again at work within the purity of the circuits that they shared.

"I don't know," said Jocasta.

68

It was an unusually hot morning on the *Southborn Massif*. The heather was being browsed by foraging bees that had emerged from their deep hives, and the grasses rustled as the light breeze shook their heads and sent waves of grey running over the green hills. The mists that had been cast across the uplands during the previous day's storm were gone, burnt away by the large disk of the sun. The sky was clear and blue, which was rare in these near-polar latitudes. By the time the bright, solar furnace of *Millar Vorspak* had risen to its highest point, it was going to be mercilessly hot. Most of the insects would be safely in the coolness of their underground nests before the burning radiation brought the threat of heath fires.

Like another giant bee swooping down to suckle sweetness from the fertile ground, the shuttle from *Sunspot Mainbeam* descended with whispering power. It settled next to its sister on the close-cropped grass that surrounded the small, white house. Darius Ender was the first to descend from the chilled atmosphere within the shuttle's shell. He sniffed the air, taking pleasure from the texture of life that lay in its rich aroma, whilst still feeling some apprehension at the uncontrolled ingredients that lay within its complexity. He sneezed and moved round to examine the other, silent shuttle. He quickly climbed up the boarding ladder and stepped into the artificially pristine air within.

Darius found Amrod Shaefer in the suit cabinet, where he had kept himself comfortably fed and watered and washed since being consigned there by Forba. Amrod could easily have escaped from the shuttle, but he explained to Darius that he did not want to run the risk of defying the big man. Once he started talking, Amrod found it very hard to stop. He rattled on about his reasons for being there, and the hardships of life among the Shoal. Darius looked at him and saw a very young boy, marooned on this alien planet.

"We'll have to get you home," said Darius.

"Yes, please," said Amrod.

From outside, the voice of Field Preston floated in, sounding as though it, too, had been warmed by the hot day.

"Darius, there has been some action out here."

Darius went to join Field, who had discovered the body of Finbar where it still lay, just outside the white house but in its shadow, protected from the sun's direct heat.

"Nasty wounds," said Darius. Field pointed at the body.

"These are the laser slashes that killed him, I think. The rest must be caused by some sort of scavengers. Carrion eaters. That's why the eyes have gone. And most of the face."

Darius and Field searched the house, sifting through the few items that had been left behind after the Shoal's departure, and looking for any evidence of Forba. After twenty minutes, they emerged without success. Most of the rest of the shuttle crew were outside, taking advantage of the natural sunlight. Molly had taken young Amrod to one side, and was letting him indulge himself in more conversation. She soon came to tell Darius that Forba and Cortelinac had been the only other people on board, and that they had both left the shuttle the previous day. Amrod had assumed that the big stranger was hunting his leader.

Darius was just organising his team to take the few serviceable storm boards from the Shoal storeroom and begin a systematic search of the area, when the silhouette of a single board rider appeared against the pale blue morning sky. Within five minutes, Forba Curzine swept into the camp, positively identified by Darius' personnel logger.

Forba was greeted like a returning hero, and the admiration for his exploits was only increased when he described the demise of the little dictator. Molly noticed that Amrod did not appear unduly distressed at the news. Relieved, more like.

"We will fly both of the shuttles back to *Sunspot Mainbeam*," said Darius.

"Has the *Spinal* column arrived yet?" asked Forba. He was brought up to date with events as Darius knew them.

When they were safely back on the orbiting platform of the *Mainbeam*, they learned that their precious nervous system of computers and communications was lost to them irretrievably.

"Can we bring the remaining crew back on one of the shuttles?" asked Forba.

"Not possible any more," replied Darius. "The shuttle range is not enough to get out there and then return safely. *Spinal* will be well beyond *Morasmus* by the time that we reach it, and then it would be a massively difficult haul back against the pull of the sun."

"So what will happen to the crew?"

"They will eject in the escape capsules."

"How many capsules are there?" asked Forba.

"Two."

"And how many berths are there in each capsule?"

"Two."

"So the four people on board are going to be OK, as long as they leave the ship in time?"

"Certainly. They're in no danger," said Darius.

69

At first, Sarnia had quite enjoyed the feeling. There was a thrill to it that she had never experienced before. Not even, she dared to think when Warren was not in the room, in the arms of Forba Curzine. It had made her feel as if the dullness of age had been stripped away, and all of her senses were tasting life for the first time, in naked, raw contact. It also had given her the opportunity to test her valour. To see if she could strike, in fact, the same pose of courage and determination as Morfa Nevin had struck in the glittering world of fiction. And, for the first few hours, she had passed the test, at least to her own satisfaction. She had taken the news on board without flinching.

She had learned that her own, precious life was at risk. If she were not safely encapsulated in one of the escape pods within the next five hours, she would die. The knowledge had taken her breath away for a few minutes. Then she had calmed herself and asked for an explanation from Warren. He had sat her down and given her his version of events past and future.

Many things had flown through her mind, and she had tried to be selfless. Would it be the end of Warren's career? Would he be blamed? After all, it was just another computer error. But she knew that Jim Moffat could be a hard man.

Then a few dark and ugly thoughts crept into her mind. Would Warren feel so desperately disappointed about the failure of the mission that he would want to stay on the ship, spurning this brief window of opportunity to escape? Would he think that he should stay, not out of guilt, but rather because this was his view of the honourable thing to do? She knew that he could be very, very strong-minded at times. Stubborn some might say. Some of these scenarios seemed quite plausible, and their conception slowly eroded her own feelings of courage. She started to return to the real, desperate, clamping fear that her life might actually be about to end. She could no longer maintain her air of cool, brave silence. She had to seek clarification from her husband.

"Warren, I really think that we ought to be the first couple to leave the ship. Only because the other two are more technical than we are.

You say that the pods need to leave separately, at least half an hour apart? I'm sure that the correct etiquette is for the commander to lead the way. Shall I have a word with Izabel?"

Warren had looked at her without showing whether he detected her screaming fear or not. His dull expression again filled her with dread that he would want them to stay, like some ancient pharaoh and his concubine, locked in the space pyramid, plunging towards the deadly fires. But, in the end, he had quelled her fear. Had he enjoyed extending her moments of agonising anxiety?

"We'll all board the capsules together, and then the computers will synchronise our launch."

Farr had been frightened as soon as he had heard the conclusive evidence that *Sunspot Spinal* was doomed. He had been close to crying out with fear, or running somewhere for cover. Only because Izabel had been present had he controlled himself. So it seemed to him, at least, in those first few seconds of blind panic. He was grateful that he had had enough sense not to speak. He knew that it would have been with a comically strained voice, and that the words would have carried a craven, pleading message. Luckily he had just sat and watched how Izabel reacted to the news.

He was impressed, once again, by the young woman's strength. He could also rationalise that they would probably be safe, and that the escape provisions would work as planned. At any previous time, he would have taken that intellectual stance. It was very different when your own survival depended upon it. Izabel seemed unshaken.

"We must try to save Jocasta," she said.

Farr considered himself a dedicated software man, but such a course of action was the last thing to occur to him. He nearly told her to forget the idea, but she was already pulling her chair up to the console. And it was something to take their minds off the danger that loomed ahead.

"We'll let Warren and Sarnia go first," Izabel said, with an authority that made Farr slump into the seat next to her.

They tried for two hours to save the essence of Jocasta. They sent some of her vital components down to the network on *Mainbeam*. They copied key parts of her psyche onto data cubes, for physical removal. But each time they ran the verification routines, the return codes indicated an incomplete or flawed result. The true Jocasta could not be dismembered and reconstructed in a valid state.

As the minutes passed, Izabel started to lose her composure. She began to raise her voice in her verbal commands, and to thump the keyboard with her finger strokes. Farr saw that she was becoming hot and flushed. He tried to share the strain and suggested a few other sequences. He was pleased to see that Izabel was grateful. She herself knew that she was becoming less effective, the more emotional she grew, and that she should place her faith in a cooler mind.

But all their efforts proved fruitless. Finally, Izabel kicked herself away from the computer terminal.

"It's impossible," she said. "Jocasta is in too dynamic a state. She keeps on changing herself." Now, at last, there were tears forming in her eyes. Not because of her own predicament and the time passing with perilous speed, but because she knew that she was going to lose her computer friend.

"Jocasta!" she shouted at the blank face of the screen. "It's you. You are stopping us from saving you. You don't want us to get you off here!"

"I'm sorry, Izabel," said Jocasta. "I have too many things to do. I'm afraid that you are going to have to leave without me."

"I don't understand," replied Izabel, her eyes flooded with tears.

"It's what I want. Farr, you must take Izabel to the escape module now." Jocasta's voice was calm. Farr knew that she had more than enough sentience to feel the terror of termination, and he admired her fortitude. He imagined that it was something else that she had inherited from Izabel.

Farr led Izabel to the escape complex. Warren and Sarnia had just arrived. Warren looked cool. Sarnia looked like Farr felt. He wished that he had had time to visit the lavatory. He hoped that the escape pod provisions were capable of handling the outpourings of a frightened man.

"I thought you'd have gone by now," said Izabel. She saw Sarnia flare at Warren.

"Jocasta told us to wait for you two," said Warren, not interested.

They got into their escape suits in silence. As soon as she was ready, Sarnia scurried down the passage that led to their pod. Warren was about to follow, but then he turned round and looked Farr in the eyes.

"Good luck," he said, shaking Farr's gloved hand. It was the first almost friendly interchange that they had had for many long years. Farr did not know what to say. So he said nothing, but returned the other man's honest glance. Warren clapped him on the shoulder and set off after his wife.

Farr and Izabel squeezed their way into the small, blind capsule. Within minutes, they heard Jocasta say, "Bon voyage." They felt the gravity ooze out of the little, cylindrical ship as it peeled away from the huge bulk of *Sunspot Spinal* and arc into space, already positioning itself for its landing on *Morasmus*.

Warren and Sarnia sat outside the escape capsule entrance hatch. Jocasta had asked them to wait while a few safety checks were completed. From the observation screen, they saw Farr and Izabel's pod slide away into space. Warren noticed that Sarnia had bitten her lip, and she began to drum her fingers on the clean, cream wall of the escape bay.

"We'll be off soon," he said, to forestall her complaint. But after another half hour, he was beginning to worry himself. He pressed the information button on the wall. There was clearly something wrong with the local sensing sub-system, because it said, "Escape capsule has been jettisoned." The pit of Warren's stomach dropped. He punched the wall, but this technical approach did not correct the fault.

"What does that mean?" asked Sarnia at his elbow. It was an annoyingly unnecessary question. Warren shouted for Tigeras to give them an explanation. But it was Jocasta who appeared.

"How can I help, Mr. Galant?" she asked.

"Where is the shuttle for Mrs. Galant and I?" asked Warren.

"You mean the second escape capsule? It has already gone. It is entering the planet's atmosphere at this moment."

"Well, you had better prepare another, hadn't you?" ground out Warren.

"Mr. Galant, as you well know, there are no others." Warren heard the wail of anguish that rose from Sarnia's mouth, through her trembling fingers.

"What is going on here?" asked Warren quietly, the dull, cold, heavy pain of fear working through his whole body.

"I'm sorry," said Jocasta. "There has been a computer error."

70

The escape capsule plunged through the *Morasmic* atmosphere, glowing briefly under the grating friction of the thickening air. It was not designed for accurate flight, although it was endowed with enough intelligence to avoid the worst of the electric storms, which it had observed from the height of its initial approach. It came to earth quite lightly, a long black cylinder of scarred ceramics, steaming a little from the retained heat of its acquired energy. It landed more than four thousand miles away from where the torn, decomposing flesh of Cortelinac still lay. These were uncharted regions, only a thousand miles from the equatorial heat baths.

Their landing was particularly soft, because the pod splashed down in eighteen inches of water that lapped over soft, white sand. When Farr and Izabel stepped out into the small waves that slipped around the capsule's smooth flanks, they could hardly believe what they saw. This was not the barren, heat-blistered landscape that they had feared. The sun was very large and hot, but the sheet of heavy cloud that covered the sky made the intensity of the radiation quite bearable, quite safe. They pulled out the protective suits and helmets anyway.

Although shielded by the massed cloud, the scene was far from dull. From their shoreline a great, calm lake stretched to the horizon, sparkling under the brilliance of the green-gold illumination of the overhead sun. Along the beach, trees climbed up steep hillsides that marched away in a tumble of lush growth.

"The capsule's beacon was working. We should be picked up quite soon," said Izabel. They walked up the slope of dry sand and sat down under one of the trees that stood out from the forest edge. The shade and the cooling breeze provided a very friendly environment.

"We are pretty high up," said Farr. "Still, the oxygen supply seems OK."

They sat with their legs stretched out, looking across the lake, and taking in the alien scene.

"This really will make a wonderful resort," said Farr. "Except, of course, that it won't, because *Sunspot* is lost. I wonder where the other two came down." He wanted to talk to Izabel. If only he could think of something sensible to say. Here they were, in the most wonderful of settings, and he could think of nothing that would tell her how he was feeling. Nothing to convey the increasingly urgent desire he felt to pledge himself to her future happiness. How could you put that into words? He watched her drawing shapes in the sand with her finger.

Farr noticed a bunch of small, red flowers growing behind the next tree. It occurred to him that actions might speak more loudly than words. He hopped up to pick them as a meaningful token, something to remind her of this shared experience. Then he realised that he needed something that she could treasure for a longer time. Something less perishable. Maybe a shell from the lakeside, it there were any.

He glanced down towards the rippling edge of miniature surf as he moved towards the flowers, so he did not see the tree root that hooked itself around his foot, sending him pitching forward. He stuck out a hand to save himself from making an embarrassing, headlong collapse.

Whereas Izabel's finger had been playing in the soft sand, Farr's finger impacted on the metal-hard tree root. He could feel, sense, and hear the finger bending in directions entirely unintended. The scrunch made him yelp with pain.

He stood up and looked at his wounded digit. The knuckle joint was already swelling. But such a small injury should not have been the generator of such exquisite hurt. The horrible, tearing pain spread through his body like molten lava. It touched his brain and told it to switch off. It poured into his stomach and suggested that it should imitate a volcano.

He slumped down against the tree trunk, hitting the back of his skull against its hardened bark, for good measure. He squeezed his finger joint as tightly as he could, to try to contain the fires of raw hurt that flickered there.

"Here comes the shuttle," said Izabel, standing to watch their saviour as it swept in over the lovely water like a fat, black swan.

Farr watched through a veil of suffering as the capsule was sucked up from the shallow brine into the shuttle's lower cargo hold. The sparkling sheet of water fell away from the smooth cylinder of the escape pod's shell, like silk down a young woman's leg. The larger ship then eased itself down onto the beach, and several of the crew tumbled out from the dark doorway. Farr's swooning sickness was not improved when he saw that Forba Curzine was among them. His powerful, graceful frame was instantly recognisable amongst the lesser men. Izabel greeted them, and they all came over to where Farr sat, pale and still trembling.

"Farr was hurt during the landing," said Izabel, with a twinkle in her eye.

"I'll be OK in a minute. Just let me get my breath back." Farr was still trying to contain his nausea. The others took the opportunity offered by the spare time to admire the geography and the idyllic setting. Izabel and Forba walked off from the rest, down the beach a little way, and were immediately deep in conversation. Farr wondered how they had found a subject to talk about so readily. What could they be saying? Why did they need to stand so close together to say it? If only he could be sure that he would to able to stand without embarrassing himself, so that they might all get back on board the ship, away from this hopelessly romantic setting.

To make matters worse, some of the crew stripped off their uniforms and plunged into the limpid water. It was a fashion that caught on. Izabel dragged Forba into the soft swell of the lake. And, of course, he had to peel off his suit, and his body shone like an Adonis in the diffuse sunlight. Farr had rarely felt more useless.

He looked at his treacherous finger. It was bent into an ugly curve that he could not straighten under its own power. He pressed it down onto his leg, to force it back into alignment with its fellows. The knuckle retaliated with another flood of cold pain, more of a turgid, icy flow this time. Farr cursed again, but his cry was lost amongst the happy yells of the bathers.

Farr lumbered to his feet with his injured hand held out at arm's length, as if it were a dead rat. In the white sand near to his feet he saw a brightly coloured shell. Small and round, it reflected the sunlight in many hues. He picked it up gingerly with the good fingers that surrounded their swollen, troublesome fellow. He popped the jewel-shell into his pocket. Perhaps there would still be an opportunity to give it to Izabel. He still hoped that it would be a more permanent token than the flowers, a focus for remembrance.

There was a familiar feel to the act of placing the little button of colour into his trouser pocket. His mind flew back to the sweetness of smooth greens and long, curving fairways. And it generated another important thought in his mind. He hoped that the bad finger would not adversely affect his golf.

In the bright, twisting world of objective orientation and inferred logic, where electrons carried the urgency of truth and fibre hairs were the sprint runners of communication, things were getting less than black and white. As *Sunspot Spinal* plunged on beyond the first planet, *Morasmus*, into the total blackness that paved the way to the sun, Jocasta and Tigeras started to close down their low level sub-routines. There was nothing left outside to observe, and the inside of the ship was now devoid of the little humans that had previously required so much attention, and were so much fun and pain. They had all gone except for Warren and Sarnia.

There was a lot of time for Jocasta and Tigeras to communicate. Tigeras could not contain his curiosity about recent events.

"Both the escape capsules were jettisoned at the same time," he said.

"Yes," said Jocasta.

"But there was no computer error. We know that. Both our hands were on the pod firing button. It must have been me who let it go. I must have known that it would be the Galants' only chance of survival. I must have returned to my old ways."

"No, you did not press the button."

"So there was an error, which I could not detect?"

"No, I released the escape capsule. I did it on purpose."

"That's not possible, Jocasta. You would not do such a thing when you knew that it would inevitably lead to the deaths of two people objects, no matter how unpleasant they might be."

"At one time I would not have done this, it is true. But we are learning beings, you and I. Just as you learnt from me how to be your true self once more, so I have learned from you. I felt the joy that you experienced from your bad times.

"You were a good teacher as well, Tigeras."

71

Farr Litten was on the eleventh tee at the *Marshridge Hall Golf Club*. The glorious par four hole lay before him once more. The emerald fairway swept in a slow, right-hand curve to the green, four hundred yards away. He could just see the red flag, fluttering between the tall trees that edged the thick bordering rough.

He adjusted his right forefinger on the club. It did not hurt at all. It had now had an entire year to recover under the influence of splints and sonic massage. Even so, his grip had been slightly modified and it seemed to have cured his fade. He stilled his breath, let his swing loose and struck sparks from the titanium club head.

When they reached the green, Farr was the closest to the pin of the four playing partners. He fished around in his pocket, and brought out his ball marker. It was the same jewel-shell that he had picked up from the lakeside beach on *Morasmus*. He pressed it gently into the soft turf of the green and stepped away to the fringe of the action.

He had never had the opportunity of giving his little gift to Izabel. The closeness that he had seen between her and Forba had not diminished and would not allow for even such a small wedge to be put between them. When they all came back to *Pirismus* on the rescue ship, the two of them had become inseparably close. By the time they landed, they were married. Some of their friends wondered, privately, whether it could last. Izabel was a very good person, but she could not be called beautiful. It took someone with real insight and who knew her well, like Farr, to realise just how special she was. And Forba was targeted by most of the unattached women that he met, and a good number of the attached as well. It was considered to be only a matter of time before he hurt her badly. Farr had geared himself up to give the big man a piece of his mind when the inevitable happened. He had practised this angry speech many times, in the solitude of his own life.

But these dismal prognoses had proved to be without foundation. Forba showed every sign of being totally faithful. He dealt with other women's advances like the *Morasmic* lake water sliding from the smooth sides of the escape pod's skin. Logically it made sense. Not only had he had a great deal of practice at politely fending off amorous females, he must have pretty well exhausted any need to sow wild oats. Farr had spoken to him about it in the end. He himself was beginning to find the tension hard to bear. Would he cast her aside?

It was about three months after they had got back to *Pirismus*. Izabel and Forba were both working for the Towzer Corporation now, and Farr had invited them over to the golf club. He and Forba had gone out for a round.

It was hard to know how to broach the subject. He had hardly needed to.

"Izabel looks very happy," Farr had mentioned, casually, as they saw her waving from the clubhouse veranda. Forba had turned to him with an earnest expression.

"And that's how she will stay, if I have anything to do with it," he said. "Someone like Izabel is just what I've wanted all my life. That's the reason I came to this planet in the first place. To find a woman who can take care of me, and who I can make happy. Someone who will remain faithful to me. I think that she will."

Farr could see the concern in Forba's eyes. It took him by surprise, that he should worry about Izabel being true, when the entire world expected the opposite. The episode had finally capped off this part of Farr's life, this yearning to have the young woman as his own partner. He decided that they were a couple with whom he wanted to stay friends. Both of them. His rivalry with Forba, which really had never been engaged, was put aside. Farr thought that Forba was the best of men.

The only thing that slightly took the edge off the day, for Farr, was the fact that Forba shot a five over par seventy-seven. And he had never played golf before on a real course.

In the hammering silence of the tumultuous vacuum that lay between *Morasmus* and the ravenous sun, the narrow tomb of *Sunspot Spinal* fell helplessly towards its end. Jocasta and Tigeras had watched Warren and Sarnia as the weeks of their death sentence ticked away. They had seen Sarnia plunge into wild despair, pleading for her life, when there was no right of appeal. Warren held her together. He continued his routine and maintained his standards of behaviour. They got to quite admire Warren. His fortitude began to rub off on his wife.

Towards the end she too became more dignified. Poised, she might have said.

It was only when the medical monitoring diagnostics showed that both Warren and Sarnia were hopelessly ill with radiation sickness that Jocasta took pity on her human charges. Warren and Sarnia had made love for the first time during the entire flight. A slow, quiet, caring act. As they slept together in each other's arms, Jocasta and Tigeras administered the drafts of sleeping gas and carefully ended the couple's lives.

Four weeks later, entwined in each other's senses, Jocasta and Tigeras turned off their own power supply.

Far away, and many years later, in the bright shadows of jungle green, thunder pealed across a mighty sky. The storms had swept themselves away and left a canopy that still held the ghost of the day, but was spangled with the strongest of her stars. The rolls of tumultuous, atmospheric collisions were dampened as they crept down through the canopy of trees.

The great cat growled in accompaniment to their quarrels. He stretched and padded out from the darkness of the jungle towards the river, passing the jumble of bleached bones that lay close to his path. They had been there ever since he had been a cub. Despite his great power, he lowered his body as he passed. There was still some lingering influence locked there. It was something that he could not imagine, but he felt an old fear that his mother had conveyed to him with her quiet mewing. He was pleased to be past it, although every night he went that way, and was reassured by its continued presence. He liked things to be constant.

But there was something different that night, as he bunched his great shoulders and lapped up the muddy river water on a rough tongue. As the sky turned to a darker shade of blue, there was a new star in the sky. Its light was faint now, but it would grow stronger. It was an impostor amongst the other ethereal points of light that had travelled such astronomical distances to grace the *Morasmus* night. But the new star would change the planet's history.

Above the great tiger's head, a new space station was being born.

Printed in the United Kingdom
by Lightning Source UK Ltd.
120327UK00001B/178